MW00437880

Jacob's Hollow

By Duane Vadron Evans

In loving gratitude

This book is dedicated to Jinx, who taught me the
meaning of love.

Table of Contents

Forward

By the author

The American West is a land all her own whose people are recorded in history and legend. The myths speak as much about the character of the men who shaped this unyielding frontier as do the actual events.

No story is complete that does not portray the hopes and fears, the courage and failings of its heroes. In the end, it is the human experience that matters most.

Jacob's Hollow is a fictional story set among actual events. The year is 1880. In researching this time period I found something surprising. The account of the actual events differed depending on who was telling the story. What we see is the perspective of not one, but many cultures. Each wrote their own history. The truth, or as close as we can get, must be found in bringing the many stories together. It is like printing a picture, where each color is laid down one at a time, and it is not until all colors are combined that the actual picture is revealed in its true glory.

It is said that history is written by the victors, and so much of what we see is painted by a heavy brush in the hands of our adventurous European ancestors. The white settlers, both civilian and military, had the advantage of being highly literate, thus the color they put on the canvas of the American West is far more vibrant.

The Apache Indians did not have a written language, nor was it their custom to speak of the dead. As such what is left is highly romanticized. Yet there are wonderful oral stories handed down from father to son, giving us a glimpse into the hearts of their people that is as important to history as the actual events.

The Buffalo Soldier painted his color with a smaller brush. His stories are often of individual battles as seen by a lone trooper with a gun placed in his hand by someone else. He did not make policy or even understand it. It was his part to do or die.

In researching the history of this small corner of New Mexico, I finally put aside the myriad of history books that gave only one view stripped of emotion and started collecting out-of-print books written by people who had actually lived and suffered during that turbulent time. My room is filled with stories by white officers, lowly Buffalo Soldiers, and translations of Apache Indians.

I do not pretend to be a scholar, nor to compare my fictional story with any great historical piece. What I have tried to convey from this moment in history, is the human heart.

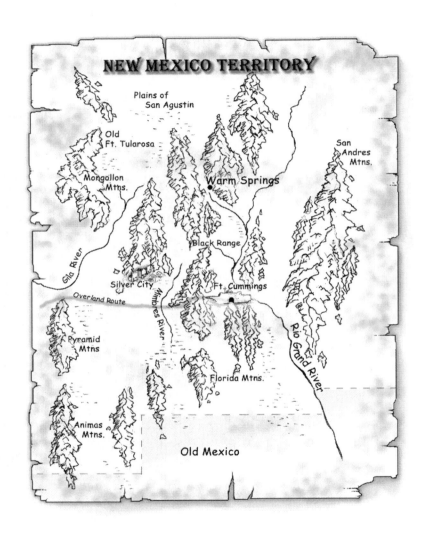

NEW MEXICO TERRITORY

Plains of
San Agustin

Old
Ft. Tularosa

San
Andres
Mtns.

Mongollon
Mtns.

Warm Springs

Gila River

Black Range

Silver City

Ft. Cummings

Overland Route

Mimbres River

Pyramid
Mtns

Rio Grand River

Florida Mtns.

Animas
Mtns.

Old Mexico

Chapter -1-
The Meeting

The world abounds with beautiful places where lush green landscapes flowering with the pageantry of life melt into soft pastel blue skies. This wasn't one of them. By the time God got around to the dry, crumbling mountain rising from the abysmal plane, He no longer gave a damn. The scorched terrain lay barren and broken. Here, in a forgotten corner of the desert, Sholo's trail came to an end.

"Give it up Jacob. He ain't left so much as a shadow."

"I can see Jube."

"Then ya ken' see Sholo done slipped away. We's follin' a ghost trail."

Sergeant Jacob Keever raised his battered binoculars. "If we turn back now, there'll be hell to pay."

Prodding his tired mount a step closer, Jubaliah removed his weather beaten hat, polluting the air with a gray, chalky cloud that seemed to settle right back on him. "That was the chance ya took when ya disobeyed orders. Told ya , I did."

The sweat-stained corporal cast an anguished glance at the parched earth before him. "Anyway, 'doubts they could find a worse detail 'n this. 'Ceptin' you 'n me might be privates again."

Intent on the distant hills, the sergeant ignored the grumbling man beside him.

Jubaliah spit the grime from his cracked lips. "You is pushin' too hard Jacob. What if he is here? We been doggin' ol' Sholo most a year. We hast to stop 'em, but why now? Best wait 'til we have him dead to rights. This purgatory is his choosin'. You is followin' a wolf into his den an' ain't nobody comin' to save our sorry hides."

Squinting his sunburned eyes, Jacob cursed. Behind him lay the vast empty desert, ahead an angry mountain. Shadows stretched out from rock and crevice, devouring all hope as the last rays of the pale March sun played out across the distant cliffs.

No sane man would have come this way, and right now, he felt like a damn fool. A thousand troops would need as many days to search this tortured land. The sergeant led only six weary trail worn soldiers barely clinging to their saddles.

Maybe Jube was right, Sholo had escaped again. "Damn it." Jacob didn't care about catching hell, he just hated being wrong.

Grudgingly, he tugged the reins but couldn't help stealing one last glance. Suddenly something pulled him back. His intense gaze strained against the encroaching night. Something…there it was.

1

In the distance, a thin wisp of smoke danced for an instant in the last twinkling of light, then was gone. The sergeant's eyes glinted as the old fire rekindled. Come sunrise, he would lead his soldiers into battle.

"What is it, Jacob?" asked Corporal Jackson.

Jubaliah Jackson was Jacob's oldest friend. He had been with Jacob through the war. That was a long time ago. Now they were known as Buffalo Soldiers, black troops given the worst details in the army. It was their thankless task to chase the dwindling bands of renegade Apaches across the harsh New Mexico Territory.

"What is it?" Jube repeated.

For the first time in days, a tired grin eased the deep lines in the sergeant's face.

"Jube, come morning we're having breakfast with the Injuns, and we will serve it hot."

Saddles creaked as weary riders suddenly came to life. Eyes begging sleep opened wide. Battle, with all its evil, offered the young black troops a measure of dignity seldom accorded them. When they engaged the Apaches, they would be soldiers. No one could take that away.

Doubting his own ears, Zeke Potter, a boyish faced lad, prodded his bony mount closer. "Does you mean it Sarge? We's finally gunna fight the Apache? It's been most a year of nothin' but trail."

The sergeant turned his horse into the graying night, and barked over his shoulder, "Fill your cartridge belt, boys. If killins' your want, the day has come."

A clamor of excited voices rose from the circled riders. Young Toby needed to hear the words out loud. "Good God almighty, bugle n' saber, we is really gunna fight the Apaches."

Erupting in a loud whoop, lanky Tyrell Brown chimed, "Wish we had a bugle. That'd be somthin'! Chargin' in, a flag waving an all."

"Ain't nobody gunna be laughin' at us this time." Zeke bounced in his saddle, then squared his shoulders. "Yessir', we will ride through them fort gates with our chins in the clouds, everyone knowin' we finally drew blood."

This was the moment they dreamed of. The thrill of battle fired Tyrell's imagination. "Ain't never kilt me n' Apache before."

Zeke wrinkled his brow and scoffed. "Hell, you ain't never kilt nothin', Tyrell."

The tattered youth would not be discouraged. "Well, it don't matter none, there'll be glory enough come sunrise."

Toby repeated his words. "Fight the Apaches."

A year had come and gone, with endless forays into the desert, only to return covered in dust and empty handed to the amusement of the white soldiers. The boys yearned for glory, but lost hope it would ever happen. A real battle – it was hard to believe.

Private Rolley Dupree, a few years older, had remained silent, viewing the impending battle more philosophically. "Yessir', killin' Apaches n', I guess them killin' us."

The soldier's dour decree played like a funeral dirge.

"Damn, Rolley." Zeke drew out his dismay in a raspy exhale of air. "What'd ya say a thing like that fo'?"

The tenor of the short lived cheer changed to one of pensive doom.

Unsettled by the disapproving glare of his comrades, Rolley defended his somber observation in a high pitch wine. "Well, bullets fly both directions."

Their short lived glory squashed as quickly as it started, Toby bemoaned. "First time we gets a reason to celebrate... well, ya ain't helping morale none Rolley."

The dispirited troopers stared at each other in awkward silence. Their young hearts protested Rolley's edict, but there was no denying the truth. Bullets care nothing for the color of a man's skin.

In a hollow victory, Rolley's gravelly voice punctuated the discourse. "Killin' will be done. Best screw ourselves to it, ain't everybody on this mountain gunna see the morning sun."

One by one the troopers prodded their haggard mounts away from the circle as though it might put distance between them and the uncomfortable reality.

Young Toby held back. Barely sixteen, he had lied about his age to get into the army. He was a boy trying to figure out life, and Rolley's words stuck in his mind, *someone was going to die.*

There was never a question of right or wrong when the black regiments were sent west. The red man was one color too many. Apaches became the enemy, and if your job is hunting Indians, its just human nature not to think too fondly of them. As Jube had said. "It eases the soul ta see 'em as a pack of snarling wolves."

Orders for the Buffalo Soldiers were clear: Herd the filthy savages back to the reservation or leave them face down in the desert sand. No one cared which. They were an animal that needed to be culled.

During their lengthy campaign, the thrill of battle was never more than capturing a lone straggler, maybe a young boy searching for adventure or a drunken old man reliving past glory... but never Sholo. Somehow the Mimbre chief always managed to slip through their grasp. He was becoming a symbol to his people. Sholo was a flame that had to be extinguished, and with luck this night would see it done.

A brooding ride carried the uneasy troopers deeper into the shrouded hills where they picketed their horses in a dry creek surrounded by scrub oak.

The impenetrable gloom reminded the troopers there are things darker than the night. Victory was not certain. Their guns, and even their horses, were worn castoffs from the white troops, no longer deemed reliable. Like their gear, they too were given little worth. Apache or Negro, it didn't matter who died on this lonely mountain, good riddance to them all. It played on their minds.

Jubaliah found his friend standing alone, staring into the dark, and eased beside him.

"Jacob, men kin only get so ready."

The sergeant didn't break his gaze. "It will happen soon enough, Jube. This will be a real battle – first for most of these boys."

Jube started to speak, but Jacob was already planning the next move. "We need to send one man to locate the Apaches' camp."

Humor crept into Jube's voice. "Bet ya itchin' ta go. Me too. But seein' as you n' me are 'bout as big as our horses, n' couldn't step on a shadow without it squeelin' fo' mercy, I reckon you'll be sendin' Private Tomes?"

Luther Tomes was as scrawny as Jube was big, a rangy young lad with just enough meat on his bones to hang a uniform if you buttoned it up tight. It was Luther's nature to never stand out. Most soldiers at the fort didn't know his name, and those who did called him Weasel. It seemed to fit.

A backwoods boy from Tennessee, they say Luther was tracking raccoons as soon as he crawled from his mama's womb. You could blindfold him, spin him around, and he would always point north. The trooper's talent was as singular as his gangly appearance.

Returning to the silhouetted figures, Jacob spoke in a low whisper. "Luth, dig out your moccasins, your turn to be a hero."

The young soldier froze, knowing every eye was on him. His comrades understood the honor, and the danger. Following a cold trail was one thing; tracking Apaches alone into their camp was another. Luther did his best to sound calm.

"Yes sir, Sarge. When do I leave?"

"As soon as you're ready. Pack light, you got ground to cover."

Setting his heavy 45-70 Springfield carbine aside, Luther checked his Army Colt .45 then slipped it back into the tattered holster; it was all he would take.

The men stopped what they were doing and gathered around to listen to the deep resonant voice of Private Rolley, "So, Weasel, when ya sneak up on them Injuns, do ya think you could paint bright red targets on their backsides?" Aptly named, Rolley was about as big a man as you could put on a horse.

"Heck, Rolley, I'll paint a target on my own backside. With your aim, it'll be the only thing safe."

"I told ya my gun pulls to the right."

"If it pulled any more to the right, ya d shoot yourself in the head."

4

Rolley gave a guilty laugh. "Maybe so, but you be careful, Weasel. Them Chiricahuas are closer to animals than men n' can see in the dark better'n a bobcat."

Zeke quickly agreed. "Animals they is, they can out sniff a bloodhound."

Jacob broke in, "Keep it quiet. Luth, you best be off."

"Sarge, I'm as good as ...," Luther vanished into the night.

Normally a detachment of Buffalo Soldiers is led by a white officer, or at least it had been lately, since hostilities towards the miners had picked up. Under pressure to get results, the colonel required an officer to lead each patrol. In this case, that would be the great Lieutenant Lawrence Reinhart, but the swaggering lieutenant found these tiresome forays beneath him. So, despite what the colonel thought, Reinhart was not in the habit of leading his own men.

He would start out with them, sure enough, the colonel would have his hide if he didn't. Reinhart paraded the soldiers, all spit and polish, right through the sally port gate and then a good march straight to Cora's whorehouse. He called it field headquarters. There he would send them on their way.

It was rumored that Reinhart actually owned the whorehouse with Cora. He even had his own private room. If nothing else, Reinhart was enterprising. "Report back here to Fort Temptation if you see anything boy," he would tell Jacob. "I'd go with ya but you darkies smell funny after a week of not bathing, it's more than my civilized nose can bear."

He would laugh at his own tired joke. "Instead, I'll be smellin' the sweet perfume of Cora's band of angels and protecting the rear if you know what I mean."

Jacob was used to this kind of talk. It might have bothered him, if he had respected Reinhart, but as it was, he was happy to be rid of the arrogant bastard.

Reinhart knew Jacob could handle any situation and Jacob knew enough to keep his mouth shut. So as it was, the two men reached an understanding that was to both their liking.

As Jacob peered into the night, he was glad Reinhart was not here to second-guess him. This was his play; tomorrow he would end the game of cat and mouse with Sholo.

While chasing the elusive Apache to the ends of an endless desert, the two adversaries had gotten to know each other quite well. The trail leading to this lonely mountain spanned a year of burning sand and icy gales, where the warrior and soldier matched wits.

The Apache was clever and the sergeant relentless. The troopers often remarked, "They know each other like brothers." There was not a sunrise that Jacob didn't think of Sholo, nor a sunset that the Apache didn't cast a wary eye over his shoulder. Yes, they knew each other well, even though the two men had never met.

Recently Sholo had started raiding outlying ranches, with what seemed like little more reason than to say, "Look at me, I am somebody."

Some cowboys finally got shot, which got the attention of the hungry press. Colonel McCrae, the commander of Fort Cummings, put the spurs to his troops. This time, there would be no returning Sholo to the reservation. Dawn would see a fight to the death. The only question was whose would it be?

Cold hours crept by. Jacob sat wrapped in his tattered wool blanket on an exposed outcrop of rock listening intently to all things unseen. The only sound was a soft icy breeze whispering off the jagged stones. A damp haze set in, hiding the stars.

"How 'bout a little firewater ta warm the soul?" came a soft chuckle. Corporal Jubaliah stepped close. "Liberated it from a drunken Injun, I did." He pulled the cork with his teeth and talked through the side of his mouth. "Offered me his squaw to get it back. Pretty thing."

"Not tonight Jube, save it for morning and we'll drink a cheer."

Jube took a swig and stuffed the flask back in his pocket. "It sure is a black night."

He laughed. "Our brave lieutenant would say, 'Blacker n' a darkie's ass.' Guess he'd be right."

The corporal slapped his hands against his arms, protesting the cold. "Speakin' of asses, ain't too late ta put ours in the saddle before that ol' wolf Sholo takes a nasty bite."

The sergeant let silence be his answer. Jube figured as much. "Ya think we gots'em this time, Jacob?"

"I do, I can feel it deep inside. But…," Jacob raised his head towards his friend's voice floating in the inky black. "…But, it don't feel good, Jube."

"Killin' never does, Jacob. Killin' never does."

Pulling his blanket closer, Jacob continued his lonely watch. As the cold numbed his mind, his thoughts drifted. Jacob was a hard, simple man, shaped by a life of limits and rules in which he had no say. But the long days on lonely trails gave Jacob plenty of time to dream. And Jacob was a dreamer. He dreamed of a better life, a life without limitations where he answered only to himself. He had an idea of how life should be, but years in the army left him only guessing without any real understanding. It was like seeing a serene painting on a wall and wishing you could be in it but not knowing how.

An idyllic dream had taken root; a little spread all his own with a small cabin, a clear creek to water a few cows and most of all… a wife. Jacob dreamed of a beautiful wife. He didn't talk about this to his men, he would not be laughed at or teased, but a wife would complete his picture of what he thought a perfect life should be.

6

His dreams might have been small by others' standards, but for Jacob it was about the biggest dream he could imagine.

Chasing Apaches had led the Buffalo Soldiers far and wide. With each new hill and valley Jacob would picture a little farm perched on a grassy ridge or tucked away in a shaded glen.

Increasingly, his dream consumed his mind, fueling a growing hatred of his hard, violent life. For a Buffalo Soldier there was no happy ending. There would be no one to weep his passing.

A man has to walk boldly into his own dream or forever play a small part in someone else's. These were Jacob's deepest thoughts.

"I found 'em." The sharp voice of Luther sprang from the darkness, startling Jacob back to reality. "Geez, Luth, how about some warning... cough, step on a twig, or break wind!"

The boys quickly gathered round to hear Luther's report.

"Sarge, they're bedded down in a grassy hollow, sheltered by the cliffs. They don't seem to be expecting nothin', not even a sentry. I think Sholo done slipped up this time, Sarge, I had my sights right on that murderin' Injun. Iffin' I'd wanted ta join him in hell, I could a'killed him right then and there."

A murmur rose and trailed away. The boy savored his moment before continuing, "There's a bubbling spring just east of them that will mask a little sound, but it blocks us from coming that way and getting behind them without a lot of splashing. The good news is that there's a small line of trees in front of the hollow that will give us high ground and some protection, not much but some."

"And the bad news?" cut in Rolley.

Luther paused and sucked in air, "The bad news is Sholo's got some recruits, there's a baker's dozen."

A collective groan filled the darkness.

"And it gets worse, they got spankin' new Winchester repeater rifles."

"Hell," rasped Jube, "they's better armed than we is. Where do a bunch of savages get guns like that?"

"It doesn't matter," Jacob's voice took control. "You're just gunna' have to shoot twice."

"You better damn well believe I'll shoot twice," returned Rolley, his voice rising. "I'll be chuckin' boulders n' pushing over trees iffin' I live long enough. Thirteen Injuns with Winchesters for Christ sake! And we gots' hand-me-down single shot Springfields."

Zeke butted in, "Thirteen is an unlucky number."

Jacob's voice rose stronger, "It doesn't matter. We are U.S. Cavalry, damn it. This is what you've trained for. So set your minds to it. If there's no more complaining, and there ain't, let's move out single file. We leave the ponies here. Luther, you got the lead. I'm next, Jubaliah, then Brown, Potter and Toby. Not a word from you, Rolley, about bringing up the rear.

Move out."

A whisper stole through the darkness. "Thirteen."

The deer trail Luther led them on snaked steadily up a succession of rough, rolling hills crossed by small, steep ravines of loose rock. The mountain seemed like an endless stair that crumbled with every step. Knees ached and ill-fitted boots made for riding soon wore painful blisters. The exertion did little to quell the nerves of the young boys. They were headed for battle.

Eventually the dusty smell of the desert gave way to the heavy scent of sagebrush. An hour passed and Jacob let the troopers take a breather. Aching bodies quietly spread out along the trail, each finding their own hole in the dark.

This would be young Toby Waters' first battle. He had not yet fired a single shot at a living thing. Toby made a point of sitting next to Corporal Jackson. Jube sensed the boy's tension. He could hear it in his breathing.

"Mr. Jube, sir, how do you think it'll go? I mean, well, it bein' kinda' lopsided in their favor and all."

"No one lives forever. Come sunrise, it'll be over one way or ta other."

The boy went deadly silent. Jube regretted his flippant answer. "But I suspect we'll win quite handily. Ol' Jacob knows what he's doin'. Kept me alive during the war, n' he'll do the same for you. Mark my word, Sarge can handle Sholo. All we gots ta do is follow him. Just stick close and do as he says. Yessir, I suspect this'll be the last Apache sunrise so to speak. Not just for Sholo, but for all his people, their time is fading. With Geronimo run off to San Carlos and Victorio bein' hunted to extinction, battles like this'll be found only in history books. And you is lucky to get in on the tail end, so to speak."

After a pause, Toby's voice seemed calmer, "Thank you, sir. I'll most certainly follow Sarge's orders. You can count on me."

"Never doubted it, son. When we gets back ta town you can buy me a tall beer n' we'll spin a few yarns for them books."

Young Toby fell silent and let the darkness engulf him once again. He thought how strange it was that some nights are filled with sounds and other nights are deathly silent, as though even the crickets sensed impending doom. This night all he could hear was the beating of his own heart.

Leaving Toby, Jube moved on up the path looking for Jacob. The deer trail was worn deep by sharp hooves and flash rains. A sliver of moon breaking through the clouds cast a pale, eerie blue light on the wavy leaf oak, making a spidery canopy.

As he often did, Jube found his friend standing alone, searching what lay before them, not just in distance, but in time. Jube knew that Jacob was already fighting the battle that was yet to come.

Sitting down next to him, Jube broke off a sprig of sage and idly chewed the end. "I was jes' talkin' ta young Toby. He's a good boy, but a might edgy. Not too sure about what lays ahead."

He paused for a bit. Jacob offered no response, so the corporal continued. "Not too sure myself. Ain't never been too good at figures, but we is out numbered almost two ta one, and them Winchesters can probably fire five rounds to each shot from our Springfields. Don't know what that adds up to, but..."

"Tell it all, Jube. You're thinking it. They got high ground. They know the terrain, and excepting you, me and Rolley, the rest of the boys are just green kids mustered back east, who ain't never seen a fight."

Jube chuckled. "While we's being so cheery, might as well point out, they is dog tired n' Sholo's braves will be rested. Could also say, they got ponies and we is on foot."

It did sound absurd, and Jacob joined with a nervous laugh. "Is there anything else you think I'm forgetting?"

"No, Jacob, I don't think you is forgettin' nothin' at all. Guess you already gots the battle won in your head. My question is why?"

Again Jube waited, letting his concern sink in. "Ya know I trust ya , Jacob, you saved my skin too many times not to. Still there are boys back there that I gots to worry about. You have never taken chances with their lives before, but even that crazy general George Armstrong Custer might say this is a bit nuts."

"You sayin' turn back?"

"No, I ain't saying no such thing. I just want you ta be certain why. All the soldiers at the fort know it's you who really leads these patrols, not Reinhart. You is a proud man Jacob Keever, n' every time we comes back empty-handed, you takes a lot of laughin' n' jeerin' from the white soldiers. You say nothin', but I sees it in yo' face. Poor dumb colored, playin' soldier."

Jacob shifted, uneasy in the darkness. Jube knew he had hit a nerve. For a long time Jacob said nothing. Picking up a rock, he weighed it in his hands. "Jube, I care about those boys back there too. Not just their lives, but their hearts. Each time we come back empty handed they die a little. How long can it go on? Eventually their spirits will be so low they won't be able to fight. We've been given a chance; if we turned tail, what would it do to them? Those boys know what they are up against, and they believe you, and I think they can do it. Come dawn, we will be taking one hell of a risk at the top of this mountain, but there's a bigger risk if we don't Jube. I can't watch them die any more. They believe in us, now we got to believe in them."

There was an awkward silence. Jube had not expected so much passion from his stoic friend, but he had got his answer and then some. Slowly the corporal stood. "Guess we best be headin' for that breakfast you was talkin' 'bout."

Moving down the trail, Jube roused the boys. Each came to their feet and continued on as before. Aching muscles finally grew numb to the pain. Jacob slowed the pace to quiet their breathing. Apaches sleep light. He was determined that this night, his troopers would fall upon the enemy as silent as rolling fog.

Heavy sage gradually faded to the light scent of Ponderosa pine. Soft ferns and grasses replaced the stiff oak and mountain mahogany that scraped loudly on their wool uniforms. As they approached the appointed hour, their luck was holding. Still, Jube's words echoed in Jacob's mind. They were outnumbered, outgunned and Sholo seemed to live a charmed life.

But a lopsided battle like this would have plenty of glory. The kind of glory that garnered medals and speeches. So Jacob had made his decision, there was no turning back. History would decide if Sergeant Jacob Keever was a hero or a damn fool.

The land began to level off, and the men sensed the presence of the great cliff towering in the darkness, a forbidding barrier where they were to meet their doom. Sounds no longer came from directly ahead; even the light breeze was stopped by that great wall jutting hundreds of feet above them.

Without the benefit of sight, other senses take over. Luther truly seemed to have the instincts of a weasel. None of the other men could have tracked the Apaches in the dark. Their respect grew for the scrawny man they had named in jest.

The soldiers inched forward, knowing the trail was coming to an end. Eyes and ears strained against the night. Rifles were held before them. Finally their procession stopped. Luther leaned into Jacob, "We're here."

Anxious troopers flattened against the ground, knowing the Apaches were just yards away. It wouldn't be long now. The cold night's march was over, dawn was near. Tension grew with every second. Black faded one shade. The sun was coming and with it, an inevitable conclusion that no man could stop.

As soon as Jacob could see his hand in front of him, he sent each man up the bank one at a time on cat paws, spreading them across the top of the knoll. Somewhere a short distance away waited the enemy. They could be docile rabbits, snuggled deep in sleep, or cunning wolves waiting to spring.

Jacob placed Toby nearest to the spring and gave his shoulder a reassuring squeeze before moving away. He eased back down the knoll several feet and crawled west along its base, finally taking up a position on the far west end where the knoll met the great cliff. Here he found a huge pine. Silently, Jacob inched up into a standing position and leaned against the tree for a better view. He struggled to control his breathing.

Dark forms began to appear among the grasses as shadows receded. He counted, then counted again until thirteen shapes lost the protection of the night. The eyes of the troopers danced between the sleeping Indians and Jacob. He raised his rifle to his shoulder, and six more silently took aim. Now was the time to strike; Jacob's duty was clear... kill them now. But it seemed wrong, they were sleeping men. Jacob hesitated. This was not a battle. How does one draw a line between war and murder?

In the growing light, Jacob looked to his corporal, kneeling, gun at ready. Jube leaned his head towards the Indians, his eyes bulging, pleading for the order to fire. Jacob looked back to the Indians and held a moment longer.

Softly in the distance, the song of a meadow lark heralded the dawn, an Indian stirred in response, then sat bolt upright, sensing more. His eyes opened wide, locked with Jacob's. The sergeant screamed, "NOW!" A deafening roar filled the hollow. Blue smoke billowed in the clearing and caught the morning sun.

Being outnumbered no longer mattered; the first seven shots from the heavy Springfield carbines pounded into seven sleeping forms wrapped for eternity in their blankets. The remaining startled braves exploded from their sleep, stunned and confused, scrambling wildly. Screams mixed with the sounds of fresh cartridges being slammed into the carbines.

Again, the order was given, "Fire." Six Apaches raced for the trees. The guns roared. Four braves made it – three with rifles. The Winchesters now barked with all their savage fury, hungering for a target. Another volley from the soldiers and only one Apache remained. Sholo stood alone.

The brave warrior, unwilling to accept defeat, dashed to the edge of the cliff in a desperate attempt to squeeze past a tall Ponderosa and make it to freedom in the last fleeting shadow. His movements a blur as he dodged limb and rock, one blinding leap brought him to a small opening in the brush next to the wall.

As his eyes focused, he saw the large bore of Jacob's carbine waiting for him. Sholo frantically brought his rifle to bear. Jacob squeezed the trigger. The Apache slammed violently back against the cliff. His body arched with pain, then crumpled in defeat.

Jacob slowly lowered his gun and moved forward. There before him lay his foe. Kneeling beside the dying man, he reached down, gripping the Apache's shoulder. His instinct to kill was replaced by compassion.

Sholo looked up in recognition. His bloody hand took a hold of Jacob's. Their eyes burned into each other's soul. One word left Sholo's trembling lips, "Brother." Then the Indian closed his eyes forever. Sergeant Jacob Keever of the Ninth Cavalry and Sholo, the valiant Apache chief... had finally met.

Corporal Jubaliah stepped through the trees. He stared at the dead

Indian, lying in a dusty patch of light. A faint wind whispered a final breath off the cliffs and silence returned to the hollow. The meadowlark was gone.

Taking his first look at the isolated stand of trees beneath the high cliff where their long march had ended, Jubaliah shook his head and lamented, "What a lonely place to die."

Jacob slowly raised his eyes and gazed past the bubbling spring, across the lush green hollow of tall pines capped with crimson clouds floating in the soft pastel blue sky. A smile softened his face. "Or a beautiful place to live."

Chapter -2-
Another Trail

In the clear morning air, brilliant sunlight filtered through the lush green hollow. Sparkling drops of dew crowned each blade of grass and weighted the moist pine boughs. Blue showy daisies and small yellow sunflowers sprinkled about the thick green mat made the glen seem almost cheery. The beauty belied the sad reality that a short time ago, this gentle place had been the scene of great carnage.

Musings of the soldiers blended with morning sounds. Squirrels chattered, woodpeckers drummed, and the bubbling spring that masked the early morning attack, percolated its soothing tune, uncaring of the dead Indian lying on its bank, his hand floating amongst the tall reeds.

Under the shadows of the tall pines, young Toby kept busy cleaning his gun, hoping the other soldiers wouldn't notice his trembling hands.

Jubaliah walked alone, moving between the bodies with his worn leather journal in hand. He made note of what he could about each Apache. Occasionally, he would thumb to the back of the book and jot a personal note.

The official entry he had just written said, "Injun six and seven lying in the center of the hollow. No identifying marks." In his personal pages he wrote, "The two savages favored each other, like betwixt father and son. The boy, maybe 14, dragged himself out of his blanket before dying, his hand reaching to the older man." Jubaliah moved on.

Jacob sat alone on a rocky point beyond the pond that was fed by the spring. From here he could see the vast emptiness, unbroken by mountains. The desert spread out forever until it was lost in the distant blue haze.

Before him, the borderland sloped away in gentle rolling hills. These barren knolls hid the thick vegetation in the deep ravines that the soldiers had secretly traversed in the dark. How different it looked by day. Sunny mornings have a way of changing everything. Sholo was dead. Nothing was going to change that.

Jacob tried to think other thoughts, but the searing image of Sholo staring up at him kept pulling him back to that final moment. He fired his last shot a hundred times. Sholo's telling eyes pierced Jacob's heart more deeply than any bullet. Here was a man his own equal, not just a nameless savage, but a brother at arms. His death was more profound to Jacob than his life. Sholo was not the first Indian Jacob had killed, but he was determined he would be the last.

The sound of the dry yellow dirt crushing beneath heavy boots pulled the sergeant from his thoughts. "Jacob, I tell ya , this here battle is gunna' make our great and glorious Lieutenant Reinhart a real hero. He'll probably get a medal and promotion to major. The Battle of Apache Springs, or some such thing," It was the familiar caustic wit of Jubaliah. The corporal continued, "How many of them bloodthirsty savages does you suppose he killed while us po' dumb coloreds huddled in fear? Can't ya jes' see him, standing tall, saber in one hand, smokin' pistol in the other, surrounded by dead n' dying heathens. Makes ya jes' quiver with patriotic awe."

Jacob raised his head. "I'll take that drink now."

Producing the flask, Jubaliah took the first swig, then held it high. "To the great Lieutenant Reinhart."

He passed the stout drink to his friend, who took a long slow draw and spoke in a solemn tone, "To Sholo."

"That's you, Jacob, always rootin' for the underdog." Jube's brow wrinkled. "Jacob, why did ya hesitate to fire this morning?"

"It lacked honor."

Taking another swig, Jube mulled it over. "Honor don't mean nothin' to Apaches. They is violent primitive savages who don't fit in this here civilized world. Good riddance to 'em all."

Stuffing the flask into his pocket, Jubaliah adjusted his coat with animated pomp and came to attention. "What's your orders, Sarge?"

Jacob stood, thrusting his large finger towards a wide yellow clearing at the base of the cliffs several hundred yards past the pond. "I want thirteen separate graves dug there."

Jubaliah grimaced, "Sarge, that'll take all day."

The crusty sergeant shot him one of those *no argument* glances and added, "With some kind of marker for each one."

With that, Jacob followed a deer trail into the woods. He heard the soldiers moan as Jubaliah said, "Men, let's hike down and get the horses. We's gunna' dig us a cemetery."

It was early afternoon when the men tossed the last shovel of dirt on the graves. Ezekiel Potter gave the mound of dirt a final pat with the flat of his shovel, then tossed it aside and started looking for a suitable stone marker. "Yes sir," he said to anyone listening, "iffin' I'd knowed' I was gunna' have to bury them red bastards, I would've let some of 'em slip away."

He hefted a large rock with a groan. "Tell ya, I weren't too sure about the outcome of this here shindig when ol' Jacob led us up here in the dead-o-night, but Sarge, he sure knows what he's doin'. He ain't never steered us wrong yet."

Potter thrust the stone down hard into the earth. "It may have took the better part of a year, but like Jacob said, Sholo can slip away from us twenty times, we only have to catch him once. Today we sure as hell caught him, we did. And he ain't gunna' slip away never no more."

Zeke Potter stomped a dusty boot on Sholo's grave as if to prove his point, then looked around for some response. "Well, Toby-boy, what ya think, this being your first battle and all? You killed your first Injun and even got shot yourself."

Toby touched the bandage on his left shoulder where a bullet cut its path. It was deep enough to leave a scar – a badge of honor or a permanent reminder of something he would rather forget. "I don't know Zeke. Don't know what ta think. Just glad it's behind us."

"Amen to that." Tyrell Brown agreed wholeheartedly. "Amen to that."

Rolley came stumbling up the ridge, grunting under the weight of a gigantic stone and dropped it at the head of Sholo's grave. "Figured he ought to have the biggest one."

Luther stepped up silently behind him. "Well, ya, said you'd be chucking stones at 'em, but Rolley, I bet ya never imagined it would be this way."

Toby turned to Jubaliah, who had just walked in on the conversation. "What do you suppose Sarge is doing off alone like that?"

"I suspect, lookin' for somethin' he may not find. Anyway, that's his business. As for you, I suggest you eats while ya can, cuz' if I know Jacob, we'll be heading out as soon as he gets back."

Jacob had followed the deer trail after his morning talk with Jubaliah, without any thought of where he was going. It didn't matter. As he walked, he felt better, so he kept walking. He gave his soldiers their first victory. After a year of humiliation, their young faces beamed with pride. But for Jacob, the battle burned in his chest like bad whiskey and he wanted to forget.

The trail meandered through a large stand of pines in a wide ravine following the base of the cliffs. Here, water pouring off the sheer walls during the rains aided a lush vegetation. Jacob marveled that he had ridden through the flatlands surrounding this crumbling mountain before, yet never noticed this small forest. There must be several hundred acres of trees, he surmised.

The hollow, gouged by ancient glaciers, had hidden the old forest from the eyes of the few brave travelers who hazarded to take the dangerous route across the center of the desert. There simply had never been any reason to leave the main trail and climb the steep foothills only to be stopped by the cliffs.

Moreover, this land, until recent years, had been Mexican territory. The Gadsden Purchase by Congress had opened it up to Americans. This was the secret that Sholo knew. Ultimately, the safety he felt in these woods had been his undoing. In this solitude, yet unclaimed by civilized man, Jacob felt the same peace.

With the sun rising high, Jacob finally made his way back to the hollow. The sergeant saddled his horse, then rode up to the larger grave stone. "Is this one Sholo?"

"It sure is," said Rolley with a mixture of pride and aggravation. "Do ya want us to say some pretty words over 'em?"

"I don't think they would value anything we had to say," replied Jacob. "Mount up and ride."

Without further comment, the soldier turned his horse and headed back the way they had come. The old bay quickened his pace, sensing they were going home. Jubaliah climbed to the saddle and spurred his mount to catch him. Settling by his side, the two friends rode on in silence.

The young men fell in behind, keeping some distance from their leaders. Over time they had learned to tell when the older men wanted to be alone to talk.

As they left the foothills the horses slowed their pace, accepting the long journey ahead. The trail broadened and the vegetation quickly fell away.

"So, Jacob, ya wants ta tell me what's on yo' mind?"

Jacob turned his head as though he was going to speak, then stared forward again. It was clear he was trying to put something to words. "Jube, how long have we been soldiering together?"

Jubaliah gave a husky laugh. "Jacob, I don't remember a time when we wasn't. We was babies on the battlefield. Ain't had no other family to speak of."

"Have you ever wanted something different?"

Pausing for a moment, Jubaliah scratched his head. "Sure, I always thought it would be great ta be Colonel McCrae, sittin' behind that fancy carved mahogany desk of his, smokin' fine cigars n' give'n orders. Everyone sayin' 'Yes, sir,'" saluting n' all, but I'm a little dark for that. The best somethin' different I can hope for is that one of Miss Cora's sweet golden angels will get curious about darkies and give ol' Jubaliah a free tumble. Cuz' I sure is curious about them." He laughed like a braying donkey.

"No, Jube, I mean something completely different, like not being soldiers, having a ranch with a wife and family, no one telling you when to get up or where to go."

"Are ya sure one of Sholo's bullets didn't crease yo' head, or go plum through? Ya better take a good look at the color of yo' skin, boy. Beside, ya don't know nothin' 'bout ranchin'. You'd starve ta death."

"Sometimes, Jube, you have to walk into the storm and trust the wind will fill your wings. I believe a man can do anything if he's got a burnin' desire in his heart. Jube, this is the only desire I feel. It is so great there's no room for anything else.

The corporal shook his head. "So, Jacob, ya gots desire, who ain't, but where is ya gunna find a woman around here anyway?"

Then Jubaliah remembered that Jacob had always favored a petite little colored girl named Rosie. Above a squalid back street saloon in the crowded mining town of Silver City was one of the several traveling whorehouses that followed men seeking gold. It differed from the other whorehouses in two ways. One, Madam Sarah Dane tolerated blacks if they came up the back stairs, and two, here dwelled Rose Montier, a whore, and the only black girl within a hundred miles worth a second look. Candy for the eyes, Rose was beautiful by any standards, which allowed her to cater to the more affluent businessmen of this budding town. Her charm and singularity certainly helped Jacob overlook her profession. Though being the only black woman of note, she still would have garnered Jacob's attention.

Jubaliah brayed again, "It's Rosie, you's sweet on... little Rosie. Ya been thinkin' of getting hitched and startin' a ranch with her. Is that what's been pounding in yo' bony head all this time?"

Jubaliah seemed to be none too sensitive to how serious Jacob was about all this. "Boy, when ya goes to thinkin' ya don't know when to stop."

"Okay, keep it down, Jube. There is nothing wrong with a man wanting a home of his own."

"Ya gots' a home, and you's sittin' on it. We's genuine born-to-the-saddle Buffalo Soldiers and that's as good as it gets in this white man's world. Considering the options, it ain't a bad choice."

Jacob's resolve was firm. "One choice is no choice at all, Jube. It is time to ride another trail."

"Jacob, you's runnin' away from what you is, and a life that works for ya. Nothin' can come of it but trouble. Ya ain't no rancher, and I ain't never gunna be Colonel McCrae. The difference is... I'm willing to accept it."

Jacob let a long silence calm the tension between them, then started again. "What if it had been different up on that mountain this morning? What if Sholo's bullet had found my heart? I'm serious about this, Jube. I would have died without ever having known love or family. Life is better than this. And I would rather die chasing my dream than spend an eternity hungering for it. So laugh if you want, but I'm getting out."

It was Jubaliah's turn to be silent. His horse stumbled a bit. Water splashed in his canteen. A meadowlark called in the distance. They rode on. "I ain't laughin' at ya, Jacob. Jes' wish ya d give it more thought."

"I have, Jube, more than you'll ever know."

"So, ya really leaving?"

"Did you know it's March fourth? My enlistment ends today. Sholo and I both quit fighting on the same day. Jube, we have been in the army so long, everybody just assumes that is where we will always be. We're like crumbling stones in the mud walls of that old fort, we're just there and ain't nobody cares. Yep, when we get back, I'm saying my goodbyes."

The large round sun resting on the distant horizon colored the alkali dust kicked up by the horses with a soft amber glow. The victorious Buffalo Soldiers crested a shallow rise overlooking Rabbit Springs. Here beneath the crimson plane, dark green grasses laced three small pools together. In stark contrast to the dry expanse, the simple springs were heaven sent.

With a sudden flutter of wings, a small flock of mud-hens took to the air, breaking the evening tranquility.

Prodding his pony forward, Rolley joined the two older men, already stripping away their saddles. "Me and the boys passed the hours on the trail re-telling the battle. It gets better each time."

Lowering his heavy girth from the stirrups, Rolley continued with a punctuating grunt. "If we hadn't stopped ol' Zeke, he would've had them Injuns spittin' flames an' ridin' wild bears."

The big man paused, waiting for a response, then started again. "Guess the two of you was recountin' the fight..."

Jube tossed his saddle to the ground. "Good hell, Rolley! Iffin' ya is burning ta know what we was jawin' on, jes' ask."

The shrill whine emitted by the stout trooper seemed at odds with the big man's size. "Well, you was looking so dang serious n' we could tell it had nothin' to do with the battle, it plain soured our celebration."

Pulling a curry comb from his saddlebag, Jube cast a quick glance at Jacob and started vigorously brushing his horse. "The boss is getting out."

Instantly, the young troopers milling not so inconspicuously behind Rolley, pushed forward in disbelief. No words were needed to voice their obvious question. It hung plain on their faces.

Leading his horse away from the troubled boys, Jacob tried to end the matter. "I'm leaving the army, nothin' more to it."

Rolley's voice rose to a higher pitch. "What's to become of us? You's suppose to do the worrying and we's suppose to do the complainin'. It jes' won't work without ya Sarge."

"Sholo is dead. Did what I set out to do and I ain't going to wait around in this dusty side of hell for another bloodthirsty redskin seeking glory."

Taking his leave, Jacob led his horse to the farthest pool. Young Toby hurried to catch up. "Sir?"

"I ain't no *sir*, Toby."

"Well, I wouldn't feel comfortable calling you by your first name, anymore than I would my own father, if you know what I mean. So begging your pardon, Sir, ever since I joined the army I wanted to be like you. Now you're saying that ain't good enough."

18

Jacob cut in, "Just be yourself." He smiled at the boy. "When I was your age the army was good enough. I learned a lot that I'm thankful for, but if a man is standing where he started, at the end of his life... well you get what I mean. It's time to move on. Toby, the next battle is yours. Fight it well."

****

On the second night a cold wind picked up, followed by a light rain. No one felt like bedding down in the mud, so they pushed on through the dark. A hazy moon cast a pale blue light as the dark procession slowly wore away the miles.

Pulling his collar close to his neck, Jube broke the silence. "We's less than an hour from Cora's place. Gots to wake the lieutenant or make camp in the rain n' let him know in the mornin' he's a hero."

Jacob's eyes narrowed at the mere mention of the lieutenant's name. "Before I leave this man's army, I would sure like to have the last word with that arrogant, pasty face, son-of-a-bitch."

"Best you forget that. We's already two days late cuz' ya disobeyed orders. Sure he's spittin' bullets and losin' sleep wondering where we is and what he's gunna' tell the Colonel."

Throwing his head back, Jacob broke into a hearty laugh. "Well, we most certainly don't want to wake the poor dear." His laugh turned to a wicked chuckle. "Let's finish off that whiskey of yours."

Jube brayed, "Does ya mean the tin flask or the bottle I gots stashed away in my saddlebags?"

In the gray mist stood the unpainted two-story farmhouse, home to Cora and her girls. It was raised on a large old porch that surrounded the entire structure. A small rickety barn and a rare three seat privy were the only outbuildings. It was clear to the observant eye that the only work being done on this farm was inside.

The dilapidated house evoked happy memories for the soldiers, partly because on warm summer days, the girls, a rare commodity in these parts, would often sit cooling themselves in the open windows in various states of undress.

The scantily clad beauties enjoyed teasing the black soldiers who could only look but not touch. Still, for the desperate men, it was as close to a woman as they could get, and the sight of a bare breast was bragging rights to be retold on long trails and lonely nights.

The farm also held a fondness for Jacob because it was where he took leave of the haughty lieutenant when going on patrols. Tonight he would get rid of him for good.

A loud belch erupted beneath the starless sky. An empty bottle dropped to the ground, accompanied by a second burp. Trying to stifle

19

laughter, Jacob shushed the men, seemingly unaware that most of the clamor was coming from him.

With a jolting stop, the old horse pulled up short outside a broken down picket fence. The celebrating sergeant tumbled from the saddle. "Climb down here, Jube, the ground's fine, and bring that journal of yours."

Jube, having forgotten how to dismount, missed his stirrup and fell on his butt. "Damn horse."

Ignoring his disgruntled friend, Jacob struggled with the latch on the badly leaning gate. It proved to be too much of a difficulty, and the whole contraption broke off in his clumsy hand with a loud clatter. "Shhh, Jube." He handed the glossy-eyed corporal the tangled boards. "Here, you'll need to come back an' fix this. Take it out in trade."

Jube whispered, fouling the air. "Heck, for one of them milk white darlins' wearing naught but a smile, I would build Miss Cora a fence around the whole dang territory."

The gate tucked under his arm, Jube followed his friend up to the front porch with an animated crouch due more to the spirits than stealth.

By the time they climbed the stairs, they were both laughing like little boys. Jacob put his fingers to his lips. "Careful not to ring that ol' bell. Tear me a page out of your book, we are going to leave our brave lieutenant a note. It would be rude to wake such a gallant hero."

Jacob leaned against the wall to steady his hand and did his best to scribble out his message. Sidling up close, Jube laughed out loud before he could stop himself. The letter read:

> *Dear Lieutenant Reinhart,*
> *Congratulations! Showing*
> *uncharacteristic courage, you defeated Chief Sholo*
> *and a dozen warriors during a fierce battle in which*
> *only you could have prevailed. We coloreds,*
> *unworthy of basking in your glory, have gone on to*
> *the fort. If you prefer that Colonel McCrae not find*
> *out your men came in without you, I suggest you get*
> *your lily white ass in the saddle before he wakes and*
> *calls for report.*
>
> *Yours respectfully,*
> *Mr. Jacob Keever*

Dropping to his knees, Jacob slipped the note under the door. The two friends scrambled back to the waiting men and made a hasty getaway. If Reinhart got the note in time, he would certainly explode with rage at Jacob's affront to his authority.

His tirade would no doubt be cut short as a wave of panic swept over him at the prospect of Colonel McCrae finding out about his dereliction of duty. Needless to say, seven very tired troopers went to bed laughing. Jubaliah's last words as he drifted off to sleep were, "Boy, they sho' is gunna to be a price ta pay come mornin'."

Jacob slept in as he thought civilians did. The men were up early though and on the parade grounds waiting for the excitement to come. Their heads bounced between the door to Colonel McCrae's office and the front gate. Sooner or later one of them was going to open and decide the lieutenant's fate.

"I don't think he's gunna make it. No sir. His ass is cooked this time. Ol' Jacob's got 'em." Zeke bounced on bended knees and giggled like a naughty schoolboy. "White folk always sleep in. Ain't nobody gets up early at a whorehouse."

Tyrell Brown shoved both hands deep into his pockets and talked to his dusty boots in a slow sarcastic draw. "Ah, he'll make it. Good men gots bad luck n' bad men gots good luck. Devil takes care of his own. He'll make it."

Zeke craned his neck out the gate before disagreeing. "Well, that third Injun, we's arguin' over which one of us kilt, iffin' the lieutenant makes it, I'll say you done the killin' n' iffin the lieutenant don't make it in time, then I kilt the Injun. Is it a wager?"

"Done."

The boys stepped back against a wall where they could watch both the gate and the door, but everyone was too nervous to stay put, and soon they were all milling around. Even Jube seemed a might anxious. He raised his eyes to Rolley and shook his head. "Either way, a price will be paid."

Just as they thought, time for Reinhart had surely run out and as the Colonel's adjutant stepped onto the porch to make his summons, hoofbeats could be heard racing toward the fort.

Trying to look without looking like they were looking, the men could see Reinhart whipping his poor horse with a fury no doubt meant for the black sergeant. If the animal survived, it would be a miracle.

The gate beneath the sally port that was usually open, was quickly closed by unseen hands before the lieutenant's terrified gaze. The men climbed onto the roofs that made the rampart as Reinhart pulled his coughing steed to an abrupt halt. There were grins from ear to ear and laughter behind the wall. Reinhart shouted, "Open the gate."

Rolley risked a little retribution of his own, "Who goes there?"

Reinhart's face went bright red as his neck bulged beneath his collar, "Open this damn gate now or you will be busted back to…," He realized that Rolley was a private and could go no lower. "Rolley, open the gate… please." His voice broke more than he intended.

Rolley chuckled and ordered the gate open. Reinhart raced through the entry and dismounted. His eyes shot to Colonel McCrae's door, then to Jubaliah who took his reins. Jubaliah could see the unspoken question and said with a smile, "It looks like ya made it in time sir. I trust ya slept well?"

Reinhart hardened as his confidence returned. His words hissed like steam from a boiling kettle. "Where the hell is he, corporal?"

"The colonel, sir?"

Reinhart bristled, "You know who I mean, where the hell is Sergeant Keever?"

Jubaliah assumed a knowing air. "Mr. Keever," he corrected, "is in his quarters. He chose to sleep in late today."

Reinhart asked no more questions. Storming off towards the barracks, he flew through the door on a wind of rage. Jacob was finishing up his last button. Reinhart exploded, "I'll peel the black hide off your bones, boy. What in Sam Hill do you think you are pulling, disobeying my direct orders and leaving that letter, you dumb son-of-a-bitch?"

Jacob raised his chin, "That's Mr. Keever to you. I quit."

Reinhart was stunned. "What the hell do you mean you quit?"

"My enlistment is up. I'm done. You no longer have any authority over me. After report this morning, I'm walking out the gate a free man. You are going to have to do your own work from now on, no matter how bad it offends your civilized nose."

Reinhart's anger was unabated. "But you are not out of this fort yet, so mind your place boy, or I'll bury you here."

Jacob's eyes narrowed, "Nor have I given my report, so maybe you better mind yours, Sir."

Reinhart's face contorted with a fury he could not vent. Hissing through his teeth, he stood toe to toe with a darkie and it galled him, but there was nothing he could do. The sergeant had made his point.

Holding the short end of the stick, the lieutenant thought it better to change tactics. "Look, we can make this easy on both of us. You're talking crazy. Maybe I will overlook this, one time. There is no place for you in civilian life, and I still need a good boy to handle the coloreds."

"You better get Jubaliah a promotion if you don't want to do your own work, 'cuz this boy has plans."

Jacob wanted to end the discussion. "Any second you are going to have to give your report to the colonel. Would you like to know what it is, sir?"

Reinhart swallowed back the bile boiling in his gut and grudgingly nodded. Jacob filled him in with the highlights and then added, "Lieutenant, it might be wise to give the men their credit this time. You will be the hero regardless. The thought of the men getting some recognition might cloud my memory on some of the details."

In Colonel McCrae's office, Jacob stood at attention one step behind Reinhart as the lieutenant echoed the report Jacob had given him, adding a few embellishments of his own. "Colonel, there were twenty warriors. We were outnumbered more than two to one and they were firing down on us from high ground with brand new repeater rifles."

The officer cast a nervous glance over his shoulder at the sergeant. Jacob thought the repeater rifles were a nice touch since he had not mentioned it to the Lieutenant.

Reinhart's mouth was dry as he concluded his recount. "Why sir, the men were most valiant. They stood fast when even white soldiers might have cut and run. All I had to do was hold the line."

Colonel McCrae listened excitedly, then spoke. "Captain, you are too modest. This is going to get written up in the papers. They will hear of it in Washington. Lieutenant, you are a hero."

Reinhart risked one more glance at Jacob who stood silently at attention, then smiled with relief.

After they were dismissed, Jacob stepped forward, "Colonel, sir, I would like to talk to you about my enlistment being up."

Reinhart stood by the door, wanting to leave but not daring to move. The colonel took his chair while shuffling documents, "Just submit the paper work as usual."

"No, sir, you don't understand. I'm leaving the army, sir."

McCrae looked over his spectacles, "Are you sure about this?"

"Yes, sir. Absolutely, sir."

"The army has been good to you, Sergeant. You may find it harder out there than you think. Is there a problem here at the fort?"

Jacob turned toward Reinhart and waited a moment to let him sweat. "No, sir. It's just time for me to follow a different trail."

"Very well, there will always be a place here for you sergeant. You're a good man. You can pick up your pay from the quartermaster. I hope you know what you are doing, son. You are excused."

Reinhart waited on the porch for Jacob to close the door. "I'm not going to forget this stunt, you uppity nigger. You think you are pretty damn smart, but you jeopardized my career…"

"Don't forget," Jacob cut in, "remember it for the rest of your days and let it sour every one of them."

Reinhart clenched his fist, then caught the cold glint in the big man's eyes, and shrank back. "If you are not out of the fort in thirty minutes, I will have you arrested." The lieutenant stormed off.

Twenty-nine minutes later, Jacob rode through the weathered adobe walls of Fort Cummings with everything he owned in his saddlebag. A bedroll and coat were tied behind the saddle. In a scabbard on the right side of his horse was an army carbine, which he bought for one dollar. On the left side hung another scabbard holding a shiny Winchester with some

Apache beadwork embedded in the stock, a remembrance from a noble Indian Chief. Lastly was a worn money belt, with his life's savings socked away from a career in the U.S. Army that had started in his childhood. Wages collected, but unspent, and winnings from playing Five Card Monty late into the night, amounted to eight-hundred and forty-three dollars and twelve cents. Jacob Keever, at thirty-three years of age, was finally a free man.

Chapter -3-
Companions

𝕿he windswept hilltop was bare, save for an ancient bristlecone pine. Thousands of years ago, when the tree was young, a lush green forest had spread for miles in all directions. Changing climates had slowly killed the weaker trees, and finally even the hardiest pines gave up the fight against a harsher land. Now this noble bristlecone stood alone, for how many ages, no one knew or even cared. The fact that it existed at all mattered only to the tree. Every year it dropped new cones without despairing that in a thousand years not one cone had brought forth new life. Still, the old tree lived like it truly believed there was a better tomorrow.

A weather-beaten rider slowly crested the hill. The lope of his horse showed he was in no hurry. Easing out of the saddle, he stretched his stiff joints and leaned a lanky frame against the sturdy old trunk.

The man's age was showing, he was no longer a starry-eyed kid, but there was plenty of fight left in him. In a land of Indians, Mexicans, and Anglos, who cared nothing about him, he chose to make his stand. With unfailing courage, he would hold against all that beset him to prove, if only to himself, that he did matter. He believed there was a brighter tomorrow.

Jacob looked back down the trail he had traveled. Everything he knew was behind him. He had been gone two days from the fort, but it seemed like a life in a distant past. There was no going back.

Turning, he gazed on his new path. The land opened wide before him. Ahead, he would make his dream a reality. The old bay nuzzled against him as if to say, *what are you waiting for, let's go.* Jacob smiled, "Alright Major, we still have a few hours of daylight to burn." He named his horse Major because presenting his posterior to an officer amused him.

As they moved from the shelter of the old tree, a wind coming up the slope filled his nostrils and stirred his spirit. It reminded him he was a free man. Jacob had entered the Union army as a young boy of just fourteen. As far back as he could remember, someone else had told him when to get up, what to eat, and when to go to bed. From now on every decision, big and small, would be his.

Jacob laughed for sheer joy. He shouted out loud, "I'm free!" He spurred Major forward into a gallop. For the first time it truly hit him. "I'm free damn it, I'm free. Why has it taken me so long?"

The horse obliged his master's merriment by racing to the bottom of the hill, where he settled into his familiar lope. "Yes, sir, Major, no one is going to tell me what to do ever again."

Jacob paused and reflected on this with a chuckle, "On the other hand, I'm no longer in a position to give orders either. It cuts both ways, I'd never considered that." He patted the horse's neck. "Well, Major, if I get to missing all that authority, you might be pulling extra duty, even peeling spuds. Unless we get a mangy dog to kick around, you're in for it ol' boy, so look sharp Mr. Horse, there will be no goldbricking."

Jacob laughed again. "I wonder what else I haven't considered?"

At sunset Jacob made camp out in the open and built a fire from sagebrush wood. It broke easy, and the shaggy bark made a quick-lighting tinder. The smoke swirled, filling the cool air with a deep pungent aroma.

In no hurry, the ex-soldier brewed some coffee and boiled a little salted meat. Eating it dry would have been less fuss, but it seemed more like a meal this way, and Jacob felt a little celebration was in order. He foraged for some mesquite beans in the nearby brush and added a large handful to the bubbling pot.

A landscape bathed in red faded to burgundy shadows. The first stars polka-dotted the sleepy sky while crickets, one by one, greeted the coming night with a soft, soothing cadence. Mournful cries of distant coyotes pushed the boundaries of the night beyond the campfire light. The crackling wood burned low, and small blue flames danced over deep red coals.

Lost in languid thoughts, Jacob watched the day turn to night. The light of a billion stars above, so close you could bump your head on them, glowed in the Milky Way's brilliant silver band.

As Jacob drained his second cup of coffee, he suddenly became aware of another sound blending with the night. He listened intently. Muffled by the desert sand came the faint sound of hoofbeats.

It was a lone horse, moving slowly. Who would be riding after dark in this country? Jacob gripped the heavy stock of his rifle and slid it closer to him. Shading his eyes from the glowing embers, he cocked back the hammer and eased a little farther into the darkness. The hoofbeats grew louder as the lone rider picked his way through the sagebrush. Finally a tall horse came to a stop at the edge of the dim light, a shadowed silhouette loomed among the stars.

For a moment the silent figure stared menacingly, before his deep voice rolled. "Does ya find it a little scary out here all alone in the dark without a bunch o' soldier boys protecting yo' backside?" It was followed by a familiar chuckle.

Jacob sprung to his feet, "Jubaliah! What the hell you doing out here scaring decent folk half to death after they hunkered down for the night? I nearly shot you."

Jubaliah eased his mount into the warm glow, a big toothy grin shining in his dark face. "Now that would a been a real shame, me havin' rid all this way out here to God knows where, jes' ta tuck ya in and then you go blowin' my head off. Ya mind uncockin' that thing?"

Jacob remembered his gun and put it down. He stared at Jubaliah, waiting for an explanation.

"Ya know it ain't easy to walk away from a lifetime of seeing yo' ugly mug every mornin'. It put me off my feed. But before ya go gettin' all mushy, I have a month's leave comin' after all these years, and I figured now was a good time ta take it. Where else am I gunna' spend it?" The soldier glanced behind him. "Weren't too hard ta find ya, not but one trail ta Silver City."

Jacob continued staring in disbelief. "Reinhart let you go?"

"Hell, he pushed me out the gate and gived me another two weeks ta boot. Sholo is dead, thanks to you. They thinks things is gunna be peaceful for a spell. Besides, Reinhart is off ta district headquarters in Santa Fe givin' an official report to some bigwigs on the Battle of Apache Springs. I planted that name in his head and it stuck. My little contribution," Jubaliah brayed. "Yessir, I'm sure he's thinkin' he'll probably get some award or somethin'. Reinhart will milk it like a swollen cow's tit, that's fo' sure. I also might have suggested he didn't need me hangin' around the fort while he was gone, spillin' the truth and all. So here I is."

"I wouldn't mess with him, Jube. He don't forgive easy."

"Well, now, you is a fine one to talk. He turns bright red anytime a body mentions your name, and there's plenty of that goin' on too. It riles him somethin' fierce that he has ta share the limelight with you, but yo' name is in it this time. A little bit of the truth has to stick."

"I'm out. Reinhart can't bother me no more, but you best watch your step."

Jubaliah tossed his saddle near the fire. "Oh, I'll be careful, but he's needing a new sergeant, so I can't let him get too high and mighty. Now, let's finish off that coffee and I'll tuck ya in."

****

Silver City was your typical boomtown – a mixture of fools and fortunes. For every miner with a handful of gold, there were saloon keepers, gamblers and whores eager to pry it from his dirty fingers. From liquor, cards, or pleasure, to holier-than-thou preachers or less than holy politicians promising a better life, it all required a little silver.

With the hustle and noise of people coming and going and new stores opening daily to accommodate the growth, Silver City was a stark contrast to the routine of Ft. Cummings where change was often measured by the seasons.

The dusty companions rode into town by late morning. With sounds of boots scuffing on the boardwalks, wagons clattering in the streets, and a late rooster having his say, the pair's arrival was of small matter.

"Is you going to see Miss Rosie first off?"

Jacob slapped his shoulder, and a cloud of dust filled the air, "Not looking like this, I ain't. First thing off, I'm going to find me a lawyer to help me with the homestead. I can't wait on that." He puffed out his chest, with a smug grin. "Us private citizens all got lawyers. You being in the military wouldn't know nothin' about that, Jube." Jacob laughed. "Then a shower and a sit down meal. After I'm presentable, I'll pay my respects to dear sweet Rose."

Jacob remembered seeing a law sign hanging in a window on a side street the last time he was in town. It was a street frequented by Mexicans. Legal matters were unfamiliar territory, and the thought of a well-to-do white attorney looking down his nose at him was a bit discomforting, so a Mexican lawyer would do just fine. Probably cheaper, too.

As they made their way up the side street, Jacob could see that the wooden placard with the single word "Law" was still there.

Most of the buildings were run together with covered boardwalks, and even though the office was in the poorer side of town, it had lots of windows, creating an impressive look. The trim was painted dark green with a generous coating of dirt, making it look older than it was. Jacob and Jubaliah tied their horses next to a watering trough. Patting off some dust, they walked inside.

A little tin bell on top of the door announced their arrival. The room was small and filled with desks, tables and plenty of chairs. It was cramped, but the windows made it seem airy. The lower half of the walls were tongue-and-groove. Green patterned wallpaper hung above, covered in spots by a framed diploma, a simple oval mirror, and a paper calendar with months torn away up to March 1880.

At the end of a hallway, past several doors, was an open office. Inside the small room, a short, stocky Mexican in business attire was lost in conversation with a distinguished older Mexican couple.

Jacob could not make out the words, but the tone was one of great distress. The stocky man appeared to be trying to console the distraught pair.

Looking up, the Mexican smiled in acknowledgment at Jacob. He then ushered the couple into another room while keeping up a reassuring composure, with a lot of smiling and head-nodding as he backed out of the room and closed the door after him. The gentleman then turned with a broad infectious smile and made a smooth transition from the anguish of the old couple to a warm, eager greeting for Jacob and Jubaliah as he came down the hall. "Welcome senors, my name is Victor Ramirez. How may I be of service to you?"

The lawyer had a genuine honesty about him that made Jacob feel like he was truly glad to meet them. "Good day to you sir, my name is Jacob Keever and this is my friend, Jubaliah. I'm planning on homesteading and could use your help in going about it."

Bursting into a hearty laugh, Ramirez offered his hand. "So this is not an official call?"

Confused, Jacob paused for a moment then remembered their uniforms. He had no insignia on his plain blue shirt, but he was still wearing his army trousers and riding boots. Jubaliah was in full uniform. It was Jacob's turn to laugh. "No, sir, I'm no longer in the army, and my good friend is only here because he doesn't believe I can take care of myself."

Ramirez ushered them into the office at the end of the hall, and they were quickly seated. The office was as warm and assuring as the gentleman himself. Sentimental bric-a-brac adorned the room. Tintypes of a large family, mementos signed by friends, and bright colored drawings from children decorated every corner.

Ramirez went right to business and swiftly jotted the details on the land. It was clear he knew exactly where it was, though there was great astonishment in his eyes. "It is hard to imagine there being trees and flowing water tucked away in such a barren place, but the desert is full of surprises. Not the least being that you are planning on homesteading where no one else has ever wanted. At least you are aware that under the Homestead Act, all homesteads are 160 acres of free land, provided you live on the property and make improvements."

Mr. Ramirez' demeanor changed. He leaned back in his chair and placed the tips of his fingers together, his eyes focusing in the air above his guest. It was clear, he was forming his thoughts and about to speak on something he felt was of great importance. The attorney's expression became deadly serious, "Senor Keever, you are aware that much of your acreage is desert alkali, and growing anything on it is going to be very tough? Many would say impossible."

Jacob glanced sideways at Jubaliah, knowing his friend must be thinking him a fool. "Mr. Ramirez, I thank you for your concern, but I assure you I know what I'm doing. I don't need much, and what I need (comma needed ater need) the land will provide."

"Senor Keever, I mean no disrespect but as your lawyer, it is my responsibility to make sure you know what you are getting into. It is apparent you know your land very well. But perhaps I can give you some understanding of the land surrounding your own and make you aware of a serious danger you may have to face if you go through with your plans."

Jacob stiffened in his seat. "If it's Apaches, I'm well aware of that danger."

Mr. Ramirez quickly interjected, "No, Senor Keever, that is not it." He paused again and slowed his voice. "Before I continue, I would like to ask you a question that will seem most improper, but I assure you, if you will indulge me, I will explain myself momentarily."

The thick muscles in Jacob's chest, tightened. He was beginning to feel increasingly uncomfortable, but there was little choice. "Go ahead and ask your question Mr. Ramirez."

Ramirez licked his lips and held a deep breath, as though he dared not ask. Then he blurted it out, "Do you have four hundred dollars?"

Jacob gripped both arms of his chair, "What?"

"Please, Senor, I do not ask for me."

Jacob again looked to his friend, who had stopped breathing. Jube's astonishment matched his own.

Releasing his grasp on the chair, Jacob's eyes narrowed, "Yes, I have four hundred dollars."

Mr. Ramirez gulped a deep breath. "Do you have it on you?"

The question was so bizarre, Jacob did not know what to do but answer. "Yes, Mr. Ramirez, I do."

The light came back into the little man's eyes and the familiar smile returned. "Thank you, Senor Keever. Please excuse my rudeness but time is critical. Maybe there can be a happy ending for everyone."

The attorney took one last breath. "Now as I promised, I will explain myself and the danger I spoke of."

Settling back in his chair, Mr. Ramirez made himself comfortable, as though he was going to talk for a long time. "Your homestead is in a very remote part of a territory that itself is a forgotten corner of the world and I am sure that no matter where you look from your land, there is only empty desert as far as the eye can see, (perhaps end sentence after see) but I assure you, it is not as isolated as you might think.

Your homestead sits on the edge of several million acres of open range. It is too dry to run cattle, so the land has been ignored – up to now, that is. Your coming here today at this time is a most extraordinary coincidence as is the location of your secret hollow. Most extraordinary indeed, but that is how life often happens."

Gazing out the window, the Mexican muttered, more to himself, "Destiny draws us all together at the appointed hour."

He sat for a moment, then shaking off the thought, he returned to his story right where he left off. "You see, this open range and the land to the south and east of your homestead is bordered by an old Spanish land grant of nearly fifty-thousand acres. The western part of the Spanish land grant is alkali desert, but the eastern half is grassy foothills, suitable for ranging cattle.

Mr. Ramirez leaned forward. "This land is owned by the couple sitting in the next room, waiting for me. The Rincons. They are very nice people." He studied Jacob's face and continued. "Now to the west of the open range is another big ranch almost as great as the Rincon's. It is a much different story. This property belongs to a ruthless rancher who believes in taking what he wants. His name is Damon Mathers. He and his two sons run a large herd, and they are determined to own the whole territory. They supply beef to the army."

Jacob interjected, "I've heard his name at the fort, but I've never met the man. So what has this got to do with me, my 160 acres, and my four-hundred dollars?" The soldier's words came deep and terse letting the attorney know an answer was due.

Leaning forward, Ramirez quickly obliged. "Your four-hundred dollars may be able to buy you a lot of land, and in doing so, make you a good friend, and possibly a dangerous enemy if not handled carefully.

"You see last year, Senor Rincon got into a deep financial difficulty. The Indians and the Mexicans have never gotten along. The Apaches keep raiding his herd and driving off the cattle. There has been little to sell. Damon Mathers was only too eager to loan him money to get by as long as he put up his ranch as collateral.

"Well, with the raids continuing, Senor Rincon has not been able to pay the loan. The four hundred dollars is the last of many payments. With each installment Senor Rincon made, Mathers became more demanding. It became apparent he wanted the land, not the money. This is a poor territory, and money is scarce. Senor Rincon has done his best, but there is no cattle to sell."

Ramirez gripped the arms of his chair, his knuckles turned white. "The loan comes due at noon today – in less than one hour. Damon Mathers is over at the bank waiting to foreclose and kick the Rincons out of their home. These dear people are hoping I can pull off a miracle, and I think you might be that miracle, Senor Jacob.

"If Mathers gets his hands on that land, he will run cattle between the two ranches and he won't think twice about running right across your little homestead. When he finds out you got water up there, he will not hesitate to move the herd right through your home. He is just that way. You would only be an obstacle to remove. You look like a fighting man, Senor Jacob, and somebody would get killed."

Mr. Ramirez's smile returned. His eyes glinted with devilish delight. "Here is what I propose to foil this vulture. The desert land is not important to Senor Rincon, it is keeping his home in the foothills for his wife and children. The Rincons have lived there for generations. If you give him the four hundred dollars he needs to save his ranch, I am sure he will be very happy to deed over to you a very large track of land. There is no time to quibble. Let's say ten-thousand acres."

Victor Ramirez paused to let Jacob come to grips with what he had said. The ex-soldier sat in disbelief. He jerked his eyes to Jubaliah and saw a mirror of his own expression. Jacob mouthed the words, "Ten thousand acres."

Mr. Ramirez continued. "Granted, it is just more alkali desert, but it would give you a strip of land that extends southwards to Sand Creek. The creek dries up in the early summer, but it is extra water when it runs and a definite border to your property which is important when staking your claim.

With luck, you would be able to graze maybe a few dozen cattle. A number too small for Damon Mathers, but it might fit your needs, and it is far more than you could feed up in your pines. More importantly, Damon Mathers won't have a reason to run his herd over your land, and he might go back to thinking of it as nothing more than the empty desert on his border.

If you would agree to this proposal, Senor Rincon wins; you win. Mathers gets the money he is owed, and a lesson for his greed, and I get to sleep well tonight having pulled off a miracle."

Jacob sat in numbed silence. His mind was racing, but going nowhere. What the attorney told him was certainly a lot to digest, with little time to do it. Ten thousand acres. He looked to Jubaliah and took a needed breath.

Jubaliah's eyes were wide with amazement. Feeling Jacob wanted him to say something, he forced air into his lungs and blew it out long and slow. Words came haltingly. "Good God, Jacob, ya comes here for a 160 acre homestead and now you're lookin' at ten-thousand acres, and a whole passel of excitement. This is more than I can wrap my mind around. That's a whole lot a desert. It's either a chance of a lifetime, or the biggest mistake you'll ever make."

Victor Ramirez looked at the grandfather clock sitting in the corner. Jacob raised his eyes too. The ticking of the clock, unheard before, became deafening with each swing of the large brass pendulum.

Jacob crumpled his hat in his big hands. A part of him wondered if maybe he really was just a darn fool of a darkie being enticed by a slick lawyer with a get-rich-quick scheme. His first decision as a free man, and he didn't have the wisdom to make it. He studied the Mexican long and hard. Something in the man's eyes told him he was honest.

Finally in a slow exhale, Jacob began to speak. "I'm not a rich man, sir. The truth is I'm probably a poor man. Four hundred dollars is a lot of money to me." He paused, gaining control, then continued in a firm voice. "I don't know what is the wise thing to do, but I do know what is the good thing to do, and that is an answer I can live with no matter how it turns out."

His decision made, Jacob wrinkled his brow, then with rising resolve, grinned wide. "Mr. Ramirez, you are one hell of a salesman. You've got your miracle."

The little man exploded from his chair, "Yes sir, yes sir!" He grabbed Jacob's hand shaking it in both of his, then Jubaliah's hand, then Jacob's hand again before bursting out the door yelling, "Senor Rincon! Senor Rincon!" – all composure gone.

Jubaliah stood shaking his head. "Jacob, for a quiet man, you seem to be havin' a most spectacular year. Yessir, a most spectacular year indeed. I'm sho' glad I came. The boys gots ta hear this 'un."

Victor Ramirez returned, leading the Rincons. The old couple pressed through the door with large glassy eyes searching the face of their benefactor for confirmation of Victor's news. Jacob shook Senor Rincon's hand. The lawyer, regaining his professional demeanor, ushered them all back into chairs. "We can do formal introductions later. Right now, we have documents to draw and a ranch to save."

Chapter -4-
Rosie

$\mathfrak{D}$reams of wealth kept boomtowns like Silver City a swarming hive of activity from sunup to sundown, but it was sundown when Silver City truly came to life. At the center of the late night commotion, grizzled miners with sweat-stained faces and large toothy grins, squandered their fortunes. Waving fists of silver, they danced through the crowded saloons boasting their claims. Morning would find empty pockets, but tonight they were rich, and all who cheered them might share in their wealth.

Beady-eyed gamblers staked their claim behind the tables like mountain lions hunting for prey, a pile of tempting coins stacked high as bait. Cowboys whooped into town to wash away the trail dust with as many cold beers as it took, and a few more for good measure. Every night in every saloon on every street was one continuing celebration charged with the electricity that only a boomtown could fuel. Silver City flowed with silver and gold.

Jacob backed out of Red's barbershop and into the mayhem. He squeezed a zigzag path down the crowded boardwalk, balancing a bottle of champagne in his hand – an expensive treat, but Rosie loved champagne.

The noisy confusion that swirled around Jacob mirrored the confusion within. It had been quite a day, and it wasn't over yet. Tomorrow there would be time to weigh the wisdom of his decisions. Tonight all thoughts were on Rosie Montier. He pushed forward, making slow progress through the bustling crowd. After awhile he opted to trust his luck with the horses and stepped into the street. Here he could breathe the cool night air.

Now a civilian, Jacob took a chance and wore his uniform. He did not want Rosie to know of his great plans yet. This evening he would be her gallant soldier one last time.

On a side street, off a back street, a narrow alley led between tall unpainted slat wood buildings. The harsh desert climate had aged them beyond their years. On the other end of the alley, the darkened doors of several shops surrounded a small irregular shaped yard with barely enough space for a privy, a woodpile, and a rickety staircase climbing to Madam Sarah Dane's House of Pleasure. This was the quick exit for respectable men in need of discretion. It was also the only entrance for coloreds.

In an adjoining saloon, a piano banged out the latest tunes from the east, while a barmaid poured filthy water into a basin. It burped from a drain pipe flowing past the rotting base of the steps and disappeared down a broken culvert.

Jacob raised his boot over the foul smell and climbed the stairs. Each wooden step creaked and bent under his weight, moaning a threat, it might break. The handrail leaned several inches when he grasped it, offering more danger than help.

Halfway up the stairs a drunken cowboy sprawled, passed out. Steam curled from his whiskey-soaked buffalo coat. His tattered, sweat stained hat lay crumpled over his face. Jacob held his breath and stepped over the putrid lump, then disappeared inside the door.

Never had any door had two such different sides. The outside, exposed to the weather and filth, hung neglected and unpainted, blending with its dismal surroundings. A dented tin doorknob protruded from a loose plate missing all its screws, and a rough cracked board with bent nails served as the threshold.

Inside was a different story. The varnished door was polished to a high shine and surrounded by ornate trim. A cut crystal doorknob reflected the flickering light of a tall kerosene lamp sitting on a hand carved table in the beautifully wallpapered hall. Flowered carpet covered the floor in extravagance. Sweet perfume hung heavy in the air, hinting of the inhabitants of the second floor.

The muffled tin sound of the piano filtered up from the saloon. Off key, the bawdy music did not fit with the elegance of the hall, yet they blended together giving the place a surreal feeling all its own.

Quick light steps in an adjoining hall preceded a pretty young girl scurrying haplessly around the corner. She came to a sudden stop when she saw Jacob, her lithe body lifting on bare toes. A soft smile disappeared momentarily, then returned as she decided she liked the cut of the potential business in a dashing blue uniform.

The delicate girl was wearing a tight-fitting white-laced petticoat with bare shoulders. Tiny pink satin ribbons tied on the sleeves and just below the knees, shimmered in the dim light. Her casual demeanor showed it mattered nothing to her that she was in a state of undress in front of a strange man. The gaping expression of the tall soldier let the girl know it mattered to him.

Leaning against the wall, she tilted her head and tugged a golden curl, while peering through the corner of her eyes with a mischievous grin. "Lookin' for somethin', general?"

Jacob froze. He had been too long in wild places, and now this giant of a man stood captive to the petite, scantily clad nymph before him. In a battle with Indians he knew what to do, but how do you fight lace and curls?

She reached out with a pointed toe and gently traced the length of his polished boot while waiting for an answer. All the while enjoying the power she had over him. This was her battle ground. Jacob swallowed hard and regrouped, offering a nervous smile. "Yes, ah yes, madam, er' miss, is ah, is Miss Montier, ah, free?"

The girl gave a deep sigh, and shrugged her soft shoulders in disappointment. A small pout replaced her smile. "I should have guessed."

She pointed a delicate finger at a door, "Rosie is alone in her room." Jacob bowed, sputtered a thank-you and slid past the girl, pressing tightly against the wall.

Reaching the safety of the door, he raised his hand to knock, when the sweet coquette tucked her head in a naughty grin, "Hey, general, have you ever tried two girls? You can have the second one for half price."

Jacob coughed and fell into the room unbidden, then quickly shut the door behind him. Struggling for composure, he held his back tightly against it, fearing it might burst open at any second.

Again the different side of the door changed everything. Outside, Jacob sought escape, inside, complete surrender. There sat Rose across the room on a red velvet vanity bench facing a large oval mirror, singing a whimsical tune, her slender back towards him. She was lost in thought while running a silver brush through her hair.

Apparently, Jacob's clumsy entrance had gone unnoticed. He gazed at Rose, her slim form was draped in a sheer evening gown covering but not hiding a tightly cinched burgundy corset adorned in satin and lace. Her hair was a mass of cascading ringlets. Rose's delicate features were visible in the mirror, a button nose, full perfect lips, and huge dark eyes that always seemed to hide more than they told. If given the opportunity, he could have stared at Rose for endless hours.

Jacob's boot scuffed the floor as he unconsciously came to attention. The angelic beauty looked up as if coming out of a dream and caught Jacob's reflection. A smile of recognition lit the room and fired the big soldier's heart.

"Jacob!" she cried in an excited little girl squeal. The silver brush went flying through the air as she swung her bare legs over the vanity bench and sprang to her full height with arms flung wide. Screaming with delight she leaped, trusting Jacob would catch her. Her gallant soldier did, lifting her high over his head, laughing and spinning around and around.

Slowly he lowered her. Rose's soft arms settled around his thick neck, in a long embrace. She raised her head planting several quick kisses amid giggles, and then one long slow silent one. He tucked his arm under her knees and carried her to the canopied bed with pink satin sheets.

Jacob lay wide awake in the darkness holding the fragrant, sleeping form in his arms. Her tiny waist was smaller than the thick bicep cradling her. She slept soundly on his chest like a small child without a care in the world. For Jacob, sleep was out of the question. These visits were rare. He wanted to remember every moment they spent together.

Memories of Rose made the lonely nights on the trail bearable. His mind wandered to the first time he saw her in a plush Victorian parlor in Santa Fe four years ago. He was drawn to a room off the main saloon by rare feminine laughter. There sat a profusion of fancy pale-skinned girls clustered together on a long couch in bright shiny dresses and layered white slips, like ornate dolls arranged on a shelf. In the middle was Rosie, the dark center of a beautiful flower. She was wearing a red satin dress. Her sparkling eyes captured the quiet soldier's heart, making his world disappear. Never had he imagined a girl so breathtaking.

From then on Jacob thought of no other. The course of his life changed forever in that moment. The army was no longer enough. Rosie awakened emotions he had never felt before.

Together they would live the future he secretly dreamed. Soon, he would build his ranch with a grand house, suitable for a girl of Rose's refinements. It would have to be the best he could afford, a vase for his delicate Rose.

Jacob meant to rescue her from this demeaning life that circumstance had forced upon her. There was much to do and little time to waste. His visit in town would have to be short.

Morning came too quickly. The sounds of the outside world awakening began to filter in. Details slowly seeped into the room tinged with a warm red glow. Jacob kissed her hair and she stirred. Large sleepy eyes batted as Rose left her dreams behind. She nuzzled under his chin and wetted her lips, "What are you doing up at the crack of dawn, soldier boy? I ain't heard no bugle."

Jacob touched her nose with his thumb, "Your snoring kept me awake."

A delicate hand slapped his chest. "I don't snore."

"Well, then it must be that pasty face banker you got hid under the bed."

Her body tensed. "Jacob, are you being jealous again?" Her tone was reproachful.

"No. But Christ, Rosie, he is married."

The brief moment of tranquility seemed lost. "You should be happy he's married; do you want him to be handsome and single?"

"No, girl, but ..."

"But what, darling? Would you rather I starve? With as little as you come around, I would be skin and bone."

"No, a girl's got to make a livin', and God knows it's a harsh land, but you can't be mad at me for wanting better for you, can you Rosie?"

"Please don't start that again. This is the way things are, and it's a frustrating waste of time to think it's ever going to change."

Jacob hugged her tight. "Rosie, if you had a chance to get out, you would, wouldn't you Rosie?"

After a pause came a low surrendering "Yes," that she knew he wanted.

Jacob relaxed. "That's all I need to hear. I just want a better life for you."

Rose was anxious to change the mood. She pushed her hands against his chest and raised to a sitting position. The silky sheets fell away. Amber rays from the morning sun piercing the wooden shutters set her firm bare skin aglow, and stole the soldier's breath.

Grabbing Jacob's hat off the nightstand, Rose plopped it on her head with both hands. Sparkling eyes and a huge smile lit the girl's sweet face. "If you want me to have a better life, I will march down to the city council this very instant and tell them stuffy gents I want to be the next right honorable mayor of this fair city."

Jacob laughed. "Dressed like this, they would give it to you."

They both laughed. Rosie straightened the hat and kneeled at attention in the middle of the tangled sheets. "Trooper Montier ready for inspection, sir." She gave an animated salute.

Jacob's hands closed around her slender waist and pulled her to him. "I do love inspecting the troops."

The morning became as magical as the night. Day would wait a little longer.

****

Jacob hurried into the Dona Anna Hotel. He was supposed to meet Jubaliah, and was late. Halfway up the stairs, he looked down into the adjoining cantina and saw his friend reading the morning paper. He waved to him and continued up to the room to change.

When he returned, Jubaliah was hunched over the table, nursing a cup of coffee. He was lost in some article, and sporting his ear-to-ear grin. "Looky here, Jacob. If this don't beat all."

Jubaliah held up the front page of the Silver City Gazette. The headlines read, "Heroic Battle at Apache Springs." Beneath it was a dramatic drawing of a violent combat between Buffalo Soldiers and Indians.

Jacob stared in disbelief, while Jube cackled. "Heck, Jacob, news travels fast, but if this is the battle I was in, I must've been hit on the head. It says here, 'Lieutenant Reinhart, leading just seven Buffalo Soldiers of the heroic Ninth Cavalry, fought a furious hand-to-hand skirmish with the famed renegade Mimbre Apache Chief Sholo and a large war party of blood thirsty braves. The soldiers were outnumbered six to one.' We's good, Jacob, but I din't know we was that good. Six to one, do you believe it?"

38

Jubaliah brayed his donkey laugh and started searching through the paper. "The article continues on other pages; it's like a dime novel. Wish I could read better'n I do. Somewhere in here it says yo' name and that you is a hero."

Jacob frowned, "Look Jube, it use to be that every day was pretty much the same as the next, but ever since that morning, my life has been a runaway train gaining speed. I'm having a hard enough time believing what is real is real without reading lies about me printed as the truth, so just put that paper away and let me eat my breakfast in peace."

"Well I ain't never been printed about in no paper, truth or lie."

"Jube, Reinhart probably put the story out to further his career. The newspaper just wants to sell copies so they add their exaggerations to it and in the end, it don't mean nothing. Just fiction."

Jubaliah looked over the paper. "Some of it's true. Sholo caused a lot of fuss around here. So if people who thinks, 'Good riddance to him,' read in print that we done his killin', then that's the truth that'll stick. If Reinhart is gunna' profit by it, then it ought to at least get us a few free beers from the good and thankful citizens."

Jacob rolled his eyes in frustration, "Jube, you can't live a lie"

"All right, all right, I's' puttin' it away. You won't hear no mo' from me. Eat your damn breakfast in peace. Not another word."

A pretty Mexican girl waiting tables made her way over and offered a sweet smile. "What would you like, senor?"

Jubaliah pushed the paper towards the girl. Tapping the picture with a big finger, an eager grin enveloped his face. "That's us."

The livery stable at the edge of town was their first stop after breakfast. Jacob bought a used buckboard and an old Shire mare. She was past her prime, and while plowing all day might be a bit too much for her, she would do just fine for hauling supplies when needed.

Peaches, that was her name, now stood patiently in front of the dry goods store while Jacob, Jubaliah, and Floyd Barns, the very happy proprietor, loaded all the necessary supplies for building a home.

Jubaliah secured a tin of lamp oil in the last available space. "Jacob, I think Mr. Barns can go fishin' 'til July since you emptied his store."

"I spent fifty-four dollars. Don't think that's too bad, considering."

"Yeah, and you spent as much at the hardware store, and then there's ol' Peaches here. Pretty soon you'll have to be tradin' on yo' hero status that ya don't wan'na hear nothing 'bout."

"So you got us a free breakfast and saved us four bits. All it cost was half the gall dang morning while you regaled the patrons of the cantina with more lies than were in the paper."

"I didn't lie; it's called drama. Ya gots ta build it up. Besides ya got an extra helpin' o' taters."

"Yes, Jube, and ten people to watch me eat them. Now climb on the wagon, and let's go before you have me signing autographs."

"Now there's an idea."

Jacob snapped the reins and Peaches headed out of town with Major and Buck in tow.

Jubaliah didn't wait a moment before he pulled the folded paper from his large pocket and flipped it open. "It says here this is the true and accurate account as related to this reporter, Barnabas Kane by one Lieutenant Reinhart and a colored soldier, Rolley Dupree. No wonder you's getting so much credit. I didn't think ol' Reinhart would be that gen'rous where you is concerned."

Jacob shook his head, "Jube, it just keeps gettin' better. Now Rolley's in it. He likes jawing as much as Reinhart likes tootin' his own horn. And these two are writing history."

"Don't forget, I came up with Apache Springs."

Chapter -5-
Stones

The journey to the Hollow took three long, dusty days. Most of the third was spent cutting a road big enough to get the wagon across the dry ravines that had kept outsiders away from the cliffs all the many years. They crested the rim and came into the Hollow early on the fourth morning. Jacob was home. The secret forest beneath the towering cliffs was now his.

Holding the reins loosely in his large weathered hands, the soldier sat in silent awe. He had traded the only life he knew for a dream. A peaceful smile softened his broad face. It was a good trade.

"Listen, Jube, you can hear the wind whispering through those dark green pines. It's so peaceful, a place all its own, unchanged by time. Jube, hear that bubbling spring. It washes away the painful memories of what happened that morning. This Hollow is a healing place. There's something here that gives a man pause. Jube, don't you just feel it?"

"Yeah, I feels it in my back." Jubaliah jumped down from the wagon with a loud groan and stretched. "Don't know why I been sittin' on a dang wooden plank, bouncin' my innards all the way up this rocky purgatory, when I gots a perfectly good saddle horse trailing behind."

"Jubaliah Jackson, you got about as much soul as dried beans."

"What did I do?"

"Nothin', just nothin,' let's get to it."

The men wasted no time. There was work to be done, a dream to fulfill, and they could not have asked for a better day. It was still early in the year. Tall, billowy clouds hung in the deep blue sky with a steady breeze pushing them slowly from horizon to horizon. It was just enough to cool the sweat off a working man's back. The morning was spent finding just the right place for the house.

Jacob took long strides in one direction, then another. He would stop at a possible location, study it, then pace off an imaginary wall before hurrying to another location and doing it again.

Jubaliah followed him around offering comments on each site, but his opinion was usually ignored, so Jube went off and busied himself building a makeshift corral from fallen aspen logs.

Finally, on a small rise to the west of the spring about a hundred yards from the cliffs, Jacob knelt on one knee beneath a stand of ancient pine. He had returned to this spot several times. An inner voice told him this was the place. Here he would build his home. The ground was level and clear. The gravel-sized stones eroded from the cliff would provide a solid base with good drainage.

Lifting his head, Jacob imagined himself resting on a wooden bench under a shaded porch, overlooking his farm. The front of the cabin opening to the Hollow, greeted the morning sun dancing on the quiet pond. Beyond the barn, the dark green cattails swayed in the breeze, bowing under the gentle weight of red-winged blackbirds. All the while the bubbling spring laughed its merry tune.

Jacob did not have to imagine very hard. The only thing missing was the house and the barn. He turned and looked the other direction. The house would be tucked under the tall stand of shaggy Ponderosa pines with their massive trunks, where gray squirrels were playing tag on the thick red bark. Yes, this is the place. Jacob grasped a large stone in his gloved hand and pushed it into the earth. The building began.

As a young boy on the tobacco plantation in the back hills of Kentucky, Jacob often peered through the cracks in the rickety slave shack. From his dreary shanty he would stare wishfully at the master's large house. Even then he longed for a roof that didn't leak and glass windows to block the winter's icy wind.

Then the war came, making it even worse for young Jacob. After running away to fight for freedom, a tent became his home when he was lucky, but usually just a bed roll on a muddy patch of ground.

Out west the barracks weren't much better, often quickly thrown together with whatever material was available. You baked in the summer, froze in the winter, and learned never to complain.

As a Cavalry soldier Jacob had spent the last decade on the back of his horse. The only home he could claim was his saddle. It was this harsh view of life that now drove this ex-slave, ex-soldier to demand exacting perfection for the house to be. He would build the master's home, but this time he would be the master.

Unable to stay away, Jube wandered back and surveyed the outline Jacob had drawn on the ground. "What's that?"

"My house."

Walking to the other side to get another view, Jube scratched his head. "Ain't no cabin that big. Yo' measurin's off."

Jacob dropped another stone at a corner of the house and did his best to tolerate his friend. "It's got four rooms."

"Good God Jacob, four rooms! Whatcha' need a house with four rooms for? Ya jes' bein' ridiculous."

Jube spun around in the center of the area marked off for the main room. "No need to build a barn, ya kin' jes' move the chickens and horses in here. That leaves a room for you and Rosie and two more for God knows what."

Intent on his measurements, Jacob continued with his work. "Ain't nothing wrong with having four rooms."

Jube spun around again and flapped his arms. "That family up on Stany Creek got eight children n' they only gots' one room."

Jacob thrust a stake into the earth with more energy than needed. "They're a poor, Mexican family."

"The Irishman on Barley Point, one room. The Swede, Johansson over in Dollar Gulch, one room, and the crazy man on Indian Mesa, all gots' one room cabins."

Groaning, Jacob rose to his feet. "They're all a bunch of queer miners without the sense to piss outside. They spend most of their time underground anyway."

"Still, I jes' named four homesteads and ya gots as many rooms as them all put together. Jes' ridiculous."

"Jube, Rosie is not some miner's squaw. She's used to finer things."

"Well she sho' will find it a plenty. Jacob's Palace. Are ya gunna' have maids? You ain't the King of England. Hell, ya ain't even the King of Africa. Bet he ain't got four rooms."

"Jube, did you have a reason for coming all the way up here?"

"Jes' trying to help. I'll keep quiet, but if little Rosie wears her po' self out on her way to the bed, don't come cryin' to me cuz' you ain't getting any."

The rest of the day was spent measuring. Jacob squared the floor by pulling a length of rope diagonally from corner to corner, making an "X."

Looking a might puzzled, Jube scratched his head again. "What ya doin' pullin' the rope all crisscross?"

Keeping his eye on the taut line, Jacob answered without looking up. "When the rope measures the same length across both directions, I know the house is square."

"Well ain't that clever! Guess that's why ya got your sergeant stripe first. You is a thinking man, Jacob."

The ground was pretty level, but to get it perfect, Jacob dug a small rectangular trench around the outline of the house, just a few inches deep. He filled it with water bucketed from the spring. Then, marking the water line he was able to make sure the floor would be perfectly level. Jube couldn't help but tease his demanding friend. "Good hell, Jacob, ya wastin' time. Iffin' it looks level it is level. Ain't nobody gunna' be fallin' and breakin' their necks cuz' you was half an inch off across yo' four room mansion. The earth curves ya know."

"I ain't going to sit here for the rest of my life cringing every time somebody drops a pea on the floor. There is never time to do it right, but there's always time to do it over."

The first days were spent laying out the floor of the house with large flat flagstones hauled from a crumbling finger of a cliff further down the ridge, courtesy of Peaches and the rickety buckboard. The stones were of even thickness of about three inches. Most of them measured several feet across. Together, the two burly men were able to lift them into the wagon. Jacob chose each stone as carefully as though it were of the finest Mississippi marble. Despite their great weight, each stone was nudged, twisted and hammered until it fit perfectly into the mosaic of the floor. Then the cracks in between the stones were filled with white caliche mud hauled from the desert below. The mud dried hard as the stone, making a solid, smooth, and level floor.

Jacob wanted a beautiful home for Rosie, and a beautiful home it would be. In the back of the house, from end to end would be two bedrooms – one for the kids. The inner wall of the bedrooms would be the middle of the house, rising to the full pitch of the roof, providing incredible strength against heavy winter snows. The doors to the bedrooms would face each other in a small alcove that separated the two rooms. It would be easy to check in on the children.

A third door, centered in the recessed alcove, would face out into the main room. This small door would open to a real bath, with a store-bought tub and a cast iron stove for heating water – maybe even a floor length mirror to sit in the corner. There would be a back door off the bath, giving easy access to firewood and water.

From the door, a stone path would meander a short way into the trees to the privy. The eaves of the house would extend several feet to provide shelter for the woodpile when it rained, and shade for the walls of the house on hot summer days.

The great room on the east side would occupy the rest of the home from end to end. A traditional country kitchen with a polished blue steel, six-hole stove centered on the south wall would face a long kitchen table in the middle of the room with plenty of chairs.

On the other end of the main room would be the living area with a stone fireplace built into the wall nearest the cliff. For a mantle, a huge ponderosa log would run the entire length of the wall.

The front door would be in the center of the house, and a covered porch would extend the entire length of the front wall, supported by thick cedar logs. Jacob even ordered four glass windows, one for either side of the front door, and two smaller ones for each bedroom. There would be thick wooden shutters that bolted on the inside in case of Indian attacks.

Spreading from the porch, the hard-packed yellow gravel flattened out for a short distance before dropping to the mossy stream. At the edge of the porch would be two long hitching rails on either side of the steps leading in.

A gentle path would curve down to the spring, and then continue over a low footbridge to the barn. The north side of the barn facing the cliffs was sheltered from the winter winds and would be open to the corral.

Against the east wall of the barn, facing the small pond, would be a chicken coop with long thin poles for roosts, and higher up, nesting boxes.

Heavy stones buried deep into the ground would keep out foxes and raccoons.

At least that was the dream. Right now, there was the floor of the house surrounded by the first tier of stones for the walls. Jacob took one last look and got back to work.

From sunup to sundown, the men toiled in a race against time. The two structures, three if you counted the privy, took shape. The barn gained a real corral for the horses. With a little luck, Jacob thought he might get a cow and a calf in the spring.

Sometimes Jacob and Jubaliah worked together trading small talk, keeping each other company, and remembering the years from boyhood to Indian fighting. At other times Jacob would continue on the house while Jubaliah worked on the barn.

Jubaliah took extra pride in the barn. It was his handiwork, and Jacob let him design and build it as he liked, while Jacob concentrated on the house. Despite the way he ribbed teased his friend, Jubaliah quietly competed with him, making sure he built the barn with the same craftsmanship Jacob was putting into the house. Jube saw it as more than just a barn; it was something of permanence that he was building with his own two hands. It was the only lasting evidence that a poor black man named Jubaliah Jackson had walked the earth.

Taking a breather, Jubaliah wandered over to the house, "Looks pretty good, Jacob, but ya gots that last row of stone upside down."

Jacob straightened from his work. "Well, I needed to put a few chinks in it so it doesn't show up that overgrown doghouse of yours. That loft is so high, you'll probably kill the horses the first time you throw hay down to them. Figured you would build it the size of the privy with all the grief you've been giving me about my palace."

"Well, Peaches is a big ol' girl, so I gots ta make it big. But Rosie is so little, ya only need a doll house."

Jacob was a man of few words, and he knew that if he didn't let Jubaliah get in the last remark, work would stop while the banter went on all day. Instead, he turned over a few stones he had placed in the wall and went back to work.

As Jubaliah wandered away feeling he had gotten the better of the exchange, Jacob took a moment to study the barn. Jube had really impressed him. There was a quaint mix of stone walls and exposed timber for the loft, as far as it had gotten. His friend had shown skills that had been hidden all those years on the trail. He was a surprising man. Jubaliah had not even asked for Jacob's help setting the huge timbers in place. Instead he had rigged a hoist and used Peaches to pull the logs into position.

Building this way, Jube was able to use larger timber. That, along with the barn being completely open on the corral side, meant it was going up faster than the house. Jacob knew he would get some ribbing for it.

In the days that followed, the men took a break from their competition to build a fourth structure. Closer to the cliffs, where the clear water passed under a huge, spreading Ponderosa, they built a small stone blockhouse just big enough to duck into.

The icy cold spring water flowed through the loose stones in the floor keeping the air inside nice and cool. There was just enough room for a milk can or two, some butter kegs and a couple sides of venison. The ice house would make dealing with the daily meals a lot simpler. So far the men had lived on wild game, but hunting took time, and right now they wanted to make the best use of Jubaliah's dwindling days. More than a month had passed. Another week, and Jubaliah would have to return to the fort. After all, this was Jacob's dream. A well deserved sergeant's stripe awaited Jubaliah.

Still, with two strong men breaking sweat from sunup to sundown, a lot of work was getting done. While the labor was precise, it was mostly piling stones and stacking logs. The little place was really taking shape.

When they tired of building, the men would take the buckboard and gather wild grass to store away in the barn. They hoped it would keep the horses through the winter.

A garden and a couple acres of alfalfa could go in next spring. Jacob was a good hunter, but he knew little about farming, so he focused on the tasks at hand and hoped the future would take care of itself.

He had reason to be optimistic. The little ranch was becoming a sight to behold. His demand for perfection in the military was paying off as the house went up with exacting detail. Jacob plumbed each course of stone in the walls with a tight cord stretched level between his end posts. Every window fell on the exact same line; no slipshod work would be tolerated. The house stood as straight as the finest home in the big cities. Using a stone dangling on a rope for a plum bob, he made sure of it. Everything was measured, and measured again.

"I declare, Jacob, this little ranch of yours looks charmin' enough ta be a picture postcard. Or one of them stereo viewers ya see sittin' in fancy parlors. Who would'a thought a no-account, dung-shovelin' colored boy with manure between his toes would ever have a ten thousand acre spread as pretty as this. I 'spect people's gunna' ride fer' miles 'round ta see yo' beautiful...barn."

As if on cue, the faint sounds of horses and the creak of wheels were suddenly heard over the bubbling spring. Casting disbelieving eyes at each other, the men jumped up in utter astonishment and ran through the trees to the lip of the Hollow.

Jube started laughing as Jacob stared slack jawed at the approaching site. There, struggling up the last ridge was a four horse wagon with Luis

Rincon whipping the reins. Elena Rincon sat stoically by his side, and perched on a canvas tarp in the back was a younger woman with long, raven hair flowing across a frilly white dress.

Riding alongside were two young vaqueros on beautiful piebald pintos. The Rincons were famous for their horses. Though the vaqueros were little more than boys in their early teens, they looked quite formidable at a distance, armed with pistols and rifles. After all it was still Indian territory. Another surprise was the last rider. Bringing up the rear was Victor Ramirez on a fat dappled gray.

Jube clapped his hands. "Well I'll be, best put our shirts on, Jacob; we got's company. Guess the fame a th' barn's already spread."

Jacob stood dumbfounded as Luis Rincon pulled the wagon to a stop. The old man smiled, "Thought we would be neighborly and drop by." He waved his hand toward the girl. "My daughter, Carmelita, wanted to see the man that saved our ranch and meet the Hero of Apache Springs. Not every day you get to meet a double hero."

"What about me?" Jubaliah interjected while sliding a shirt over his thick muscled body. Carmelita blushed and turned away from Jubaliah's broad grin.

Victor half climbed, half fell down from his horse, and in his usual politeness offered his hand to Jacob. "Greetings my friend, it is good to see you."

He stepped past Jacob and took in the Hollow. "This is truly beautiful, Jacob. Who would have thought such a place existed out here?"

Luis agreed. "My family has lived in this territory for a hundred years, and we never knew. If a man is willing to walk a little farther or explore the unknown, who knows what treasures await. This is wonderful! And look at what you have built!"

Jubaliah leaned into Carmelita, "The barn's mine. I take on the big jobs."

Jacob finally thought to speak. "Please, hop down and rest. We'll find something to eat."

Senora Rincon spoke up. "We didn't expect two hardworking men to feed us. Carmelita and I packed plenty of food for us all. Besides, we never got to truly thank you in a proper fashion for what you did for us. You men talk, and us women will take care of things as always. Now give me your hand."

Jacob helped Senora Rincon down, and Jubaliah reached into the wagon unbidden, lifting Carmelita to the ground. "Haven't lifted anything so light in weeks. Sergeant Keever works me like I was a buck private. He forgets that I outrank him, being a sergeant myself and all. He's got this girl on his mind and he forgets."

"Jube! Don't bother the lady with your rambling."

Carmelita was quick to his defense, "I do not mind his ramblings, Senor Keever."

Jubaliah dawned a big smile, "Did ya hear that Jacob? Finally, someone with taste appreciates my ramblings."

"Give her time, Jube."

Unable to remain silent any longer, the two boys edged forward, eager to meet the Hero of Apache Springs. Old Luis laughed at their obviousness. "Before they burst, I'd better introduce my two young vaqueros." Reaching out a hand, he scooted the boys towards Jacob. "These young rascals, Roberto and Juan, have been best friends since they were babies. When they found out we were going to pay you a visit...well they just had to come."

The boys blushed, but their excitement over meeting the Buffalo Soldier kept them from running away in embarrassment. Jacob nodded politely and shook their hands. "Welcome to my ranch. It's not much to look at yet, but someday it will be."

Senora Rincon interrupted. "Nonsense. This is truly beautiful. It is a pity that our son, Vicente had to stay and take care of the ranch. He will be jealous when we tell him about your wonderful home. Now, show us where we can have Roberto and Juan unload our supplies."

Luis winked. "Elena was worried you were starving to death out here in the wilderness, so I am afraid she has packed enough food for the whole ninth Cavalry, should they happen by. She forgets that you are a great Indian fighter who is used to living off the land."

"There is eating, and then there is eating well." Elena retorted. "Today we eat well. After all, these men are heroes and deserve a hero's meal."

The house still had no roof, and with the walls being only to the tops of the window frames, a table was hastily constructed in the barn. Jube's rustic building had most of the loft to serve as a ceiling.

Jacob caught Jubaliah's grin and stopped him before he got a word out. "So help me Jubaliah, not one more boast about your dang barn..."

"I didn't say a thing." Jubaliah protested, then turned to Carmelita. "The house is mos' def'nitely more suited for entertainin' reg'lar guests though it only has four rooms."

He took her arm and led her inside the barn, speaking just loud enough for Jacob to hear. "Now, iffin' Jacob was entertainin' a king, or a beautiful lady such as yo' self, then the grander settin's ya see here is far more fittin'."

His voice trailed off as he led the blushing girl out through the open side of the structure to see the picturesque view. "I believe ya can tell a lot 'bout a man by the way he treats his animals, don't you, Miss Carmelita?"

Elena was right. There is eating, and then there's eating well. Chewing a handful of meat off a sharp spike seemed okay this morning, but after eating a full meal on china plates, Jacob guessed a strip of charred rabbit would come up somewhat wanting tomorrow. It was during dinner that Victor and Luis announced their plans to stay two days and help with the house-raising. Jacob was elated.

Counting the boys, who seemed eager to help, it made a six man crew. He knew they would have the roof on before it was time for them to leave.

Evening was coming, and Carmelita wanted Jubaliah to show her where the battle took place and the Indian cemetery that she had read about. Elena busied herself cleaning and unpacking while ordering the boys to partition off space for privacy in the barn with the tarps.

The men settled in the confines of the house walls, making themselves comfortable on piled stones around a small fire in the half built fireplace. The moon was rising full and the sun not quite gone, but the fire would ward off the evening chill when it came. "This is mighty nice of you to come all the way out here like this. You sure surprised us."

Victor made light of it. "It is our pleasure. Life gets boring in town and we were most curious about how you were doing. In fact, many people in town are curious, about a lot of things, Senor Jacob."

"Curious! Why?"

Victor settled on a broad stone and placed his hands on his knees. "Several reasons. First, you are a hero. I can see you are uncomfortable with the word hero, but Sholo had kept all but the bravest bottled up in town, and the mining is restricted to the bigger claims where there were plenty of men. His raids nearly ruined poor Luis here. Yes, you are a hero. Have you not read about it in the papers?"

Jacob frowned. "I've tried not to."

Luis joined in. "It is true, Jacob. You did my family and the town a great service. People love a hero and are naturally curious. They love someone new to talk about. It is just human nature."

Jacob looked at both men. "There's more you have to tell me isn't there?"

Victor glanced at Luis then spoke. "Damon Mathers. He is mad as hell. He confronted Luis in town and says he cheated him. He wants to know where Luis got his money. We have kept that a secret between us, but Mathers has heard about you and your ranch."

Victor paused, "He knows Luis gave you a lot of land. He checked at the land office. Mathers put two and two together. He is mad, real mad, and he was thundering in the saloon a few days back that he was going to pay the Land-Grabbing Nigger a visit. I am sorry, but those are his words, Senor Jacob."

Jacob shook his head. "You'd think that way out here in the middle of the most unwanted land on earth, a man could lose himself, or at least that any dangers he might face would come from wild savages and not some wealthy rancher. How can a man I have never met hate me so bad? I can't believe I'm that important."

Luis spoke up. "With a man like Mathers, believe it. He wants to be a cattle baron, a king, and taking down the Hero of Apache Springs would only add to his fame. He does not need much reason to hate you. We had to warn you. It is the least we could do."

"I thank you. If he comes, he comes. There's nothing I can do about that; but if he comes hunting trouble, he'll find it."

Luis pushed his hand through his peppered gray hair. "He has read about you and knows you are a fighter. If he comes, he is sure to bring his two boys; they're just as mean as him, but without sense to know when to stop. He also has a couple dozen cowhands."

Jacob chuckled, "Haven't you heard? I killed that many Apaches right here single handed."

Victor chimed in, "I heard it was fifty."

Carrying a pot of fresh coffee in one hand and balancing a tray of cups in the other, Elena stepped through the doorway. The men changed the subject to light-hearted talk, regarding the work they would do on the house come morning.

Elena was excited about the bath and interested in how a bachelor might furnish a home. Jacob never mentioned Rosie or his plans, but Elena could tell Jacob was a man with his sights on a family. "Senor Jacob, you are going to make a fine catch. Many a woman would be quite thrilled to settle into marriage in a house this wonderful. With the pond and all, it is right out of a fairytale, with you being the hero."

Jacob smiled awkwardly. He had never thought about Rosie hearing about him being a hero. He wished it had been fifty Indians.

As stars began to take up their position overhead in the blue gray sky, Roberto and Juan wandered in from brushing down the horses. The boys were wearing their pistols and cradling Winchesters in the crooks of their arms. Jacob smiled at the boys. "Armed for bear, I see. Not likely we will be attacked by Apaches tonight."

Juan twitched uncomfortably at being teased by the man he most wanted to impress. The shy boy slipped into the shadows behind his taller friend. Roberto, being bolder, nodded to Luis and offered a defense. "Senor Rincon said we could come see your ranch, but we were to protect the women folk."

Bolstered by his friend's courage, Juan edged closer to the light. "Si. He said if we let any harm come to the women, it will be our necks."

Old Luis laughed. "That I did, and I meant it."

Elena waved her hand "Oh posh, I think we are safe enough without all these guns."

The two young boys squirmed, fearing their hero saw them, not as brave vaqueros, but as little children at play. Jacob could see their misery.

"You've been given a job to do, so never mind our teasing; just stand your ground. Remember, Sholo let his guard down, and paid with his life beneath this very tree." Jacob pointed up through the open roof. "We wouldn't want history repeating itself."

A smile burst anew as Juan gripped his rifle and came to his full height. The realization that it all happened right here where they now stood left wonder telling on their young faces. Being with the actual hero made them feel a part of it. It was a flirt of danger that took them a tiny step closer to manhood.

In the distance, Jubaliah's laughter signaled his return from his walk with Carmelita. The men stood as she stepped through the doorway with Jube close behind. The girl's raven hair shimmered blue beneath the silver moon. Quiet and shy, her delicate beauty, in stark contrast to the rustic setting, was enough to steal any man's breath.

The starry-eyed girl timidly approached Jacob for the first time. "Senor Keever, you have done so much for my family and I have read all about you in the papers. Jube, I mean Senor Jackson has told me all the amazing feats that the articles left out. It is truly an honor to be a guest at your wonderful ranch."

Jacob cast a glance at Jubaliah. "Jube will have to tell me about all those amazing feats sometime, but thank you very much for your kind words. You and your family are always welcome."

Everyone retired early. Victor and the Rincons bunked down in the barn. Roberto and Juan chose the open loft, thinking it would be the best place to keep a look out for Indians. Carmelita had told Jubaliah earlier how excited the boys were. On the journey to the Hollow they had let their imaginations run wild, fantasizing about fighting blood-thirsty Apaches with the famous Sergeant Jacob Keever of the Ninth Cavalry.

Jacob and Jubaliah laid their bed rolls out under the stars as they had since coming to the Hollow – as they had most of their lives. A small fire crackled between them. When it burned low they would go to sleep with the coals for warmth. Jacob broke the silence. "Jube, I don't get all this hero stuff. It's all anyone talks about. Surely one article in a no account mining camp rag can't cause such a fuss."

Jubaliah raised on one elbow. "Well ol' friend, people want heroes ta believe in. Guess it's jus' yo' turn. And it weren't one article, it was three. Carmelita said that reporter, Barnabas Kane, sold the first story – the one ya wouldn't let me finish – to an eastern newspaper. So he wrote two more n' he's plannin' a book. Maybe he got a might fanciful when he ran out of facts. Money and fame'll do that."

Jacob lay silent in thought for a moment. "I imagine Rose has read about it by now. What did that first article say about me Jube?"

Jubaliah chuckled and reached into his saddlebag, "I knowed' curiosity would get to ya eventually."

51

Jubaliah leaned next to the fire and thumbed the pages. "Here it is. The beginnin' of the article is 'bout Apache depredation n' such leading up ta the Battle of Apache Springs. But it says, that after the courageous Buffalo Soldiers drove the blood thirsty savages back against the towerin' cliffs, the horrific battle finally ended when the notorious Apache Chief Sholo, seein' all his braves slaughtered by the fierce black troops, charged out of the woods like a great wounded bear. His Winchester frantically spittin' a hail of lead 'n flame at the one soldier who stood between him and freedom – Sergeant Jacob Keever of the valiant Ninth Cavalry. Sergeant Keever appeared before his adversary from a swirlin' mist of smoke, his face stained by battle. He stood alone, unwaverin', like a mighty oak facin' Sholo's ferocious onslaught armed only with his Springfield single shot carbine. The brave soldier must a' been protected by God Almighty, for not one of Sholo's screamin' bullets touched him. Sergeant Keever ignored the fiery hail of death that rained down upon him and took steady aim. He fired his single round, drillin' the Apache chief right through his black heart, sendin' the murderous heathen back to the fires of hell from whence he came.

"It goes on to say that, while Lieutenant Reinhart's skillful leadership 'n bold charge routed the savages, it was Sergeant Jacob Keever's courageous stand that brought Sholo's bloody reign a' terror to an end. Sergeant Jacob Keever, no matter the color a' his skin, is a true hero deservin' the respect 'n gratitude of all men."

Jubaliah folded the paper. "That's mighty pretty writing. Seems like everyone wants ya to be a hero but you. Hell, even Reinhart profits from ya bein' a hero. The boys back at the fort are prob'ly splittin' a gut making up stuff fer this here Barnabas Kane feller ta print, though it don't seem he needs no help.

Carmelita says even I'm mentioned by name in the last article. Guess he's runnin' outa stuff ta print. Jacob, like I said, the truth's there. Sholo's dead n' you kilt' him. They'll paint what they want 'round it and ya can't stop it no more'n ya can bring Sholo back ta life. It ain't no longer yer story. You's now a part a' theirs."

"Hero! I ain't no such thing. Jube, they got it all wrong. It's not real, and it makes my dream less real. I don't even seem real; least ways not how people see me. My dream finally comes true, and I'm somebody else. I can't do it. I can't be what they want. I'm going to live my life on my terms. History will have its truth and I will have mine."

"Spoken like a true hero."

"Don't you start."

"Jacob, just so's ya know, while we's talking 'bout truth, I'll give ya mine. Maybe your truth ain't no more real n' theirs. That dark mornin' I was there in that battle by yo' side, as I've been countless times before, ever since the battle of Island Mound where ya bayoneted that Reb' who had his musket ta my head, and you not much more than a half growed' kid with an' empty gun. Told myself right then n' there, 'here's a boy I's' stickin' to.'

"I know ya, and you's more of a hero than ya think. Have ya ever wondered why me n' the boys followed ya so willin'ly all these years, and why they's saying all them things now? It ain't jus' for jest, they want ya to get the credit you really deserve. Over the years ya showed your mettle in more battles than jus' this 'un n' no one ever sung ya no tune. Now ya s gettin' the whole chorus. You's a hero to me, old friend, and now you's a hero of the people, where ya b'long. Be yo' self, but don't be thinkin' everyone else a fool."

There was a long silence. Both men had said their piece and it was a darn sight more than either had planned. Jacob faced away from the fire. "Good night, Jube."

****

Jubaliah pushed out of his bedroll, drawn by the smell of strong coffee borne on the fresh morning air. A rattle of pans and the song of a whippoorwill welcomed the day. Far beyond the cattails, Jacob could be seen taking his morning walk as he always did. Juan and Roberto were scurrying after him. Luis was proud of these boys. They were good kids. Both were the same age, yet Roberto was a head taller than Juan.

Juan had the quicker wit, with darting eyes. Still it was Roberto who was the leader, not because of his size or strength, but because of his confidence and easy-going manner. He was comfortable in his own skin, a rare thing in boys that age. Roberto was more like Jacob, strong and serious, a person you could trust.

Juan, on the other hand, often set the older men's heads to shaking by his foolish actions, done more out of nervousness than a lack of common sense. He let fear cloud his judgment. But Juan tried hard, and so it was that everyone took a natural liking to him as much for his vulnerability as for his good humor.

The one thing both boys shared was their awe of Sergeant Jacob Keever, hero of the Battle of Apache Springs. Boys of that age dream about courage in battle, but few ever got to meet a real live hero. So here they were in his magical Hollow, entwined with the events that made him famous. It seemed the most amazing thing.

While Jacob might not have understood the boys' hero worship, he did see their eagerness to be with him and he made an effort to be pleasant, which didn't come easy to a crusty, tight-lipped army sergeant used to barking orders. Questions danced in the boys' eyes, but fortunately for Jacob, the youngsters were too shy to speak, and settled for tagging along.

Jubaliah watched them until they disappeared into the pines, then sauntered to the barn, rubbing and scratching his rumpled form.

Elena was stirring some sizzling bacon with a two-pronged fork over a hastily constructed makeshift hearth next to the feed trough. Peaches was eyeing a basket of tortillas perched on a wooden stump nearby. Victor and Luis sat on their cots looking little better than Jubaliah. "Mornin' everyone; where's the sleepin' princess?"

Elena nodded towards the canvas wall. "Sleeping."

Jubaliah stepped over and knocked on the post. From inside, Carmelita's sleepy voice wailed, "Go away, my hair is a mess."

"It ain't gunna' get no better layin' in there. Come on out n' face the laughter."

A small shape wrapped in a blanket shot out from beneath the tarp and headed straight for the pond.

Jubaliah watched her go. "I've chased Injuns that ain't moved that fast."

The men chuckled. Elena spoke without looking up from her work. "A young girl's vanity. I suspect, Senor Jackson, the Indians you mentioned weren't smitten by your charming ways."

With a bit of frustration, Luis added. "She should be smitten, at twenty-two she is almost a spinster."

"Now, Luis, don't you go getting on her again. Pickin's out here are mighty slim … No offense Senor Jubaliah. A big strong dashing soldier like yourself, doesn't come riding into a young girl's life every day. Senor Jacob isn't the only hero, at least not to Carmelita's eyes."

Jubaliah stood dumbfounded. Somehow during the night he had become an acceptable marriage prospect for the first time in his life, and he kind of liked it. Maybe the Hollow was a magical place after all. Jubaliah rubbed his stubbled face. "Guess I ought to clean up."

Elena took on an air of authority. "Both of you could do with a little scrubbing. If you and Senor Jacob have other outfits to change into, I will wash the clothes you have on. It looks like it has been awhile since they have seen real soap."

Jacob stepped into the opening with the two boys in tow. Jubaliah hurried past them. "It's washing day, Jacob. Iffin' we turn our duds over to Mrs. Rincon, she'll accept the courageous task of washin' 'em. They's heroes all over the place this mornin'. I'll have ta check my wardrobe and see what I's got ta wear."

"You only have two outfits, and they are both more dirt than thread."

"Ain't so, Ain't so a'tall!" Jubaliah protested as he ambled off.

The men and boys sat down on a split log bench at the plank table which Elena had covered with a fine white cloth. Victor helped Elena set out the knives and forks, while Luis sat patiently waiting.

In the center of the table were serving plates piled with bacon, potatoes and refried beans. Elena had even gathered stonecrop from near the cliff which she cooked up as well.

The primitive surroundings had not prevented her from setting an elegant table. It was obvious that Elena was a woman of breeding. One could sense the grander days long past, before the coming of the gringos. Even the elegant hand-painted china she packed spoke of a better time. Like her daughter, Elena had been a beautiful woman in her day.

Carmelita came walking back from the pond rubbing a towel against her long black hair. Before she reached the table, Jubaliah appeared in the door dressed in his starched military blues. Carmelita's eyes sparkled. Jubaliah pulled her chair from the table with an exaggerated bow that did not fail to impress her. "Miss Carmelita, you look lovely this mornin'."

The girl blushed and ducked her head. "You do too. I mean..." Her words trailed off as her blush deepened.

****

After breakfast one final surprise awaited Jacob. Luis showed him the contents of the wooden crate in the wagon. It was the windows Jacob had ordered. This meant the house could truly be finished by the time the guests were to leave.

The day was spent in great activity with everyone doing as much as he could. Jubaliah kept to his barn, vowing he would keep pace with the five men working on the house. With his shirt stripped away, his muscles strained and rippled under the labor. Carmelita was never far away.

Jacob and the boys laid rock at a fast pace. Juan and Roberto did their best to match Jacob stone for stone. Victor meticulously installed the windows, showing he was no stranger to manual work, while old Luis proved his carpentry skills by fashioning a pair of sawhorses. Then from an old box of tools, he produced a drawing knife and set about crafting the doors and shutters, mainly from the window crates.

Elena did not have the brawn of the men, but she didn't let that stop her. Behind the house, Jacob had a huge pile of caliche left over from the floor. He had brought up a whole wagon load. This she planned to use for plaster on the two walls that faced out in each bedroom. The cream color would brighten up the rooms and stop cold air from seeping in through the cracks. The rooms would have the quaint mixture of stucco and stone since the interior walls would be left alone. She also intended to plaster all the walls in the bathroom.

Elena had the boys shovel the caliche into a makeshift trough where she mixed it with bucketed water to a thick paste using a heavy wooden pole almost as tall as herself. Elena added prickly pear cactus to the mix, which she boiled down in a large pot. Its sticky gum helped the plaster adhere better to the walls. Jacob was concerned that she had taken on too much, but Luis told him not to worry. She had plastered most of their hacienda herself and was equal to any man when it came to mudding.

Carmelita stayed with Jubaliah helping him however she could, from holding planks in place to handing up tools and even working right along side him, hammer and nail. She wanted to prove that she was not afraid to dirty her hands.

Clatter and chatter rang through the Hollow. Hard work cemented new friendships that would last a lifetime and endure the harshest winds.

At day's end the final stones had been laid into place. The peaks of the house reached to their full height, tied together by the long center wall. Even the large log rafters were notched and all set firmly in stone. The change in one day was simply amazing.

True to his word, Jubaliah had completed the front side of the barn's roof with split planks. Standing at the right angle, the barn looked finished. He did not let it go unnoticed.

The exhausted men slumped against its heavy timbers, while Elena tended a huge pot of stew. Vegetables and meat swirled in a thick brown broth. Somehow Jubaliah found the strength to go for one more stroll with Carmelita. This time they followed the last rays of sun into the ancient woods that bordered the cliffs.

Elena looked after them with a mother's concern. Jacob patted her shoulder. "Don't worry, Jubaliah will keep her safe from savage or beast. She will come to no harm." As an after-thought, Jacob added, "Jubaliah may not be an officer, but he is a gentleman." Elena smiled and returned to her work.

Jacob was already bedded down when Jubaliah returned from a long stay at the barn. After stoking the fire back to life, Jube fussed around with his gear, making more noise than warranted. Then he cleared his throat several times, and added another log to the fire.

Rumbling a deep growl, Jacob rolled to face his friend. "I take it something's on your mind?"

The big man didn't apologize, he had to speak or bust. "Jacob, at first I thought ya was crazy ta leave the army n' follow a fool's dream. Now, well now I envy ya. I wish I had a ranch ta offer someone. I don't mean I'm planning on marriage or nothin', but being here in the Hollow, with Carmelita, well, ya know what I mean. I feel like I gots' more now than I ever had n' the truth is I ain't got nothin'—jus' a taste a somethin' a whole lot better'n I've ever knowed, an' no way ta do a dang thing about it."

Jacob sat up and looked long at his friend. "Jube, take a look at yourself. You are younger than me by two years. What you do is your choice. A loving woman will wait for a good man, so long as she knows there's a future in it. I started out with a free homestead and I suspect that somewhere on my property where it winds on down these cliffs, there may still be a few springs left to be found…and well, as long as I got a biscuit, you've got half. So if that becomes your choice, I can't think of a better neighbor."

Jubaliah stood staring at the barn. "The Rincons is decent people. They look for the good in a man and his color don't make no matter. Bein' Mexican, their experience maybe ain't too different n' mine. Thanks, Jacob. You turned it around for me. I gots a lot ta think on."

Jubaliah kicked off his boots and crawled into bed. "Jacob, iffin' I do decide ta change paths, you owe me a barn."

The second morning came with a good start. The weather was cooler with a light breeze. Overhead, large billowy clouds tinged with gray never seemed to move. Jacob and Jubaliah were both splitting logs into planks before breakfast, and after the meal all the men joined in.

Luis put his skills to work building the kitchen table and chairs. The table would be long, seating four people on each side and a person at each end. Luis came from a time when everything was handmade with care. Having no use for the new-fangled nails, Luis doweled the table and chairs with finger sized branches of mountain mahogany, making them much stronger. He then bound the joints of the chairs with wet rawhide. As the leather dried, it pulled the joints tightly together until they were as rigid as if carved from a single piece of wood. To make the seats more comfortable, Luis used a double layer of thick elk hide that Jacob had lying in the barn. This also saved a lot of time.

Standing next to a chopping block under the shade of the tall pines, Jacob motioned Roberto and Juan to him. "You ever split shingles?"

Looking nervous, the boys shook their heads. Jacob gave a wink. "Don't matter, until a few days ago neither had I, but I figured out a way that works." Picking up a short cedar log free of knots, Jacob dropped it on the chopping block. Grasping the large double-bladed ax, Jacob swung it high over his head. His powerful swing split the log with one blow. With two more quick swings he split the halves into quarters, then gave the boys a reassuring smile. "From here, it's just like slicing a pie." He picked up a wooden mallet and a froe. "Ever used a froe?"

Another blank stare was the only answer from the timid youths. "Pretty simple, just a long flat blade with a handle on one end." Positioning the froe in the middle of the pie shaped block, Jacob tapped it with the mallet. "Always start in the middle, so it don't curl. Now you just keep slicing the wedges into smaller pieces until you get them down to the thickness of your finger on the outside edge and sharp as a tooth on the other end." He made a toothy grin and clicked his teeth.

After repeating the process several times, Jacob held up a finished shingle to the amazement of the boys. "The trick is making them as fast as

I can pound them into place on the roof." Jacob handed the mallet to Roberto and the froe to Juan. "Let's see what you can do."

The boys jumped at the challenge. They found it worked best if one wielded the mallet while the other steadied the froe instead of trying it alone like Jacob had. After several failed attempts and useless wood shavings, they finally produced their first shingle. Dropping the froe, Juan proudly held it up for Jacob's inspection. "We did it, we did it!"

"Ya sure did, now six or seven hundred more, and you'll be real carpenters."

Work proceeded smoothly with military discipline. The boys split the cedar shingles with growing speed. Victor stood on the ladder handing shingles to Jacob who spent most of the day on the roof rapidly pounding away.

Elena used her time to finish plastering the walls. Luis had been right, Elena came from tough pioneer stock and was used to work. When she was done, she fashioned a broom and swept every room of the house clean. Next, she washed windows and set a neat pile of wood by the fireplace. She even arranged wildflowers on the mantle. These were a woman's touches that made a house a home.

Jacob cast a glance to the barn and could see Carmelita standing in the hayloft handing lumber to Jubaliah. It was easy to tell she had joined the competition and wanted her man to win.

Since the barn's roof was being made with long planks only, while the house was getting planks and shingles, Jube stood a fair chance of winning. The day was filled with happy commotion and eager talk as everyone rushed to the end that was now in sight.

With very nail hammered, and every task completed their excitement rose. A dream was being realized, and shared. The humble cabin was more than lumber and rocks, it was the intangible bond that binds friends and neighbors together.

At precisely three o'clock on a warm April day, the noise stopped. The last shingle was nailed in place. Jacob climbed down from the ladder and joined the group standing in the front yard staring at their creation. The little stone house was beautiful – the kind of home that would give guests pause to comment. It was as Jacob had pictured it in his dream, with a steep shingled roof and a welcoming porch.

Jacob wiped the sweat from his brow and turned to the barn. Jubaliah and Carmelita were gone. So was Buck and one of the pintos. Jube had won.

Mrs. Rincon folded her hands under her chin, "Jacob, it is simply beautiful. All it needs is a woman to love it and make it a home."

She winked at him, "I am sure you have your plans laid. No man goes to this much trouble just for himself. Now everyone clean up while I prepare a great dinner to eat in Jacob's new home."

58

Chapter -6-
Carmelita

The two older gents sat resting on the porch. Victor's hand twitched, too tired to chase away an annoying fly that refused to be dissuaded. After a long quiet moment that seemed to need some words, the attorney cleared his throat, as much to break the silence as to speak his thoughts. "Yes sir, I am sure glad we came. Have to see this place to believe it. Jacob and this quiet hollow seem to fit. Like there's nowhere else on earth for either one of them. Kind of sad, but kind of nice, it shows that there's a place for each of us. We just have to find it."

Luis rose, and turned his attention to their host who was now at the barn. The old Mexican had survived a lifetime on the edge of the desert in part by reading people. Jacob's usual strong steady demeanor had changed. There was no apparent problem, but Jacob was definitely concerned about something. The big man moved from the edge of the corral to Jubaliah's gear stacked by the wall of the barn and then back to the corral.

Not taking time to open the gate, Jacob hopped the fence. Luis cut Victor off in mid-sentence and headed to the barn with the attorney following along, attempting to keep the conversation going. When they got to the fence, Jacob was saddling Major. "Is there something wrong Jacob?" Luis's fatherly concern was kicking in.

"Maybe nothing." Jacob responded while pulling up on the cinch. "I just want to be sure."

Luis wrinkled his brow. "What do you see, Jacob? Is my daughter safe?"

Jacob paused, deciding to take a moment to answer the old man's fears. "Well, here it is as I see it. It may be nothing, but a man has got to play it safe out here, and that's what I'm doing. Jube told me yesterday that he had spotted unshod hoof prints while they were out riding. He could not tell how old they were, so he did not say anything to worry Carmelita."

Luis cut in. "But Jubaliah would not take Carmelita riding if he felt it was not safe."

"Mr. Rincon, I don't think Jube took your daughter riding."

"What do you mean? They are both gone and the horses are gone. Jacob, tell me what you see."

Roberto and Juan joined the men at the fence. If Jacob was going riding, they wanted to go along.

While answering, Jacob strapped on his Colt. "Jube left his carbine. He always takes it when he goes riding, even if Carmelita isn't with him. I think he rode out in a hurry – in such a hurry he didn't even take the time to tell us. Maybe he didn't think it important enough to worry us, but it was important enough to worry him."

Jacob pointed to the roof of the barn. "The roof isn't done. There's still one plank missing. That's not like Jube. Luis, I think your daughter got tired of waiting, or maybe wanted more attention than Jube was giving her, so she quietly saddled the pony in the barn where Jube couldn't see, and took it out through the small door on the east side. The tracks show this. The door is hanging open. Maybe she was just playing games. Jube saw her from the roof, as she wanted him to, and took off after her. He didn't even bother to put his shirt on. It's still hanging right there on the post."

Leading them through the small door, Jacob pointed to the ground. "When they have gone riding before, Jube has led. Here, old Buck's tracks are on top of the pony's. The stride is wide; he left on a run."

"That daughter of mine! If she has caused problems, well, she is not too big to spank." Luis shook his bony fist.

"I'll just ride out and take a look. There's no reason to…"

Everyone heard it. The low rumble of a gunshot as it echoed off the cliffs. They all held their breath. There was a pause, and then two more shots in quick succession.

Jacob turned to Victor, "We're going to need to borrow your horse. Then he turned to the boys. Whose paint did Carmelita take?"

Juan raised his hand.

"Saddle Victor's. Grab your guns and be ready to ride hard."

The boys jumped into action. A mixture of fear and excitement colored their young faces.

Turning to Luis and Victor, Jacob tried to comfort them. "We don't know anything. Don't worry Elena. Just keep her inside. Close the shutters on the back of the house and carry in lots of water. If something happens it could be a long wait."

Luis assured Jacob. "I know what to do. I had my dealings with Sholo too, and his father before him. Just find my daughter and bring her home safely so I can wring her neck."

Jacob understood Luis. They were not so different. It was only Luis' years that kept him from going along. He would be able to handle trouble if it came to him. The house was built to provide protection. If trouble found its way to the Hollow while Jacob and the boys were away, Luis, Elena and Victor would be able to hold out until they returned.

Jacob gripped his Springfield carbine and then set it down. As the boys rode up, he pulled a rolled blanket from inside his buckboard. Tossing the blanket aside, he held up Sholo's Winchester. Feathers still hung from the barrel. Jacob shoved it into the scabbard on his saddle and crammed a box of cartridges into the saddlebags.

"Let's hope you can stay young boys awhile longer, but if it comes to it, I'll expect you to explode into manhood with all the fire you've got in you. Now follow my lead."

Leaping into the saddle, Jacob spurred Major, following hard on Jube's trail.

****

It has always been that just a few words can change the direction of a single moment or an entire life. While Jacob and the boys had been frantically working away on the cabin, rushing to finish the last shingles. Jubaliah raised from pounding a plank into place and looked down at Carmelita impatiently. "Come on, ya lazy girl. You're no faster at work than you is at ridin' that paint. Let's get to it or Jacob'll win fer sure."

Carmelita's eyes flashed. "Here is your old board, if that is what is most important to you."

"Well, of course it is. Ya didn't think I was growin' sweet on ya , did ya?"

He winked and blew her a kiss, then went back to work.

Carmelita climbed down from the loft and stepped into the corral to take a better look at how the roof was progressing. One of the ponies came up and nuzzled her from behind. She gave it a hug. A mischievous light danced in the girl's eyes as she thought to herself, "I will show him how fast I can ride, and find out what is more important to him, me or finishing that dumb roof."

A moment later Carmelita shot out the back door of the barn. She whirled the pony around, looked up at Jubaliah, and blew him a kiss. "There is your kiss back. If you were the big man you think you are, you'd come down here and get a real kiss." With that, she turned the pony and headed into the brush. The fiery girl was out of sight before Jubaliah could react. "Stupid woman."

Jubaliah started to finish the last plank. Beating Jacob was important. He raised the hammer, held it in the air for a moment, then threw it to the ground. "Damn it. Stupid woman!"

He climbed down, and a moment later he was saddling Buck. Jube began to worry. She would have several minutes lead. He knew that the pony with little Carmelita on his back could out run old Buck carrying his two hundred pounds of weight.

Carmelita came out of the thick brush that bordered the far side of the pond. She giggled at her mischief and spurred the pony through a clearing, then charged down the hill.

Her father had not allowed her to ride the open range during the last year while Sholo had been making his raids. Her younger brother who was only nineteen and now the ranch foreman got to ride wherever he wanted, and it galled her. She had taken care of him growing up, and now he was in charge. To add salt to the wound, even her little brother had forbidden her to ride.

Jubaliah did not treat her like a child. In the last days, he had taken her hiking and riding across breathtaking country, giving her a taste of what she had been missing. She felt free for the first time, and she didn't want it to end when they finished that silly barn.

Carmelita whipped the reins and turned the pony off the trail and down into a shallow ravine bordered in Scrub Oak where there was shade. She would go no further. The pony needed a rest, so she slowed their pace to a walk. Besides, she did want Jubaliah to eventually catch her.

The end of the ravine poured out on to an open knoll surrounded by pinyon and juniper. She figured she had ridden less than a third of the way down the hill to the flats below. The Mexican girl really had no idea how long it would take Jubaliah to catch her, and now she feared it might take him a long time. She giggled again, knowing she was going to catch hell from him when he did find her. The horse moseyed along from clearing to clearing, grazing as it went.

Finally Carmelita heard hoofbeats coming towards her. A huge smile spread across her face. She ducked her head under a branch and shot into the next clearing to take her punishment. "It's about time you…"

To her utter shock, Carmelita burst into a circle of armed Apaches. The nearly naked savages gripping bows and rifles stared back at her with astonished grins. She froze, unable to will her body to move. Her stomach knotted with fear as the sick feeling grew until she shook uncontrollably. Suddenly she was a little girl again, helpless and in trouble.

There were five braves. One rode forward and took the reins from her hand. She did not resist. All of them were young, the biggest not being any older than herself. She tried to think, but even that was beyond her power. Would they kill her, or worse?

The savages pushed their ponies in around her. The youngest boy, not more than fifteen and riding an old gray faced mule, leaned over and flipped her hair. She pulled back in fear. A murmur of laughter rose from the Indians. Pointing at her, the braves made comments in their own tongue. The words she did not understand, but the laughter was vulgar. Carmelita shrunk deeper into her saddle. Her eyes glistened with fright.

The oldest boy kicked his pony closer, pressing his bare leg against hers. He did not hide his unholy intent. Lifting her chin, he held Carmelita's eyes until the first surrendering tear rolled off her cheek. He smiled approvingly, then with the back of his knuckle, slowly traced a line down her slender neck, staking his claim.

Carmelita wore a simple Mexican blouse that hung loosely, offering no protection. The savage hand brushing against her skin caused

Carmelita to tremble for the brave's amusement. He refused to let her look away. Her humiliation brought him more pleasure than her flesh.

Hooking his finger in the thin cloth, he slowly bared her shoulder. Carmelita's eyes darted to the hungry faces of the boys. It was only a bare shoulder, but she felt naked under their stare.

The young brave licked his lips. They were the same age, but she was his prize. Decency did not apply. The rules of war allowed him to take her, perhaps even demanded it. This was a rule they both understood.

The boy moved his hand slowly down the neckline, tormenting her. Eyes glinting, he gripped the flimsy material between her breasts, ready to rip it off. Carmelita gasped. An involuntary squeal rose from deep in her throat rebuking the degrading silence.

Suddenly the brave stiffened, and looked around. His hand instantly retreated to his rifle, leaving the poor girl shattered but covered. The other braves reacted to their leader's concern. He realized that young girls did not come this far alone.

Some words were exchanged and the other braves were instantly alert. Fearing she might be followed, they headed out of the clearing in single file, using gestures instead of words. The second Indian held her reins while she sat meekly gripping the pommel of her saddle with both hands. She reeled from what might have been, and still could be. It was only a reprieve. Her breath came in feeble sobs, as she fought back tears.

They rode with hardly a sound for several minutes; Carmelita had not yet spoken one word of protest. What good would it do?

Deep inside the Mexican girl, a will to fight began to grow. They had no right to take her, to touch her. Perhaps she could warn Jubaliah, or at least let the savages know she was not afraid. She thought of the boy's hand inside her blouse. "You bastard!" She screamed at the top of her lungs, filling the air with her injustice.

The ponies pulled to an instant stop. Anger burned in the leader's sneer. He turned his pony around and came back to Carmelita, a fire smoldering in his eyes. She did not look away. The young brave clenched his jaw, then suddenly backhanded her hard across the mouth.

Recovering her balance, Carmelita brushed the hair from her face and raised her chin in defiance. The Indian snarled and raised his fist high, but she did not flinch. Her stare matched his.

Slowly he lowered his hand, spun his pony around, and the procession continued. Now was not the time for a noisy scene, he would deal with her later.

Carmelita's face stung. The taste of blood salted her lip, but the girl was glad she had shouted. She had taken back some control of her life.

Her heartbeat slowed, but Carmelita wanted Jube... Maybe he was still building that stupid barn and didn't care.

The Apaches left the deer trail they were following and headed straight up the backbone of a long steep ridge. It was hard going, and the ponies struggled for footing on the loose rock. Carmelita wrapped her arms around her pony's neck, holding on as tightly as she could.

Just as the leader neared the top of the ridge, a thundering of hooves exploded above them. All hell broke loose. Carmelita looked up to see the belly of Buck come flying through the air. It looked like he would sail right over them. Instead, the old horse aimed his feet, and came down in a steep angle, crashing into the lead pony, causing it to rear and fall over backwards.

Jube had come for her! Carmelita could see murderous rage in his eyes. As long as she lived, she would never forget that look, or forget that it was for her protection. Jubaliah drove Buck into the second pony, sending it rolling down the hill.

Screaming horses, eyes wide with terror, fought to keep their balance in the confusion, their riders helpless to control them.

On a dead run, Jubaliah's huge arm caught Carmelita around the waist. Sweeping her out of the saddle, he cradled her against his chest. The soldier pushed Buck on down the ridge. A powerful kick from his left boot sent the next Indian flying off his mount and sailing through the air. With flaying arms, the brave landed hard, rolling down the steep face.

The last two Indians were trying to bring their weapons to bear, but Jubaliah's charge had caught them off guard. Jube drove a massive fist into the face of the next Indian as he passed him and, pressed Buck into the flank of the last pony, spinning him sideways, launching his hapless rider into a patch of prickly pear.

It was over in an instant. Jubaliah left the ridge heading south, trying to get out of the line of fire. As they dove head-long into the trees, a single shot plowed into the pinyon next to them, scattering bark. Two more shots were fired as they crossed the next ridge, but they were out of range.

Several minutes of hard riding brought them to another wooded gully. Jubaliah pulled Buck to a halt. The old horse was spent. He was white with lather and coughing hard.

Jubaliah jumped down, with Carmelita captured in his arms. He held her tight, her feet dangling in the air. His body was as hard as iron, but he was trembling. "Stupid woman. If anything had happened to you..."

"Please, I can't breathe."

Jubaliah eased his grip. Carmelita looked up at him. The rage was gone from his eyes, replaced by fear, born of love. She felt guilty for the danger she had put him in, and what he had to do for her.

The sides of his arms were cut and bleeding from the race through the snarl of scrub oak branches. Tears flooded her eyes. Jubaliah softened. No matter what she had done, he couldn't bear to see her cry. "Ya don't get off that easy." He said sternly. "I believe ya owe me a kiss."

Carmelita tried to laugh but melted into sobs. She threw her arms around Jubaliah's neck with all the strength left in her and kissed him long and hard.

Finally, taking a quivering breath, she pressed her cheek against his and fell silent. Jubaliah held her for a tender moment, then let her slide to the ground while he caught his breath. "Wow, for a kiss like that, I owe ya a few more Injuns."

Again Carmelita tried to laugh, but too many emotions sat too close to the surface. It would take time for her to be all right. Still struggling with tears, she sniffed. "That has got to be the bravest thing any man has ever done, charging five armed Apaches without a gun. You went through them like a plow through sand."

She touched his bleeding arms. "Oh, Jube! Are you okay?"

Jubaliah grinned. "Nothin' a whole lot of lovin' won't cure." Carmelita stifled a laugh. "It's not funny. I could have gotten you killed."

Buck coughed hard again.

"Is he going to be alright?"

"I think so, but we better get ta walkin'. When them Injuns get themselves put back together, they might get to rememberin' how pretty you is."

Fear clouded Carmelita's face. "Jube, I was so frightened, I couldn't move. They just came up and took the reins out of my hand. I wasn't brave like you. I feel ashamed."

"Ah, don't worry. Heck, first time, I wasn't brave like me. It takes a few times of getting' knocked down before ya start fightin' back."

His words helped. Carmelita touched her tender cheek and raised her chin in proud defiance. "I called them bastards."

Jubaliah gently brushed his thumb on a small bruise; his eyes narrowed. "If I'd knowed' 'bout this, I wouldn't a been so gentle on 'em."

She marveled at how easy humor came to him on the heels of such terror, as though what happened was no big thing. Then she remembered the rage in his eyes, and how he had trembled when he first held her. Humor was his way of holding it together. She saw him as a man capable of emotions, and not an unreachable hero.

She was in control again. "Let's get moving. Jube, you've got a plank to put up if my father doesn't break it over my backside first."

Jubaliah laughed, "What makes ya think I didn't nail it into place a'fore I came after ya?"

Carmelita leaned against him, "Cuz' you're crazy about me."

Half an hour had passed since they had heard the gunshots. Jacob led the boys down the mountain at a dangerous speed. When they reached a steep ridge that the Roberto and Juan felt sure he would turn their course.

65

Instead Jacob just spurred Major to a greater pace and hurled down the slope at a dead run.

With no time to question, the boys followed, their hearts pounding in their throats. Juan leaned back in the saddle as far as he could, but still felt like he would tumble over the pony's head and be trampled. By the time they reach the bottom, it was more of an uncontrolled slide – rocks and dust formed a choking cloud around the ponies.

As soon as they hit flat ground, they were off and running again across the next plateau. They followed a long winding deer trail, jumping fissures and tearing through brush. The harrowing ride seemed like it would never end.

When Juan felt he could go no more, the mesa suddenly fell away before them, bringing them to a quick stop at a rocky cliff that afforded them a view of the land below. Jacob leaned forward on Major, peering through his field glasses. The boys steadied their mounts next to him, welcoming the breather.

Juan did not know how much longer he could have held such a pace. He tried to hide his shaking. Was this how grown men rode into battle? Was he ready?

Thrusting a finger, Jacob shouted. "Look! There! Five Indians traveling along the bottom of that arroyo. I don't see any sign of Jube or Carmelita, but the last Indian is leading a riderless pony. Juan, is that your pinto?"

Juan squinted his young eyes, "Si, that's his markings!"

Jacob slapped his reins, "Let's cut them off! Keep a lookout for more!"

Roberto and Juan exchanged glances as they spurred their horses. They were outnumbered, but it didn't matter to Jacob. It was as they hoped and now feared. The boys were riding into battle with the Hero of Apache Springs.

The arroyos spread out like splayed fingers from the mountain above. Jacob led them down an arroyo which opened into a flat plain that was joined by the arroyo where the Indians rode.

His heart pounding as they twisted through the narrow gully, Juan glanced back at Roberto looking for assurance, but his friend's expression gave him none.

Nausea rose in his stomach. Juan was going to be sick. He was riding into battle with his hero, and he could see himself by Jacob's side, heaving his guts out.

Finally, the arroyo leveled out into a thicket of junipers spreading into the one the Indians would have to come through. Jacob slowed the ponies to a walk and came out well in front of the Apaches. He pulled to a stop in a long grassy clearing and took position in the center of the trail. "Move to the side over there; keep in the shadow of the trees. Stay out of sight until I signal to you, then ride out slowly, guns raised high. We want to talk to them, not fight them unless we have to. If it does come to killin', choose your targets and empty your guns like hell was opening beneath you. In a gunfight – there is no second place."

The frightened boys hurriedly found a spot deep in the Scrub Oak, not seeing how this could end peacefully. There had been shots fired, the Indians had Juan's pony, and Carmelita was missing. This was a renegade band of Apaches, and they weren't looking for polite conversation.

Juan's young hand was sweating against his rifle. Wondering if he could even shoot, the boy looked to Roberto who was sitting straight as a ramrod; his resolute manner had returned. His friend would fight if it came to it, no doubt about that. As always, Roberto would do the right thing. Juan's question was, would he? The doubt clawed at his gut. "Roberto, what if they fire at us?"

"We stand." Roberto was grim. "It was our job to protect the Senorita and we didn't do it. We stand 'til we fall."

Juan swallowed hard. He hadn't thought of it that way. It was a matter of honor. The boy sank into his saddle. This would be his first life and death decision. Could he find the courage of his friend?

While Juan struggled for an answer, the plodding sound of horses rose through the junipers. He glanced from the thicket to the big man sitting erect on the great horse. The butt of Sholo's Winchester rested on the pommel, the barrel pointing towards the sky.

To Juan, the stoic soldier looked like a statue he had seen in a book – powerful and magnificent, hard as granite. The boy trembled in his saddle and looked away, every breath he took rattled in his chest. Was he the only one frightened out of his wits?

The Indians came into the clearing about fifty feet from them with their heads down. They looked beat. One brave barely clung to his horse with cuts up and down his body. Another had a face so swollen, Juan doubted if he could see. Whatever happened, the fight was knocked out of them. The warriors saw the lone rider blocking the trail, and came to a sudden halt.

For a moment no one moved. Then Jacob raised the palm of his hand, signaling he wanted to talk, and urged Major forward. The Indians gripped their weapons, but a cold flame blazed in the eyes of the big man, freezing them in their tracks. To oppose this stranger was death. He growled in their tongue. It was clearly a command.

Jacob motioned to the boys. Slowly and calmly, Roberto pushed his mount forward, reins in one hand, rifle pointed high in the other. Taking a deep breath, Juan followed Roberto's lead. Fear boiled in his stomach, but he wasn't going to show it. The Indians jerked their weapons towards the young vaqueros as they appeared from cover. Juan started to aim his rifle in response. "Keep your barrel up." Roberto cautioned under his breath.

Juan regained his composure. The warriors twisted nervously on their ponies, unsure of what to do.

Waving his hands, the lead Indian frantically pleaded with his braves not to shoot, an order the frightened Indians willingly obeyed. None wanted to die.

Roberto stopped less than ten feet from the line of Apaches. Pulling up by his side, Juan struggled to calm his breathing.

The lead Indian faced Jacob. His voice was high and weak. It was clear he did not want to fight. They would talk.

Jacob asked questions, the Indian answered. At one point, the boys could see Jacob fill with anger. The Apaches could see it too. The leader quickly recounted a story, using huge gestures. It was obvious as he jerked about as though being hit, that they had been on the losing end. He could not hide his disgrace.

The questioning continued. Juan looked at the young Indian holding the reins of his stolen pony. The boy was no older than himself. He was poor, wearing only a tattered loincloth and ragged bindings on his feet. His bare skin was stained with dust and long streams of sweat. Scratches covered his starved body. Crouched on the back of an old gray-faced jenny mule, he stared back at Juan who by contrast was handsomely garbed in vaquero fashion with a large sombrero and a pearl handled revolver at his side.

The Indian's soiled face showed envy and shame. He knew what Juan was thinking and he hated the Mexican, whose mere presence made him feel like dirt.

Juan could not help feeling sadness for the Apache's discomfort. No one should be so wretched. Fear was something Juan understood all too well, and in the naked Indian he saw a measure greater than his own.

Jacob's grilling finally ended. The young brave slumped in relief. Dismissing him, Jacob lifted his eyes to Juan, and motioned "Get your pony, son. We're leaving."

The Indian boy spoke broken English and understood the soldier's command. His young face twisted in anguish. Perhaps the older boys would not have let him keep the pony, but while he held the reins, this beautiful stallion was his to cherish, a foolish dream for a one who knew that no dreams were possible for him. He stared at Juan, unable to hide his pain. Tears rolled down his cheeks. His humiliation was plain for all to see. He was told to be a man, but he was just a boy.

Juan sat silent for a long moment. The braves hung their heads in disgrace. Taking the prized stallion from them like they were children was the final indignity.

A tender smile slowly softened Juan's troubled gaze. "Senor Keever, would you please say for all to hear, that this is my pony to do with as I want, and I give the pony to this fine brave to honor him for having the courage not to fight."

A flicker of surprise broke across Jacob's stone face. "Are you sure, son?"

"Sir, for the first time I am truly sure of something."

Accepting the boy's decision, Jacob repeated Juan's words in the Indian tongue. A murmur of astonishment rose from the braves. The Apache youth stared at Juan in disbelief, his teary eyes searching the Mexican boy's face, fearing it was a cruel joke. Surely he would never give such a fine horse to a wretched enemy.

Juan returned his rifle to its scabbard and nudged his horse forward, offering his hand in friendship. The young brave was overcome by joy his small body could not hold. Speechless, he leaned over and took Juan's hand in his and held on for as long as he dared.

Finally his eager eyes turned to his new pony. In an excited scramble, he changed mounts as quickly as he could. Climbing up, the boy sat proudly, his back straight, his head high. The young Indian turned to Juan, a quizzical look of deep appreciation brightened his face.

Juan could not help be overcome with emotion of his own. "Let this day end in friendship."

The Indian boy's eyes teared again, but this time he felt no shame. Prodding the beautiful stallion forward, he handed Juan the bridle of the gray mule. It was the only gift he had to give. Juan accepted the old jenny graciously and backed away, allowing the proud boy to ride past. As the Indians left the clearing, the young brave turned one last time and looked at the Mexican. The hard line of enemy and friend was forever blurred.

Jacob smiled at Juan with growing respect. "Will wonders never cease? We come with guns at ready and you turn it into Christmas. I'm proud of you, son."

Jacob rode off down the trail.

Roberto shook his head and grinned. "Let's hope Senor Rincon will give you another pony, otherwise you are going to be riding that mangy old nag until she keels over dead, which don't look like it will be too long."

Roberto spurred his pony to catch up with Jacob. "What did you find out?"

"According to the leader, they found a young woman and were protecting her when a huge buffalo man tore through them like a wounded bear, and took the woman away without giving them a chance to explain."

"Do you believe them?"

"I believe Carmelita is safe." Jacob spurred his horse. "We'll back track and find them."

Juan trailed behind, lost in thought. There was no great battle, no heroic charge, nor a single bullet fired, but a victory had been won. Like

Jacob had faced Sholo, Juan had faced this destitute Apache boy, but with a different outcome. Not all conflicts had to end in death. This was a lesson learned.

A soft smile lit Juan's face. Fear no longer hold him so tightly. He had grown some, and for now that was enough.

In time the trail led them within a mile of the house where they found Jubaliah and Carmelita walking along in the red glow of the evening sun. They were leading Buck and holding hands like sweethearts out for a Sunday stroll. Jacob looked down at the couple as he rode by. "Dinner's gettin' cold." That was it.

Back at the house, Jacob made light of the whole affair. Elena was still emotional and not easily calmed. Luis's anger melted away with a big pouting hug from his only daughter. Sometimes it is better to let a happy ending just be. The dinner was a thanksgiving feast Elena had cooked to stay busy. It was a special occasion, the first meal in Jacob's house, made even more special by the safe return of Carmelita and the gathering of friends. The little house in the Hollow would have other gatherings, but Jacob would always remember this one with great fondness.

****

Morning found everyone slowly packing the wagon under the boughs of a large pine. No one was in a hurry to leave. Together they had labored, strengthened friendships and averted a crisis; some had even found love by the bubbling spring. Yet even the magic of the Hollow could not stop time.

Jubaliah joined Jacob by the corral where he was feeding the horses. He stood without speaking. Jacob looked up with a knowing smile. "You're leaving."

The soldier hung his head in silence.

Jacob reached out a gentle hand and patted Peaches' nose. "Is that so hard to say? The only time you aren't gabbing is when you should be."

Jubaliah leaned on the fence and stared into the distance. "It's jus' that the work's done here and with the Injuns, the Rincons would be safer if I went along. Besides, in four days, I got's ta return to the fort."

"How about for the first time in your sorry life, you are head over heels, crazy in love, and you're too big and tough to admit it. Maybe when you were babbling on about me and Rosie, you didn't know a damn thing you were talking about, and now you don't have the guts to say I was right."

Jubaliah gave a sheepish grin. "You was right. But you's still an arrogant bastard."

"So are you going to stay in the Cavalry?"

"I don't see my future clearly yet. I don't see the army as my future no more, but I don't see me as a sod farmer neither. Maybe a little time at the Rincons' ranch, seein' Carmelita in her surroundin's will help me find a way, but for now I'm gunna stay put and hope she'll wait. It's all I can do."

"Don't take as long as I did."

Elena fixed one last breakfast for the hungry men, and left Jacob some dishes and pans.

Luis pulled the wagon in front of the house. Everyone was scurrying about as people do when packing for a trip.

Finally the moment came for good neighbors to say their goodbyes. Assembling on the front porch, they looked around for Jacob.

With a loud snap of the reins, Peaches came around the barn, harnessed to the buckboard with Major in tow. Jacob pulled up alongside the Rincons' wagon. "You all worked so hard there's nothing for me to do here, except put that last plank in place on the barn." He cast a glance at Jubaliah, "So I thought I would ride as far as Rabbit Springs with you and then tomorrow morning, accompany Victor into town and get the bathtub and stove and whatever else I got money for."

So the small wagon train rode out of Jacob's Hollow. At the edge of the trees, Jacob paused and took one last look. It was just as he had pictured it, a serene mountain home tucked under the tall Ponderosa pines. Beyond, the cheery spring bubbling forth from the base of the yellow cliffs flowed gently through the center of the Hollow and past a rustic barn, then on into the sparkling pond surrounded by lush green cattails. Here, nature and the human heart breathed as one. Now, save for a few squirrels and some deer, the ranch would sit empty until Jacob's return.

Chapter -7-
The Proposal

$\mathfrak{F}$orty-eight dollars and nineteen cents. Jacob tipped back in his wooden chair and stared out the window at nothing in particular. Forty-eight dollars and nineteen cents. All that remained of his life savings was stacked in a small pile of tattered greenbacks and assorted coins on the table before him. It sure didn't seem like much. Perhaps he had been a bit extravagant, but as he admired his shiny blue six-hole stove, he realized that he had created quite an extraordinary home.

On his trip to town, Jacob had also picked up a copper bathtub, a small cast iron stove with a side tank for heating water, and a full length floor mirror along with several pairs of new Levi jeans. Then there were other supplies like flour, tins of food, cartridges and such. Jacob turned his head and looked towards the fireplace. Sitting in front of it was a large plush diamond-tucked high-back leather chair that Floyd Barns, proprietor of the dry goods store had shipped in all the way from Kansas City. Now maybe that was a bit extravagant.

However, Jacob figured the house belongs to the woman and a man needs a throne to stake his claim. Sure it was expensive, almost ten dollars, but it was the only item he had bought for himself. He would have denied that he secretly envied Colonel McCrae's high-back chair, even though this was almost an exact copy.

Besides, he saved money by building the two beds, even if he did buy the mattresses and feather pillows. Then there was the suit. A man should get married in a suit. Rosie would expect it. Still, if he was frugal, forty-eight dollars and nineteen cents should last him through the year. It was now late May. Jacob had delayed his proposal of marriage to Rosie until everything was perfect. As he looked around, the time was now. If things got anymore perfect, he'd be broke.

His last trip into town had been exciting to say the least. Rosie had read of his exploits and was so giddy with questions she could hardly contain herself. She was in the company of an honest-to-goodness hero. He was famous. The other girls were envious and she loved it. Rosie had to keep a tight rein on him; several of the ladies were offering their services for free.

Fortunately for Jacob's plans, the articles in the paper mentioned nothing of his leaving the army. As for his civilian clothes, he just told her that when he was in uniform, the girls wouldn't leave him alone.

Jacob's bag sat by the door. His suit was packed along with one final item he had purchased – a gold wedding band. The former soldier was ready to complete the final part of his dream. He couldn't wait to see

Rosie's joy when on bended knee, he offered to make an honest woman of her, and then surprise her with the ranch.

Marriage was something women in her profession dared not dream of, and a beautiful home of her own would be heaven on earth. This was a day long in coming that he would remember forever. Jacob picked up the bag and walked through the door.

"Howdy, Jacob. Ya brought Peaches n' Major again ah see." Old Man Tatum, proprietor of the livery stable, looked as rough as his weather-beaten barn, but he always softened his edges with a kind word. If he had a first name, no one knew it. Or maybe Tatum was his first name.

He was wrinkled leather topped with a white shock of hair that defied combing. He had a welcoming smile despite his lack of teeth. Oddest thing about him was his bare feet – not a good idea around either end of a horse. In a land of colorful characters, old Tatum stood alone.

"Mr. Tatum, it's not safe to leave a horse unguarded in a corral up in them hills with mountain lions and Apaches. Anyway, I suspect I'll be hauling more furnishings if that old buckboard you sold me holds up." Jacob smiled, thinking of Rosie's personal effects.

"The rig is 'most as old as me. Surprised it's held up this long with the loads you been packin'. It's a buckboard, not a gull dang freight wagon. Poor ol' Peaches might as well be hitched to a plow."

"It's the only exercise she gets. Besides, I think she misses you."

Old Tatum broke into a toothless grin and patted Peaches on the neck, "Well, ah take good care of her n' Major while you go 'bout your doin's."

Jacob noticed a large white stallion stomping in the nearest stall, "That is some nice horse flesh you got there."

Tatum pulled a sour face, "Mathers an' 'is boys are in town. From what I hear, bes' you sidestep 'em."

Jacob frowned, "I've got no beef with Mathers or his boys, but thanks for the warnin' just the same." Trouble was the last thing he wanted on what was to be the best day of his life.

Evening came with a welcoming breeze. Jacob quickly closed the back door at the top of the rickety stairs and stood quietly in the familiar hall. He cut quite a figure in his new suit, despite his great size. The flowers in his hand made the hulking giant look a bit silly, but he had an idea of how it should be done, and he was going to do it right.

As he stood in the shadows waiting for the chill to leave and a little courage to strengthen his knees, Rosie's door opened, a balding man stepped out and hurried down the stairs. Jacob's shoulders tensed, nearly ripping his suit, then he noticed the towels in the man's arm and remembered he had seen him doing odd jobs around the hotel.

Jacob knew there were other men, but he had never encountered

73

them, except the banker early on. Since then, Jacob always checked to see if the "Do Not Disturb" sign was on the door. Fortunately it was not.

Hoping to surprise her, he crept into the room unbidden. It was an opulent room, meant to impress its guest. Bawdy artwork and candles adorned the papered walls. Rosie was not in the room, but her angelic voice, humming a whimsical tune, drifted from an adjoining alcove. Like some of the more profitable girls of the establishment, Rosie had a private bath. The patrons seemed to enjoy it, all part of the service, for a few coins more.

Floor length curtains hanging from a pole parted as Jacob quietly stepped through. The dark-skinned beauty was covered in bubbles with more splashed on the damp wooden floor. Her bare legs were gently swinging back and forth over the end of the small copper tub.

Luxuriating in the fragrant suds, Rosie's eyes were closed, her head thrown back in total relaxation as she savored her warm bath.

Jacob plucked a single rose from his bouquet and pressed it ever so lightly to Rosie's breast. Her hand slowly reached up, finding the flower. She smiled and gently opened her eyes. "Hey, hero," She whispered in a whimsical voice. "You're getting' to be a regular around here." The delicious girl squirmed and pulled in her legs, playfully arching her back. "You must like what you see."

Rosie sat up noticing the bouquet, "For me? Well, aren't you the romantic? And look at that suit! You are nigh on as pretty as me."

Jacob risked a little water, and scooped Rosie out of the tub. "Ain't nothin' as pretty as you."

He set her feet on the floor and gave her a firm swat on the bottom. "Come on. Put on your prettiest dress. I'm taking you out for dinner."

A small table in a dark recess off the saloon downstairs was about as much going out as the back street angel would do. Here she felt safe.

Pushing her plate away, Rosie smiled and leaned forward on tapered elbows. Her hands tucked under her chin held a delicate wine glass by the rim. She was wearing a beautiful lavender dress trimmed in black lace with a deep neckline. A cameo fastened snugly around her slender neck with black satin ribbon made her seem as fragile as the glass.

"You show up in a Sunday-go-to-meetin' suit with flowers and dinner. All this hero stuff must have gone to your head."

"Did you buy that dress over at Floyd's dry good store?"

"I most certainly did not! It was imported all the way from New York!"

Jacob laughed.

Rosie frowned. "You knew it didn't come from Floyd Barns."

"And you know, I would never let this hero stuff go to my head. Can't a man have his own reasons for getting dressed up?"

Purring soft as a kitten, Rosie batted her eyes. "Long as I'm the reason."

She was the reason, Jacob's only reason. The suit, this romantic dinner, the ranch and his leaving the army, Rosie was the only reason in Jacob's life. Every breath he took was spent thinking of her. From a slave shack to a ten thousand acre ranch, his journey served only one purpose— to make this angelic creature his earthly bride.

Reaching into his pocket, Jacob fumbled with the gold wedding band. His heart quickened. The moment had come, but he couldn't just hand her the ring. She deserved words – beautiful words. Jacob's lips parted hoping his heart would know what to say. "Ros…" All of a sudden, the piano player started banging out a loud noisy tune. Jacob slumped. He would wait for a more romantic song. The moment had to be just right.

Releasing the ring, Jacob pulled his hand from his pocket and picked up the bottle of champagne. "Let me refill your glass."

As Jacob poured, he noticed a large, well dressed man with an air of importance staring at them from the shadows at the far end of the saloon. "Well, there's a guy that looks like somebody just kicked his dog."

Rosie took a quick glance over her shoulder and turned back to Jacob. Hiding her face, she began to tremble. "Please, take me back to my room." Rosie slid off her chair and hurried for the back stairs without waiting for his response.

Jacob stood up and met the stranger's angry glare, neither man willing to break eye contact.

"Jacob, please!"

Jacob turned; Rose ran up the stairs. He had no choice but to follow. Her door was ajar as he reached the top of the landing. Rose met him as he pushed through the opening. She had her shawl. "Not here. Take me for a walk."

Rose headed for the backdoor. It was clear that the man must know which room was hers.

Jacob knew there were other men, but naively denied their existence and pretended they were faceless strangers who came and went, meaning nothing, giving nothing, taking nothing.

A cold blast of air swept through the door as she stepped on to the dangerous stairs. Jacob grabbed her arm, "Rose. We don't have to leave."

"Please, Jacob! For me. Let's go."

They hurried through the alley and down the street. The gaiety and noise of the nightlife surrounded them, tempering the mood. Rose hurried on down the boardwalk. She wouldn't let Jacob see her face. He let her run herself out a bit, then grabbing her by both shoulders, he pressed her into a darkened doorway. "I've never run from anything, and I don't feel like startin' now. Let's go back and finish our champagne."

"Jacob, you are a colored man for Christ sake. He could kill you, and no one would do anything about it."

"It wouldn't go that way."

"What, you kill him? They'd hang you for sure."

"I'm not afraid."

Rose buried herself against his chest. "Maybe I am. Maybe I'm afraid for me."

"Rose…"

"No! Don't say anything. We were happy. You wanted to take me out, so we're out. Let's enjoy ourselves."

Rose pushed back from his arms and stepped through some late night revelers. Glancing back at Jacob, she turned, hurrying on down the streets. Jacob caught up with her, and they continued in silence. After a while he ushered Rose onto a quieter side street that led down towards the livery stable.

A narrow alley opened to their right. Slumped against a coal bin was a drunken miner. He was snoring loudly, and Rose risked a soft laugh as the shabby man snorted loudly. He was out cold with a bottle of whiskey in his hands and another one stuffed in his coat pocket. Jacob leaned over and plucked the bottle from his coat.

"Jacob, what are you doing?"

"It's not champagne, but you wanted a night out, and I'm not gunna' let anything spoil it." They both laughed. Jacob held Rose close, giving her a kiss, then continued on down the dusty street. Minutes later they came to the livery stable.

Opening the shadowed door, Jacob pushed Rose inside. She gave a startled scream. He silenced her by pressing his lips to hers, long and hard. Stepping back, he gave Rose a quick shove and she fell into an unseen stack of hay, squealing in surprise.

A soft light burst through the dark as Jacob put a match to a lantern sitting on a wooden barrel. The lamp was low, and the light was lost amongst the high rafters.

"Rose leaned back on both of her arms. "That's no way to treat a lady."

She looked around and whispered. "Where is that strange old man, Tatum?"

"Out getting drunk like everyone else."

Rose pulled some straw from her clothing. "This hay will ruin my new dress."

Jacob took a swig from the bottle and wiped his mouth. "Take it off."

"Here in a barn? I will not!"

Jacob kneeled down, took Rosie in his arms and kissed her tenderly. All night there had only been one thought on his mind. It couldn't wait any longer. "Then marry me."

Rose was astonished. "What?"

"Marry me, Rose. I love you."

"Jacob, don't kid around."

Jacob pulled the gold ring from his pocket and pressed it into her hand.

"Marry me. Let me take you out of this town."

Rosie stiffened, her eyes growing cold. "Marry you and live in the army barracks with you and your... your soldiers?"

"No, Rose, I left the army."

"You what?!!" Her warm ebony skin turned cold as marble.

"Rose, I knew the army life was not good enough for one so gentle. I own a sprawling ranch in the desert, with a stone house that I built for you."

Rose stomped to her feet and straightened her dress. Anger was clearly visible in her narrowing eyes. "Jacob, stop it. It can't be."

"Yes it can, my love. You don't have to live like this any longer."

Suddenly Rose laughed out loud in disgust. "Live like what?"

She pulled away. "How many farmers' wives, toiling from sunup to sundown, can say they dress as well as I do? Do you have money?"

"No. But..."

"Do you have four thousand head of cattle? ...Hundreds? ...Any?"

"Not yet, but..."

"A rancher without cattle is just a dirt farmer. Do I look like a dirt farmer's wife?"

Jacob was dumbfounded. This wasn't the way it was supposed to be. "Rose?"

"Jacob, we have fun. Don't ruin it. Let's keep things the way they are and forget this nonsense."

Jacob felt like he had taken a cannon volley to the stomach. He didn't understand. "Rose, I'm offering you marriage and a home. It's a good home. I, I built it for you, for you Rose." His large trembling hands reached out to her. "It has a bubbling spring."

"A spring! So you have water. Big deal! I have all the water I want right here, and I don't have to wander for days in that filthy desert. Does your spring bubble champagne?"

The big man's voice shook. "Rose, I love you."

Losing her patience, she shouted, "Oh, Jacob, stop it! Don't be a fool. What could you offer me that I don't already have? Does your home have one single room as beautiful as mine? Does it have large closets for all my beautiful dresses? Do you expect me to give them up for a soiled apron, so I can cook your meals and suckle your brats? A dirt farmer!"

His head reeling, Jacob rose weakly to his feet. Anguish twisting his once hopeful face, he stared in disbelief – a hollow shell where a man once stood.

Rose angered at his pain. Her beautiful face curled in revulsion at Jacob's ignorance. "Men shower me with money and gifts. They give me anything I want, and all I have to do is let them touch me while I stroke their ridiculous egos. They all know it's a game. But not you, ya big, dumb, hulkin' fool. You fall in love like you're someone special, better than all the rich white men, Hero of Apache Springs."

The once lovely voice mocked him in a shrill pitch.

Jacob grabbed Rose. "It's that dandy in the saloon isn't it?"

Rose sneered and jerked away. "Damon Mathers? He bought me this dress. You couldn't have bought me this dress with a year's pay. Jacob, wake up. For what I do my color doesn't matter, but you're just a poor dumb colored boy dreamin' in a white man's world. You'll always be lickin' their boots and eatin' their scraps. Don't expect me to do it with you. If Damon Mathers and other high and mighty white folk want to pretend I'm their fancy little dark-eyed doll, then let 'em, as long as they pay."

Rose showed no sympathy for the stricken man. "You put your little pittance of silver on the nightstand when you ride into town, like you're some great benefactor and I'm supposed to be grateful as hell." She flung her arms wide showing her disgust. "Damon spends more on me in one night than you could ever imagine. I took pity on you, and this is the thanks I get for my kindness."

Giving a shriek, she shoved both hands against his chest, pushing him away, not hiding her revulsion. The burly man, weakened by her vicious assault, stumbled backwards.

Her cruel words struck like fists, hammering him down until he had nothing left. Everything he had worked for, his great dream, so close only to be crushed by the vile mocking of a whore he never really knew.

Rose finished her outburst. Her voice softened, once again candy sweet. She stepped forward and slipped the ring into Jacob's pocket. "So you became a hero; that don't put silk on a girl. Go back to the army Jacob, where you belong. Come around in a few months and things can be the same as before. I'll forgive you for messing up."

Jacob took a quivering breath but couldn't hold it. Nausea churned in his stomach. With fumbling hands, he picked up his saddle and stumbled into the shadows, wounded more deeply than by any bullet. He had been such a fool. The soft petals had fallen away from his beautiful Rose revealing cruel thorns that any child could have seen. The girl he loved was dead. His dream was dead. He wished he were dead too.

Chapter -8-
Lost Dreams

"Whoa!" Jubaliah held his hand in the air, bringing his troopers to a halt outside the low adobe wall surrounding Luis Rincon's grand Spanish home. "Keep the line straight men, and yo' faces too. If any of ya is thinkin' of makin' me look a fool, so help me, you'll be on officers' latrine duty through the hottest, smelliest, fly-infested days a' summer. You'll be diggin' from the bottom up an' prayin' for whitey to piss on ya just ta wash away the stink."

Rolley gave a high-pitched hyena laugh, "Oh, we knows enough to be good in public, Sarge. Since you've been sweet on Miss Carmelita, you been sweet on us too."

The men snickered, but straightened up quickly when the large wooden door creaked open. Carmelita pushed through it, stepping lightly onto the path. She was wearing a long white dress, typical of her people. Her waist-length raven hair scattered the sun in the morning breeze. The fine threads of her shawl danced with light, creating a glow about her. Against the stucco backdrop of the old two-story hacienda, Carmelita held the regal air of her Spanish ancestry.

Jubaliah was smitten. She was more lovely than when she was in Jacob's Hollow. There, her beauty was contrasted by the land. Here, she was in total harmony.

Jubaliah had once met Rose Montier. She was truly a rare beauty, but it seemed to sit on the surface as it were. Carmelita Rincon's beauty had depth. Her face glowed with youth and innocence, yet a timeless presence seemed about her as though she had always been. In her, there flowed an ancient blood.

As the trail worn men gazed upon the delicate girl, there was one emotion in every heart – envy. Carmelita slowed as she approached the starched line of troopers. She was sure Jubaliah had cautioned them to be on their best behavior. His shoulders were thrown back, looking every bit the proper soldier. She knew he wanted to impress her and he had, all the more because it showed he cared.

Carmelita folded her hands and tucked her head to hide a telling smile. "Sergeant Jackson, it is so good of you to stop by."

"Just on patrol, Senorita Rincon. It's our humble duty and pleasure ta make sure the ranchers is safe."

Carmelita's large brown eyes greeted every man. "You and your brave soldiers are most welcome. Please, climb down."

Jubaliah deepened his voice. "Troopers dismount. Troopers... ah, ah, oh, go guard that hitchin' post over yonder."

Swinging down from the saddle, Jube eagerly escorted Carmelita in the opposite direction. "Where is your father?"

"The men are moving cattle. Father likes to supervise. It makes him feel less old, I think."

"Darlin', I got your note ta come as soon as I could. It sounded urgent, so I made a wide detour, following Injuns, of course," He gave a quick wink.

Carmelita glanced at the soldiers and tucked her arm inside Jubaliah's. She was silent for a moment, concern building on her face. "Oh, Jube, it is so terrible. Roberto and Juan came back from town last week very distraught. Damon Mathers is talking around. Some people are just born to make trouble."

She stopped and looked up into Jubaliah's eyes. "He is telling everyone that Jacob came to town thinking he could get a wife, because he was a big hero and all, that he proposed to a whore and she turned him down cold. The woman laughed right in his face. Mathers is making Jacob sound like a fool."

Jubaliah looked stricken. "Has anyone heard from Jacob?"

"Nobody has seen him. It is a long hard ride to the Hollow now that the days are growing hotter, and it is still dangerous, with other warriors looking to fill Sholo's place. Father is too old to take off on horseback alone, and not many people around here know Jacob well enough to, to be, well..., discreet. Jacob is a proud man."

Carmelita leaned against Jubaliah. "We are worried. Father was hoping you..., he said, 'Tell Jube, he will know what to do.'"

"Thank your father. I 'appreciate ya sendin' for me."

"Jube, do you think it is true?"

"It ain't what it seems, darlin'. I 'spect Mathers' words are true enough, but it's how people choose ta hear 'em. It weren't that way for Jacob. He loved this girl. What she was didn't matter, but there's enough truth there that Mathers can twist it n' make a good man look bad. People love heroes, but they also likes to see 'em fall."

"Jube, can you go to him? Can you see if he's okay, let him know that we care? Let him know that to us, he will always be a hero."

Jubaliah scratched his head. "There's an upstart Mimbre buck named Cota that's left the reservation, stealin' horses and chickens. It's rumored that he's hidin' in Sholo's old haunts. Maybe I could take an extra couple a days without too much fuss from the Colonel. Reinhart's off hobnobbing with senators, so's he won't care."

Jubaliah took Carmelita's hands. "I'll do it. Don't worry yo' pretty little self no more."

Light returned to the girl's sweet face. "Do you think you could spend today here?"

"Sure, if ya don't mind visitin' me in the stockade."

Carmelita's innocent smile puckered to an injured pout. "How disappointing. There is a delicious breakfast prepared for the vaqueros; your men will be sad when I tell them you couldn't spare the time."

"Well, now, even the colonel knows the army travels on its stomach. I think we can spare an hour."

Carmelita raised on her toes, kissing Jubaliah on the lips. "Or two?"

Jubaliah looked to his troops who were grinning ear to ear. "Stockades ain't so bad."

****

The sweltering days of an early summer slowed both men and horses. Jubaliah pushed the mounts as much as he dared across the hostile land. After two days, Jacob's mountain appeared from the shimmering waves of heat rising from the burning desert sand.

The barrier had been crossed, and in a deep-shaded arroyo about an hour from the Hollow, Jube had the men make camp. He and Jacob had found the arroyo while hunting. Hidden in the stones was a seep. The men dug into the sand and water slowly pooled. No good for cattle, but with a little nursing it would take care of the troopers' needs.

Jubaliah watered Buck from his hat and headed out alone. If he hurried, he would reach the cliffs by sunset, and they would quench their thirst from the bubbling spring.

After a short while, Jube found the wagon trail that he and Jacob had cleared. Save for a few deer tracks, it had not been used. Buck settled into a steady gate. Jubaliah gave him his head and lapsed into thought.

Jacob was a private man. He never wanted to be a hero, but no man wants to be called a fool, especially over a woman. If Jacob had a failing, it was too much pride, and now Jubaliah feared it would be cutting him like a dull knife. The one dream that alone had sustained Jacob was gone. For the first time, Jube was not looking forward to meeting his old friend.

The final rays of the hot June sun turned the rough stones of Jacob's house a dark, blood red. Shading his sunburned eyes, Jube saw no signs of life, save for an old owl, anxious for the cool of night. Tying Buck to the rail, the tired soldier dusted himself off with his hat. The easy part of his trip was done.

Jubaliah hesitated at the door, then knocked. There was no answer. He pounded harder. Finally a stirring of footsteps could be heard shuffling on the stone floor. The door opened a crack. In the murky light, Jubaliah could see Jacob's dark, whiskered face, drawn and gaunt. There was no smile to greet him, only a morose indifference.

Jubaliah stepped closer. "I thought I'd come visit. Ya gunna' let me in?"

With a shrug of resignation, Jacob reluctantly opened the door as he

81

glanced at the clutter on the floor. "Not really presentable for entertaining guests."

"Jacob, we've been ankle deep in horse dung together, do ya think I'm gunna' be too picky?"

Relenting, Jacob let go of the wooden latch and moved aside. Stepping past him, Jubaliah took the lantern. "Do ya mind if I burn a little extra wick?"

"Suit yourself, but I warned you."

The yellow glow of the kerosene flame told the story. Jacob stood barefooted in the middle of the room, his shirt unbuttoned as though it were just thrown on. The air was heavy with the putrid smell of rotting food, and foul odors long trapped behind a tightly closed door. Dirty plates and pans were piled on the table along with uneaten meals. A few whiskey bottles lay empty on the floor, save for some that had been smashed against the stone walls.

"Maid's day off?"

"I warned you."

Jacob fell back and slumped into his chair. "I would offer you a drink but I ran out the first night. If you hadn't noticed by looking around, sweet little Rosie turned me down. Sweet, cold, heartless Rosie."

He looked up at Jubaliah, rubbing his bearded face. "But I'm willing to guess you knew that. I don't think you just happened to drop by."

Taking a wooden chair from the table, Jubaliah spun it around and placed it next to Jacob, then sat on it backward and rested his gloved hands on the top rung. "No way ta make it easy on ya . Mathers' been havin' fun with it 'round town."

Jacob's fingers dug into the thick leather arm of the chair. Anger darkened his face. "You know, I'm beginning not to like that man."

Jubaliah smiled. "Well, he certainly ain't a model of western hospitality."

Jacob sat expressionless, staring into the lantern. "Remind me to kill him."

He coughed and clutched his stomach. "I suppose everybody knows. Where's Rolley and the boys?"

"I bedded 'em down 'bout an hour south a here."

"Protecting poor, foolish Jacob. Why didn't you just bring them up here so they could all have a good laugh and get it over with?"

"Ain't nobody laughin', at least none of yo' friends, and ya got's quite a few of 'em."

Jacob pounded his fist. "No, they're not laughing. I got their pity, and that's a damn sight worse."

"It looks like ya got enough pity of yo' own, ol' friend."

Bolting from his chair, Jacob exploded with rage. "I'm a blind fool, ain't even good enough for a damn whore!"

"You were in love. What she was didn't matter."

Grimacing in pain, Jacob clutched his stomach again. "It should have. Did you know she was never a slave? Her family came from New England. She chose to be a whore. That's how much honor she has. I knew it, and I ignored it."

"What, the great Jacob Keever ain't entitled to make mistakes?"

Leaning his head against the wall, Jacob beat the stones with his fist. "Go home, Jube. There's nothing here to see. Just a colored dirt farmer who didn't know his place."

Stumbling to the window, Jacob ripped the curtains open. "I convinced myself this was a ranch when I don't even own a single cow. Not one damn cow. How big of a fool is that?"

Jube had heard enough and raised his voice. "It's a good dream, jes' the wrong girl."

"You don't know! You don't know. There's just a big empty hole. I put everything I had into a fool's dream and now it's a big black empty hole. It's black. All I can see is black, her black heart."

Jacob paced the room and laughed. "Oh, and did I tell you I'm broke? Even too broke to get soused. I ain't even a decent drunk."

"Ya never was."

Rising from the chair, Jube stepped close to his friend, and continued. "It weren't long ago that we had good times under these trees and there weren't no Rosie Montier here either. If ya want, it can be happy again. Ya said the Hollow was a healing place, but ya gotta want it. Keep the dream, jes' find another girl."

"I got nothin' left Jube."

"Ya don't have Rosie, but look around ya . You still gots' more than the rest of us. I know what you's gunna' say. 'It's only half a dream.' Well, think of what ya had when ya was livin' out of yo' saddle! Now that is all I gots' to say. Next time I come a ridin' all the way up this dang mountain, I expect ya to be back to yo' old nasty self n' greetin' people proper like. One last thing. It may not seem like it, but ya ll find another woman. One that's worthy of ya ."

Jacob looked weary and spent, but a lot of the anger that had been eating his insides had finally been vented to someone who cared. His body relaxed as he slumped into his chair.

Jubaliah went to the door. "I'm goin' to toss some hay to the horses 'cause the way they's fussin', I 'spect you ain't been takin' care of them neither. Then before I go, I'll see what kind of meal I can scare up for us 'round here."

The next morning, Jacob awoke while the sun was still low. It wasn't early, but it was a start. He moved toward his chair, then stopped. For weeks now he had done nothing but sit in that chair and stew in his own anger. Today the chair held no comfort. He had swallowed all the

83

bitterness he could stomach. In his shame, he had felt he would never be able to look another human being in the face, but Jube's coming changed all that. What Jube had said made sense, and it gave him the first glimmer of hope. The hole wasn't so dark.

Jacob looked around at the filth and clutter with disgust. He thought of Mathers and the townsfolk. "Well, they may laugh at what is done, but I won't give them more reason to laugh. Jacob's Hollow will be spit-and-polished. I will have a ranch, if I have to grow the cows from seeds."

Jacob had found resolve, but he felt dead inside. The joy had gone out of life. Still he didn't let it stop him. Falling back on his regimented army training, he started putting his ranch back to rights. After he got the house cleaned up, he began making improvements. He built stables in the barn and a chicken coop on its east side, with plenty of nesting boxes.

There were no chickens, no feed if there had been chickens. It was the work that kept him going. Still, no matter how hard he toiled, Jacob couldn't drive the image of Rosie's vile scorn out of his mind. It was always there, just under the surface tormenting him. Sometimes he would boil over and throw a hammer in rage, or bloody his fist against a wall, but he kept going.

He built two square stone pillars five feet high on either side of the road where it crested the knoll, entering the Hollow. From each pillar, a log fence went out along the ridge until it disappeared into the woods and then stopped.

Next he built a stone smokehouse up against the cliffs. When not working on the ranch, he filled the barn with grama grass and the blockhouse with venison. He would do anything to keep busy: build a bird house, a better latch on a gate, a stone pathway, and finally he built closets for the bedrooms. There was nothing to hang except one nearly new suit, but there were closets just the same.

So went the building at Jacob's Hollow—a lovely place to see, if anyone were to pass by. It was an inviting ranch—only without cattle, without love, without laughter. The only sound that could be heard was the bubbling spring.

Chapter -9-
Neighbors

On silent feet, the young coyote edged towards the smoldering campfire in the cold gray dawn, ready to spring away in an instant.

Above the dying embers, a tempting morsel of charred rabbit hung on a sharpened stick from the night before. Its beckoning smell had drawn the hungry coyote from a mile away.

Beyond the swirling smoke lay the ominous form of a large man wrapped in a blanket and covered with canvas, deep in slumber by the sound of his heavy breathing.

Closer, closer, steady, closer, the coyote's eager jaws snapped shut on the tender prize. A quick blur, and all was gone. The branch impaling the meat flipped across the rocks, showering ashes and coals over the sleeper as it ripped through the embers.

Jacob awoke with a start. He saw no evidence of what had just taken place, but there was no time for wondering as he beat out the hot coals scorching his bed. "One hell of a way to get rousted from my dreams. Find out your breakfast has gone south, and you're on fire to boot. That's just the way life is going." He paused and looked around, seeing nothing but sagebrush and greasewood.

Jacob flicked off the last cinder and glared. "Major, you were standing guard, ya old nag. Couldn't you have opened your sleepy eyes and snorted or stomped your lazy foot? Keep it up and you'll be busted to private."

After dusting himself off, Jacob grabbed a clump of sagebrush and tossed it on to the coals. Moments later its shaggy bark glowed with crackling red flames. He filled his tin cup with water from his canteen and balanced it on a burning log. Then, dropping a hand full of coffee beans on a flat rock, Jacob crushed them with the butt of his carbine and scooped them into the steaming brew. While waiting for his first cup, he pulled some stiff jerky from his saddlebags and bit off a piece. "This'll have to make do, Major."

The soldier swallowed a hard piece of gristle. "Guess that tar weed you been nibbling on ain't much better, ol' friend."

Jacob had not meant to spend the night on the desert; he had gone farther than he planned. There was little left to do at the Hollow, so he decided to survey his ten thousand, one hundred and sixty acres and see what he really had. For the most part, he decided it was a whole lot of hot and empty. Just large expanses of baked earth dotted with sparse thorny brush more suited to horned toads than cattle. Thinking on it, he muttered to himself. "If grease wood was gold…"

Shallow gullies carved by rain broke up the monotony of the flat desert, making the land difficult to traverse by horse and darn near impossible by wagon. Rosie's words rang in his head. Dirt Farmer.

Giving up on the tough jerky, Jacob drew a crumpled, hand drawn map from his coat pocket. He shaded his eyes and took his bearing from the rising sun. Then drawing a fix on a familiar peak in the distance, he made a mark on the map with a stub of a pencil. "That should put us right about here, Major."

Jacob stuffed the map back into his pocket. He was not relishing the long ride back to the Hollow. The desert gives a man time to think. Unfortunately, Jacob's thoughts often drifted to Rosie. Traversing the barren land was hard enough. Replaying that night in his mind across the endless miles took a painful toll.

The only consolation was that surviving the desert had its own pain. When it got bad enough, it drove out even the torment of a cold-hearted woman. Maybe deep inside, he needed to be out here. The desert was his whiskey. Yet a harsh land breeds a harsh man, something Jacob did not understand as he walled himself off from all human contact. He was changing. His face was drawn, his eyes sullen, his once-proud heart had grown cold. Hiding away in his Hollow, he'd not seen another living soul in over a month.

The sun peeked over the distant hills; it was time to shake off his dark mood and make tracks. On the western horizon lay a thin blue-green line. Maybe a stand of trees. It was someplace to go, and it couldn't be any worse than where he was. Gathering up his gear, Jacob forced himself to stand. "Come on Mr. Horse, let's get movin'. If we're lucky, maybe we'll get snake bit n' die."

Sick of self pity, Jacob found other thoughts to occupy his mind. Early yesterday he had come across a cattle trail, which he followed until it got dark. The trail was old, but what was strange was that it was even out here. Why would anyone be driving cattle across this part of the desert? It just didn't make any sense. A day of following the trail didn't make it any clearer, and Jacob lost interest. The thin blue line on the horizon was more inviting than another day of swallowing dust, so for now the cattle trail would have to remain a mystery.

****

Little in life is more heart wrenching than helpless screams, pleading for mercy to the sick laughter of a cruel tormentor. So it was in a lonely stand of junipers at the edge of the desert.

"Hold her, Raithe, but don't bust her. We'll save her for later."

Wyatt Mathers laughed as he turned his attention to an old Apache, striking the Indian hard across the face with the back of his hand. The old man in a thick, hoarse voice, pleaded in his native tongue, while the buckskinned girl tucked under Raithe's left arm like a sack of flour screamed obscenities in English. Her arms stretched to a beloved grandfather she could not reach.

Wyatt yelled again. "You thieving redskin. Ain't no animal lower than a damn Injun."

Clutching his victim by the neck, Wyatt laughed and hit him again. "Only thing worse than a Injun is a stinkin' Apache."

Reveling in his own brutality, Wyatt grabbed the old man by a fist of white hair and hurled him to the ground. The decrepit Indian landed with a jolt on his hands and knees, tearing his flesh on the sharp rocks.

With the blunt toe of his boot, Wyatt kicked him hard in the ribs. A grunt caught in the old man's throat, his eyes rolled against the pain.

Wailing screams emptied the poor girl's lungs until her gaping mouth could utter no more sound. Her entire body convulsed with anguish over the old man's humiliation. The vile laughter of the brutal boys crackled in her ears like distorted howls in a surreal nightmare.

Wyatt at nineteen, and Raithe at seventeen had more meanness than ruffians twice their age. A brutal father had left his scar. No act of kindness was ever shown the boys, so they had none to give. Wyatt straddled the old man and jerked his braids like the reins of a horse. Reaching back, he slapped the Apache on the rump. "Come on, crawl, you worthless bag of bones. You ain't fit to walk the earth like a man, maybe you can crawl like a dog."

With a gasping breath, the old man raised his bloody hand trying to move under Wyatt's prodding, but crumpled to his elbows. Life is fragile, and there was precious little left in the aged warrior.

"You can't even crawl. What good are ya? I'll do the world a favor."

Wyatt slipped his gun from his holster, then pressed the cold steel barrel to the back of the Indian's head. With a sideways grin to his brother, he cocked it.

The girl's eyes widened in terror. She thrashed wildly trying to reach her grandfather. Raithe shifted her weight on his hip as if she were a bawling child easily ignored. "Do it, Wyatt! Do it! Splatter his brains in the sand." His laugh was pure evil.

Above the din, a deep voice rang loud and clear. "I wouldn't, if ya want to go on livin'."

Every human sound stopped. All eyes save the old man froze on the newcomer. Wyatt stared into the large bore of Jacob's Springfield carbine. He gave a nervous laugh and licked his lips. "Well, what do we have here?"

The arrogance of the father was apparent in the son. "You must be the famous land-grabbing Hero of Apache Springs that everyone's jawin' about. Raithe, look, we got all sorts of color here today."

Raithe's gun hand twitched but he made no move under the big man's icy stare.

Jacob's voice hung cold in the hot desert air. "Drop your gun."

Wyatt cursed, uncertain of his next move. False bravado edged his voice. "Ain't no old colored boy gunna tell me what to do."

The older brother weighed his chances. His gun was drawn and cocked. Could he turn and fire before Jacob could pull the heavy trigger of the army carbine? Jacob wondered too, but the truth was he didn't really care. He was simply doing what he'd always done, protecting those who couldn't protect themselves.

The soldier's eyes narrowed as he readied for battle. If he took Wyatt, there was still Raithe to deal with. The boy would be a difficult shot shielded by the girl.

To improve the odds, Jacob taunted the younger brother. "Hiding behind a girl. Won't daddy be proud?"

Raithe was young and took the bait. He dropped the girl in the dirt and squared with the big man, his jaw clenched in hate, but fear still held his young hand. The boy's eyes darted, pleading with his brother. "Shoot him, Wyatt. You can do it."

Wyatt shifted nervously. "You can't get us both, soldier boy. Best you get your ugly black ass out of here while you got the chance. Go back to chasing whores." Wyatt laughed at his own humor, knowing his insult hit the mark.

Jacob's face darkened. "Let's make this clear. Don't matter who finds courage, you or your noisy brother, this bullet is for you. So make your play."

Wyatt's curled lip twitched involuntarily, but his hand remained frozen in the grip of self doubt. He had never faced a man so calm. If he could shake him, he could slow his hand, but the black soldier was cold as death.

"Wyatt, take him. Shoot, damn it!"

Wyatt looked from his goading brother to the indifference in Jacob's eyes. Sweat rolled down the boy's face.

"What're you waitin' for? Shoot him!"

"Shut up. Just shut up, Raithe!"

Wyatt turned back to Jacob. He hesitated, his hand shaking with a fury he dared not satisfy. Suddenly he threw his gun to the ground and cursed.

His brother screamed. "You coward! You damn stinkin' yellow coward! You let a darkie face you down!"

The sobbing girl crawled frantically to her grandfather.

Jacob turned to Raithe. "Then show your big brother how it's done. Take your chance, little boy."

Raithe spit. He had twice the rage and half the brains of his brother.

Folks said he was just plum crazy. "Ain't no nigger going to treat a Mathers like dirt."

Caught somewhere between a boy and a man, he couldn't keep his gun hand from twitching. Fear and some vestige of sanity raged a battle in his tormented mind.

"You're seconds from hell, son."

A sudden thought came to the boy's head. His father would be furious with him if he got himself killed. It made no sense, but such was the father's control.

Raithe trembled, tears stung his eyes. "My pa will kill you for this."

It was Wyatt's turn to taunt. "Yeah, Raithe, hide behind Pa. Who's the coward now?"

"Time's up, boy, unbuckle your gun or I'll kill you where you stand."

Raithe's shoulders shook weakly as he broke into sobs like a beaten child. Obediently, he let his holster fall. Wyatt laughed at his brother's shame to ease his own. Then he turned and cursed Jacob. "You're going to hang for this. Pa ain't gunna' stand for it."

Jacob kicked their guns aside. "That may be, but I suspect the first thing he's gunna' do when you tell him what happened here, is whip the hide off your backs for turnin' yellow. Like you said, we got all sorts of color here today."

The boys looked at each other and paled with fear. Their pa would accept no excuses for a Mathers cowering before a darkie. If he heard the truth, he would tear into them like a crazed grizzly, kin or not. Each of them carried scars on their backs from the old man's wrath. Realizing their predicament was hopeless, they stood like little boys waiting to be punished.

Spineless, Wyatt whined a defense. "This thieving Apache bitch stole one of our horses. We were within our rights. You had no call to interfere."

Jacob pulled their Winchesters from their saddles. "You are on my property. That's cause enough." Then he turned to the Indian girl. "Did you steal their horse?"

Clinging to her grandfather, the terrified girl looked up from the sand with a tear-stained face and runny nose. Her breath came in gasps as a threat of death once again loomed over her.

In a thick Apache accent, her lips quivering, the girl pleaded her case. "My, my grandfather is old and, and wants to die on sacred ground. He is very old, and I was taking him there. He is sick and could walk no further, I took one horse. They had many more than they could ride. I only took one. Please, just one."

Her slight body shook as she broke into sobs, knowing her plight meant nothing to the gringos.

Raithe yelled. "It don't matter, it's still horse stealin' and we could hang 'em for it."

Taking a long quivering draw of air through a down turned mouth, the Indian girl looked anxiously at Jacob, awaiting his verdict. Would the big man give her back to the cruel boys?"

The Apache was not Jacob's problem, but the young girl's pleading eyes let him know he was her only hope. Turning to the hateful brothers, Jacob's face twisted with disgust. "I rather think she was just exercising him for you. Take the sorrel and go."

For the boys, his answer was a reprieve. He gave them their freedom when he could have killed them, as they surely would have killed him if their fortunes were reversed. The Apaches were nothing, just amusement, and they would have their vengeance on the arrogant Buffalo Soldier another day.

Wyatt turned to Jacob. "It's a long way home. What about our guns? Pa would be mad if you took our guns."

Wyatt was the older of the two brothers, but his weakness of character was evident as he groveled before the big man. Though cruel and twisted, he was almost effeminate. "We need our weapons sir. Besides, we're no threat to a soldier who has done the killin' you have."

'Killin.' The word danced on the boy's lips like it was a compliment. He had no comprehension how it weighed on the heart of a decent man.

Jacob stuffed their pistols into one of the saddlebags. "Tell me son, just how many did you hear I killed?"

Wyatt swallowed hard. "Some say that when the battle was over, you'd slaughtered most of fifty by yourself, and ya would have killed more but ya run out of bullets."

Towering over the boys, the soldier broke into a wry smile. "Well, I got plenty of bullets now."

The brothers sickened at the implication.

Jacob shoved the reins of the sorrel at Wyatt. "Hold 'em tight."

Pointing one of the Winchesters into the air, he fired. The two saddled horses bolted. Jacob fired again. The ponies took off at a dead run. "There are your pistols, go after them. I'll keep the rifles. Wouldn't want you brave Mathers back-shooting me from behind a cactus."

Raithe swore. "You expect us to ride double and bareback?"

"I don't care what you do. Just get off my property."

Whining like kicked dogs, the boys climbed on the sorrel and hightailed it after their ponies. There would be hell to pay if the horses got back to the ranch without them.

The girl looked up, her face drenched in tears, her injured voice trembling, "You should have killed them."

"Maybe I should have, but once killin' starts, it's hard to stop."

Cradling her grandfather in her arms, she rocked gently. "They're very evil gringos. They will murder someone yet."

90

The old man coughed weakly. His eyes were glazed, his body as rigid as dried wood. Blood trickled from an ugly gash on his cheek. Kneeling in the dirt beside him, the girl shook with grief for the old man as her tears flowed unbidden.

Giving her time, Jacob busied himself tying the rifles behind Major's saddle. Eventually the girl rose to her knees and pushed back her tangled hair. Large questioning eyes, now visible, fixed on Jacob, still fearful of the black giant. She took a deep breath, trying to control the trembling in her breast. "Thank you, buffalo man."

Her tear-stained face lifted towards him in the bright sunlight. She was petite but not a child as Jacob had first thought. Only young by contrast to the old man, who was ancient. She was maybe twenty. There was a boldness about her that made her seem older, but a child's face with small features. Maybe her anguished expression made her appear more than her years. It was hard to say.

The old Apache coughed again, then struggled to one knee. He remained expressionless. Twigs and dirt matted the ancient warrior's snow-white hair. His granddaughter tried to brush the filth away. "He is too weak to walk." She cast a reproachful eye at Jacob. "We really needed the pony."

The last months had been filled with more bitterness than any man could swallow. Jacob just wanted to be left alone to lick his wounds. He clutched the reins, wishing he could ride out and be done with it. They were just Apaches. Wasn't saving their wretched lives enough?

Kneeling with her arm around her grandfather, the girl watched. She could tell what the big man was thinking. Jacob wanted to yell at her, 'Stop looking at me' but he wasn't that kind of man. It appeared that his punishment for saving this feeble old Apache and his horse-stealing granddaughter was that they were his responsibility, at least for the moment. Jacob sighed. "Let's get him on my horse."

It was not yet noon, and the desert sun was tempered by thin hazy clouds. The heat was bearable. Jacob kept to the foothills to catch the breeze as it lifted over the mountain.

With the brittle old man jarring on Major's back, a slow pace seemed best. Still, with luck they would make the Hollow in three or four hours if the old Apache lived that long.

They walked the length of the dusty ridge in silence. The girl could see anger in the tense muscles of the giant. Maybe it was because they were Apaches. She was used to people feeling that way.

Looking back at her frail grandfather brought her sadness. He sat straight in the saddle like a great warrior on a noble steed heading for battle, ignoring that others held his reins. The girl knew it was his feeble attempt to hold on to the tattered remains of his dignity after his humiliation at the hands of the boys.

In the last years, he had lost so much. Age and encroachment of the white man had left little for a once proud warrior. The Apache braves had failed to protect their women and children, and now he could not even protect himself. All honor was gone.

The old warrior had been a great man respected by the elders of their village. When the girl was young, he would pick her up and toss her high into the air. She remembered the strength in his laughter as he would catch her then hold her close. Now he looked so small sitting on the back of that great horse. Her heart ached for him. She turned to Jacob. "Your horse is big and fat."

Jacob feigned a smiled despite his annoyance. "You should see Peaches."

They continued walking side by side, leading Jacob's fat horse along a deer trail now hidden in the thick wavy leaf oak. For the moment there was shade. Jacob looked down at the sad-eyed girl. He was a foot taller and easily twice her weight. "One of your little Indian ponies couldn't carry me."

Even though they were walking slowly, she would occasionally take a double skip to match Jacob's long strides. Her doeskin moccasins fell silently and left no tracks in the dried earth. Jacob's boots fell heavy, leaving evidence of a big man.

"The bad gringos called you a soldier."

"I was... once."

She took several steps in silent thought. "Soldiers hunt my people. Did you kill Apaches?"

The brash question gave Jacob a start. "I never killed anyone that wasn't lookin' to kill."

"Maybe they kill because you hunt them?"

"Maybe I hunt them because they kill."

She accepted his answer and changed subjects, her voice a little lighter.

"Where is your home?"

He pointed. "Beneath those yellow cliffs."

The girl almost danced. "That is near where my grandfather said we were going."

"Is your ranch big?"

"I guess... you're on it now."

"Do you have many cows?"

Jacob frowned. "No cows."

"You can't have a ranch without cows."

He raised his voice. "Well, I do."

"Do you have chickens?"

"No!"

"No chickens, no cows, it sounds like a dumb ranch."

"Can we change the subject?"

"Do you have a dog? I like dogs."

"NO!"

"No dog, no chickens, no cows…"

Jacob nearly burst. "Look! My horse is fat. I was a soldier. My ranch is dumb. Do you have any other complaint for the man who just saved your life?"

The girl seemed genuinely sad. "I am sorry. I did not mean to hurt your feelings."

"You didn't hurt…Can we change the subject?"

Lowering her head, the Indian girl walked in pensive silence trying to think of something she might say to ease the tension. "Is Peaches your squaw?"

Jacob groaned from deep down inside. "Let's talk about you."

"I am Apache."

She said no more. He waited patiently for her to continue. Her eyes cast about taking in the winding trail as though her thoughts were now elsewhere.

"That's it?"

The girl laughed, realizing the big man expected more. "My people are the Aiaha N'de, what you call Chiricahua Apache. Though we do not use the word Chiricahua. They are the people of Cochise. My people are known by many names, the Red Paint People, the Gila, Warm Springs, even the Victorio's. The list is many. It seems everyone has a name for us, but nobody knows us.

"We call ourselves the Chihene, it is our name, but now we are called the Mimbres by the white eyes who named us for the mountains. It is an honorable name. I am called Mea-a-ha. My father was a brave warrior and a leader of our people. He is dead now. My mother died too of white man's disease. I have two brothers, Teowa and Daniel. We have not heard from Teowa for a long time." Her voice lowered, "He is a warrior, I worry for him. It is sad.

"The Apache are scattered, and news does not travel much any more. Daniel has a Christian name. Priest came to our village when he was born." She raised her head adding importance to her words. "The priest told a story of a boy who was put in a mountain lion's den by bad soldiers, but the lions would not eat the boy. Mother said the name has magic and that the soldiers would not be able to harm Daniel."

She hurried her step, dancing sideways to face Jacob. "Does your ranch have a pencil and paper? The priest taught me the white man's letters. I can spell my name. M-e-a-a-h-a." She smiled with pride, looking young again. "We wrote with sticks in the sand. Our words did not last. The priest brought paper from his church on which he wrote. Once he let me use a pencil, and I wrote my name on a piece of paper. He gave it to me and I would unfold it and look at my name. 'Mea-a-ha.' It lasted for a long time. I would like to write my name again."

"Yes, my ranch does have pencil and paper." Jacob smiled.

"Then maybe your ranch is like a church."

"Some might think that."

"If your ranch is like a church, then maybe it does not need cows."

Mea-a-ha continued with hardly a pause. "My brothers and I lived with my grandfather on the reservation at Warm Springs, but my brothers left with other braves to be free or fight the soldiers if they must." Her voice trailed off in thought. "If you were a soldier now, you would hunt my brothers."

A sadness came over her. "One rainy night on the reservation, the soldiers came returning braves they had captured. The warriors told us my father was dead. It was the first time I saw a Buffalo Soldier. They looked black and mean. Mother was crying and I was very scared."

She sniffed hiding a tear. Again, her emotions changed. "You do not seem mean to me, but…" Her voice trailed off.

"But what?"

"I am a little scared. Will you send my grandfather back to the reservation before he can lie in the sacred hills?"

The Apache girl turned and stepped before him. Her large brown eyes raised upwards demanding an answer from the towering man. She was defenseless, yet she boldly faced her greatest fear, a soldier.

Seeing courage in one so small awoke feelings long buried in a cold heart. Jacob had stopped caring, but from this girl, emotions flowed freely. Her innocence amid such tragedy held strength he envied. For the first time since that dreadful night in Tatum's stable, Jacob's heart began to beat with compassion.

Placing his callused hands on her petite shoulders, Jacob spoke with tenderness. "It is no longer my place to return your people to the reservation. My big fat horse and I will take your grandfather to the mountain. And Mea-a-ha, you don't have to be scared of me. I won't hurt you."

It was a simple kindness but the girl was overcome. Kindness was not something the Apaches were given. Closing her eyes she leaned her soft cheek into the giant's hand. His unexpected offer meant their long ordeal was finally over. It had been this young girl's enormous burden to get her sick grandfather across the sweltering desert to the sacred mountain, and now a stranger had instantly lifted the great weight from her shoulders. Her eyes opened wide as her joy bubbled over. "You would do this?"

A caring smile on the big man's face was her answer. Bursting with excitement, the girl turned to her grandfather, and told him in the Apache tongue that the mighty Buffalo Soldier would take him to the sacred hills. For the first time, life stirred in the old man. His chest swelled and he simply nodded his head.

"Grandfather is happy."

They walked on for a long while without talking, the girl making shy sideways glances. The black gringo had an honest face. She believed him. For the first time since Mea-a-ha and her grandfather started their grueling trek, she felt safe. It lifted her spirits so much that she skipped down the trail, erupting in tiny giggles.

Suddenly she turned to Jacob. "What is your name?" He told her. She repeated it several times softly to herself. Then she held out her hand as if she were a fine lady from the east, and bowed sweetly. The priest must have taught her more than letters. "Mea-a-ha is pleased to meet you, big man Jacob," she laughed.

Jacob took the tips of her fingers in his hand and made a deep exaggerated bow. "Jacob is pleased to meet you, little Mea-a-ha." They laughed together and continued on.

The girl's mind never stopped. Once more she lifted her chin. "The Mimbres make beautiful pottery. It is not an easy thing, much work. If a branch is turned into a lance or a piece of flint into a blade, they are still just a stick and a rock. Our pottery is fashioned from the earth until it is something that did not exist, like the white man making the metal gun." Her eyes shone with pride. "We have much skill, and our pottery is the finest in all the land."

Jacob knew she expected him to be impressed. He nodded approvingly.

After a while they came out of the trees on a plateau that looked across the vast desert. The empty land spread on forever without any sign of mankind.

Mea-a-ha stepped close to Jacob and gazed at the expanse. "Jacob, you are free to go where you want. We are told that the Great White Father says that we should not be free, that he wants the Apache to live on reservations. He has decided that this is what is best for us. But he has never asked us if we are happy. We are told that the Great White Father loves us, but I do not think this is true. The soldiers come and say they bring good words that will make life better, but life is not better. It seems the words say that the Apache should politely die and not be a problem. It is hard to understand."

A pang of guilt stabbed deep in the soldier's chest. He had only seen the Apache as a problem to manage. Yet this Indian girl's outpouring of emotions seemed so human. Jacob tried to be consoling. "It is hard to understand. All I know is we have no say about what life is when we start out. We just have to keep walking so we don't get run over, and hope that someday we will find a place where we can stop."

Mea-a-ha turned to Jacob and motioned to the land. "Jacob, have you stopped walking?"

Jacob paused in thought. "A man walks in many places. In some I have stopped. In others I am still walking."

A look of understanding showed in her eyes. "When we find peace, we stop walking."

She looked to her grandfather. "The Apache are sad. I think maybe my grandfather will have to walk after he dies. Maybe he will find peace then."

The girl's words touched Jacob's heart. "Maybe he finds peace in his beautiful granddaughter."

She looked at him with surprise. Her wondering eyes sparkled. "Maybe Jacob should be the Great White Father."

Jacob laughed despite himself. "That will be the day!"

Chapter -10-
Guests

There was little more than a wide space free of trees and rocks to evidence a trail to Jacob's Hollow. The infrequent travel of horses and wagons had yet to leave a lasting scar that might someday be a road. Shaggy junipers and stunted pinyons sprinkled at the edge of the inhospitable desert gradually gave way to larger pines.

The wide path dipped into the secluded hollow weaving through the border trees, rising and falling in respect to their mighty roots. A soft green light filtering through the thick pine boughs created a tunnel of deep warm emerald and yellow hues along the grassy trail.

Jacob hesitated by the stone pillars protruding from the dense line of ponderosas surrounding the Hollow. The ranch lay hidden just beyond. Once he had thought his home beautiful, but that was before Rosie ridiculed it as the stone hovel of a dirt farmer. Pangs of anxiety tightened his chest. Would Mea-a-ha laugh as Rose had? He found himself growing angry at her for an offense she had not committed.

Drawn by a sense of wonder, Mea-a-ha quickened her step as the canopy of trees gave way. Suddenly, there it was, a humble stone house, with its high-pitched shingled roof sheltered beneath the boughs of the ancient trees. A rustic barn of log and stone stood silently at the edge of a turquoise pond laced in deep green cattails. The tranquil meadow lay nestled in huge dark pines against a backdrop of towering cliffs reaching into a clear blue sky, and as always, the music of the bubbling spring.

Maybe the Hollow amplified the soothing sound. Perhaps the cliffs echoed the bubbling tune, layering the notes. Whatever it was, it filled the Hollow with its enchanting song.

Mea-a-ha threw her arms wide, spinning around and around. "Your ranch is beautiful." Suddenly she stopped and lowered her arms with her palms facing outward. The Indian girl closed her eyes as though she were communing in some ancient Apache rite. Her body remained motionless. Then silently, almost a whisper, "Listen, spirits dwell here. They speak. Jacob, your ranch is like a church."

Jacob breathed a gentle sigh. Why, he didn't know. She was just a primitive savage who would be awed by the simplest trappings of civilization. Still, he was eager for her approval.

The old man had survived the long ride. Without encouragement, Major lumbered up to the porch and stopped. Jacob and Mea-a-ha eased his weary body from the saddle, supporting his arms as they guided him through the door.

Mea-a-ha's bright eyes pried into every corner, wonder telling on her

97

delicate face. She had never been in a house before.

While she was distracted, the old man shook free of her grasp and headed straight to Jacob's leather chair. He planted himself with firm resolution, looking like an ancient king on his throne. The hair on Jacob's neck bristled. "Wouldn't he be more comfortable in a bed?" His voice was flat with a tinge of angst.

Mea-a-ha knelt by her grandfather and lovingly patted his wrinkled hand. There was not the slightest motion from the old man. His gray face could have been carved from stone. "He is happy."

Jacob turned away in annoyance. "How can you tell?"

Rising from her grandfather, the wide-eyed Apache girl floated around the room, her fingertips trailing across the tops of chairs, then on to the long table, where she eagerly peered into an empty black pot. Jacob came close. "Have you eaten today?"

She pulled back, embarrassed that her thoughts were so easily read. Folding her hands, the poor girl looked down and shook her head. Her famished expression made Jacob doubt if she had eaten anything in days. He himself had only a bite of jerky since his meal of rabbit had disappeared.

There was still a side of venison hanging in the smokehouse, which Jacob retrieved. The meat was cut into chunks and tossed into a heavy metal pot along with plenty of wild potatoes. Scrounging about, he added pan-fried flour biscuits to the menu, and boiled some beans with a little salt pork and molasses for flavor. It was the last of the store-bought meat.

Mea-a-ha stayed close, trying to help with the cooking, all the while in awe of the wondrous blue steel six-hole stove. She had only cooked over open fires, contending with ash and smoke. This was truly a splendid invention.

Jacob sent her to the spring to pick some fresh watercress. As each new item was added to the meal, Mea-a-ha's excitement grew, her little hand stealing samples of sticky biscuit dough and crunchy uncooked beans. Inquisitive fingers stabbed into crocks of salt, flour and sugar then were licked clean, each invoking a telling expression on her child-like face.

And so it went, no sooner would Jacob put something down than the girl would pick it up and examine it, marveling. Sometimes she would look up at Jacob with a quizzical expression. He would smile. "It's a salt shaker." Little things that were taken for granted by a civilized people filled her with wonder.

"These are called spoons, yes?"

Jacob nodded. "Yes."

She smiled, proud to have gotten it right. "You have so many spoons. Little ones to eat with and big ones for cooking and then even bigger ones."

"That's a ladle."

The excitement of his starry-eyed guest turned the simple meal into a banquet. Her infectious good humor even elevated Jacob's spirits. Darkness that had weighed so heavily was slowly lifting.

Jacob reached into a wooden box and set three china plates, compliments of Elena Rincon, next to the knives and forks. Mea-a-ha carefully picked up a plate in her tiny hands, and tipped it, letting it catch the light. Her stunned expression reflected in the beautiful glaze. The painting was very intricate, not like the dull colors of the Mimbres. Mea-a-ha lifted her eyes to Jacob, and spoke meekly. "It is very pretty. Is it white man's pottery?"

Jacob nodded. Mea-a-ha set the plate down. "Our pottery does not compare." She hid her face. "You must think me silly, boasting of our mud pots."

Jacob could see the her discomfort. She had so little to be proud of, and now as a new world unfolded before her, even that was taken away. He picked up a plate. "It is beautiful, but cold. The white man is skilled, but they no longer take pride in their work. I have seen the Mimbres' pottery. It is more than mud; there's magic from the Apache hand that makes the water taste sweeter. Your people care, and I would gladly trade this old plate for a Mimbre vase any day."

The girl looked to her host with grateful eyes. "We do care."

She was happy again, and turned back, eager to help this kind stranger cook the great feast.

With the aroma of food filling the house, even the old man began to fidget. Secretly Jacob hoped the delicious food would entice the Indian out of his chair. It didn't. Mea-a-ha wound up fixing her grandfather a plate and placing it on his lap. Jacob accepted the failure and sat with Mea-a-ha at one end of the long table.

During the meal she laughed and talked, bubbling with the excitement of a child at Christmas. Mea-a-ha's joy was contagious. For the first time since the terrible night with Rosie, Jacob actually felt happy. The Indian girl chattered without punctuation. "Are you a rich man, Jacob?"

Her question caught him by surprise. "Do you know how much nineteen dollars is?"

With bright wondering eyes, and a completely innocent face, she shook her head no. "Is it enough to buy a great herd of cattle?"

Jacob laughed. "No, Mea-a-ha, it is not. Maybe I could buy a few chickens?"

The girl quickly added. "And a dog?"

Jacob laughed again. "Yes, a few chickens and maybe a dog."

"Then that is what you should do. You would have a beautiful ranch with chickens and a big friendly dog."

"And what would I do for money, when I really need to buy something?"

"I do not have money. Grandfather does not have money. We survive. You will survive. You have your own place where you can stop walking. You can come and go, and the white man does not hunt you. I think you are rich."

Jacob stared at Mea-a-ha in wonder. Suddenly he no longer felt like a foolish dirt farmer. With a few words from this simple girl, his dream took life once more. If only Rose could have seen through Mea-a-ha's eyes. Rose. His smile faded. "Oh, I don't know about the white man hunting me, though. After shaming the Mathers boys, their father might come after me pretty quick."

Mea-a-ha filled with anguish. "Jacob, I am sorry if grandfather and I have brought danger to you."

He had not meant to sadden her. "It was not your fault. Men like Mathers and his boys look for excuses to cause trouble. You just crossed their path. So did I, I guess."

"But we are still a burden to you. I can see it."

Perhaps the truth showed in Jacob's expression. Her large soulful eyes searched his face, and he felt guilty for his unkind thoughts. "Well, while you're here, you can earn your keep by cooking and cleaning – doing woman's work. I would rather wrestle a grizzly than scrub those pots."

Bouncing in her chair, the girl smiled eagerly. "Thank you for your kindness. I will work very hard, for grandfather and me. You will see."

"Speaking of your grandfather, what should I call him, besides 'Old Man'?"

She laughed. "He has been Grandfather so long, few remember his name, most people in our village call him Grandfather. You can call him Grandfather too."

"Then Grandfather it is. Now, shouldn't we be getting Grandfather into bed?"

Mea-a-ha slid from her chair and gave the old man a hug. There was something timeless about him. He had walked the lands before the coming of the white settlers. This ancient warrior was the last vestige of a lost race. He and Mea-a-ha were both Apache, but they dwelled in different worlds.

Jacob showed Mea-a-ha to the little bedroom. Heat from the warm day hung in the thick stone walls; the night would be pleasant. The little room was sparse. On the outside wall there was a small square window next to a narrow closet. The ceiling sloped steeply from the high inside wall to just barely a man's height by the window.

In the corner sat a small rough hewn wooden stool with three stout legs. A sturdy log bed, big enough for two filled the center of the room. It

100

looked soft and lumpy. White sheets were folded down over a worn gray army blanket with two large feather pillows placed on top. Next to the door a short wooden shelf hung on the wall with pegs beneath it. Sitting on the shelf was a dented tin lantern flickering with a warm light. An elk hide served as a carpet on the stone floor at the foot of the bed.

The only color in the room came from a pair of green and red plaid curtains covering the window. Floyd at the dry goods store, a true salesman, had given Jacob a great deal on four sets of curtains when he bought the windows. The room was tidy, but Rosie would not have approved of its furnishings – not even for a child's room. Jacob's face clouded.

Mea-a-ha helped her grandfather to the bed. The old man laid his head on the pillow, and immediately closed his eyes.

Jacob glanced around the humble room once more. "I'm sorry the room is so small and plain, but I hope you'll be comfortable enough."

Mea-a-ha looked over her shoulder at Jacob and left her grandfather's side. She stepped very close, the toes of her moccasins almost touching Jacob's big boots, her head was cast down. "Your small room is much nicer than our wickiup of sticks."

She raised her bright moist eyes to meet his. "Jacob, you do not know. Here in your room no cold wind blows through. Rain cannot get in. You have finely woven blankets instead of hides. The door does not open to sagebrush and sand."

The young girl filled with emotions. Without thinking, her delicate fingers reached for the security of Jacob's hand. "I have never slept in a house before and I have only heard of beds. The room is wonderful and beautiful. On our journey across the desert, we spent so many cold nights curled on the ground, frightened with no weapons. Tonight I will sleep without fear. I know that you will protect us, and tomorrow there will be food. Do not apologize for offering me more than I have ever dreamed. To me you are rich. I am ashamed to take so much after all the problems we have caused. Thank you for your kindness to a poor Indian girl." She hung her head again.

Jacob froze in awkward silence. Gently, he gave her hand a reassuring squeeze. Everything this little Apache had said today surprised him. She was a mixture of childish wonder and deep wisdom. How many times had he ridden through Indian camps, regarding the women with disgust as the frightened, mindless cattle of savage men?

The women, clad only in dirty animal skins, most of them not civilized enough to cover their breasts, suckled their naked offspring, never speaking or showing any signs of intelligence. And now, one stood before him, short with a round face and ruddy complexion, looking little different. But when Mea-a-ha spoke, there was wisdom. Her words reached through the darkness. The girl's innocent laughter and gentle thoughts soothed a gnawing hunger deep inside. "You best get some sleep." Jacob turned and left the room.

****

The soft warm rays of the morning sun peering through the dusty window panes found Jacob sitting quietly at the table as he often did. Warming his hands on a tin cup of coffee, Jacob wondered if he should peek in on his guest, when suddenly the front door burst open bathing the room in brilliant light. Mea-a-ha danced in beaming with excitement. She was out of breath and her moccasins were wet. Spying Jacob, a smile of perfect white teeth brightened her face. "Jacob, there were deer drinking from the spring. I was getting so close, when all of a sudden this giant gray horse, the biggest I have ever seen, trotted from the barn and whinnied at them. I think I met Peaches." She laughed.

Jacob grinned. "So do you still think she is my wife?"

Mea-a-ha blushed at Jacob's little joke. "No. She is much too pretty."

Giving a chuckle, Jacob returned to his tin cup. Mea-a-ha sat in a chair next to him and pealed off her wet moccasins, then proceeded to braid her long black hair, all the while talking about the morning, the Hollow, and how well she had slept in a bed. The cheery girl was an endless stream of conversation that seemed to need no reply, other than an occasional nod from Jacob to show he was listening. Finally, with her hair done, she turned to more immediate matters. "Will you show me how to use the metal fire box and let me fix the morning meal?"

With great delight, Jacob consented.

The most ordinary tasks were done with excitement as she scurried about the kitchen with an endless supply of energy. She marveled at the matches, holding the little wooden stick delicately in her fingertips, looking for the hidden fire.

Jacob's stone face slowly softened to a smile as he showed Mea-a-ha the operation of the stove with its many doors, lids, and side tank for boiling water. Then he found her glazed pots and metal pans to cook with. Items that Rose would have fingered with disgust, the Indian girl held as treasures.

Finally her attention turned to cooking, and she pushed Jacob back into his chair at the table. Having gotten caught up in the excitement, he relented with a bit of disappointment and contented himself with simply watching as he sipped the last of his coffee. The comforting aroma of flapjacks soon filled the house.

So taken with watching the girl work, Jacob was shocked when he turned and saw Grandfather sitting in his leather chair, stoic as ever. A tight lipped frown replaced Jacob's new smile. His throne had been stolen right from under his nose.

Holding a wooden spatula in one hand, Mea-a-ha skipped quickly to her grandfather and gave him a kiss on the cheek, then just as quick, she was back at the stove flipping the final flapjack on to a tall stack. "The fat tortillas are done."

Flapjacks were Jacob's idea.

As before, grandfather ate sitting in the chair while Jacob and Mea-a-ha sat at the table. Jacob watched with growing annoyance as Mea-a-ha drowned her breakfast in syrup. The gallon jug was to have lasted him all year. He wondered how long his house guests would stay. The old man had taken quite a beating from Wyatt Mathers. "Mea-a-ha, how long do you think it will be until grandfather is ready to travel to his sacred burial ground?"

Mea-a-ha rose from her plate. The smile from enjoying the sweet syrup faded as she looked to her grandfather. "Grandfather is hurt bad. I can see it. But I think he will not die until he has finished his journey. Maybe he will be ready to travel in a couple of days, or maybe many days. I do not know."

Jacob grimaced unconsciously. Mea-a-ha noticed and bowed her head. Everyday of her life had been a bitter struggle for survival. Jacob's Hollow with its simple gift of food and shelter was heaven on earth, a sanctuary for a desperate heart.

Caught up in her joy, she had forgotten they might not be wanted in paradise. It hurt. Bravely, she struggled for words, trying not to cry. "I am sorry we are a burden."

Realizing her pain, Jacob cringed, ashamed of how cruel he had become. Was his heart so black that he could wound someone so innocent? He slid to the edge of his chair. "No, Mea-a-ha, it is me who is sorry. I have lived alone too long, and have forgotten how to treat guests."

He placed his hand over hers and held it softly. "I have enjoyed your conversation, you have brightened my home. Please forgive me."

With a big finger he wiped a speck of food from her cheek and smiled. "Now finish your plate of syrup, you have a lot of cleaning to do."

Lifting her hopeful eyes, the girl's smile returned. Maybe they were wanted?

For the rest of the morning Mea-a-ha merrily skipped in and out of the kitchen, carrying water, scrubbing dishes and pans with the joy a little girl might have playing with her first tea set. The table was cleaned; the stove was wiped and polished until it shone brighter than it had new from the store. While she hurried about, she would pause to smooth her grandfather's hair or give him a hug. Her fascination with the strange new house continued. She loved the windows especially – they let you see through walls but kept out the wind. With attention bordering on reverence, she cleaned them of every last speck of dust.

Then there was the little room between the bedrooms, with another stove and a huge kettle in the middle of the floor. "What is it for?"

Picking up an empty bucket, Jacob gestured to the stove. "You heat water and bathe in the tub."

"Swim indoors?" Her expression was one of sheer amazement. "In warm water?"

"It beats a dip in an icy creek on a snowy morning," Jacob replied with a grin.

Mea-a-ha knelt, her hand sliding along the curled edge of the copper tub. "How often do people bathe?"

"Oh, a feller might bathe once a month, but I hear some fancy womenfolk bathe every day." Jacob pointed to a small shelf with pegs below. "There's the soap and a towel, when your chores are finished, you might like to have a soak. I keep a barrel full of water outside the door; you don't even have to go to the spring."

The Indian girl stood. "Gringos think of everything; it is so amazing." Leaving the room, she paused at the door, taking one last longing look at the shiny tub.

Jacob wasted the morning watching Mea-a-ha from his wooden chair. The Apache girl chattered away, offering her thoughts on everyday life. Her unique views were refreshing, so different from his ideas born in a no-nonsense army life. Mea-a-ha's thoughts were more spiritual, more feminine. Whether insightful or amusing, she chased away the dark clouds that shadowed his mind.

Knowing he had stayed far longer than he should, Jacob reluctantly took his leave and went hunting. It looked like he might have guests for some time.

In the days that followed, the icehouse and the smokehouse again began to fill with elk, deer, rabbit, and wild turkey. Jacob was a good shot and provided meat, but did little about other foods like nuts, berries and roots. Gathering such foods took patience; a trait found lacking in Jacob. So little thought had he given to these necessities, that while building an icehouse and a smokehouse for the meat, he never considered digging a root cellar.

After a spell of meat three times a day, which was fine with Jacob, Mea-a-ha started taking time from her chores to pick acorns, wild grains, berries, yucca root, nettles and yellow dock. The pickings were sparse on the edge of the desert, but it was early in the year and food was to be found if one looked hard enough.

When tortillas became part of the daily meals, Jacob happily accepted the variety without giving much thought to Mea-a-ha's extra effort in making this happen. Leather pouches and small handmade baskets filled with wild spices, seeds and dried berries began to fill the corners of the kitchen. The soldier, who thought he had planned so well, who built nesting boxes for chickens that did not exist, never thought of cupboards

104

where a woman might want to store supplies other than meat.

The days progressed with slow steady change in Grandfather's health. He talked more, but travel was still out of the question. Each day when Jacob returned, there he'd be, sitting in his leather chair. Jacob began to regard him simply as part of the furniture.

Mea-a-ha was saddened by Jacob's lack of care for Grandfather. He seemed only interested in when the old man would be well enough to go away and die. True, this had been their intentions, but resting in the peaceful hollow had extended Grandfather's fragile lease on life, and each new day with Grandfather was a cherished gift to Mea-a-ha. Still, it was Jacob who made these added days possible, and she would never forget how he'd saved their lives. In her mind, Jacob owed them nothing, and she was grateful for everything he gave them.

She came to understand that Jacob had his moods, both cheery and sad. There was darkness inside him. At times, she thought it might be because of her and Grandfather, but deep down, she knew there must be something more. Her feminine intuition told her it was another woman, but as to what the story was, she dared not ask.

So Mea-a-ha tried harder to please Jacob. She promised herself that when he came home this evening everything would be perfect, and so it was.

In the late afternoon, Jacob pushed open the door to a delicious aroma that instantly told him the his resourceful guest had been cooking all day. The table was set as it had been their first night, with dishes, cups and flatware placed with care. A heavy pot with an iron handle sat simmering on the stove.

When Jacob dropped his gear on the floor, and slammed the heavy door, it was answered by a loud splash from the small room. The door opened a crack and Mea-a-ha, dripping wet, clutching a towel, raced into the bedroom scolding as she went. "You're early. Don't you dare eat until I say."

Jacob looked to Grandfather who sat on the edge of the stuffed chair eagerly eyeing the food. Something told Jacob that even the old man had been warned, 'No eating without the cook's permission.'

Moments later a fully dressed, but still damp girl appeared, looking a bit reproachful, but she quickly broke into a delightful grin. "Sit down, dinner is ready."

Bowls of steaming salsify root, maguey, prickly pear fruit, blackberries and roasted pine nuts in maple syrup already adorned the table. This time Grandfather eagerly left the padded chair and joined the banquet.

As the two hungry men waited, Mea-a-ha reached up and took a pan of golden fried biscuits down from the warming oven and put them on the table, followed by the main course, a hardy pot of venison chili. She filled their plates then sat down watching Jacob's expression.

Taking a large spoonful, the big man's eyes closed as he savored the delicious meal. His stomach rumbled, impatient for its turn. Jacob dug in.

There was little time for talking as both men gave their full attention to devouring the scrumptious feast. Jacob filled his plate several times, and even Grandfather was smiling and asking for seconds.

To her delight, Mea-a-ha's hard day's work was quickly consumed. The biscuits were the tastiest ever. Jacob sopped up the last bit of chili with one more than he needed, then slid his chair back from the table with a contented glow. Even Grandfather's returning to his padded chair didn't bother him.

Thinking back to all his days in the military, Jacob could not remember a meal so fine. Little Mea-a-ha kept stealing glances at him, knowing she had done well. Finally he spoke, "You never cease to amaze me. You have an opinion on everything, and now I find you can cook Anglo, Apache, and Mexican dishes. If I didn't know better I would think that you attended some fancy finishing school back East."

Mea-a-ha did not understand everything he said, but she knew it was a compliment and blushed with embarrassment. She skipped across the room and knelt by Grandfather, speaking to him in Apache. "He may growl too much, like an old bear, but he can be very sweet and say nice things too. I think he likes us."

Scurrying back to the stove, she started cleaning up. Jacob sat quietly for a moment, then spoke casually. "I suppose you're right." Mea-a-ha continued her cleaning. "Right about what?"

"Oh, I don't know." Jacob's voice was laced with a bit of humor. "Everything... I growl too much, and I have grown to like you and Grandfather, but do you really think I'm an old bear?"

Mea-a-ha whirled around wide eyed, sending pans clattering to the floor. She frantically gathered them up and turned back to the stove. Her voice was small and shaky. "You speak our tongue?"

Jacob laughed. "Quite well, actually."

Her tone was sullen, but a tinge of humor crept in. "That is very mean of you not to let me know, and you are a grumpy old bear." She tried to stifle a giggle. "But you do like us? You said so."

Jacob chuckled. "I suppose, you have a way of growing on people like a cute little squirrel that chatters all day. And I don't know if I could ever go back to my own cooking after yours. The question is... do you like grumpy old bears?"

Now it was Mea-a-ha's turn to be honest. She held her tongue for a moment, searching for the words. "As long as the grumpy old bear does not bite the head off the little squirrel." She giggled at the thought. "The bear is great protection. Yes, we like him, but he should remember that a cute little squirrel has teeth too. And she can play her jokes as well."

106

Jacob carried his plate to the stove and stood next to her. "At least we understand each other a little better. The bear will try not to bite the little squirrel's head off, and the little squirrel will... well... just keep being the cute little squirrel. Truce?"

Mea-a-ha looked up with a shy smile. "Truce."

In bed that night, with her hands folded behind her head, Mea-a-ha found herself wide awake enjoying the memories of the day. It had been a good day, and Jacob had not growled once. She smiled to herself and wiggled her toes. Yes, it had been a very good day.

From the great room Mea-a-ha heard the squeak of Jacob's leather chair. She slipped out of bed, wearing a long blue shirt of his that he had given her to sleep in since she had nothing of her own. He actually gave her two shirts, sort of. The other she borrowed, and over time it kind of became hers. She thought the old shirts were the most beautiful clothing, softer than hides and she loved the way they twirled about her. One was her night shirt, the other her day shirt. To make them different, she tightened the day shirt about her petite waist with a thin beaded belt. When no one was looking, she would sneak into the small room and stand in front of the mirror, admiring her dresses as she called them. They drowned her, falling to her knees and the sleeves had to be rolled several times. Even with all but the top button buttoned, the collars often slid off one shoulder. Still, they were the only things she owned, and they made her feel rich.

On tiptoes, Mea-a-ha peeked around the corner, and found Jacob resting quietly in his chair. Sensing her presence, his eyes blinked open. Mea-a-ha timidly stepped away from the wall. "Sorry, I did not mean to disturb you."

Mustering a tired smile, he raised to meet her. "You didn't. In fact, I was just thinking about you."

"About me?" Her face brightened.

From the fireplace mantle, Jacob retrieved a brown leather box. He took Mea-a-ha's hand and led her to a chair at the table. A lantern in the middle cast a dim yellow glow. "I was thinking of you and the talk we had the first day on the trail."

Jacob sat next to Mea-a-ha and placed the leather box before them. Resting both hands on the lid, he gave a sly grin. The girl's eyes grew wide with anticipation. He teased her for a moment, then folded back the lid. Mea-a-ha gasped with delight. "Paper!"

Unable to contain herself, she reached into the box, plucked out a sheet and held it up to the light. "Oh, Jacob! You remembered."

"Well, go ahead, write your name." He coaxed her with a grin.

Mea-a-ha placed the paper on the table. Taking a pencil from a small drawer in the bottom of the leather box, Jacob handed it to her. Reverently, the Indian girl rolled the pencil in her tiny fingers then started writing very slowly and carefully, saying each letter out loud as she did. "M-e-a-a-h-a, 'Mea-a-ha'... there."

She laughed aloud and wiggled in her chair. Then she handed the pencil to Jacob. "Now you write your name."

Jacob printed his name with Mea-a-ha saying each letter as he did. Next she took the pencil and wrote his name again. "J-a-c-o-b."

Again she handed the pencil to Jacob, "Write Grandfather."

The next hour they spent together with Mea-a-ha saying a word or a name for Jacob to write and then she would copy it. Some of the words were things she could spy in the dim lamplight: pot, table, chair, stove, man and girl. Others were house, ranch, Major and Peaches.

Letters were bits of magic that lit her bright face with wonder. Each new word was knowledge for a hungry mind. Even a sheet of paper was a precious gift beyond value to one so deprived of simple pleasures... and so the evening went.

Finally rising from his chair, Jacob stretched and yawned. "Well, I'm goin' to bed. Mornin' comes early. Feel free to write as long as you like. There's plenty of paper."

Mea-a-ha's eyes followed him as he shuffled to his door rubbing sleep from his face. He turned to say goodnight one last time and found her standing.

Bathed in a soft warm glow, clad only in his thin shirt, her hair falling loosely about her, Jacob saw her for the first time as a lovely woman, not a little girl, not an Apache, but a very attractive woman. He was surprised he had not noticed before. She was small, but every curve was feminine. Her soft bare shoulder and delicate neck quickened his breathing, yet it was her large hungering eyes that held his gaze. They were filled with a thousand questions.

Suddenly, with quick light steps, Mea-a-ha crossed the floor between them, her bare feet hardly touching the stones. Before Jacob knew what was happening, she threw her arms around his waist and buried her head against his chest in a strong hug. "Thank you."

Just as quick, she scurried back and leaned against the table. Resting her knee on the chair and tucking her head, Mea-a-ha peered at Jacob, unsure of his reaction.

Taking a deep breath, Jacob went back to the table, knowing now was not the time to walk away. He circled her waist with his big arms, lifting her onto her toes, and returned the hug. "Thank you, Mea-a-ha."

A second squeeze, and he let her slide to the floor. His hands lingered for a moment on her slender waist, her sweet scent awakened old feelings. For an instant he leaned close, but fear stayed his hands. They dropped to his side. Turning, he crossed the floor in three large strides, and disappeared into his room.

Mea-a-ha melted into the chair and sat quietly. Suddenly she giggled and kicked her feet with girlish delight. Her smile lingered as she picked up the pencil and continued writing, "J-a-c-o-b."

Chapter -11-
Secret Places

𝕸ajor plodded through the broken rubble, occasionally stumbling as he picked his way across the rock slide at the base of the high cliffs. The trail was rough going, but there was shade from the blistering August sun. Sweat evaporated quickly in the dry air, leaving scratchy salt stains on Jacob's soiled shirt. His jaw hung open in a face gaunt with fatigue. Dust caked in a mouth too dry to spit. The canteen hanging from the saddle horn had been empty for some time, but Jacob shook it just the same, wishing for one last swallow.

Game was getting scarce, and Jacob had been away from the ranch for three days. Fortunately he had managed a long shot out in the open desert, downing a scrawny antelope at full run, it lay across the pommel of his saddle. Flies buzzing over the carcass bit at his face. For Jacob it was just another day. You got used to it.

From beneath the worn brim of his hat, he looked up at the towering cliffs. Swirls of dust kicked over the edge by a high breeze gave evidence that it was cooler on top. He often wondered if there might be a hidden trail to the rim. The thought of a cool breeze was inviting, but for now the cliffs would remain a mystery.

****

The sun sank below the trees, casting long shadows. Mea-a-ha stepped through the door and started sweeping the stone porch as she had several times since early morning. It had been three days since Jacob had gone hunting.

Indian women knew that when the braves rose with the sun in search of game, they might not return by dusk. There was no point in coming back empty-handed, but Jacob had always managed some game each day, if only a couple of rabbits, and she was worried. In the desert there were many reasons why a man might not return.

Each night without Jacob increased her anxiety. She did not sleep well when he was away. Sweeping harder, she tried to push the thought out of her mind that she might have feelings for him. The lonely evenings did not help.

She often thought of the night several weeks ago, when Jacob hugged her. Did he have feelings too? The hug was not talked about, but things had changed. They stood closer, but often lighthearted conversations ended in awkward silence.

Perhaps it was understandable; they were from different worlds and there were too many uncertainties in these violent times. Mea-a-ha was beholden to Jacob for so much, and that is not a good way to start a relationship. Then there were his dark moods.

Mea-a-ha had vowed to keep a distance between them and she did her best, but on the morning he left, while he tightened the saddle cinch, the inches between them seemed to disappear and she found herself giving him a quick hug. She hadn't meant to, it just happened, like when a woman hugs her man goodbye. 'Her man!' Mea-a-ha stabbed the broom into the dusty porch. Now things were even more complicated.

The door creaked opened and Grandfather shuffled past her as she stared longingly into the distance. Gentle days in the Hollow had worked wonders, and the old man's health was improving steadily. His mind, still sharp, missed nothing. Pausing, he cleared his throat. "He is a good man. You will need someone."

Mea-a-ha's eyes flashed, "Grandfather!"

Her Grandfather grinned. "What, because he is not Apache? Do you think I should disapprove?"

She returned to her sweeping. "Maybe you should disapprove."

The old man's face held understanding. "You have been a good granddaughter and I do not wish you to die with me. Take what life offers. For the Apache, gifts are few."

Mea-a-ha launched an effusive protest. "There are too many stones down that path Grandfather. Besides! I don't feel that way about him." Her voice trailed. "And maybe he doesn't feel that way about me."

Grandfather placed a wrinkled hand on her shoulder. "Sometimes the path worth traveling has the most stones. Face it with courage and honesty. Don't pretend to feel different than you do."

Mea-a-ha blustered. "Well, I don't."

Grandfather turned and walked slowly towards the spring, amused by his granddaughter's denial. "And the white men will go away, the buffalo will return, and I will never die."

He glanced back at her without stopping. "And if you could see with half the wisdom of this old Apache, you would see your man coming through the trees."

She looked up. "Jacob!"

Grandfather put an aging finger to his lips. "Do not shout his name, granddaughter; he might think you care."

When the old man turned his back, Mea-a-ha stuck her tongue out at him, then bent her eager gaze to the dusty figure. He came riding in from the east where the cliffs dropped steeply into the dry lands below. Major headed straight for the pond. The man and horse drank long before continuing to the barn.

Jacob was grooming Major when Mea-a-ha stepped through the door. He cast her a glance and kept brushing. For a moment she leaned against the shadowed wall, hesitant to close the distance between them. Her telling eyes darted furtively in the awkward silence, fearful she might reveal her hidden feelings. She must say something.

Taking a nervous step forward, Mea-a-ha spied Jacob's hat lying on the saddle tree where he had tossed it. The old hat was a part of him that allowed her to be close without actually going to him. She fingered the dusty brim then plopped it on her head. It hung over her ears, making for a comical scene.

Speaking in a deep husky voice, the Indian girl did her best to imitate a cowboy. "Howdy, stranger."

In spite of his exhaustion, Jacob chuckled. "Have I been gone that long?"

"Yes." There was a tinge of reproach. Mea-a-ha looked at the antelope hanging on a hook from the rafters. "It's not much bigger than a jackrabbit."

Jacob shook his head. "Pickin's is getting' slim, mighty slim. I guess that's why no one lives out here. Life evaporates with the water."

Mea-a-ha stepped nearer giving a reassuring smile. "It will be okay. We still have plenty of meat in the smoke house." She lingered by his side, hungering for his embrace. "I made lots of jerky and pemmican while you were away. It is flour and meal that I worry about."

A pout returned to her face. "Squirrels beat me to the acorns."

Extending a finger, Jacob tilted the hat back so he could see her beautiful eyes. "Don't be hard on yourself, they're bigger n' you."

Pulling the hat from her head, Mea-a-ha batted Jacob on the shoulder. "You try to find enough tiny acorns to fill a hungry old bear."

"Well, what's for dinner tonight?"

Mea-a-ha brightened. "I made another pot of my venison chili you like."

A flash of approval lit his face but he quickly cocked a brow. "You were sure I'd return?"

Embarrassed, the girl cast her eyes down. "I thought if I acted like you were coming home, you would and here you are so there. If I was worried it is because you got chores to do. I'm tired of feeding that giant horse and chopping wood for you. So come on in and eat, but you can forget about any biscuits tonight."

Heading back to the house, they paused on the wooden footbridge, spying Grandfather sitting under the trees by the spring. "Your grandfather looks healed."

Mea-a-ha clutched the rail. "Healed from the beating, but not old age. Still, the time here in the Hollow has done wonders. Even if we had never met those evil boys, I do not think Grandfather would have lived this long. I am thankful for each new day with him, but I fear it will not be much longer. He has plans of his own. For several days now he has walked to the spring. He drinks the healing waters, then sits in that very spot, looking off into the distance. His thoughts are elsewhere."

Jacob put his hand on the small of the girl's back and ushered her towards the house. She accepted his kindness. "Jacob."

"Yes."

"If you don't find game, it's okay to come home each night. We'll get by."

For the next few days Mea-a-ha watched Grandfather take his daily walks to the spring with growing concern. He would gaze at the clouds, his hands occasionally lifting as though he was conversing with an unseen guest.

In the Indian girl's short life, there had been many deaths. Sadly, all were lives cut short. Grandfather's passing was different, like watching a dark horse approaching from a great distance. Maybe that was why the old man stared beyond the horizon; he could see the death horse coming for him.

Jacob stayed closer to home to Mea-a-ha's relief. They relied on the dwindling food storage, trusting that more game would come along. Even so, when Jacob returned with a squirrel he killed at the edge of the Hollow, he was severely chastised, and the poor animal was buried. Apparently the squirrel had a name. A rule was made that there was no hunting in or near the Hollow. That night Jacob had beans.

At last a day came when Grandfather returned from his communing much earlier than usual. His eyes were clear. He seemed at peace.

As Mea-a-ha prepared dinner, Grandfather struck up a conversation with Jacob. The two men had been talking more since his health improved. They had traveled many of the same trails and realized they had stories in common.

The old Indian recounted a skirmish where he had shot the hat off a reckless young Buffalo Soldier. Jacob gave a start, remembering having his hat shot from his head during his first encounter with the Apaches. Both men laughed.

Hearing them talk made Mea-a-ha happy. She stirred her pot and pretended they were a real family.

Since Jacob's return to the Hollow, the old man had been taking dinner at the table with them to Mea-a-ha's relief. There was no more awkward silence. Jacob and Grandfather continued their lively conversation right through dinner. Occasionally, they would try to include Mea-a-ha, but the young girl knew little of battles, and was quite content to listen to their amazing stories.

While Mea-a-ha cleared the table, Grandfather remained. The flickering shadows of the kerosene lamp darkened the deep wrinkles in his weathered face, yet his piercing eyes danced with an urgency. In a moment of silence when Mea-a-ha's chattering and the clattering of dishes died away, he spoke. "It is time."

Concern growing on her face, Mea-a-ha returned to the table. "Time for what, Grandfather?" She hadn't really needed to ask.

"This old body is as healed as it can be. I know your thoughts, granddaughter, but we started this journey knowing how it would end. It is time. Coming to Jacob's Hollow has not changed this. It is a healing place where magical waters have flowed from under the sacred mountains since before the Apache walked the earth. Life is long here and the Hollow has blessed me with extra days, but even the Hollow cannot stop time. If I stay here, I will die here, and that is not my wish.

My beautiful granddaughter, you walked with me on my journey. You can walk a little further, but the final path is mine. Help me finish my journey while I still can."

Mea-a-ha's shoulders slumped in resignation. She knew the truth in the old man's words. There could be no protest. "When do we leave?"

"In the morning."

Mea-a-ha gasped. Her eyes darted to Jacob, but his expression offered no hope of changing Grandfather's mind. She slowly stood, hiding her sadness in the shadows. The old Indian turned to Jacob. "You have opened your home and befriended us, even though it was not in your heart to do so. It speaks well of you. There are times when we all walk in darkness. Jacob, I think maybe Mea-a-ha has been a light for you as you have been for us. Who knows why the gods bring us together. Do not dismiss their gift lightly."

Jacob glanced nervously to Mea-a-ha. She met his gaze, but neither spoke. The old Apache continued. "If you will indulge this old man a little longer, I have one last request. My legs will not take me where I need to go. Would you and your great horse carry me a little farther?"

"I would consider it an honor, Grandfather. Major will, too."

"Then it is done. Let's fill our cups with more of your delicious cider and be merry."

Mea-a-ha tipped the earthen jug to the empty cups, then turned and faced the wall. The three of them were in agreement on what must be, but each heart carried a different emotion... peace, sadness, despair.

Morning came bright and beautiful; both meadowlarks and ravens heralded the new day. Grandfather was up at dawn, warming his old bones in his usual place by the spring, while young squirrels played about his feet. To the old Apache they were a good sign, a reminder that life goes on.

Mea-a-ha opened the heavy door and placed a large sack on the porch, then stepped back inside. She returned a moment later with a smaller sack and placed it next to the first.

Raising her eyes, she could see Jacob saddling Major by the barn. A light morning breeze carried the faint, familiar scent of the old horse.

Since she was a little girl, the musty smell of horses had been comforting for her. It meant the coming and going of braves. It was a smell she associated with men and their freedom to go where they will.

Now it was Grandfather's journey. She reminded herself that it was not a journey he chose, but one that chose him.

The old man pressed his wrinkled hands against the rough log and straightened his stiff frame. Even standing required effort. Slowly he started back towards the house. Jacob slipped his glove around the bridle and lead Major to the hitching post. Stepping onto the porch, Mea-a-ha closed the door behind her. No words were necessary. They each knew it was time to go. The sacks were tied behind the saddle, and the ancient warrior took his place on the great warhorse.

Leaning down, Grandfather took the reins. "On this, my last ride, I will lead."

Major responded to the gentle prodding of the old man's moccasins and the journey began. Mea-a-ha turned and took one last longing look at the Hollow. The little house of stones had been her home for one moon. It had been the only time she had felt safe and truly happy since she had been a small child. Her sweet face flushed with emotion and she wondered if she would ever see it again.

Heading west behind the house was the old deer trail that Jacob had followed the morning after the fateful battle with Sholo. It twisted through the ancient trees, meandering back and forth as it made its way over rock and root.

On the east side of the trail, the ground rose steeply to meet the cliffs. Here the steep terrain was strewn with rubble. Thick gnarled brush armored with sharp thorns struggled for life in the thin strip of sunlight where trees could not grow.

To the west of the trail, the land fell away gently. A thick mat of pine needles made a soft carpet beneath the majestic trees. Lush dark ferns huddled in the patches of pale green light. It was as though the shaded path was a border between this secret forest and the harsh world that lay beyond.

At times the trail would climb quickly, heading towards the cliffs, then suddenly turn sharply away as it dipped into a deep ravine. On the other side, it would switch back and continue on.

Eventually the wandering path moved to the center of the old forest, settling into a long, deep hollow beneath the tall trees. Here and there, smaller trails branched off to the west.

To Mea-a-ha each was inviting – an adventure for the taking. But their untold stories must wait for another day, and perhaps another pair of willing feet. The destination of the somber travelers lay elsewhere.

Even though the old man had been to the sacred mountains in his prime, he had never traveled this secret route. It simply headed in the direction he knew he must go, so they followed it.

A musty smell hung in the ancient woods. The forest was old. Like the Hollow, these towering trees held a magic that resisted time. Mea-a-ha paused and looked straight up, marveling at their tremendous height. They made her feel like one of the small woodland creatures scurrying in the shadows on the forest floor.

Everything was big. Jacob was big like a bear; even Grandfather sitting on the giant horse was big – everything but Mea-a-ha. Most of her life she had felt small and this old forest was a reminder. Being small was not always bad, but now and then she wished she could be big and protect those she loved instead of always needing protection. If only she could protect Grandfather now.

Morning passed and the trail eventually narrowed. Jacob moved from Major's side and settled in behind with Mea-a-ha. She welcomed his company, though they walked in silence. It was not a time for words. Maybe it was the solemn purpose of their journey or a reverence for the ancient trees. If gods walked the earth, they would surely do it here.

When the trail smoothed out, the old Indian dozed. His sagging head bobbed from side to side. They were in no hurry, and the beauty of the great woods was a pleasant distraction for his loving granddaughter.

Flickers and scrub jays flittered from tree to tree as gray squirrels raced through the upper branches, their high-pitched chatter proclaiming through the glen, "There are strangers in the woods." Far below their scolding tongues, the quiet procession traveled on.

Like the Hollow, the old forest had its borders. Gradually cedars dwindled, replaced by small sparse pines, which gave way to clumps of junipers. The trail was drier now and dust rose from their weary feet.

Mea-a-ha paused and took a breath. Ahead, the trail rose straight and steep past one last ancient cedar standing majestically at the top of a stony ridge. For years beyond time, the stately guardian kept watch at the edge of the secret forest, for at this point the trees and even the land itself seemed to fall away. Here ended the tranquil woods. Ahead lay the unknown.

When they reached the great tree, Jacob helped Grandfather down so he could rest in the shade. Mea-a-ha fell against the massive trunk of the cedar, more tired than she had realized.

Sagging boughs hung like old moss, and huge roots spread out, finding purchase among the lichen covered rocks. The dampness in the dark forest had made their trip pleasantly cool. Now the hot, dry desert air assailed them if they stepped beyond the shadow of the towering cedars.

Mea-a-ha retrieved several pieces of pemmican from one of the sacks and shared them with the men. This they washed down with water from the big canteen that always hung from Jacob's saddle.

Grandfather was weary. It was now noon, and after the old man finished eating, he leaned back against the tree and dozed, cradled by the spreading roots.

After a short rest, Jacob rose and hiked to the top of the trail. They had climbed considerably from the Hollow without knowing it.

The path leveled out on a high sandy ledge covered with sparse, dry grass. From here Jacob could see the vast desert far below, stretching both south and west.

To the north, the long narrow ledge ended at a jagged cut in the towering cliffs. Each side leaned away as though it had been ripped apart by giant hands.

Toward the south, the trail – or what was left of it – dipped over the edge, angling steeply down to the desert floor. It dropped quickly, more than five hundred feet before sloping off.

Over the years, deer and bighorn sheep chased by mountain lions with little choice of escape had worn a thin scar into the crumbling stone wall with their sharp hooves until it became a trail just inches wide. No doubt many had given their lives in the effort.

There was no way Major could keep his balance on such a thin ledge. Mea-a-ha joined Jacob at the rim and gasped. She timidly pushed a small stone over the edge with her toe. It dropped and bounced, gathering speed, flipping high into the air then crashing back into the face, dislodging other stones along the way, until it finally hit the bottom in a torrent of rubble, obscured in a thick cloud of dust. Filling with alarm, she turned her eyes to Jacob's. He shook his head. "Imagine what a man on a horse might do instead of a little rock."

Mea-a-ha clutched her throat. "Must we go this way?"

"If we were being chased, but we are not, so I think we will change direction here at the edge of my property."

Mea-a-ha looked surprised. "You know where we are?"

"Yes, but I haven't come this far. Never had much luck hunting in these old woods. It's funny, I've looked up at that old cedar from the bottom of the trail before, but never bothered to hike up to it. Something seemed to say this was the end, so I turned back without ever seeing this ledge. It's amazing. The view is incredible.

Jacob stepped to the edge. "Do you know where we are?"

Mea-a-ha returned her gaze to the desert below and shook her head.

Lifting his long arm, Jacob pointed to the south. "About three miles down, at the edge of the foothills and maybe the same distance east, is where you tangled with the charming Mathers boys."

Mea-a-ha cringed and pressed against Jacob. "Then, definitely, let's not go that way. I never want to see that place again."

Jacob pulled her from the ledge. He turned his attention to the jagged cut in the cliff. The ledge narrowed to a point where it met the cut about a hundred yards from where they stood. Hoping there was a trail to follow,

Jacob started hiking up to the gaping scar.

Not wanting to be left behind, Mea-a-ha slipped her hand into Jacob's. It was a steep ascent and they were both breathing hard by the time they reach the top. Their knees ached from the effort.

They were now squeezed against the cliff where the ledge played out. The last several yards, the couple slid with their backs pressed to the wall.

To their surprise, just over the edge, a small trail headed up the cut. It was flatter and wider than the one that dropped to the desert floor. Jagged outcroppings protruded from the walls of the narrow ravine. The trail looped over these exposed rocks like a draped ribbon. Rising steadily up the wall, the thin path climbed until it veered out of site heading back east. It wasn't much of a trail, but it was better than the alternative.

Mea-a-ha eyed Jacob hopefully. "We can make it up this?"

Steadying his breathing, Jacob weighed their chances. "As far as I can see, but if the trail breaks, we will pay hell trying to turn ol' Major around. Still, it's either that or go back the way we came."

They helped Grandfather remount and minutes later, with Jacob holding the reins, Major edged over the lip. Mea-a-ha walked behind. Grandfather had to pull his right leg up so the horse could press close to the wall, and still Major fought for solid footing on the crumbling ledge. Finding nowhere to place his hooves, he would paw the air, then stretch farther or make small leaps to surer ground. Each time the old horse jumped, Mea-a-ha held her breath, fearing that Grandfather would fall to his death on the rocks far below. Their progress was painfully slow.

Jacob dislodged loose boulders with the heel of his boot, clearing a way for the brave horse. A cloud of dust rose about them, making breathing more difficult. As they climbed up the face, the steepness of the trail became more of a concern than its narrow width. Jacob was covered in sweat as he pulled tightly on the reins, while stumbling backward and often falling on his backside.

In back, Mea-a-ha slipped continually, the toes of her soft moccasins finding little traction on the steep, sandy slope. It was more of a scramble than a walk, her hands clawing the steep path as she leaned forward. When they finally reached the bend heading east, the trail leveled out for a bit. It was wider and they found shade beneath the high cliff. Jacob slumped to the ground, his sides heaving with each deep gulp of air. "Let's take a breather."

Edging past Major, Mea-a-ha settled next to him. They dangled their legs over a hundred foot drop and tried to calm their nerves. His chest heaving, Jacob forced a tired grin at Mea-a-ha. "And to think I almost brought Peaches for you to ride."

The girl laughed. "Well, at least you didn't bring the wagon."

Grandfather, who had remained silent through the ordeal, came to life. "Army horses too big, mustang ponies much better. Apaches always get away in the mountains. We just needed more ponies, and more mountains. Never had enough ponies."

He continued on talking more to himself. "The Apache long ago had much land, but the Comanche came and pushed us south. Never liked the Comanche. They have too much pride."

He made a big sweeping gesture towards the mountain. "These mountains belong to the Apache. We hold them sacred. It is a good place to die."

Mea-a-ha lowered her head in strained silence. She understood their journey, but could not accept it. For her, the trail could go on forever if it slowed the dear old man from reaching its end.

After their nerves had calmed, Jacob helped Mea-a-ha back to her feet, the worst of the climb was over. The final stretch might have been called bad anywhere else, but after what they had gone through, it seemed pretty good. Grandfather took the reins again and prodded Major up the final yards of the trail which switched back under an overhang of rocks, then through a very narrow cleft. Finally the tired travelers stood on the rim of the yellow cliffs. It seemed impossible, but they had found a way to the top.

Mea-a-ha stepped next to Jacob and followed his eyes. The cliffs snaked for miles in either direction, broken only by occasional deep canyons that dissolved in a labyrinth of craggy ridges.

The view of the desert was breathtaking. They were standing on an immense mesa that lay at the base of the mountain. Jacob realized, to his bewilderment, that the yellow cliffs towering over his secret Hollow were just a mere step to the mountain that lay beyond.

The desert range was not spectacular. There were no majestic snowcapped peaks or towering pinnacles. Instead, the high ridges were worn and barren, scarred with many small canyons and ravines in which a man could be swallowed up. It was easy to see why travelers had skirted around this hostile terrain. The Apache had found sanctuary here, but little else.

The rest of the day was spent crossing the broken, rock-strewn mesa. Cracks spreading from inches to several yards wide covered the hard stone surface.

In some places, the fissures were twice as deep as a man's height. It forced the companions to walk a zigzag trail, often backtracking. The mesa was covered with scrub oak and low-growing mountain mahogany. Small cottontails and gangly jackrabbits darted about while hungry eagles cried overhead.

Grandfather was drawn toward his destination by ancient memories. Occasionally he would pause, trying to remember, then shake his head and move on.

Near evening they finally made camp at the opening of a canyon where a low outcrop of stone curved in a semicircle. The rim was secluded in wavy leaf oak brush, making a natural shelter. They had made it across the mesa before dark.

A cool breeze picked up as the sun sank beneath the horizon. At dusk, temperatures on the desert can drop from scorching to freezing in a few hours. The day's hot dry zephyr became an icy breath, whistling across their exposed skin.

Dog-tired, the travelers huddled around a small fire, each holding a cup of beans that Mea-a-ha hastily cooked up. It wasn't much, but it was warm.

Exhaustion had overcome Grandfather. He held his blanket tightly around his neck with a trembling hand, fitfully drifting in and out of sleep. The fire burned low, Jacob and Mea-a-ha were too spent to make a serious effort at keeping it burning. It was clear they were in for a cold night. The small blue flames dissolved into the icy black sky, offering little light. Overcome by fatigue, they sat without talking, staring into the dying embers – their minds drained.

Jacob's head jerked up. The blurry eyed soldier realized he had been dozing and wondered how long. Across from him, Grandfather was sleeping soundly, snuggled against the rocks, wrapped in several blankets. Next Jacob spied the small form of Mea-a-ha curled in the dirt next to the smoldering fire pit, clad only in her deerskin dress. His heart melted. The brave little girl, if it were in her power to add one more day to Grandfather's life she would, no matter the cost. Apaches can handle cold better than anyone, but Jacob knew by morning she would be freezing.

Roused from a fitful sleep, Mea-a-ha found herself lifted softly. "Come little princess," he whispered. "You will share my blanket."

Mea-a-ha laid limp against him, eyes shut, allowing the big man to cradle her in his arms.

Tenderly, Jacob covered her bare legs, then tucked the other end of the blanket about her face. He smoothed her hair, and with a bent knuckle, gently traced the outline of her cheek. Jacob hugged her close, his lips almost touching hers. "Goodnight."

After a long pause, Mea-a-ha whispered, her voice barely audible, "Goodnight, my hero." A billion brilliant stars looked down as distant coyotes summoned the moon, but no one heard a single note. They were engulfed in a deep and dreamy slumber.

Chapter -12-

Mogollon

𝔄 soft, cool breeze kissed Mea-a-ha's cheek, coaxing her from a gentle sleep. Stars filled the morning sky, with just the faintest tinge of amber, revealing a distant horizon. The crisp air stung her nostrils with the scent of juniper and sage. She wanted to return to her dream of snuggling in Jacob's arms. Mea-a-ha wriggled deeper into the blanket. The only sound was Jacob's slow, heavy breathing. Her eyes opened wide with a sudden panic. Her dream was real. A gasp caught in her throat.

Had she spent the night nestled in Jacob's arms? Her mind was racing. In their month together he had never said a word about how he felt, or if he felt anything at all, and yet here they were in a tender embrace. The comfort of her slumber changed to the paralyzing fear of a trapped animal.

What if he were to wake? What would she say? Would she pretend she was not cradled in his arms, or act as though it was perfectly natural? Could she say nothing? Would her silence say something, exposing her, laying her heart bare for his inspection? What would he say? What if he woke and kissed me? — What if he didn't?"

She tried to silence her thoughts. Her head was swirling. "This is ridiculous, I am lying here wrapped up like a baby, afraid of, of, of what?" His shoulder twitched. "Is he waking?" The girl held her breath. He relaxed, still lost in sleep. She was safe, for a moment.

Mea-a-ha liked the feel of his muscles against her. He was a man, and there were few available men left in her village. The years had been empty for her. She hid her loneliness in caring for her aging grandfather.

Jacob had the strength that she missed; she could feel it in the ease with which he held her. There was power in this man. Nothing frightened him – neither man nor beast. He had a code that sustained him. When it came down to it, he would do what he believed was right, even if it meant death. She admired him for this. He was a man worth holding on to. Mea-a-ha was a proud Apache, yet she had waited too long, and there was nothing left for her.

Grandfather was right; she should take what gifts life offered. Mea-a-ha took a deep breath. In that moment, the young Indian girl admitted to herself that she cared for this big man. It broke in her consciousness like a loud crashing wave washing over her with joy and panic. Her heart beat wildly. The time had come to push aside her fears and be brave.

Somewhere in the dark, a coyote cried to the coming sun. The camp was suddenly awake.

Shaking off sleep, Grandfather coughed, clearing his gravelly throat.

Reaching an icy hand out of the blankets, he grabbed a branch of sage wood and threw it on the pile of charred limbs in the fire pit. The old man stared with a blank expression. The wood did not ignite. "Damn! It looks like the Apaches must swallow their pride once again and ask the Buffalo Soldier for one of his magical fire sticks." He looked across at Jacob and assessed the transformation that had taken place overnight. "What changes morning brings!"

Jacob and Mea-a-ha stared back blankly like raccoons caught in the act of stealing. A thin sheepish grin appeared on Mea-a-ha's face from under the blanket that flopped down, nearly hiding her large brown eyes.

Grandfather feigned a gruff posture, but without much conviction. "Young man, what are your intentions toward my granddaughter?"

Mea-a-ha twisted to face Jacob. "Yes, what are your intentions toward his granddaughter? Do you think you can scoop a girl up in the middle of the night and not tell her your intentions?"

Jacob stared back in shock, completely at a loss for words. He had not expected this.

Mea-a-ha persisted, "Well!"

Grandfather interrupted. "You can have her for a match. I am freezing."

Mea-a-ha shot a glance at her grandfather. "I will decide what he can have her for."

She turned back to Jacob. "Or if he can have her at all."

Jacob awoke to a startling dilemma, and things were quickly getting out of hand. He knew he had better say something, anything. The Indian girl opened her mouth but he cut her off. "Now wait, just a minute. How do I know she's worth a match?"

Mea-a-ha shrieked and kicked her way out of the blanket. "Let go of me, you great big lumpy mattress."

She stomped to her full height, jerked the blanket around her and stormed off into the chill gray morning. Astonished, the two men watched her disappear into the brush. Jacob was pretty sure his little jest wasn't the something he should have said.

Grandfather kicked a foot from under his blanket at the burnt wood. The charred debris collapsed in a plume of cold black dust. "Maybe half a match?"

When Mea-a-ha returned, the fire was burning higher than needed. The men, not sure what to do where a woman's emotions were concerned, continued to pile on the tinder. Grandfather had wandered off to collect more wood for the bonfire. Jacob was kneeling, warming his hands.

Still wrapped in her blanket, Mea-a-ha stepped behind him and stood silently. Jacob continued to stare into the flames. "Mea-a-ha, I am not without feelings. You should know that."

She slowly knelt beside him. "I know."

After a pause, he continued. "Some of my thoughts are about you, but some are not."

Mea-a-ha's eyes darted towards Jacob, then returned to the fire, her voice low. "Another woman?"

His jaw tightened. "No. Not really, just the shadow of a woman. It's not something I can explain. Other thoughts trouble me. There's what I am, what I've been all my life, and there's what you are. It is difficult."

Mea-a-ha leaned against him, her small brown fingers twisting the fringe of her dress, then smoothing it across her bare knee and twisting it again. "I am sorry. You have done so much, it wasn't fair of me to make demands of you."

Taking a long deep breath, Jacob exhaled slowly. "You have squared the debt and then some." He looked away, far away to the distant horizon. It was like he wanted to be somewhere else.

She waited for his gaze to return, but it did not. "You are not happy. Do you regret holding me?"

"No. I have no regrets. And I'm not unhappy, at least not about you, not really."

Jacob turned to face her, giving a nervous grin. "No, I'm not sorry for holding you last night or hugging you, it's been wonderful. Mea-a-ha, the years have been harsh and often violent, so it's nice, real nice to come home to a warm hug. I think about them when we're not together, but it sure has created a lot of tension between us."

Mea-a-ha managed a fragile smile. "I think that is why I blew up this morning. It has been driving me crazy. Everything is left unsaid. You say you are not without feelings, but…" She let her words trail away, hoping he would finish the sentence.

Jacob tugged at his hat, then picked up a stick and poked at the burning embers. "Mea-a-ha, this here fire, I'm drawn to it. It gives me warmth, but I can't touch it. This fire and me are about as different as… as. You are an Apache, and I have spent my life hunting Apaches. I'm sorry to say, sometimes killing them. It's not something you just change," his voice trailed off.

Mea-a-ha pressed her forehead to her knees. A tear rolled down her cheek. Then more came. She did not try to hide them. For a moment she sobbed, then suddenly raised her head, her eyes ablaze. "Jacob, anger flashes in you like black lightening. You hide behind it, and push me away."

The girl's heart was tormented by injustices left too long unspoken. This moment, she would be heard. "Hatred is a circle of tears. The gringos use the Buffalo Soldiers as dogs to hunt their prey. They despise you, and still you hunt for them, hoping for their approval, which you will never have. You turn your anger towards the Apache. The Buffalo Soldiers are wiping my people from the face of this land. Our men are driven into the desert and slaughtered. The women, empty of milk, watch their babies die of hunger."

Welling with grief, she broke as visions of death seared her mind. She had seen too much in her short years. Clenching her teeth, she struggled on. "I will not be part of the circle. If you find reason in your heart to hate me for the color of my skin while condemning the gringos for doing the same to you, then you are not the man I believe you to be. My heart waits, but remember this fire that gives you warmth; if it is neglected too long, it will die."

Mea-a-ha folded her arms and set her jaw. She was silent, yet flames smoldered in her eyes.

Jacob cupped her face and wiped away her tears. She was not ashamed of them, nor did she let his tenderness weaken her will. His hands lingered. Finally a thin smile of resignation twitched at the corners of his mouth. "Damn it girl, if you don't always speak your mind. I wish I found it that easy." He lifted her chin. "I care. That is the best I can do right now Mea-a-ha. I care about you. Okay?"

A glimmer of forgiveness softened her sweet face. "Okay."

Jacob took a deep breath. "Is it over?"

"Yes." Mea-a-ha gave a mischievous grin. "For now."

She laughed and threw her arms around Jacob in a big hug. The couple stood up together, laughing. Mea-a-ha turned her attention to the crackling flames. "You build a fire like a white man. How do you expect me to cook anything on that?"

"Well, you roasted me pretty good."

****

Grandfather rested his worn hands on the pommel of the saddle, contemplating the cold gray canyon before him. For want of a trail, a sandy dry wash was the only choice, yet his eyes looked beyond the rounded stones, beyond the vale of the mountain, even beyond time.

Memories of old friends rushed to greet him. The sounds of war drums and spirit dances took him back to his youth when he was strong and full of life. Passing years rob a man of strength, but even time cannot age memories. Faces from the past hung vividly before him, and he was young again.

Rising above the drums he heard the gentle cry of gulls and saw a shimmering light dancing on a great water.

Amid the sparkles appeared the smiling face of an enchanting maiden. He knew her and his heart raced. She had come to him before... calling him. Her distant, melodic voice blending softly with the cry of the gulls and the lapping of the water on the warm sandy shore. It was music, not words, but he understood her just the same.

124

This time the maiden seemed to step beyond the vision. Her once familiar fragrance suddenly filled his lungs. A tear came to his eye; how could he have forgotten?

Smiling gently, the maiden reached out her hand and touched his face, calming him. "My brave, Naytennae, it is time..."

He reached for her, when suddenly a flock of birds lifted from the top of a tree with a great flutter of wings. The war drums faded. Grandfather wiped an aged hand across his eyes, then smiled at the young couple before him. "These are the sacred mountains of my people. Hidden in these hills are the graves of our greatest warriors. It is here I buried old Compa. Much sadness."

For a moment he paused in reverence, then continued. "Among their spirits, I am not alone. With each new day, I can speak to them more easily. This is where I belong. Here there is still honor for the Apache."

Mea-a-ha leaned her head on Grandfather's leg. His gentle hand, like soft leather, lovingly patted her shiny black hair. "Granddaughter, I know your heart. Be at peace. There is no sorrow in my passing. I have lived long beyond my time. My brothers and sisters died ages ago. My children are all dead. My beautiful Seaowa, love of my life, waits. Everyone I played with as a young boy is gone from this earth. They call to me now. To not die would be rude."

Taking his hand, Mea-a-ha placed a tender kiss in it, then held it to her cheek. "Grandfather, I am still here."

The old man looked down. "Yes, you are still here, my loving granddaughter. You who are my heart, but it is time you live for yourself and not as the handmaiden of an old man. Granddaughter, you should be pregnant."

"Grandfather!" Mea-a-ha cast an embarrassed look at Jacob. "You say things like that to silence my emotions."

"I say it because it is true."

"Grandfather, I know you are going. I just have not found the way to say goodbye."

"That's the problem. You don't say goodbye. I will be with you always. With the waking of each day, you say, 'Good morning Grandfather' then listen to the wind. It will carry my love and my words. Each morning I will say---I will say, 'Why aren't you pregnant?'"

Mea-a-ha pressed her forehead against his leg to hide her smile.

Grandfather smoothed her hair. "I will say, 'I am here, child. Be at peace.'"

Tilting her head back, Mea-a-ha smiled lovingly at the old man, her eyes sparkled. "Be at peace, Grandfather. I can let you go, as long as I know you are not going too far."

Mea-a-ha stepped back from the horse and let her arms fall by her side. Without any prodding, Major continued on.

The twisting canyon was not difficult to travel, but many draws opened up on each side making their route confusing. A gusty breeze, forcing its way up the mountain, kicked up dust, bending heads against the blowing sand. The day would be cooler, maybe rain. Mea-a-ha rested her small brown hand on the big horse's flank for balance and kept pace.

Signs of animal life were rare in this dry environment. Only the mournful cries of ravens circling overhead broke above the wind. There was a disquiet, more than a quiet. Breathing was labored, as much by anxiety as the thin air.

Major plodded forward while Grandfather recounted old stories of life for the Apache before the white man, before the Mexicans, and even some before the Spaniards. These were ancient stories, told from father to son. While speaking of happier times, he would stop his tale in mid-sentence. A distant stare of his wrinkled eyes hinted that he was back in the past, greeting old friends.

Jacob and Mea-a-ha walked quietly, not wishing to intrude. The soft hissing of the wind filled the silence, then just as suddenly Grandfather would start talking again, sometimes right where he left off, or in the middle of a completely different story.

About mid-morning they came upon a narrow cleft in a wall of gray stone, smaller than many they had passed. There was nothing extraordinary about it. The cleft formed a passage, little more than ten feet wide with vertical walls too tall to climb.

Grandfather headed Major in this new direction. Here, sunlight never touched the floor. The narrow passage was breathtaking in its stark beauty of rock carved by water. Smooth walls twisted and curved, resembling frosting swirled on a cake.

The wind blew across the top of the gorge whistling like air over a bottle. A haunting, wailing tone echoed down the passage. The pitch would change, dying away to a whisper, then rise to a deep reverberating roar. Grandfather spoke, "This is a trail you find, not with your eyes, but with your ears. The white man does not listen to the earth anymore, so the trail remains hidden."

The floor of the gorge was tightly packed gravel with occasional depressions where damp sand began to appear. As they continued, the gravel eventually gave way to the hard rock below. In places it was worn into smooth bowls where water collected. The walls narrowed, Mea-a-ha spread out her slender arms and touched both sides.

At first the pools were easy to step over, but eventually they became several feet long and knee deep. The secret trail became more of a watercourse. Mea-a-ha walked barefoot, her moccasins tossed over her shoulder. With doubting eyes, she gingerly lifted the fringed hem of her dress above the water.

Near the end of a long straight passage the path began to climb up a sandy incline. Here the gorge took a sharp turn to the right. As her toes dug into the cold sand, she hoped they were finally above the water, but it was not to be. All of a sudden they were facing a long passage filled with a stagnant pool from wall to wall. A layer of green scum floated on top.

Forlorn faces stared at the dark, foul water. It held the stench of death. Grandfather, who had been dozing as Major trudged along on his own, awoke and shrugged his shoulders. "Don't remember this. Everything has gone to hell since the white man."

Major sniffed the green scum, then jerked his head back in disdain. Holding the unwilling horse's bridle, Jacob steadied himself and stepped into the water. The smell made him wince.

What he had taken for an old log floating just under the dark surface, drifted in his wake. It was the rotting carcass of a deer. Jacob clenched his teeth and in no time was knee deep with slime sucking into his boot. He glanced back at Mea-a-ha who was wrinkling her nose.

Returning to the bank, Jacob unbuckled his sidearm and hooked it over the pommel of the saddle then faced Mea-a-ha. She could smell the odor rising from his clothing, and pulled a face, fearing that a similar fate awaited her. Jacob saw the Indian girl's distress.

Taking Mea-a-ha by the waist, he placed her behind her Grandfather. "That will keep you dry, provided the water isn't too deep."

Jacob took the reins and eased back into the pool. Major followed, sinking deep in the foul slime. Mea-a-ha pulled her bare feet up, balancing herself on Major's broad back. "Now I wish we had Peaches."

Jacob flashed her a smile over his shoulder, as he pushed through the chest deep water. "Peaches is a lady. I doubt we could get her into this ooze."

The prospect of being dipped in the green, smelly muck did nothing for Mea-a-ha's temper. "What do you think I am?"

Jacob chuckled nervously at his unintentional insult and trudged slowly forward. "I once saw a lovely water lily floating in a southern swamp. If it gets me out of trouble, you're like the lily."

She was in no mood to be charmed. "I don't know 'swamp', but if being a lily means I wind up floating in this muck, then I better remind you of a little bird."

Jacob continued forward, his chin dipping into the green slime. He managed a smile over his shoulder. Mea-a-ha sneered as she watched unthinkable things float by. Her brown toes wiggled on Major's back, trying to find purchase.

Finally, as they neared the other bank, she could see Jacob slowly rising above the black water, and gave a sigh of relief.

A short distance from the shore, the gorge opened into a small bowl strewn with boulders and logs. Here they stopped. Jacob reached up for Mea-a-ha. She pulled back. "Don't you touch me, until you clean up. I will get down myself."

Mea-a-ha slid off Major's back, slipping in the process. Her arms flaying in the air, she landed hard on her rump in the sand. Embarrassed, she glared up at Jacob from the ground. "Don't you dare laugh."

Jacob wandered off muttering. "No matter how hard a feller tries, he's always in the wrong when it comes to women."

Leaning against the rock wall, Jacob drained the muck from his boots, then pulled his shirt off over his head. Mea-a-ha watched as Jacob wrung out the soiled clothing. His arms and chest rippled with each powerful twist of his hands. Never had she seen a more muscular man. Her heart was beating faster. Growing angry at herself, she turned away in frustration. Mea-a-ha laced up her moccasins and tried to think of other things. Jacob returned, carrying his wet shirt only to be met by her disapproving frown.

At a loss to satisfy her, Jacob protested. "There's only so much I can do."

"You still smell."

"Well, what do you want me to do, go running around like a naked Indian?"

Mea-a-ha's eyes flashed. "You don't have to be nasty!" Then she grinned delightfully at the thought. "Well, maybe."

Jacob arched his brow. "Well, maybe you wouldn't mind the smell so much, if we both stunk. How 'bout one of those hugs."

Mea-a-ha backed away, eyes wide with fear, but it was too late. Jacob scooped her up with a big wet bear hug and swung her around in a circle. Mea-a-ha screamed. "I will get you for this!"

Laughing, Jacob wrapped his arms tight around her and hugged her slender body against his.

Mea-a-ha pushed away with her hands, but to no avail. "Ick! You have just put this little Apache on the warpath," She was laughing. "If I had a bow and arrow, you would never sit again. Now put me down."

"Then maybe I should never put you down."

"If my brothers were here, we would roast you good. Now put me down before I throw up."

"First we must have a peace treaty."

"Peace, but I will still get you for using me as a towel."

Jacob roared with laughter and let Mea-a-ha slide to the ground. As she slipped through his arms, he quickly kissed her. Mea-a-ha stepped back, straightening her dress all the while, searching Jacob's face for a meaning to the kiss. Was he caught up in the moment, or did he care more than he was willing to admit?

She could see the struggle in his eyes. He wasn't sure himself, it just happened. Mea-a-ha leaned forward and gave him a forgiving hug.

They let the moment pass. Jacob held her tight, nurtured by her warmth, and thankful for her kindness. "Ya know, swamp smells good on you."

"If you think that is flattery, you've got much to learn about girls. Major smells better than you... Major!"

Her body tensed. "Grandfather!"

Grandfather and Major had disappeared. There was only one way they could go, but how far ahead were they? How long had Jacob and Mea-a-ha been playing?

Mea-a-ha grabbed Jacob's hand. "Let's hurry."

She hollered for her grandfather, but her voice was lost in the low rumble of the wind. The weather had worsened, and dark clouds were gathering overhead. The air felt moist and cold on her exposed skin.

Matching Jacob stride for stride, Mea-a-ha's voice broke shrill with worry. "Why would he go off?"

Jacob pulled her up the twisting corridor. "He may have given Major a kick and dozed off again, or he may be drifting in the spirit world."

Mea-a-ha shook free of Jacob's hand and started to run. Following her through the deepening gorge, his heart went out to her. The mountain was too big, and she was so small, but he knew she'd never surrender. They hurried on for several minutes without any sight of Major, adding to her distress.

Aching lungs gasping in the cold air forced them to finally slow their pace. Mea-a-ha leaned against the limestone wall to catch her breath. Struggling with emotions, she looked to Jacob. Alarm was visible on his face. He walked a few steps past her and stopped. "Grandfather has both guns. This isn't the best place to be without a weapon."

Thunder rumbled deep and low. Jacob looked at the black clouds squeezing together, like there wasn't enough room in the sky. "This isn't the best place to be at all."

When Mea-a-ha was able to control her breathing, they hurried on again. The narrow gorge continued to climb as it burrowed deeper into the lonely mountain, deeper into the graying mist.

Raindrops began to fall in light staccato beats, almost soothing, like a sweet summer song. Then in the span of a few minutes, it quickly intensified, turning to a raging downpour. Drowning in the desert became a real possibility. Jacob instinctively put his hand on the smooth stone walls; there was no way out. His own heart began to beat. Every fiber of his body told Jacob now was the time to run!

He knew that the weather at this altitude could change quickly. If it did, a roaring wall of water would wash them to their deaths. Logs wedged between the walls high above their heads warned of the danger this narrow canyon held.

He looked at the Apache girl before him. It was no use. There was nothing he could say to dissuade her. Even though Grandfather had come to die, she would not abandon him, even if it meant they would all perish.

Swallowing hard, Jacob wiped the water from his face and pushed on leaving his fears unspoken. The rocks darkened as the rain grew harder until tiny rivulets began to trickle down the steep walls. Soon a small stream flowed beneath their feet. The water quickly pooled.

Jacob cursed under his breath. The situation was beyond his control. Mea-a-ha glanced back with anguished eyes, then hurried on. Her wet buckskin dress clung to her body, weighing her down.

Up ahead, a great boulder was lodged between the walls of the gorge above the path, making the narrow gully look like a dark cave.

Catching up, Jacob took Mea-a-ha's hand and ducked under the huge stone. A high ceiling gave him enough room to stand. The growing stream washed over the toe of his boots, but for the moment they were out of the rain. Mea-a-ha clung to Jacob, resting her head on his chest as she fought for control, but just for a moment. Heartsick for her grandfather, she pushed away, ready to struggle on.

Stepping from under the massive boulder, she gasped. On the other side of the passage, the gorge opened into a huge gray grotto, its towering cliffs lost in the thick black clouds boiling overhead.

The floor of the grotto spread wide before her, and sloped steeply to her right, ascending thirty feet or more into a great undercut in the shear wall.

Her eyes could not believe the sight! Beneath a great ledge high above, were magnificent stone houses, dwellings of an elder race that lived ages before the Apache. Mea-a-ha had seen their ruins in the desert, but not like this. These were not crumbling or covered in weeds and sand. The densely packed lodges were unchanged by time, as if chiseled from the cliff itself. Stone upon stone, the dwellings were stacked four and five high, a silent city of dark windows and gaping doors, long empty.

Falling back against the cliff wall, Mea-a-ha was overcome by an ominous presence that stole her breath. It was as though voices long silent suddenly cried out at her unwelcome intrusion. She clutched her throat.

The towering stone city filled her with awe. Jacob came to her side. Mea-a-ha's voice trembled with reverence. "This is the city of the Mogollon, 'The people who have gone.' Of them we know nothing more."

Thunder rumbled again, shaking the very walls. Breaking free of the spell, Jacob ushered Mea-a-ha on up the center of the immense grotto.

Despite the danger of the impending storm, Mea-a-ha couldn't peel her eyes from the ancient city. Putting a hand to her back, Jacob coaxed her forward past the countless irregular shaped openings.

At the other end of the dwellings, the grotto floor rose steeply in a terrace of flat stones, like giant stairs. Each knee-high step spread out eight feet or more to the next. Here the grotto divided into two gorges, heading in nearly opposite directions.

From where they stood, Jacob could see the left gorge rose quickly more than a hundred feet.

Wanting to get as high as possible as quickly as he could, Jacob chose that direction. Bending his head against the pouring rain, he took Mea-a-ha's arm and dragged her upwards.

As they made their ascent up the steep slope, thunder boomed stopping them in their tracks. The terrifying report was answered by the sharp whinny of a horse. Mea-a-ha whirled around.

On a high, protruding ledge in the opposite passage, stood Major, with Grandfather slumped forward on his back. The old warrior's head was pressed against the horse's thick neck, his arms hanging limp on either side. Horse and rider looked like a ghostly statue carved of stone. Steam swirled from the great beast in an eerie mist. Mea-a-ha screamed, "Grandfather!" The wind swallowed her words.

Jerking loose from Jacob's grasp, Mea-a-ha raced down the incline faster than her small feet could run. Slipping, she rolled to the bottom, but scrambled up, frantic to get to the old man.

Cries gurgling in her throat, she ran wildly, stumbling and falling again. Tears mixed with the rain streaming down her cheeks. Struggling back to her feet she charged over the loose wet stones.

Oblivious to all, Mea-a-ha fought on with her last ounce of strength. Her only thought, 'Grandfather.'

Reason was beyond her. The girl threw herself at a higher boulder. Her soaked moccasins slipped on the slick rock, and she came crashing down hard on her chin.

Wailing, she clawed up from the cold wet stones once more, and drove forward, only to collapse into a black pool. Stunned, her strength gone, she sank face down in the icy water.

Suddenly Jacob was by her side, his big hands scooping her up. She hung limp, her long raven hair matted about her face. Jacob shifted her weight and continued forward. She fell against him, crying uncontrollably, her fist beating weakly on his chest.

Ignoring the driving rain, Jacob climbed up the narrow passage leading to the ledge where Major stood. The noble warrior's head was bent, his eyes closed. Jacob had seen death many times. The old man had completed his journey.

Taking a final step, Jacob stood silently on the ledge. Mea-a-ha sobbed. "Is he...." Jacob held her tight. "He's gone."

The girl collapsed, consumed by exhaustion and emotion. Darkness took hold, protecting her from pain she could not bear. Words could no longer reach her. Jacob did not try.

Lightning struck the upper wall with a blinding flash, sending thunder ripping through the canyon. The violence of the report shook the rain out of the dense black clouds.

Jacob looked up the gorge. The now raging water forced its way over debris in growing torrents. With an evil rumbling, logs and even boulders began to roll.

There was no hope in that direction. Jacob took Major's reins and turned him around. "You are going to have to follow me, old boy. We're in for it now." Major obeyed, trailing Jacob down the narrow passageway. Grandfather's body lay rigid on the faithful steed's back. Had it not been for the wide girth of the horse, the old man would have fallen.

The rising stream surged against the back of Jacob's legs making it hard to stand. Reaching the bottom of the passage, Jacob looked across at the steep gorge they had originally tried to climb. It had become a roaring waterfall. There was no time for regrets; an answer was needed quickly. The veteran soldier assessed the situation. He looked down protectively at Mea-a-ha. She was oblivious to any danger.

Below, the grotto widened like a courtyard to the dwellings, and the water spread out, moving slower. Jacob shifted her weight and started down the slope.

Intensifying in fury, the rain came in sheets. Amid the mayhem, the massive walls became silvery waterfalls, bursting in blinding brilliance with each thunderous bolt.

The deluge brought rocks and debris crashing down from the craggy ledges far above. It sounded like a battlefield. The souls of lost Indians might claim victory at last. Mingled in the maelstrom's roar, Jacob imagined he heard laughter. He shook the thought from his head and hurried on.

At the base of the dwellings, a small path climbed steeply past the gaping doorways. It was their only chance. Jacob drove Major before him, up the steep slope. A solid curtain of water pouring over the top of the cliff hung between him and the dwellings like a veil to the past. He hesitated.

At that moment a terrifying sound burst from above the din, drawing his eyes upward into the abyss. A huge pine tree torn from its rocky perch hundreds of feet above, hurled out of the black clouds straight at him.

Jacob slapped Major, driving him up the incline, then fell back into the surging flood. He curled about Mea-a-ha covering her with his body. The giant tree crashed on the stone floor, sending a shock wave that struck Jacob like a mighty hammer. He was blasted from the water. The tree exploded on impact, showering Jacob with a violent wave, charged with splintered timber. His body raised again slamming helplessly against the sharp stones. Pain shot through him like a dagger.

Sputtering to the surface, Jacob struggled to his feet, lifting Mea-a-ha above the churning foam. The veteran of countless battles knew he was seriously injured. Looking down he could see a jagged shard of wood sticking through his boot. It was bad.

His arm was bleeding from a deep gash and more blood flowed from his head, blinding his eyes. Jacob gritted his teeth. His concern had to be for Mea-a-ha who hung cold and lifeless, numb to the hellish nightmare engulfing them.

Major had charged up the narrow pathway. The brave horse dove under the curtain of water and stopped next to the lowest dwellings waiting for his master. Wild eyed with steam blowing from his nostrils, he stood fast against the terror.

Jacob shook off his pain and burst through the pounding water after the great horse. Dragging himself up from his knees, he grabbed for the reins; it was all he could do to stand.

With Mea-a-ha cradled to his chest, he clung to the side of the horse and limped up the path, a stream of blood marking his trail.

Pressed against the ledge, the curtain of water hid the boiling cauldron below. Black clouds filled the grotto, thrusting them into a surreal twilight of distorted shapes. Bursts of lightning illuminated the veil of water, then darkness, then brilliance, then darkness again. The deafening roar began to overwhelm his mind, tearing at reality.

Jacob led Major past several small doors, knowing they had to climb higher than the flood. Painfully he pushed on. The big man's strength was failing. Even Mea-a-ha's small body was becoming too much for him bear. He risked a moment to catch his breath, then struggled on up the ancient path.

Ahead, a narrow side passage wound between two walls heading back into the deep recesses of the cliff. Jacob followed it a short distance. With each step, the deafening roar lessened, muffled by the thick stone masonry.

Near the back, Jacob found a large, rounded chamber with an opening tall enough for Major to squeeze through. Flashes of light from a high window showed the floor was covered in soft gray dust.

Jacob left Major still burdened with the old man and stepped back outside, looking for another room far enough away that Mea-a-ha would not have to wake to the presence of her grandfather's body.

He proceeded back up the main path. The rain slowed, and the curtain of water pouring down from above was now broken in places allowing Jacob to see the angry rapids surging through the doorways of the lower dwellings. Twenty feet of water coursed where they had stood moments ago. He continued on.

Higher up the path, a small alcove housed five low portals. Leaving the landing, Jacob chose a door at random and ducked in. His leg was throbbing and he knew he needed rest, but not yet.

Kneeling, he deposited Mea-a-ha gently on the stone floor, then struggling to his feet, limped back to take care of Major. Sharp pains stabbed at him with each step. Staggering on, Jacob leaned against the walls, gasping for air as he went. Finally inside the tall chamber, he lowered Grandfather's body from Major's back. Despite Jacob's weakened condition, he found the old Apache's body surprisingly light. The only thing that had kept the withered man going had been his incredible willpower.

Horses are sometimes spooked by the presence of death, so Jacob removed Grandfather's body to a smaller chamber along the passage. There he wrapped him in his blanket with as much dignity as he could. Finally, Jacob unsaddled Major and retrieved the supply sacks.

By the time he returned to Mea-a-ha, his leg was numb. He dropped his bundles and slumped to the floor. The pounding in his chest eased and his breathing slowed. Now there would be time for rest.

Mea-a-ha lay curled in the shadows on the stone floor. Jacob crawled to her. She was soaked to the bone, her limbs cold as death. Wrapping the girl in his arms, he brushed the damp, tangled hair from her face. She was pale as a ghost.

Hypothermia was setting in, and time was critical. Jacob leaned against the wall and held Mea-a-ha close. Unlacing her moccasins, he peeled them from her icy feet. He hesitated a moment, then taking the hem of her soaked buckskin dress, pulled it over her head. Jacob curled her limp body to his chest, but he was drenched too. What little warmth he had would do her no good.

Stretching out a heavy arm, he pulled the canvas bed roll from the sack and wrapped Mea-a-ha in a blanket, then patted her dry as best he could. This would slow the hypothermia but he needed to build a fire fast.

There were a few sticks and leaves scattered about, but not enough, so once again Jacob dragged himself out the doorway and into other chambers, scrounging for wood.

In the dark rooms off the alcove, he gathered enough fuel to make a small fire. The exertion was taking its toll and he could no longer stand, so he crawled, holding the wood in one arm.

The big man focused all his energies on lighting the tinder. Fortunately, in one corner there was already a pit with a vent hole for smoke. This chamber had been living quarters for a family long forgotten. His trembling hands worked frantically. In the damp air, the tinder was reluctant to light. Jacob took three cartridges from his belt and removed the slugs with his knife, then poured the black power into a tiny pile. He struck the metal blade against the stone floor, it sparked. Soon, a small fire crackled, warming the little room.

Taking his blanket, Jacob wrapped it about him. When he was settled, he pulled Mea-a-ha into his lap. She was still unconscious, but she was less cold. He rubbed her arms and legs to restore circulation, but decided not to try and wake her. Let the pain she was going to face wait awhile longer. Slumping against the wall, he held her close while he rested. Her long hair was drying. In the red glow of the warm fire, she looked peaceful.

Jacob cradled her in a tender embrace, studying her features. She was an Apache woman, not beautiful like Rose. She was not fancy, nor would she ever wear makeup or sweet perfumes, but she had a loveliness all her own. Her sweet face had a mix of nobility and innocence that went deeper than any rouge. Rose knew she was beautiful and used it as a tempting prize, or a cruel knife, whichever suited her purpose.

Mea-a-ha never talked about beauty except for the kind of beauty that rests in one's heart. Her thoughts were deep and soulful. Rose was civilized, adept in polite society. Mea-a-ha was a savage, born to a stone age people, but Jacob had come to realize that despite her ignorance, Mea-a-ha was much wiser than Rose. Mea-a-ha cared about others. Rose cared about Rose.

Jacob sat alone in the shadows. His thoughts whirled, and in that moment his idea of beauty changed. Rose's face hung in his mind, hard and grotesque – a garish painted mask. He shook it from his memory, never wanting to see it again.

Smiling down at the Apache girl, he smoothed her thick raven hair, then took it in his hands and let it fall. Mea-a-ha was beautiful. She was truly beautiful. He had been so wrong. What he'd mistaken for beauty was only a thin veneer. Beauty does not fade with age… it grows.

Jacob wondered at her fragile innocence as she lay naked in his arms. He could have opened her blanket, but he was not that kind of man. He lived by codes. She was his to protect, even against his own desires. Jacob turned his thoughts away and looked down at his leg. There was moisture in his boot. He didn't know if it was water or blood. He reached over and tossed several logs on the fire, then closed his eyes.

Chapter -13-
Stone Haven

𝔐ea-a-ha woke to a warm light filtering in from a high window. Morning brought truth. Grandfather was dead. Tears came to her eyes and she wept softly for a long while. She lay wrapped in a blanket in Jacob's arms once again. Seeking comfort, she snuggled against him and drifted off to sleep. This time she would not worry about what to say when he woke.

When she opened her eyes some time later, she could tell the sun was much higher. Her spirits rose with it. Grandfather had lived a long life, and in the end, he had completed his journey. There were tears yet to come, but for now there was reason to be happy.

Mea-a-ha elbowed Jacob. "Wake up, mattress."

Jacob stirred. He raised his head blinking his glazed eyes, trying to come to his senses. All he could do was stare blankly. Mea-a-ha elbowed him again. "Had a rough night?"

He looked down at her, still not able to form a coherent thought. His lips moved and twisted for a moment before garbled words finally croaked in a deep baritone voice that came low in his throat. "You okay?"

"I am okay now. I've had my cry. It was just seeing him that way, but I will be alright." Shaking off the sleep, Mea-a-ha sat up and stretched her arms. The blanket fell away. A cold draft turned her yawn to shock. The girl snatched the blanket quickly around her and glanced at Jacob. She didn't know what to think. Mea-a-ha scowled with a disapproving air. "It looks like you had a busy night!"

Jacob twitched a feeble grin, and coughed. His voice came weak. "It was the day that like to killed me." His eyes closed.

Mea-a-ha's expression changed to alarm. She had not considered what had happened. The storm. She remembered the rain, but how did they get here? Jacob looked pale. She shifted in his lap; he winced in pain, jerking his leg. Mea-a-ha looked down and saw the jagged stick protruding from his boot and screamed, "Your leg!"

She put her hand on his face. It was cold, yet sweat beaded on his forehead. Dried blood caked his temple. Fear welled in her eyes. "You are hurt!"

He cleared his throat. "Mea-a-ha."

Mea-a-ha slid out of his lap. "Don't speak, just rest."

"Mea-a-ha... you're beautiful."

She rolled her eyes. "Now you tell me!"

Sliding down to his boot, she touched the end of the stick, Jacob's body arched. The shard was about as big around as her wrist. It struck the boot near the top penetrating into his fleshy calf. Mea-a-ha slipped her hand down the boot and gasped. On the opposite side, her finger found the tip of the stick; it had gone completely through.

"Oh, Jacob." Mea-a-ha looked around not knowing what to do. She reached for her dress. It was a soppy mess. An understanding of Jacob's effort while she was unconscious began to take hold. Seriously injured, he had carried her to this tiny room and cared for her, built a fire, and retrieved the bedroll and provisions. The pain must have been unbearable.

Quickly she opened the larger sack and found the pouch of coffee beans. Mea-a-ha dumped these onto the floor and ripped the bean sack along the seams, opening it wide. Next she stoked the fire, bringing light to the little room.

Water was needed, but Jacob's canteen was nowhere to be found. It must still be with the saddle, wherever that was. Grabbing a pot from the sack, Mea-a-ha climbed out of her blanket and ducked through the door. The damp stones were cold on her bare feet. She tiptoed cautiously to the edge of the ledge. Looking over, she quickly retreated. They were so high.

Bright sunlight painted a grotto in stark contrast to yesterday's memory. Debris was scattered about where the day before there was none. Logs were jammed against the lower dwellings. It was obvious there had been a terrible flood.

A huge splintered tree, its branches broken and scattered, lay wedged under the rock arch where they had first entered the grotto. More logs and debris had packed around it as the raging water drained through the opening. The flood was gone, but several pools remained.

Mea-a-ha hurried down the path, tiptoeing around the wreckage. On light feet, she ran to the center of the grotto and knelt on the cold limestone by the first deep pool. The water was clear and cool. Dipping the pot into her worried reflection, she paused to look at the arch through which they had come. The massive pine was there to stay, barring the only entrance she knew. A shiver ran down her bare spine as she faced the realities of a new day. They were trapped.

The Indian girl's inquisitive brown eyes scanned her surroundings. The towering cliffs loomed over her, harsh and uncaring. Grandfather was gone from her life. Jacob was hurt bad. Their provisions were few.

A feeling of hopelessness washed over her. Small and naked, Mea-a-ha crouched against the stone, wishing she could hide. Her eyes burned, but she refused to cry.

The quiet courage that had always sustained her burst anew in her savage heart. What happened now was up to her. Jacob's life was in her hands.

Mea-a-ha took the pot of water and stood defiantly facing the rows of vacant windows buried in the cliffs. She raised her chin in challenge. Her voice rang clear, echoing down the canyon walls. "I am Chihene of the

N'de. This is the land of my fathers. I will not be frightened."

She stood silently as if daring an answer. Unseen faces in the vacant windows loomed in the Apache girl's mind. "Did you hear me? I will not be frightened! You will not beat me."

A long silence followed, while her defiant heart raced.

Then, it came, a silent whisper borne on the wind. A soft cool breeze stirred her hair "I am here, be at peace." Mea-a-ha's heart pounded in her chest. The old man had kept his word. Her lips parted to call his name, but there was no need. He was with her as he'd always been.

Fear had brought her down the path, courage took her back. Balancing the pot of water and an armload of wood, Mea-a-ha hurried through the small door. The kindling and pot went onto the fire, then she turned to Jacob. He was unconscious. It was just as well for what she had to do.

Settling on the floor, she pressed her knees tightly on both sides of his boot to steady his leg. Then grasping the stick in her left hand, she pulled with all her might. It would not budge. She grabbed it tighter and twisted it, trying again. The stick loosened and slowly pulled out with a sick, sucking sound.

Blood pooled on the floor. Mea-a-ha dropped the stick and pulled off his boot. More blood poured out the top. She wondered how much blood a man could lose.

Taking Jacob's knife from his belt, she slit his pant leg up to the knee. Mea-a-ha dipped the bean sack into the steaming pot of water and washed the wound thoroughly. The shard of wood appeared to have gone between the bones, they did not feel broken. Her main worry was the size of the hole.

Wringing the water from the cloth, she wrapped his leg as tightly as she could, binding it with the lace from her moccasins. An injury that serious would take time to heal. How would they survive?

Through it all, Jacob never stirred. It worried her. All she could do now was wait. Retrieving her blanket Mea-a-ha covered Jacob and snuggled beside him. "Don't you die on me, old bear. It would break my heart."

She pressed a kiss to his lips, then laid her head on his chest so she could hear his breathing. When he woke up, she would be there.

The warm smell of food cooking roused Jacob from his deep slumber. Rubbing his face, he spied Mea-a-ha stirring a pot. He smiled weakly. "Dinner ready?"

Dropping the spoon, Mea-a-ha beamed with delight and pressed her hand to his forehead. "Yes, old bear, but not the dinner you are thinking of; that was days ago."

He swallowed hard. "How long have I been out?"

Mea-a-ha pretended to be annoyed. "Three days. Three days, I have been talking to you and pouring out my heart, for all the good it did."

Jacob tried to rise, but she pushed him back against the wall. "Just stay where you are. The Indians are in charge."

Jacob mumbled. "You've been sitting here watching me all this time?"

"No, I had things to do. Can't be wasting my time just because you get a scratch."

She smoothed his hair, then continued. "I had to find food for us and grass for Major. Yes, I found where you hid him. I had to go several miles up the left fork of the canyon to find him feed."

Her voice became somber. "I covered Grandfather with stones and sealed the door."

A single tear rolled down her cheek, but she quickly wiped it away and smiled boldly, refusing to let it get her down.

Mea-a-ha's eyes glistened. "I got some delicious rabbit stew here. Doesn't it smell good?"

Her patient arched a brow. "Where did you get a rabbit?"

The Indian girl proudly raised her chin. "Not rabbit, rabbits. Two of them. You are not the only one who can hunt. And I didn't need your loud guns either, just a simple snare." She paused, then added in a low voice. "And a large rock – that was the hard part."

Jacob muttered again. "Three days."

Mea-a-ha dipped a tin cup into the pot of stew and offered a spoonful to Jacob. He chewed slowly, savoring his first bite of food in days "Good as your chili. I'm famished. – Three days?"

Mea-a-ha echoed, "Three days."

"Was I delirious?"

She pushed the spoon towards him. A smile danced in her eyes. "Well, you did talk a bit. I guess that is delirious."

Jacob stopped chewing. "What did I say?"

Mea-a-ha paused to let him squirm. "This and that. Oh! You told me I was beautiful."

Jacob froze. Mea-a-ha leaned in close. "Do you remember that?"

Jacob swallowed hard, wishing to avoid the answer. "I remember thinking it."

Mea-a-ha stirred the spoon in the cup. "You were thinking I was beautiful, hum. Was that after you stripped me naked?"

Jacob felt his stomach tighten. "Mea-a-ha, I truly did my best not to look. It was dark. You were soaked."

She pressed her forehead next to his with accusing eyes. "Are you sure you didn't peek? Just a little?" She was enjoying herself.

Jacob's head was not clear enough to banter with her. "Mea-a-ha, please…"

"So you do think I am beautiful?" She bounced with delight.

139

She gave him another spoonful. "It is a fair question. Do you think I am beautiful?"

Jacob slumped against the wall. "Oh, Mea-a-ha, I think you are beautiful, and damn if you aren't as cruel as you are beautiful – taking advantage of a man who is sick and half-starved. You should be ashamed."

Mea-a-ha's voice softened. "Would you have told me, if you weren't delirious?"

"Maybe. Eventually."

Mea-a-ha raised another spoon to his lips. "Eventually doesn't tell a girl where she stands today. I just wanted to hear you say it when you weren't delirious, is that so bad?"

Jacob shook his head in resignation. He loved her teasing and the way she spoke her mind, even at his expense. "Little girl, you got what you went huntin' for, but be real careful when you corner a wounded bear. He may bite. Now stop your gabbing and feed me before I starve to death."

Filling another spoon, Mea-a-ha giggled with delight. Jacob would be okay.

The next few days were blissful. Jacob continued to feel better. The fog slowly left his head. Mea-a-ha had propped his leg on a small log and cleansed the wound daily in boiled chaparral that she gathered high up the left fork. It was good medicine.

She also tidied up the little room. A handmade straw broom stood in the corner, and a stack of wood was piled neatly next to the small fire. The contents of the supply sacks were stacked about, more to decorate the room than for their immediate use.

Mea-a-ha had put her skills to work and wove a large sleeping mat from coarse grass that grew out of cracks in the upper canyon walls. Beneath the mat, she placed soft pine boughs. The pitch was also good medicine. With little else to do but lay on the floor, the scented bed made her patient a lot more comfortable.

As the days passed, she busied herself while Jacob slept, doing what she could. Mea-a-ha had plenty of extra time, and used it to explore all the dwellings. For the Apache girl who had always stayed behind watching the braves come and go, it was an exciting adventure.

Mea-a-ha poked her head in every doorway, crawled through narrow passages, and climbed hidden ladders. From cellar to rooftop she explored her stone city, and not without profit. Arrowheads, flint blades and even grinding stones were treasures to be found. Everything was put to use.

Early one morning while searching one of the deepest rooms, Mea-a-ha watched a field mouse, scurry through a crack in the back wall. Curious, she pulled away the loose stones and pressed her face close to the floor, trying to see. Cool air flowed from the dark hole.

Using Jacob's magical matches, Mea-a-ha lit a sagebrush torch and excitedly pulled away more stones. Soon she had a hole big enough for her small shoulders to squeeze through.

Once inside, Mea-a-ha scrambled to her feet and held the torch high. A childlike sense of adventure set her heart pounding. The tiny light burst forth, and Mea-a-ha gasped. She was standing in a secret chamber. Her eyes widened, adjusting to the light. Shadows fell away. A natural crevice appeared to head deep into the heart of the mountain. Mea-a-ha realized she had discovered a hidden cave. The ancient ones had buried the entrance, but why?

Filled with wonder, she took timid steps down the narrow corridor. All along the walls, paintings of great hunts and battles spoke from the past. The stories were drawn with simple figures, but the Mogollons took life. They were a desert people who toiled beneath the sun, much like her own. Mea-a-ha wondered if their death was violent, or did they just quietly fade away? All things die, and man's pride does not exempt him from the same fate as other animals. She wondered, what would be the passing of the last Apache? The girl moved on.

For a moment it looked as though the cavern was a dead end, when suddenly it opened into a huge chamber where cave formations hung from the ceiling. She could not believe her eyes. On the floor of the cave, beautiful clay pottery of varying sizes lined the vast passage. Some were plain, others painted with intricate designs. Mea-a-ha hurried to one of the larger pots and looked in. It was filled with seed husks. This was the secret of the Mogollon. Once, the cool dry room had been a granary, but the mice had cleaned it out centuries ago.

Lifting her eyes, Mea-a-ha could now see the cave went on, but her dwindling torch would not. She quickly gathered several pieces of the smaller pottery into her arms and headed back to the entrance. The clay pots would be added to the treasures of their humble room.

Crawling back through the hole, into the light, Mea-a-ha paused, to carefully replace the stones. Perhaps her effort was unnecessary. No one would likely come this way again, but it was the secret of the Mogollon, and she would respect it. Like them, the story of her people someday would be told. Mea-a-ha smiled. Maybe it would be told with paper and pencil, by a small Apache girl.

Mea-a-ha hurried back. There was work to be done. Each day meals had to be found. The tireless girl had fended for herself all her life and was good with the snare, catching birds, rabbits, lizards and snakes. It wasn't steak, but there was always a tasty stew. Jacob was not squeamish, but often chose not to ask what was in the pot.

One of Mea-a-ha's greatest delights was riding Major up the left fork so he could feed on the dark grass where water seeped from cracks in the wall. She looked forward to these daily outings. For her it was the independence she imagined the braves felt as they raced away on their ponies. While she rode through the deep canyon on the great horse, Mea-a-ha pretended she was a bold powerful warrior. Foolish perhaps, but it was a time for daydreams. It was her time.

Every decision was hers to make. She loved it. Imprisoned in the grotto, Mea-a-ha found freedom for the first time in her life.

Gentle days passed, and Jacob grew stronger. He hobbled around with a crutch, yet he had lost a lot of blood and tired easily, so excursions were kept to a minimum.

Hidden from the violent world outside, their time in the grotto was carefree. Mea-a-ha loved nursing her wounded soldier, instead of always being in his debt.

Most of all, Mea-a-ha enjoyed the hours spent talking with this quiet man of another race. The Mimbre girl had many stories, and Jacob was a good listener. Often they would sit on the flat stone landing overlooking the hidden city, letting the sun warm Jacob's leg. Mea-a-ha would excitedly tell what she did that day, or show Jacob some small treasure she discovered: a carved wooden figure, or just a pretty stone. He would mostly listen, but occasionally he would join in. Mea-a-ha found that Jacob was smiling more, and even laughing. Without thinking, he would take hold of her hand while they talked. It came easy here. Life was simple.

One evening after a fine meal of quail, Mea-a-ha sat staring at the fire with her knees tucked under her chin. For a long time she had been lost in contented dreams. "Jacob, do you remember the first day we met, and you talked about finding a place where a person can stop walking?"

Jacob was half dozing, but raised his head. "Yes, I remember."

"Well, I think I could stop walking here."

She crawled across the floor to sit close to him. "I feel safe. It is peaceful. There are no soldiers, or evil ranchers… just us."

Jacob could see the emotion welling in her. He had never seen her so blissful. Yet he knew what she was thinking, and what it was leading up to. He patted her hand. "Mea-a-ha, it is beautiful here in its own way. You have managed to find food every day." He looked around the room. "And you have made this place feel right homey. It's been wonderful being here with you, but it's just not possible."

Mea-a-ha's face fell. Her eyes grew moist. "But…"

Jacob persisted. "One thing is for sure. The pools of water are going to dry up, or it is going to flood again. There is no way around it. The ancient people probably thought as you do, still they abandoned this place for a reason."

Mea-a-ha was crushed, but she knew Jacob was right and she felt foolish. "I know." She kept her head down, so he wouldn't see her eyes. "It was just a nice dream." She hurried to the door. "I think I will say goodnight to Major."

Outside the tears began to fall. Mea-a-ha ran down the path crying. Moonlight bathed the stones in a cold blue light, matching her mood. Hurrying inside the chamber she threw her arms around Major's neck and cried aloud. She cried for a foolish girl's dream. She cried for the loss of Grandfather. She cried for a love she longed for. Mea-a-ha let the tears flow.

Her life up until now had not allowed her the luxury of crying over silly dreams, but tonight they had all seemed so close. She had fooled herself into thinking they were possible. Dropping to the floor, Mea-a-ha cried herself to sleep.

It was late when she returned to their dark little room. Mea-a-ha curled up on the mat next to Jacob without speaking. He leaned in close and whispered. "I'm sorry." She pulled his arm over her and silenced her mind in sleep.

It was late morning when Mea-a-ha woke. She knew her face was still puffy from the night before and was glad Jacob had gone out. She washed with water in a clay pot, then quietly sat, looking about her lovely little room. Each memento brought emotion, but crying was over. In the distance, she could hear the clip-clop of Major's large lumbering hooves on the stones. Going to the alcove, she could see Jacob leading the horse fully saddled. Mea-a-ha went to Major's side and laid her head on his flank. "Is it to be this morning?

"Yes."

"So soon?"

Jacob nodded. "The longer we stay, the more likely of running into trouble." He paused and adjusted the bridle. "And the harder it will be for you to let go."

Mea-a-ha lowered her eyes. "How is your leg?"

"As good as it's going to get anytime soon."

Returning to her small room, Mea-a-ha took her time packing some of the smaller pottery she found, remembrances from the lost grotto of the Mogollon.

Jacob tied the sacks on the saddle, then returned for Mea-a-ha. He found her sitting in the middle of their humble chamber. It was emptier, but still cozy. She left a generous supply of firewood, a few pieces of pottery, and the sleeping mat, in a secret hope they might return someday. Jacob raised her from the floor and wrapped his arms around her. "I don't think I will ever forget this little room."

Mea-a-ha turned in his arms, searching his face. Could he ever understand how much it meant to her? It was where she dared to love and dream. While he slept, she grew. How could he understand? She had changed. Lowering her head, she stepped past him. "It's just a room."

Major struggled up the first ascent of the left fork where weeks before there had been a waterfall. The old horse strained under the big man's weight. There was no choice; Jacob's leg would never manage such a strenuous climb.

At the top, Mea-a-ha took one last wistful look into the grotto and quietly bid farewell. The sky was sunny and clear except for a few billowy clouds that never seemed to move or change shape. It was a perfect day to begin their journey.

The left fork twisted between deep narrow walls for miles, past grassy seeps where Mea-a-ha had taken Major to feed. Eventually the gorge became a gully, and the gully became a dry creek, then a shallow wash that simply vanished at the top of the mountain.

Coming into the open, Mea-a-ha marveled at the endless hills that spread beyond. A fresh breeze greeted her, blowing her hair. She turned not more than twenty yards from the rim. The gorge was invisible, lost in the endless folds of the rolling land. The rugged terrain hid the secrets of the grotto more closely than could the mightiest gate. A lump caught in her throat as she vowed silently that one day she would return.

Following the ridges of the mountain, Jacob led them almost due east into the labyrinth of low hills that had confounded the most intrepid explorers. It was a much longer route, but definitely better than the steep and dangerous westward direction they had taken from the Hollow. Going down was easier than coming up. It was a slower, gentler trail. Broken rock gave way to sandy soil. Major welcomed the soft earth.

Jacob hated riding while Mea-a-ha walked. For her, it was the Apache way, and Jacob was injured, so she thought nothing of it. But as the miles grew so did Jacob's guilt. He had to speak. "You know, I'm getting' a mite tired of talking to the top of your head. Either I need to try and walk beside you for a bit, or you need to climb up here and sit with me for a spell."

Mea-a-ha cast him a smile and kept walking. "You can barely limp around a campfire, and limping ain't walking. We would be old and gray by the time we made it off this mountain."

"Well, then, climb up here and sit a spell."

Mea-a-ha kept her steady pace. "Major might buckle under the two of us. It is bad enough he has to haul a grumpy old bear all over these hills."

Her flippant attitude, cute or not, was aggravating. The soldier in him bristled. Jacob wasn't used to people arguing with him. Spurring Major forward, he leaned down and plucked Mea-a-ha off her feet with as little effort as picking a wildflower and plopped her in the saddle before him. "First of all little Missy, remember what I said about baiting this here bear. And speaking of bear, you're coming close to getting your bare backside tanned right here and now. Secondly, Ol' Major here carried me and a wounded soldier a darn sight bigger than you for two days through the burning desert. So don't worry your little self none about him

144

buckling. My boots weigh more than you. The only danger he faces is going deaf listening to all your back-sassing."

Jacob ended his lecture with finality and clamped his jaw shut. He said his piece and that was the end of it.

Mea-a-ha sat quietly for a moment, pondering his verbose scolding. She replied softly, her words dripping with sweetness. "If you wanted me to ride with you, all you had to do was ask." Leaning forward, she whispered into Major's ear, "I know, Major, we will humor him for a bit."

Clenching his teeth, Jacob threatened, "There's a sack tied behind me and it ain't half full."

She gave him an innocent smile. "I'm being good." Undaunted, the cheery girl leaned against his chest and released a long gentle sigh. "Wake me when you have forgiven me."

"You're gunna' have a long nap."

She giggled. "What was it you said? Oh, yes, you care, and I am beautiful. Pleasant thoughts for a long dream."

"I'm not gunna' get the last word, am I?"

"Nope."

They rode on in silence, neither seeming to mind. For awhile their cares left them. They were two people lost on a vast mountain, dwarfed by towering clouds adrift in a infinite blue sky. A harsh world in its rush to nowhere had somehow passed them by.

The rhythmic beat of Major's gate lulled Mea-a-ha to sleep. Towards afternoon, she awoke without opening her eyes. Jacob was humming some tune, then he softly lapsed into singing under his breath. A low melodic rumble, reverberated deep in his chest "Oh, my darling, oh my darling, Clementine." He didn't seem to know most of the words and kept repeating the same verse over and over. "You are lost and gone forever, dreadful sorry Clementine."

Mea-a-ha had never heard him sing, or even hum before. It was comical, and beautiful, and sad. So unlike Apache songs. She wondered if he knew more, but was sure if she asked, he would say no. Eventually he went silent and she drifted back to sleep.

Towards evening on the third day, they worked their way down a small rocky draw. Suddenly the rounded knolls spotted with greasewood, yucca, and weathered rocks, fell away, opening out on to the vast desert. It was like bursting from a shaded tunnel. They squinted against the brilliantly parched earth. Mea-a-ha twisted, looking up at Jacob. "We are finally out. Is the Hollow near?"

He prodded Major forward. "We should be home by afternoon tomorrow."

She realized he had said little all morning. As the day wore on, he talked even less, leaving the conversation up to her, and not always listening. Mea-a-ha studied his dark face with concern; he was slipping

145

into one of his dark moods.

After traveling several hours in near quiet, they made their camp towards evening in the open flats. Large clumps of tall sagebrush offered some seclusion. Jacob managed to bring down a plump rabbit, which Mea-a-ha cooked. Dinner was eaten without conversation.

Mea-a-ha sat silently nibbling meat off a small bone, watching Jacob clean his guns. She had come to realize that he often cleaned his guns when he was upset. Even if he had just cleaned them. Mea-a-ha finished the meat and tossed the bone into the fire. "Is something upsetting you?"

Jacob rammed the cleaning rod down the barrel but did not look up. "Nope."

"What are you thinking?"

"Nothing."

"Have I done something to make you mad?"

"Nope."

Small talk was no use. She decided to speak her mind. "We are nearing the Hollow. Are you worried you will be stuck with me?"

He did not answer.

Mea-a-ha stood up wrapping her arms around her, wishing he would care enough not to let her fear it was true. When no assurance came, she moved away from the fire, letting the darkness claim her. She walked slow hoping he would stop her, then slower. It was no use, the girl gave up and hurried into the night.

The glow of the campsite gave way to the stars. Mea-a-ha rubbed her shoulders, feeling colder than the night warranted. Her throat tightened as a growing sadness turned to physical pain. When Jacob was distant, she felt small and lost. It was not a good time to be an Apache. It was not a good place to be a woman.

Here, there wasn't any future much bleaker than being an Apache squaw wandering all alone. The rabbit they had eaten had a better chance, and right now she was feeling like a helpless rabbit.

This was the desert, and the soldiers patrolled most of the trails, or at least the trails with water. An Apache brave would be killed. A young Apache girl off the reservation would be regarded as a plaything to amuse the soldiers and satisfy their needs. Afterward, they would discard her without the slightest guilt. She wouldn't even be considered worth the bother of returning to the reservation.

Mea-a-ha choked back tears, but they came anyway. In her heart, she was still a young girl who had never done anyone harm. She didn't understand how a world could see her as having no value. And here she was proving them right, not even able to take care of herself. Before she realized it, she was crying uncontrollably, venting rage the only way she could.

She loved a man who didn't want her. Worse, she needed him to survive. It was hard to separate the two, and it filled her with guilt. Did he understand there was nothing else left for her? She sobbed. And if he let her stay, how would she know it was out of love and not pity?

Behind her Mea-a-ha could hear Jacob's limping shuffle. She frantically wiped her face, but she couldn't silence her telling sobs. Jacob came up and placed his hands on her shoulders. She jerked free. "Go away."

Her body shook with each breath. "You make me so mad. It is not right that I should feel so worthless. Just go away."

"You are not worthless."

She stepped away. "Not worthless! You were a big soldier and you have your own ranch, but you are like a chief without a tribe. Curl up with your ranch on a cold night, then see if the best you can say is, I am not worthless."

"Mea-a-ha, I know what you want of me, and it would be easy just to go along. But if I didn't know for sure, it wouldn't be right. I would just hurt you more, and I care too much for that."

"Then don't care. It is that easy."

Jacob gripped her arms tightly and pulled her to his chest. She struggled, but he would not let go. "It's not that easy. I do care for you. You're the best thing to ever come into my life."

He wrapped his arms around her. "Look, earlier when we were riding together, everything was okay. Can't we just go back to the way it was?"

She held herself ridged. "Earlier I was not pushed out of your heart by one of your dark moods. You do not know how it feels to be alone."

Jacob released her. His arms hung limp at his sides. "Yes. I do know. Until you came along, there was only darkness. You have been the fire I dare not touch."

Mea-a-ha stood firm. "You are afraid of what gives you warmth? You... you... dumb soldier!"

"Mea-a-ha, I may be a dumb soldier, but I do know your worth."

He scooped her up in his arms and started slowly back to camp.

Mea-a-ha slapped her small hand against his chest. "I did not give you permission to pick me up."

He hugged her close, nuzzling her under his chin. "I know. If it makes you feel better, you can scalp me while I sleep."

She wrapped her arms around his neck. "Does your leg hurt?"

"Yes."

"Good."

Jacob eased down on his knee, setting Mea-a-ha gently on her bedding. She gave him a piercing glance and jerked the blanket tightly around her. She was not ready to let go of her anger.

Doing his best to ignore her defiant mood, Jacob sat near and struggled with his boots. Usually Mea-a-ha helped pull them off. He

147

looked to her, but she only watched. Her eyes burned cold.

With nothing else he could do, Jacob managed his best without her. Long minutes passed as the uncomfortable silence grew.

When the tension got to be too much, he shuffled to her. "It may get cold tonight." he gave a wicked grin. "With that icy stare, holding you might be downright freezing, but I will warm you by morning."

"You carry me without permission. You think you will hold me without permission."

The old soldier's patience was wearing thin. He set his jaw. "I think I might."

Mea-a-ha said nothing, offering only an exasperated hiss. Turning her attention to herself, she stripped off her moccasins and tossed them aside, then, pulling the blanket over her, she squirmed beneath it. The Mimbre girl surfaced with a smug pout, and extending her wadded dress at arms length, dropped it onto her moccasins.

Caught somewhere between an angry curse and an injured pout, her eyes grew moist. As is often the way of women, her mood suddenly changed. Looking cuddly as a kitten, Mea-a-ha rose on her knees and edged close to the big man. Slowly, the blanket slipped off her delicate shoulders. As she inched closer, a smooth bare leg slid from beneath the blanket, catching the warm glow of the dying campfire. Jacob smiled – he had won. His pulse quickened.

Mea-a-ha's fingertips toyed with her covering, opening it just the tiniest bit. Transfixed, the big man swallowed, waiting for it to fall away.

The girl hesitated, just a moment. The blanket parted..., then abruptly, Mea-a-ha jerked it tightly shut, and thrust her face into his, shouting, "Then let this *not worthless Apache* drive you as crazy as you are driving me!"

Whirling away, Mea-a-ha curled into a little ball and hid under her blanket. Once again, she had found a way to make her point.

Jacob's jaw went tight. He opened his mouth and closed it, then opened it again. A tortured growl rose from his throat, "Woman!"

His huge paw snatched her around the middle, dragging her, arms and legs flailing, out of her blanket and into his. A startled scream escaped her lips. Jacob took her face in one big hand. "I told you not to bait this old bear."

"And I told you this little squirrel could bite, too." She threw her arms tightly around his neck and pressed her lips hard against his. He tensed, then softened. She held the kiss for a long moment before she slowly released him. Her pained eyes searched his face. Tears welled and she retreated into a soft little ball, sobbing quietly.

Resting on his forearm, Jacob smoothed her hair and pulled the blanket over her exposed back. "Okay, you have driven me totally crazy."

Lowering himself, he rested his cheek gently against hers, snuggling

148

close. He pressed his hand against her warm bare stomach. Every muscle in her small body tensed to his touch. She did not resist, but neither would she give him the satisfaction of yielding to his caress.

Jacob let his hand trace her delicate form down her smooth leg, then slowly back to the curve of her waist. She gave no sign. Without permission, his hand captured a soft round breast, taking what warmth he could. He kissed her shoulder. "Completely and totally crazy."

Chapter -14-
Storm Clouds

In the distance lay the familiar yellow cliffs. Their long journey was coming to an end. Mea-a-ha chose to walk this morning, wanting time to herself. The night before played in her thoughts – Jacob's touch, gentle and caring. Eventually she forgave him and curled naked in his arms, but refused to let it go any further. Still she loved it. Mea-a-ha wondered if he knew what she was thinking. She smiled. How could he not.

Soon they would be back in the safety of the Hollow. Time would tell if she had a home. It all seemed so long ago when Jacob had taken them in. She had been his unwanted guest, but the journey to the mountain had changed their relationship. They were closer – a lot closer. Was it close enough?

Summer was waning; crisp breezes played in the morning air. Mea-a-ha could feel the cold ground through her moccasins. It felt nice. Immense billowy clouds towering like alabaster cliffs hung low over the vast desert. When she had fallen asleep in Jacob's arms, there had been only stars; now a sea of clouds spread to a dark horizon. Evening might bring rain.

Ahead the trail narrowed. Jacob rode next to Mea-a-ha. Reaching down, he drew her up onto the saddle before him. She welcomed the ride, but wished he had asked before snatching her from the ground. With a sideways glance, she elbowed him in the stomach. "I am not a sack, to be tossed about as you wish."

Jacob let it pass. He was anxious to get home and her slow meandering pace didn't set with his sense of urgency. A lot weighed on his mind. He was returning to a world of realities. One was the Apache girl sitting before him. He could not easily turn her out, but to let her stay might be taken as forever, something he was not sure he could handle.

Late afternoon finally brought them up the rolling foothills to the base of the majestic cliffs. Heavy clouds piled against the towering walls, covering the Hollow in dark shadows. Major climbed the last steep slope, punctuating his effort with a husky cough. Their journey was almost over.

Jacob climbed down and lifted Mea-a-ha to the ground. "Let's walk, Major's earned a rest." Mea-a-ha stared towards the Hollow. The pond lay hidden in the tall reeds several hundred yards ahead. Just beyond, stood the barn. Rising on her toes, Mea-a-ha could barely see the peak of its roof. Past it were the tall trees that sheltered the snug little home. Her heart leaped… home!

A small sandy path lined with tall dry grass led the way. Mea-a-ha knew Jacob often came home from hunting following this trail, but she had never followed it herself. Taking care of Grandfather had left her little time to explore. Besides, the path dropped off into the desert, and she preferred the beautiful trees behind the house.

Ahead, the yellow weeds gave way to a small clearing at the base of the tall cliffs. Mea-a-ha noticed thirteen stones laid out in neat rows. One stone was larger than the rest. It was obvious they had been placed here on purpose.

Taking her arm, Jacob ushered Mea-a-ha forward. She twisted in his grip questioningly. "Jacob, what are these stones?"

He stared forward expressionless, his eyes burning in his dark face, and pushed on in haste. "Jacob, what..."

His voice was cold. "A cemetery."

She gasped in shock. "Out here on the edge of the Hollow? What kind of..."

"An Apache cemetery. Let it be."

He hung on Major's bridle, making the horse pull him along. She hurried to catch up, but ignoring his injured leg, Jacob hurried far ahead. The trail was too narrow for her to engage him.

Mea-a-ha's mind filled with questions. Apache graves in the beautiful Hollow. Graves Jacob didn't want to talk about. Giving up the chase, Mea-a-ha slowed her pace, needing time to think.

The winding path through the tall, dark reed hid everything from Mea-a-ha's vision. The damp trail stayed low, skirting the east side of the pond. Red winged blackbirds played among the cattails, not seeming to worry about the impending rain. The disquieted feeling belonged to her alone.

On the far side, Mea-a-ha finally came to the corral. A span of railing was knocked down. Maybe Peaches had gotten tired of waiting for someone to feed her and took matters under hoof. Stepping through the break in the fence Mea-a-ha hurried into the open side of the barn. Jacob was unsaddling Major, with Peaches standing near by. The big horse had proven to be a barn rat. Sliding up to her neck, Mea-a-ha gave Peaches a hug. "There you are girl, you stayed home."

Slowly she turned toward Jacob who was brushing Major. His silence told her there was no use in asking questions. She scooped up the food sacks and made her way to the house.

Inside, Mea-a-ha felt comforted. The cozy home was just as they left it. She ran her fingers across the top of the stove, then looked towards the door. An uneasy pang weighed heavy on her heart. Maybe it wasn't to be hers.

Setting the sack on the table, Mea-a-ha opened the lid and struck a match as much to lay claim as for warmth. If anything in Jacob's belonged to her, it was the shiny metal stove.

Jacob came through the door, brushing the first drops of rain from his

151

shoulders. Thunder cracked outside and a gentle pitter patter floated down from the rafters. Easing himself into his leather chair, Jacob broke the silence. "What's for supper?"

Banging a tin pan on the stove harder than needed, Mea-a-ha responded without looking. "Unless you got a deer in your pocket, it's beans." She looked over her shoulder. "You don't have a deer in your pocket, do you?"

"No."

"Then, beans."

"We need water from the spring." Picking up the empty wooden bucket she went to the door. Suddenly she changed her mind. Crossing the distance between them, she knelt at Jacob's feet.

In the gloom of the fading light, her dark eyes glistened in her delicate face. Mea-a-ha rested her chin gently on his knee and pressed her fingertips into his clenched fist. "Are you going to tell me about the graves?"

Jacob's jaw twitched with memories. Slowly he reached out and brushed a lock of hair from her face, then patted her. Mea-a-ha rested her head in his big hand, quietly waiting for his words. His sad eyes held her gaze for a long moment, then he looked beyond her. In a voice thick and deep, he began. "It seems like a different time, a different world, but it wasn't, it was right here in the Hollow... not that long ago."

She was surprised; he began to tremble as he stroked her cheek. "What once was hailed as a courageous act of bravery, now...Well, it was big news, you probably heard of it. Mea-a-ha, I was a soldier and I had a duty to do. One morning, outnumbered and outgunned, I ordered an attack on a war party of Apaches. It happened so fast."

Jacob paused as he relived that fateful moment. The echo of anguished screams amid the smoke and flames leaping from the soldiers' guns. The dead and dying... Shaking his head he tried to force the terrible slaughter from his mind. The leathery soldier swallowed a lump in his throat and continued. "Afterwards, I had them buried beneath the cliff. That's how I found the Hollow."

Trembling, Mea-a-ha's eyes grew wide with fear. "Oh Jacob, Grandfather and I were in the desert for a long time; we heard no news, none."

In her breast, her heart began pounding wildly. Fighting back panic, her eyes pleaded for an answer she could accept.

In a raspy whisper Mea-a-ha forced her worse fear through her trembling lips. "Do you know who they were?"

Jacob shook his head. "No. Only the chief. His name was Sholo."

Mea-a-ha's body jolted as though she had been struck a mighty blow. Terror welling inside, twisted her sweet face in agony. "Sholo.... you killed Sholo?" A wailing scream burst from the small Apache girl. "Did any escape?"

"Darling, I'm sorry, none escaped."

Mea-a-ha collapsed on the floor in a flood of tears. Her grief could not be contained. Jacob placed his hand on her, she jerked violently away screeching. "Don't touch me! You killed Teowa; you murdered my brother!"

The girl's decree burst in his mind like the roar of a thousand deafening cannons, 'Murderer... her brother?' Jacob sickened, locked in a nightmare from which he could not escape.

Mea-a-ha pounded the floor with her fists, murmuring, "You murdered Teowa. You murdered Teowa."

Consumed by the flames of unfathomable guilt, Jacob slid from the chair sinking to his knees beside her. Nausea churned in the pit of his stomach and rose to his throat. "Mea-a-ha, I'm sorry. I didn't know. I couldn't, I...I..." Words failed. There was nothing he could say, nothing to make it right. His mind reeled. Hesitantly, he reached for her, his big hand shaking.

Screaming hysterically, the stricken girl pulled away, retreating under the edge of the table. "Murderer!"

'Murderer,' the word stabbed deep into his heart. "Mea-a-ha, darling, they were a war party bent on killing. It was my duty to stop them."

Choking on emotion, she raged. "It was you who were bent on killing. You! You ...Soldier."

Mea-a-ha spit the foul word from her mouth like bitter poison. Through burning tears she glared at the man she loved, but now she could only see the enemy of her people. Her brother, her sweet beautiful Teowa, dead. Murdered by his hand---a soldier.

"Darling, please listen to me. Sholo murdered innocent people. It was kill or be killed; there was no choice."

Mea-a-ha's body writhed in grief. "You lie, Teowa was just a boy. You murdered children."

The fury of the injured girl's words scorched his soul. "Sholo was a great chief; you are not half the man he was."

Mea-a-ha's accusations tore open old wounds, cut deep by the cruel mocking of a black whore. Anger unburied, rekindled in his chest. She was unfair. It was not his fault, but he reached for her once more. She shrieked, pulling deeper under the table. "My brother, my brother."

Her anguished convulsions were more than he could bear. "Mea-a-ha, my little Mea-a-ha, please..."

She hissed, "Don't say my name. I never want to hear it on your lips again. I will never be your little Mea-a-ha. Murderer. MURDERER!" She collapsed in tears. "Teowa, Teowa, Teo..."

Jacob's mind and body swirled in agonizing turmoil. His arms flailed helplessly. At a loss for words, his hurt and guilt mixed like tinder and flames. It was burst or die.

Balling his fist, Jacob vented his torment with a thunderous blow to the table. Mea-a-ha jerked, shocked by his rage. Jacob stormed to his feet. "Then you will never hear it again. What I said about Sholo is true, and if you can't see that, then you're just a... a dumb savage. Hide under the table like a kicked dog if you like."

He pulled away. Mea-a-ha gasped, her eyes wide in disbelief. How could he speak to her like that after his monstrous deed?

Jacob regretted the words before they left his mouth, but the damage was done. Struggling to breathe, he stumbled out the door. Mea-a-ha's hand stretched after him, then dropped to the floor.

Unrelenting rain beat down on a wretched soul beyond caring. A cold fog rolled off the pond, shrouding the Hollow. He had never been more alone. Mea-a-ha's words tore at his mind. "Murderer. Not half the man. Murderer." Jacob staggered blindly to the barn. Cursing, he punched a heavy timber until his hand was bloody. Would she ever understand? Sholo chose violence. Death was the price. Sholo understood it, why couldn't she? Maybe she would cry herself out. He would give her time, but never would he accept guilt for doing his duty.

Jacob slumped against the wall. 'His duty.' He had never questioned it. Since he was fourteen, the enemy had died before his gun, and he had never asked if they deserved death.

Suddenly the gentle face of a young boy lying amongst the reeds came flooding back as vivid as the morning it happened. There was a resemblance, could he have been Teowa? Among the dead, were young boys. He had killed children; he had killed Mea-a-ha's brother. Maybe forgiveness was too much to ask. Killing children was murder.

Jacob had never faced it like that. *Murderer*. The word stuck in his throat. He had tried to live his life with honor, but the name fit, and duty could not excuse it. The big man leaned over the rail, shaking. Water pouring off the eaves battered his jumbled mind. He vomited. 'Murder'... the word thundered and nothing could ever wash it away. Shaking from his illness, he closed his eyes against the shame. "What have I done?"

Rain drummed through the pitch black night. It was the only sound. Just a short distance to the house, yet Jacob let hours pass while he sat alone regretting his cruel words. Now more than ever he was aching to hold her, wishing for one of her tender hugs. His empty arms clutched at the air, then dropped to his side.

Unable to bear his exile any longer, Jacob rose and paced the barn. He felt like running away, but some how he found himself standing on the porch of their home. Yes, it was her home too. He knew that now.

For a moment, he hesitated at the door. Why had he called her a dumb savage? He wanted her. No, that wasn't it... he loved her. Jacob jolted. He loved her. Standing in the doorway, it came to him. Why had it taken an unbearable tragedy to make him realize he loved this Apache girl? Why had it been so hard? The truth was finally clear and he must tell her.

Trembling, he lifted the latch on the door. The house was dark and cold. "Mea-a-ha."

He held his breath. "Darling, I love you...Mea-a-ha?" The chilling silence was broken by a sudden crack of lightening. Through the small room, the brilliant flash revealed the back door hanging open. Mea-a-ha was gone.

Jacob cried aloud, and raced into the rain, screaming her name over and over. "Mea-a-ha!" His heart aching, the giant man shook with a fear he had never known. He took several stumbling steps. There was no hope of following her in the rain. What good would it do? Mea-a-ha hated him. She would never return. Jacob dropped to his knees in a black pool of water. The rain drenched him. In a moment of rage, he had chosen anger over love, and now it was all he had--his dreaded companion.

Chapter -15-
Long Walk

"Don't be afraid." Mea-a-ha whispered. She had walked the forest trail beneath the cliffs with Grandfather and Jacob once before, but now she was alone. It was night, and there was a terrible storm. Lightening cracked, freezing every muscle in her thin body. Thunder rolled down the length of the cliffs in a deep rumbling that never seemed to end.

Her heart ached, but she willed herself forward. "Don't be afraid." Beneath the boughs of dense black trees, Mea-a-ha felt lost – a small child swallowed up by the angry night.

Cautiously, she took each tiny step, fearing to disturb whatever lurked in the tangle of darkness. "Don't be afraid."

An unseen canopy high above blocked most of the rain. The dampness on her face was her own. Everything had come undone. There was no safe place for her anymore. Grandfather was gone. Teowa was dead, and Jacob...Jacob must be dead to her also...and with him, her dream. She collapsed against a tree and sobbed.

In a moment, she would regain control and go on. So it had been for many hours. Cold and hungry, she missed the Hollow, their snug little home. Maybe Jacob would come and make her go back. "No!" she wouldn't let him. Mea-a-ha pushed away from the huge trunk and struggled on.

In the gray drizzle, Mea-a-ha reached the ancient cedar at the edge of the forest. During the night, the rain slowed. A damp musky odor filled the lonely woods. For Mea-a-ha it became the scent of all things lost. It was the smell of despair. Slumping between the roots of the old tree where Grandfather had rested not so very long ago, she closed her eyes. If she could sleep maybe it would all be just a bad dream.

Mea-a-ha was exhausted, but sleep wouldn't come... only relentless pain. Teowa, she couldn't think of him without unbearable loss...and Jacob. As hurt as she was, there was grieving for his loss, too.

Consumed with despair, she struggled to her feet. Ahead was the great cut in the cliff, which led up the mountain to the grotto. Here also lay the perilous ribbon trail dropping to the valley far below. Jacob said it led to where they first met. Their time together was marked by a tragic beginning and now a tragic end. Emotions churned in her stomach, but Mea-a-ha pushed the painful memories to the dark recesses of her mind.

During the long lonely night, she had cried herself sick, she could cry no more. Mea-a-ha knew she had to move on, but which way? Her beloved grotto held no meaning without Jacob. She must try to reach the reservation, which meant going down the trail, steep and narrow.

Timidly, Mea-a-ha looked over the edge, her heart raced wildly. A warm wind rushed up from the desert floor blowing her long black hair across her face. "Don't be afraid." Ever so hesitantly Mea-a-ha placed one tiny moccasin on the muddy ledge and pressed her back against the wall. "I can do this," she whispered.

Small pebbles dislodged by her toes, tumbled down the steep face. "Don't be afraid."

Step by step, she edged downward; arms spread wide, fingers digging into the damp wall searching for a hold. "Step by step."

Her feet inched along the slippery precipice. As she moved from the safety of the rim her breath became rapid. She closed her eyes and let the panic pass. "Don't be afraid."

In the pale morning light a curious flock of swifts, riding the wind, drifted upwards investigating the intruder on their nesting cliff. On graceful wings, they hovered close, reminding Mea-a-ha that she was literally hanging in air. "What am I doing here? This is the domain of birds, and no place for foolish girls."

She looked back up the trail, doubting her choice. This was insane. Should she go back? To, to...

As if in answer, a strong gust pressed her against the cliff, robbing her breath. The wind! Grandfather's words came warm and loving. "Be at peace." She argued. But the death of Teowa... "Be at peace." The loss of love and home? "Be at peace." "Be at peace with yourself my child. What is done is done. Be at peace."

For the first time since the tragic news, she smiled. Never would she be alone again. Mea-a-ha searched the black clouds, expecting to see the old man's face, but his words were enough. It was time to bravely look forward to a new morning and turn away from the cruel night.

Courage came with every breath. She was Apache, and Apaches could go where others could not. Mea-a-ha pried herself from the wall. Each step came quicker. On and on she went. Soon she was hurrying with only one hand on the wall for balance. The family of swifts stayed with her until she reached the desert floor, then they were gone.

With a final jump Mea-a-ha landed on solid ground and raised her head high. All her life she had been small. A small girl in the violent world of giant men. Even in her own mind she was someone fragile who needed to be protected. Yet she had braved the dark forest, survived the ribbon trail and now, she would conquer the vast desert on her own.

Mea-a-ha walked quickly; each step was a triumph. Her slender legs obliged her demand for haste. There was far to go.

Hours passed and the morning came, but without the sun. She was tired from lack of sleep, still she did her best to hurry on. The barren land held its dangers, yet the girl's greatest fear lay beyond.

An Indian reservation is a terrible existence, a place where dreams are taunts of what will never be. For little Mea-a-ha there was nothing else. Nothing was left but enduring a future without hope, made worse after the joy she had known in Jacob's Hollow. The loss of what might have been, and the dread of what was to be tore at her heart. She pushed the painful thoughts from her head.

For hours the grieving maiden pushed on across the lonely expanse. Her mind would not quiet. Defiance and despair waged a teetering war inside her, and once again, despair became the heavier burden.

Without Jacob's protection she knew no matter what she encountered, man or beast, she was the prey. Teowa's death could not be forgiven, yet all she wanted was to be in Jacob's safe embrace. Was he sad she was gone, or was he happy to be rid of her? Maybe he was angry.

Suddenly she felt like a naughty child who had run away from home. No, he had not claimed her, she could go as she liked. Anger flared at the thought of him forcing her to return against her will. He had his chance at winning her heart and tossed it away. If he came looking, he would not find her sitting on his doorstep. Mea-a-ha wiped her face and marched into the endless sea of gray.

Her first trip across the desert with Grandfather had taken a long time because of the old man's poor health. Often they made camp for days while he rested. Now she was on her own. If she hurried, she could reach the reservation in less than a week. Apaches were known for their ability to travel great distances by foot. Youth was on her side, pain would be her fire.

All morning she walked at great speed, but by afternoon her growling stomach could no longer be ignored, she had hoped to continue on until sunset and capture small animals that came out in the twilight. Sunrise and sunset are the most active time for animals on the harsh desert. Mea-a-ha had visions of a fat rabbit roasting on a spit, but that required gathering materials to fashion snares. Instead, the first day's fare consisted of three lizards caught warming themselves on rocks. Three well aimed stones hurled by a small but experienced arm quickly dispatched the quarry. Pulling the raw meat from pulverized bone with her teeth was disagreeable after dining on antelope steaks and simmering pots of chili. The cold, stringy flesh brought her no joy.

In the last rays of the setting sun, the cliffs at the edge of Jacob's property were still visible. The little distance she had covered reminded her how big the desert really was. Its vastness overwhelmed her. Could she make it alone?

When darkness finally fell, Mea-a-ha found a thick juniper, with the lower branches touching the ground. There was just enough space for her to crawl under and make a bed on the fallen needles. Here she lay, hiding like the smaller animals of the desert. Wolves and cougars would find her just as tasty a meal as any rabbit. Shrinking in the darkness her tiny hand searched the ground and found a stout stick with a sharp jagged point. She clutched it to her breast. If the wolves came, they would find a rabbit with teeth.

For awhile she listened fearfully to the sounds of the night. As darkness deepened, cold found its way beneath her thin dress, chilling her spine. Fighting for sleep, her thoughts went back to colder nights on the mountain spent blissfully with Jacob, her back pressed against his warm chest, his huge arms wrapped around her. She felt guilty for wanting him now. Sleep was her salvation, but it did not come without tears.

Morning broke cold and gray, a biting wind carried a threat of more rain. Crawling out of her damp rabbit hole, Mea-a-ha wrapped her arms tightly about her and hurried on. Shivering, she scolded herself. "Foolish girl; didn't even bring a blanket."

With head bent, she pushed forward, trying to forget her plight. Strong gusts tore at her clothing. Yesterday's hard march had taken a toll. The lacing on her doeskin dress was unraveling up the side of her leg. She did her best to hold it down.

The rain came about midday, turning the desert floor into a thick gooey clay that hung on Mea-a-ha's moccasins like heavy weights. Walking became impossible as the suction of each step pulled at her feet with more force than her small legs could bear.

With each stride she sank deeper. Struggling against the mire, Mea-a-ha jerked a foot free only to lose her balance and fall face down into the sticky white soup.

Lifting her head she spit the bitter mud from her mouth. Wet hair stuck to her face in a tangled mess. Pulling on it only made it worse. Mea-a-ha drew up a knee and tried to stand, but she was caked. The desert became an unbeatable foe for which she was no match..

Erupting in a shrill scream, Mea-a-ha beat her fists against the earth. It wasn't fair.

Resigned to her fate, she crawled to a flat rock and started peeling off her moccasins. Pouting, she kicked her bare foot free in a last act of defiance. It didn't help. Feeling like a helpless child, she started sobbing. Her small shoulder shook with each quivering breath.

Utterly miserable, the Apache girl raised to her knees, and fingering the hem of her soaked dress, slowly lifted it over her head. For a moment, she clutched it to her breast, not wanting to give the soiled garment up.

Mea-a-ha plopped it before her in a soppy mess. Her arms went limp and she hung her head in despair. She was naked.

Before her, lay the last vestige of a civilized existence. A shiver ran down her bare spine, tears started to burn, but she quickly denied them. "I am Apache. I am not worthless." The sound of her own voice broke the dismal spell. She sniffed back the tears. Her chest swelled in a long slow breath.

Closing her eyes, she lifted her face skyward and held her arms high. The sound of the beating droplets quieted her mind. Mea-a-ha stopped fighting the desert squall, and let the rain bathe the stubborn white clay from her smooth brown skin.

What had been her enemy now healed her. Thick mud gently dissolved from her hair. Beads on her face flowed down her neck and dripped from her breasts, changing her color.

The Mimbre girl's body glistened as streams of water washed away every last bit of grime and soothed her troubled heart. She chanted to herself. "I am Apache. I am not worthless."

The harsh reality of the desert melted away with the mud. Surrendering to a dream, darkness slowly filled her mind.

As the rain cascaded over her, the call of seabirds carried her into distant light. She was walking naked on a vast shore, leaving footprints in the damp sand. The sun was warm and a breeze off the water kissed her bare skin.

She had never seen the ocean or met anyone who had, but she knew this was the great water. The desert with all its cruelty paid homage at its shore. Here she was safe.

Overcome with joy, she danced blissfully in the lapping tide. Giggling, she lifted on her toes, and spun full around, then suddenly stopped. Her eyes grew wide. There were footprints other than her own.

Casting about, she saw no one. The young girl was alone, but the prints told her those she loved were close by. Mea-a-ha knew each sandy impression as surely as the face of the person who made them. There was Grandfather's and Teowa's.

She knelt and lovingly touched them. The waves splashed against her, washing the prints away, only hers remained. Rising from the sand, she hurried on.

Sunlight sparkled on the sea foam. The morning colors were pure. Mea-a-ha started to run, then stopped once more. Footprints of a small boy came from over a red dune and went before her. The child was stumbling in pain.

Alarmed, Mea-a-ha hurried forward, following his tracks. The prints abruptly ended, only to be replaced by large heavy boots. Her heart quickened. She knew these too. The cry of the gulls returned.

Mea-a-ha slowly opened her eyes. How long she meditated she did not know, but the rain had subsided and she was renewed.

Tying her clothing in a tight bundle, she started off again across the vast desert, knowing it too had an end. She was small, but her heart burned with the courage of her ancestors. Tiny steps never faltering would carry her any distance she had to go. Giving up was not in her character.

Where she could, the Indian girl picked a course across higher, firmer ground. The clay slipped more easily from her smooth wet legs than from the soaked moccasins. Mea-a-ha trudged alone for several more hours. The desert took its toll but a spark that burned within sustained her. She would stumble, but never fall.

A thin stain of white clay painted her bare limbs once more. Long strands of wet hair matted to her body, she was now the epitome of a naked savage. Jacob's last words came back to her but the sting was gone.

Surviving was important, not appearance. In summer Apache men often roamed naked; she could do the same. The rain slowed to a drizzle, but an icy breeze blew across her wet skin, leaving her shivering. Mea-a-ha clenched her teeth. It would take more than a storm to stop her – a lot more. She quickened her pace.

Not far ahead was a large stretch of sagebrush spotted with junipers. It would provide shelter against the wind. Crossing a shallow desert wash, Mea-a-ha paused to rinse the clay once more. As she stood in the middle of the stream rubbing the grime from her legs, a long tree branch floated into reach. Quickly she snatched it up. It was several inches taller than her. The branch was straight and smooth, perfect for a spear. She grasped it tightly in her small fist, excitement swelled in her breast. What good fortune; the gods took pity.

At the edge of the wash were several large boulders. Mea-a-ha eagerly knelt and started grinding the end into a sharp point. Growing up, Apache girls did not use weapons – they were for the boys. So Mea-a-ha had spent her time throwing rocks. What her arm lacked in strength, it more than made up for in accuracy. The boys in her village learned not to tease her, or to do so at a safe distance.

At times when the men took the boys hunting, Mea-a-ha stole away and practiced throwing sticks until she was as accurate as with a stone. Snares took time and patience, which she didn't have right now. Her simple shaft was a gift to be cherished.

Where there is sagebrush, there are rabbits. Tiptoeing with her spear clenched ready to throw, it didn't take long before a cottontail came under Mea-a-ha's deadly aim. The spear leaped from her hand, flying straight and true. The kill was instant.

With a proven weapon and food in her grasp, Mea-a-ha found greater confidence. The rabbit would be a tasty meal after yesterday's smashed lizards. Her feast would wait until she could build a fire. It would be a well-earned treat that she planned on savoring.

The storm finally passed over and the sun broke through, lifting her spirits. Mea-a-ha climbed a large boulder at the edge of the stream. It gave her a good view of the surrounding land. Setting her rabbit aside, she lay on her back sunning herself. Warmth returned to her slender limbs, easing the day's fatigue.

After awhile she rolled on to her stomach. Resting her head on her folded arms, the girl dozed, letting the soothing rays work their magic.

She hadn't realized how tired she was.

Mea-a-ha slept soundly for some time. When she awoke, blue skies spread from the western horizon. Sunbeams cut through the remaining clouds bathing the landscape in a warm glow, even in her current mood, the beauty didn't go unnoticed.

Perched on the large white rock, the young naked girl scanned the vastness before her. Motion caught Mea-a-ha's eye, stopping her cold. Something moved in and out of the distant brush. There it was... a patch of fur. She shuttered. A large gray wolf was coming towards her. The lobo was sniffing around in the very spot she had speared the rabbit. Had he just happened across the scent of the kill or had he been tracking her all along?

Either way, the trail would lead straight to her. The weapon in her hand reassured her, but she did not kid herself about who was hunting who. If her wooden spear missed its mark, the lobo would rip her throat in seconds.

Gathering her bundle of clothes and the prized rabbit, Mea-a-ha slid quietly from the rock and hurried into the rapidly dwindling stream. Water does not flow long on the desert after the rains quit, but maybe the few inches of water would throw the lobo off her scent.

On light feet, she hurried downstream, trying not to leave any tracks. She dared not look behind her. After a few hundred yards the water disappeared all together. Maybe it was enough. Her breathing quickened as she headed into the thick sagebrush along the bank. Putting distance between her and the wolf was the only thought in her mind.

Several minutes passed as she zigzagged, following small animal trails through the dwindling cover. The further she got away from the water course, the sparser the sagebrush became.

From a small knoll Mea-a-ha looked back, her eyes darting anxiously, searching for the beast. Maybe he had lost her scent. Maybe he was heading away, following another rabbit. No! There he was racing back and forth across the stream, searching for her trail. Her heart pounded as she realized it was definitely her that he was after. There was no doubt now.

Turning, she headed forward through the last of the shaggy weeds. Some distance ahead was a low outcropping of rocks maybe twice her height that rose to a new plateau. If she placed her back to the wall of stone, he would be forced to come straight at her, giving her a chance. She would have to hold the spear when he made his lunge; it was too light to throw against a wolf his size.

The rocks were a great distance and the sparse sage had ended. If he caught her in the open, she would be helpless. It didn't matter; the rocks were her only chance. Mea-a-ha pinned her eyes on the nearest point and burst into the open at a dead run. This would be the race of her life.

Behind her the lobo howled; he had spotted his quarry. The chase was on. Raising her knees high, she pounded her feet to the ground. Already her lungs ached. Eager barks told her the lobo was closing in. Glancing over her shoulder, she saw he was already in the open, all four paws digging into the wet sand. His speed was frightening. Terror turned to outright panic.

Frantically twisting back, she stumbled and fell, caking herself again in the sticky white clay. The naked girl struggled, losing a precious moment before scrambling to her feet. She threw down her bundle of clothes and bolted into a mad run. Maybe her scent on the rags would buy her some time.

Flying past the bundle, the wolf closed the distance on his prey. In a moment he would have her.

Still gripping the spear tightly in one hand and the rabbit in the other, Mea-a-ha fought on but only seconds remained. Air could not come fast enough into her screaming lungs. The distance was too great; each heavy stride she took was slower than the last—not so for the wolf. Howls of a confident victory echoed behind her. Like a gray bullet, the distance between them vanished. With a scream of injustice, Mea-a-ha whirled and threw her prized rabbit at the gaping jaws of the drooling beast. He leaped and snatched it in mid air, it bought her time. Stumbling the last steps to the rocks, she turned and fell back against the stone, raging at the killer. "You dirty thieving wolf, that rabbit is mine. It's mine, you filthy..." Her mouth hung open in helpless rage, empty lungs no longer capable of a final curse.

For a moment the old wolf shook the limp rabbit viciously in his teeth, then cast it aside. A dead rabbit would not satisfy his lust, for him it was the thrill of the kill. Her helpless screams made him wild; he would snap her neck and toss her about as easily as he had the rabbit.

From a dead run, the lobo's powerful legs beat the ground propelling him forward in a blinding leap toward the defenseless girl. With huge fangs bared, the great wolf's arcing leap carried him downwards upon her.

Bracing herself against the wall, Mea-a-ha jammed the butt of the spear against the stone. Small delicate hands pointed the sharpened stick towards the huge beast. She closed her eyes.

Too late to turn aside, the snarling wolf plowed into small girl, slamming her violently into the wall. The vile smell of his hot breath fouled her nostrils, then everything went black.

Breathing came hard, and her arms would not move. Mea-a-ha forced open her eyes. She lay buried beneath the hairy beast. Thick warm blood coating her body told her he had not been dead long. Even now she felt it trickling down the side of her leg.

Pushing with all her might, she rolled her would be killer off, and quickly stood. There at her feet lay the great wolf, her spear buried deep in his chest, the tip sticking out of his back. Sobs turned into hysterical laughter and back into sobs again. She had survived and conquered.

Slowly her nerves calmed. Her button nose wrinkling into a sneer. She kicked the lobo with her bare foot. "That's what you get for stealing my rabbit."

Mea-a-ha kicked him again for good measure. Then climbing on the wolf, she gripped her spear with both hands and wrestled it free.

She had defeated her enemy in battle. Often the girl had wondered how men felt after combat and now she knew. Where once huddled a frightened child, now stood a triumphant Apache warrior. Little Mea-a-ha had been tested and proved her courage. For the girl who was not worthless, the change was profound.

Amid the stark expanse, the scene was extraordinary. Mounted atop a huge garish beast, stood a small naked female, her brown skin coated in white clay, drenched in blood, with her long black hair twisted and matted about her thin body. Clenched in her bloody hands was a wooden spear held valiantly. Her lungs filling with air, The Apache girl stood fearlessly savoring the thrill of victory.

While lost in the moment, a noise on the rocks behind her suddenly brought her to attention. Whirling around she raised her weapon, unleashing a fierce battle cry. Her action was met with frightened high-pitched screams escaping from two wide-eyed Apache braves standing on top of the rock ledge.

The young warriors and Mea-a-ha stared at each other in disbelief. Knees shaking, one of the braves pleaded. "Evil spirit woman, we mean you no harm. Please don't turn us into toads."

Mea-a-ha recognized the two boys; they had grown up together. She breathed a sigh of relief. "What are you saying, Sauto? You know me."

Sauto squinted. "Meeeaa-aaa-haaaa?"

Astonished, Sauto turned to the boy next to him. "Mea-a-ha!"

The second boy craned his neck still doubting. "Meea-aa-ha?"

Completely confused, she spoke again. "Who do you think?"

Sauto spoke. "Sorry, but why are you standing naked on a wolf, painted white, and bathed in blood, like a crazy woman with a killing stick?"

Looking down at herself, Mea-a-ha was aghast. Painted as she was, she indeed looked like an evil spirit, albeit a naked one. Dropping the stick, she wrapped her arms about her. "It has been a bad day."

Nodding agreement, Sauto sympathized. "It has been a bad day for everyone."

Mea-a-ha had the boys wait while she retrieved her clothes and washed in a pool of rainwater in the rocks. With her damp dress on, and rabbit in hand, Mea-a-ha climbed to the top of the ledge where the boys had built a fire.

"Mea-a-ha, you scared us good."

Kneeling beside the boys, she blushed. "Let's make a deal. You forget what you saw and I won't tell anyone you screamed like little girls."

Looking uncomfortable, Sam Walking Bird finally spoke. "Can we eat your wolf?"

"Fill your bellies, but bring me the lobo's teeth for a necklace."

"Deal."

The Indians ate their meal atop the rock and talked. Being in the company of her own people calmed her nerves, but the boys were evasive about where they had been. Mea-a-ha got the idea they were hiding something and pressed for answers.

Sam Walking Bird told her he knew of Teowa's death and was sorry. It made their news all that much harder. He stared at the fire not wanting to continue. Sauto, who knew her better, took over. "Mea-a-ha, we have been riding with Cota."

A frown crossed Mea-a-ha's face. Cota was not the great leader that Sholo was. He was quick to anger. Cota was bold, but acted without thinking, endangering the braves that followed him. Many Apaches would die.

Sauto understood Mea-a-ha's displeasure but continued. "A few nights ago we were joined by a band of young braves. Daniel was among them."

Mea-a-ha jumped to her feet. "Daniel, my brother Daniel! He is just a child, how can you expect someone so young to fight?"

Ignoring her protest, Sauto returned to his story. "With them, we numbered twenty. Cota decided to avenge Sholo by attacking the Buffalo Soldiers while they slept, like Sholo was attached. It did not go well and many braves were killed or hurt."

Losing Teowa was too much, she couldn't lose Daniel. "What of Daniel? Where is my brother?" she screamed.

Sam Walking Bird tried to calm her. "We do not know. Early in the battle, he was wounded by a soldier's bullet. His horse carried him away. More soldiers charged in, some chased Daniel. The last I saw of him, he was clinging to the pony's neck."

Sauto broke in, taking over the story. "The battle lasted for a long time after he was shot. Finally we fled for our lives, with the Buffalo Soldiers in fast pursuit. They chased us for a long way, until we scattered in different directions. There was no chance to look for Daniel."

Filled with so much pain, she went numb, unable to accept anymore. "You are just boys. Cota has no right leading you against trained soldiers."

Taking offense, Sam Walking Bird protested. "We may be boys to you, but we are Apache. When the old men refuse to fight, it is left to us to defend our people."

"Defend what? There is nothing left to defend. You ride out from the reservation, killing and dying, and when you are hungry, you ride back accepting the white man's beef. The women cry as fewer of their sons return. If you want to defend the Apache, stay home."

Defiant, Sam Walking Bird stood his ground. "The reservation will never be my home."

"I will not argue with you Sam. Do you know where I can find my brother?"

Sauto hid his eyes. "If Daniel survived, he might do as you say and try to make it back to the reservation, but the soldiers will be looking for him. He will not be safe."

The gods had turned their backs on her family. Daniel was all she had left. The young Apache girl cursed in defiance. She would find him if it was the last thing she ever did. Without another word, Mea-a-ha picked up her spear and started walking. One girl, alone against the world.

Chapter -16-
Valiant Ride

The white desert clay faded to rust as sagebrush surrendered to yucca and prickly pear. Tall saguaros stood guard over barren ground where fractured rocks lifted from the red sand.

Like elsewhere, seasons changed, but the immutable desert did not. Each breath had to be won, making life here all the more precious. Beneath an indifferent sun, a small Indian girl walked alone.

Two days ago, Mea-a-ha had sat with Sauto and Sam Walking Bird. Since then she had headed straight to the reservation, but in the back of her mind, the words of Sauto kept returning. "The soldiers will be looking for him. He will not be safe."

Daniel was young, but smart. Teowa had always said, "Daniel is the smartest one in the family." If he were still alive, he would not ride into a trap. Indian trails were now guarded by soldiers, but secret places still remained known only to the Apache. "The Ruins!" Mea-a-ha cried aloud. "The ancient dwellers."

Half a day's walk from where she now stood, hidden in a small sandy ravine were abandoned dwellings of the stone builders. They were not like her beloved grotto of the Mogollon. These were mostly fallen walls, lost and forgotten. The deserted ruins lay in a shallow arroyo, covered with centuries of blowing sand and dried tumbleweeds, but a few rooms still remained.

Toward the back of the arroyo a small, mossy spring seeped from cracks beneath the weathered sandstone. In happier times, Grandfather had taken Mea-a-ha and her brothers to the red gorge. If Daniel were able, he would seek shelter under the stone walls, safe from the soldiers.

Wasting no time, Mea-a-ha changed direction. She quickened her stride. Before sunset, she prayed she would see Daniel.

Any distance is long when someone you love may be dying at the end. How Mea-a-ha wished she were on Major's back again. Memories of riding him alone in the mountain grotto awoke warm feelings. She tried not to think of Jacob, but visions of him lingered in her mind on her lonely walk across the desert. She thought of him now.

At first the memories filled her with rage, but as the days passed without him, she found herself longing for his touch. She had called him a murderer. He had called her a savage. Could either be forgiven? Did the answer matter? She had run away, and he didn't care or he would have come after her. A lump caught in her throat. She hurried on.

Small crumbling ridges of red stone protruded from the abrasive desert sand, creating a series of tiny plateaus. Climbing over the terraces of rock would tire the strongest man. It was far better to follow the trails of the antelope. More than any other animal, antelope loved to run. Their trails were meant for speed. Even if the trail didn't head in the direction you were going, another one would cross it that did. Thus Mea-a-ha picked her way towards the red gorge. Miles of hard walking on sharp stones had left Mea-a-ha's moccasins barely hanging on her sore feet. The fast pace she had managed since leaving the boys was taking its toll.

More than anything, her thin body needed food and rest. She told herself, tonight she would rest with Daniel. "Lord, please let him be there." Hunger gnawed at her stomach. She felt hollow. Dizziness brought on by lack of sleep blurred her vision, but she hurried on.

Yesterday, she had nibbled on the last of the rabbit – today only stink beetles. As the sun sank low, the rapidly cooling desert air cut through her ragged dress which hung loosely on her wasting frame. "Tonight, I will build a great fire for Daniel and me. Then I will be warm." Stubborn courage kept her going.

Her shadow lengthened before her until it was lost in the distance. A raven circling overhead had been her only companion for a long time. Was it a kindred spirit keeping watch, or just a hungry carrion-eater waiting for her to die?

Mea-a-ha was Apache. Like the red stones, she was part of the land. There was no arrogance of being anything more. The gringos rolled over the earth like the clouds, belonging nowhere, the bringer of storms. They saw themselves as gods.

Jacob was neither gringo nor Apache, but maybe a little of both. If clouds could dwell among stone, then maybe he did belong. She thought of his lofty Hollow. The raven cawed, and with a flap of his wings, disappeared.

Finally with the large, round sun resting on the horizon, Mea-a-ha stood on the rim of the red gorge, leaning weakly on her spear. Somewhere along the way, she had lost a moccasin.

Blinking her eyes, she slowly became aware that her journey was over. Small, square rooms built into the rock lined both sides of the shallow ravine. A flat barren lane maybe ten feet wide went nearly straight between the rows of fallen walls. Sand poured over the low window sills.

Stepping to the very edge, Mea-a-ha filled her lungs. "Daniel." Holding her breath, she waited. No answer. The girl yelled again and again, her voice rang shrill with desperation. Still, no reply.

Running along the edge, Mea-a-ha climbed down to the spring. If Daniel had come this way, surely he would have sought water. Dropping down over flat stair step stones, she knelt and dipped her hand into the clear liquid. Parched lips welcomed the healing drink. Slowly, her head began to clear.

Mea-a-ha searched the damp sand. There it was… a hoofprint, maybe a few days old. It was shod, but many of the horses Apaches rode were stolen, so the fact that it was not an Indian pony did not worry her. The metal scrapings of the horseshoes were easier to follow on the soft sandstone. A short trail led to a tall thicket of willows growing between two natural walls at the high end of the ravine.

Water from the spring kept the reeds green all year long. Pushing through the thicket, her heart leaped. Hidden in the dark foliage stood a beautiful pinto. It was a horse of great breeding; she feared it was too fine a horse for a young Apache boy. Then she spied the dried blood on its withers. She cried out. Daniel had to be here. If he was hurt bad, Daniel would have tried to make it to one of the lower rooms.

Along the bottom of the gorge lay several lodgings. Only one on the west side still had a roof. The fading glow of the setting sun cloaked its door in shadow. Fighting back panic, Mea-a-ha ran to the small dwelling and burst in. "Daniel!"

She had found him. The last of her family, her dear brother lay motionless on his stomach, clad only in a dirty loincloth.

Falling beside him, she feared the worst. Mea-a-ha stretched out a trembling hand and touched his leg; it was cold as stone. Tears burst from her eyes. "No!"

Throwing herself on his body, she cried, then stopped. His head against her cheek burned with fever. There was life. "Daniel, Daniel, it's me, wake up."

A twitch of his lips was the best he could do. Carefully, she rolled him over. Caked blood covered an ugly bullet wound above his heart. "Oh, Daniel."

Again his lips twitched. Finally he took a deep breath. "Mea-a-ha." His voice sounded like a small sleepy child.

"Be still, my brother. I am here."

"Mea-a-ha, did you see him?"

"Lie still."

"Did you see him?"

She brushed his hair. "See who?"

"My horse."

Mea-a-ha smiled. "Yes, my little brother. I saw your horse; he is beautiful."

"He saved my life. No horse soldier can catch him. They tried, but they couldn't. I call him Snow Raven because of his colors, and he takes wing."

"Sleep now. I am here."

"Mea-a-ha, don't leave me."

"Sleep."

Through the night Mea-a-ha sat quietly by Daniel's side. A sleepy fire crackled by the door, bringing warmth to the little chamber. Soaking torn strips from her doeskin dress in the spring, Mea-a-ha cleansed his wound the best that she could. With more leather strips, she squeezed drops of water onto his cracked lips.

Kneeling by her brother's side, Mea-a-ha tugged at her ragged hem. What remained no longer reached to her knees. The long journey and nursing Daniel left her garment little more than a tattered rag.

The Apache girl looked at the dismal room, and sighed. A beggar would have passed it by. Mea-a-ha pieced the torn fragments of her dress together, only to have it fall apart when she let go.

Everything she owned, she had on. The last of her kin lay dying on a dirt floor. No one knew where they were or would weep at their passing.

In the faint red glow, Mea-a-ha whispered in defiance. "We are not worthless savages. We do matter."

Curling next to her brother, she cuddled his head beneath her chin. They had fire and water. If Daniel's heart kept on beating, they would have tomorrow. For that she would trade all riches.

Through the night, the boy mumbled. Sometimes he knew what he was saying, but mostly he didn't. Daniel was young when the priest had come to the village, and he had learned little of the white man's tongue. Teowa had no desire; only Mea-a-ha had cared to learn. Would Jacob have thought her more a savage if she had only spoken Apache? Even now she did not want him to think of her that way.

An unseen animal scurried past their door, rousing the girl from a fitful sleep. Daniel coughed. Leaning close, Mea-a-ha kissed his cheek.

His breathing was stronger, but he burned with fever. Without help, he would not last much longer, but who would help?

Crawling outside to think in the fresh morning air, she remembered Sam Walking Bird saying Buffalo Soldiers had been wounded and killed. Troops would be watching the reservation closely wanting vengeance. The major trails would be patrolled. There was no chance of reaching the medicine man.

Soldiers had great medicine if she was to take him in, but they would heal him and then hang him. Such was the way of the gringos. Priests were great healers too, but they traveled far – no telling where they might be now. For an Apache, no place was safe except--Jacob's Hollow. The Hollow had magic all its own. Even Grandfather said it healed him.

Jacob had the knowledge of the white men. One thing Mea-a-ha knew for sure, Jacob would not kill them. Murder was not in his heart. This she knew beyond any doubt. Suddenly it hit her. Blinded by pain, she had refused to understand. If Jacob killed Sholo, it was because he had to. He was not a murderer. Jacob, Sholo, and even Teowa, were warriors, and warriors die. In battle, the dead do not cry murder.

In the clear morning light, the crimson stone of the grotto could not have been more brilliant. Even the dark green reeds glowed with vibrant light. As if summoned by the sun, Daniel's beautiful stallion burst forth from the thicket, shaking its regal head, saying let's go.

Mea-a-ha knew what she must do. No matter how dangerous, they had to try for the Hollow. On a fast horse, the Hollow was less than a two day ride. The stallion was swift. Mea-a-ha and her brother weighed no more than a man. If the soldiers spotted them, they would give them a race they wouldn't forget.

Among the reeds there were grubs; of these they ate plenty for strength. Near the spring, Mea-a-ha gathered wild rose hips from the thicket and packed them in damp moss, wrapped in the leather strips torn from her dress. Though bland, they would quiet a hungry stomach.

Keeping just enough doe skin for a loin cloth for herself, Mea-a-ha used the rest of her dress to bind Daniel's wounds tightly. This she also packed with moss because it was good medicine.

With care, she helped Daniel up a broken wall where he could slide onto the stallion's back. Climbing behind him, she took the reins. "Hold tight, my little brother. I will do the rest."

The spirited horse rose to the challenge, climbing effortlessly from the grotto. His quick gate was smooth. "Now Snow Raven, live up to your name and take wing."

If Daniel's wound did not open, they would make good time. All morning they rode without stopping. The paint seemed tireless. It was clear he was bred to the desert. When she gave the pony permission, he would burst into a run.

From time to time, Mea-a-ha slowed the horse's pace so Daniel could rest. Then she would spur the pony on. Near midday, the trio slipped into a narrow gully, cutting into the foothills. No water flowed, but green foliage hung on the damp stones. From this the stallion took nourishment. Fortunately, Daniel's wound bled very little.

What worried Mea-a-ha more was his appearance. He sat hunched over, with his mouth gaping. Sweat dripped from his head. Perhaps the ride was too much. She feared he wouldn't make it to the Hollow. Mea-a-ha pulled Daniel back against her breast. His head fell limp on her shoulder. "Rest, dear brother. I will not let you fall. All you have to do is breathe."

Daniel managed a weak grin. "Sister, you may ask too much, but I will try."

A lump stuck in her throat. "Just hold on. I am taking you to a very special place. It is a healing place where there is no war, there is always plenty to eat, and you can sleep each night without fear."

His eyes rolled towards her. "It sounds like heaven. Are there any soldiers?"

She kissed him. "No. But there is a mighty giant who protects the

171

Hollow."

"What is he?"

Mea-a-ha thought for a moment. "He is like a huge, black bear."

A weak chuckle escaped Daniels lips. "I met a being like that; he scared me to death."

She did not understand, but hoped to keep him talking. "Oh, he can be scary, but he is kind."

Exhaustion was taking its toll. The boy's words were barely audible. "It sounds like him…"

All her prodding could not wake the boy. Only the sweat on his face told her he was still alive. Infection was poisoning his frail body, and time was against them. She knew they must keep moving, but how much could Daniel take? Her choice might be the death of him, and it weighed heavily in Mea-a-ha's heart.

The vast desert that she once traveled on foot at an aggravatingly slow pace now fell away under the steady pounding of Snow Raven's hooves. The horse showed no signs of tiring.

Mea-a-ha squinted, scanning the horizon. For some time now a cloud of dust had been growing ahead of them. It was too big for a lone rider. Either a herd of wild horses or a cavalry patrol was heading their direction. Mea-a-ha guessed horse soldiers.

Reaching down, she patted the stallion's neck. "They may be big men with guns, but I have you, Snow Raven. How Daniel came by you, I do not know, but I do not think the gods intended for us to be caught this day."

There was no real trail to follow; whoever traveled the desert just picked his way around the scattered rocks and brush that loosely covered the rolling knolls of crumbling sand. If the soldiers stumbled across their hoof prints, it would be by dumb luck. A greater concern was not to make a dust cloud of their own, or worse, be spotted. Mea-a-ha halted in a shallow depression, sheltered by a tall saguaro growing on a broken ledge of stone. Here they would wait for the fearsome host to pass.

Moving close to the ledge, Mea-a-ha tied the stallion to a creosote bush and eased Daniel onto the outcropping. Here, shaded by a few spindly plants, she made him as comfortable as she could. With a little searching, she found a sharp piece of agate and cut a large chunk from a barrel cactus. As the dust cloud slowly grew in the distance, Mea-a-ha rubbed the moist piece of pulp on Daniel's burning face. It cooled him instantly, and his breathing grew deeper and more relaxed. She then pressed a piece against her dry lips, reveling to its touch. With no provisions, it was a welcome delicacy. The cactus brought life back into her, along with an awareness of just how tired she was.

Filling her small brown fist with another large fleshy chunk of cactus, she rubbed it over bare skin, washing away the dust. A slight breeze cooled the moisture on her limbs. Mea-a-ha lay next to her brother and kissed his cheek, then closed her eyes.

She had not intended to fall asleep, but some time later she woke with a start to the high whinny of horses just over the knoll. She glanced at Snow Raven. He was well trained and did not answer the call.

Rolling onto her stomach, Mea-a-ha dug her toes into the sand and crawled silently to a depression in the knoll above where Daniel lay. Pressing herself flat, she became nothing more than one of the many rocks that dotted the sandy mound. Her small, round face matched the stones in size and color. The hot sand burned her bare skin, but she dared not move.

Moments later, the horses came into view. They were soldiers – Buffalo Soldiers like Jacob! A white officer was in the lead.

Nearing her hiding place, a large black trooper riding beside the white officer raised his hand, bringing the patrol to a halt. "Whoa."

The officer turned to the man. "Sergeant Jackson, what the hell are we stopping for?"

"Jes' listenin' to ma' horse, captain. Buck don't make no fuss for nothing.'"

Rising high in his saddle, the black man twisted his thick neck, slowly scanning the terrain. Mea-a-ha held her breath as the soldier's intense gaze moved across her hiding place.

His eyes paused over her, but then started to move on when all of a sudden, a large flapping magpie landed on a rock just above her, proclaiming its arrival with a loud cry. The black man's piercing eyes pulled back to where she lay. Electricity ran down her spine. He sensed something wasn't right, and set his eyes to searching each rock.

"Jackson, we haven't got time to stop for every little birdie you see on the way. God, there are times you make me wish that son-of-a-bitch Keever was still here. He may have been an uppity pain in the ass, but he knew the difference between magpies and Injuns."

The black man turned to the officer with a braying laugh. "Captain Reinhart, we must a been out here on the desert too long iffin' yo' is missin' Jacob." He brayed again and the men joined in.

"All right, knock it off. This ain't a party. We're out to extract retribution for a dead trooper by killin' every stinking Apache we find off the reservation, not getting skittish over magpies."

Letting the comment pass, the black soldier glanced back at the magpie, pecking at the stone beneath its feet. The man's eyes then moved to the distant mountains beyond. He sat in silent thought. Reinhart followed the sergeant's gaze. "That's where he lives, isn't it? Somewhere up in those mountains. Crazy son-of-a-bitch. I still got some unsettled business with him. Maybe we will have to ride up there one of these days."

The sergeant's eyes narrowed and his voice grew cold. "Captain, bes'

173

you leave ol' Jacob alone. We follow your orders sure enough, but if ya 'spect us to back ya iffin' ya mess with Jacob, well... don't count on it. We all owe our lives ta him one time or another, and it's a debt we will pay."

His words clearly angered the captain who turned bright red and spit. "Move 'em out sergeant."

With the silent raise of his hand, the soldiers moved forward. No more was said.

After the last horse disappeared behind a knoll, Mea-a-ha took a deep breath, blowing the sand in front of her face. Beads of nervous sweat rolled off her back.

Jumping to her feet with an angry stomp, the small girl fumed over the captain's words. His hatred of Jacob bothered her more than his threat to kill Apaches. Instantly, she disliked him.

Before returning to Daniel, Mea-a-ha wanted to make sure the soldiers were well out of sight. Her cover behind the saguaros could vanish if the soldiers chose to take to the high ground instead of staying to the sandy bottoms. Hurrying on foot, Mea-a-ha followed their trail for some distance, skirting around several more knolls to where the soldiers committed to a long shallow ravine.

Feeling comfortable that they would not be able to spot them from this lower trail, Mea-a-ha turned and headed back. The conversation she had overheard between the soldiers kept playing in her head. The officer disliked Jacob, but the big soldier would die for him. Still she feared them all. They were soldiers – enemy of the Apache. They would kill Daniel.

Mea-a-ha stepped around a ledge of rocks at the opening of the ravine. Suddenly two large, powerful hands grabbed her from behind – one over her mouth and the other around her waist, lifting her off the ground. A braying laugh broke the silence. "What've we got here? Looks like a naked little Injun girl."

Sheer panic swept over her. Mea-a-ha twisted violently, beating at the big man's arm, but to no avail. "Settle down ya naked little rat."

Angered by his insult, she gave a final kick, then relented. Mea-a-ha had no choice and went limp in his grasp, surrendering to the soldier's will.

Cautiously, the big man eased his grip around the girl's stomach and let her slide to the ground. Turning her around, he kept his hand over her mouth. "Shhh... told the captain I wanted ta do some scoutin'. Don't want him comin' back. He'll kill ya, pretty little thing or not."

With his hand on the small of her back, he pulled her face close to his. "Will ya be quiet if I uncover yo' mouth? Savvy English?"

Wide, frightened eyes peering over the edge of his big, dusty black hand nodded yes. Jube slowly eased his grasp. The girl nervously licked her lips and took a breath. She was trembling like a captured bird.

174

Sitting back against a rock so he could look her in the eye, Jube continued talking in a soothing voice. "Thought I saw somethin' back there, but weren't sure. Expected a young buck, but never this."

He brushed the tangled hair from her face. "Ya know we kill Injuns off the reservation, don't ya?"

Mea-a-ha's heart pounded in her chest. Her moist eyes burned red, and she knew her fear was plain for him to see. It embarrassed her, and she blurted out. "You don't kill me."

The big soldier took a look at his catch. Her waist length tresses hung thick and shaggy like a winter coat. He gently petted her as though she were a soft, furry animal to be stroked.

With the back of his hand, Jube pushed her raven hair behind her shoulders, uncovering what lay beneath. The girl clenched her teeth, bravely defying his unjust liberties.

Slowly, he turned her full around, her tiny feet drawing circles in the sand between his big boots. She was young and pretty, less than a hundred pounds. Tight, smooth brown skin softened her lean body.

A narrow doeskin loincloth, crudely cut, hung precariously on a leather cord so thin it looked ready to break. He plucked it with his finger, half hoping it would. A tremor ran down her spine, but she did not cry out.

Jube drew a deep breath. With the tips of his thick fingers, he gently lifted a breast. They were round and firm, hinting that she might be in her late teens or early twenties.

His hand slipped back to the tiny loin cloth, letting the scrap of leather lay across his fingers as he toyed with it. A gentle tug, and the girl would be laid bare. She was only an Apache – a wild animal without rights. Enjoying her beauty was nothing more than picking a desert flower, but...but now there was Carmelita. She would not see this simple creature as mere amusement.

With a forlorn sigh, Jube released the tattered strip and took the girl's slender waist in a firm grip, that was meant to let her know who was in charge. She did not resist.

Lifting her onto her toes, he stared into her large sad eyes. They held wisdom and sorrow. Perhaps she was older. Still, she was as poor a savage as he had ever seen – not even coverings for her feet.

She was a most curious mixture of emotions, standing proud and defiant, yet trembling under his gaze. The girl was harmless, but maybe she knew how to find the warriors who had attacked them.

Jube made a frightening sneer. "Why shouldn't I kill ya? Beneath the dust n' dimples, you is an Apache plain enough. I could jes' snap yo' pretty little neck."

175

While he examined her, the girl had time to control her emotions. Her fear changed to indignation, then anger, and now courage. "You're just trying to scare me. You won't hurt me."

Lowering his voice to a deep husky growl, the huge black soldier hunched over the delicate waif, doing his best to look ferocious. "And what makes you think I won't?"

"Because Jacob would have no friend who could be so mean."

Jubaliah gave a start. Her words stunned him. "Huh? What? What is you sayin'?"

"You are Jacob's friend, no?"

The big man stared in disbelief. "Well, yes, but..."

Taking a breath, Mea-a-ha knew she must choose her words carefully. Daniel's life depended on her winning her freedom from this man. "I know you. You are Jube. Jacob has told me stories."

Mea-a-ha let the startling truth sink in. Then wetting her lips she went on, "I belong to Jacob; I am his woman. You must let me go."

Jube's hands fell away, a mixed expression of amazement and disgust painted his face. Unable to hide her humiliation Mea-a-ha cried out. "I know what you are thinking. What would Jacob want with a worthless little savage like me? Well, I will tell you, I did not always look like this." Pride welled in her breast. "I can write my name, and Jacob has taught me other words. If he found something of worth in me, then maybe I am not the naked rat you take me for."

Mouth agape, Jube was at a loss. Before him stood a primitive savage, yet despite a thick accent, she spoke with intelligence. "Forgive me Missy, but this is very strange. It's common for men out here to take squaws, but for a soldier to take up with an Apache in these times, I don't know. Loneliness can drive a man ta do crazy things." He let his eyes slide down her body. "If you is Jacob's squaw, what is you doin' bare ass naked in the middle a' the desert?"

Whatever she told him she knew must be the truth or he would see through her, but she did not have to tell him *all* the truth.

Carefully she explained, "Jacob's Hollow has been my home, ever since he rescued me, but that is another story. What you want to know is that I ran away from him after I learned he killed Sholo." Mea-a-ha's voice broke. "And my brother Teowa, he was with Sholo." Again she stopped to control her emotions. "But I was wrong to run away and I am returning to him." Holding the soldiers stare, she added. "He is looking for me."

Jube's eyes narrowed, and he took hold of her arms. "If he was looking for ya, he'd a found ya."

Tears tried to wash away the lie in her eyes, she jerked free. "He is too looking for me, but I said some cruel words." She covered her face and sobbed.

Jube's heart melted. The poor girl looked like a small frightened child waiting to be punished.

She was hurting. Taking her by the shoulders, Jube pulled her to him. "What is we ta do with you, little papoose?"

She dropped her hands by her side. "Please, if you love Jacob as I do, then let me go to him. If you owe him a life, then give him mine. Surely the great army does not fear one Apache so small."

Shaking his head, Jube protested. "We lost one of our own a few days back. The captain would have my hide."

'The Captain!' Mea-a-ha had already made her mind up about the mean officer. Her anger flared. "Am I to die because you fear your white master?"

The big man's lip curled, he swore under his breath. "I pick my battles, n' dyin' for an Injun ain't one of 'em."

Mea-a-ha tried to swallow her emotions. It would do no good to make the man angry. Unclenching her tiny fist, she pressed her finger tips delicately to Jube's chest, and softened her voice to that of innocent child. "Big soldier, please tell me, could you forgive yourself if you let your captain kill not just a girl, but Jacob's girl. He would enjoy that, wouldn't he? The captain would gloat and throw it in Jacob's face. Jacob would come down from his mountain and he might be killed. Maybe one small Apache girl does not matter, but is Jacob not worth fighting for?"

Blowing air from his lips, Jube smiled, then chuckled out loud. "Damn, I guess as I can understand what ol' Jacob sees in ya." Releasing his grip, he raised her chin. "A cute little thing that can talk like a southern lawyer."

Mea-a-ha's tear-stained face smiled back. "Jacob says I talk too much."

Jube laughed. "Ah, he always tellin' me to shut-up."

Hope rising, she folded his big hand in both of hers, and clutched it to her breasts. "You will let me go, yes?" She bounced on her toes.

The big man shook his head. "It will probably be the ruin of me, but guess I'll let ya go."

Jube rose to his full height. "While you is condemning me to a firing squad, is there anything else I can do for ya?"

With her freedom won, Mea-a-ha thought of her modesty and folded her arms across her breasts. "Jacob would not want you to see me this way. Can I have your coat?"

An amused toothy grin spread across his face. "No, ya can't have my coat, but if ya follow me to ol' Buck, there's an extra shirt in my saddlebags ain't no one gunna' miss."

For freeing her, Mea-a-ha allowed Jube the liberty of helping her into his shirt. She stood patiently while he finished the last button. His eyes sparkled. "I can tell ya, I've had worse duties. There, ya don't look so bad. At least this shirt ain't never looked as good." Jube, stepped back. "Now is there anything else you would like?"

Mea-a-ha stood bare feet together. Stretching out a slender finger towards his canteen, saying nothing, she let her helpless appearance plead her case.

Unhooking the strap from the pommel, Jube handed her the canteen and chuckled. "The shirt off my back n' my last drop of water. Suppose ya d like a little hard tack to see ya through as well?"

Taking the food, Mea-a-ha threw her arms around Jube's neck. "Thank you. If all soldiers treated Indians like you, we would have surrendered a long time ago."

"And us soldiers would'a gone back east, penniless n' missin' our scalps."

Jubaliah turned serious. "I don't know what Jacob has got himself into, taking up with an Apache squaw, but you bes' know this is as far as I can go. If someone else catches ya, there ain't nothin' I can do, so stay outta sight."

Mea-a-ha understood. He turned her about, and with a parting swat, sent her on her way.

At dusk, Mea-a-ha slowed Snow Raven to a walk. If he was tired, he didn't show it. Daniel was a different story; his breathing had become labored. Even the slightest bumps caused him discomfort. Time was critical. If they rode through the night, they could reach the Hollow by morning. How she yearned to be there. Jacob would know what to do. Mea-a-ha looked at Daniel, and her hopes faded. After pushing so hard on horseback all day, he had nothing left. The Hollow wasn't meant to be. She knew in her heart he would never make it. A full day's ride had been a heroic effort, but it was just too much.

Daniel needed to rest or death would take him, yet without medicine he would also die. To go on was death; to stay was death. Her heart was breaking. He looked so frail, resting in her arms. Gently she kissed his forehead. In response he slowly opened his eyes. "Mea-a-ha, I am so tired."

The decision was made. "We will stay here, little brother."

It had been a good race, but she had found him too late. Carefully, she lowered Daniel to the ground and laid him on his horse blanket. She placed the canteen to his lips, but he could barely swallow. While he rested, she built a fire. If he was to die, he would not die cold.

Beneath the full autumn moon hanging low on the horizon, Daniel, her little brother, the last of her kin, was slipping away and all she could do was watch him die.

For several weeks, death had been her constant companion. First taking Grandfather, then Teowa, and now Daniel. Would it ever stop?

Alone under the cold, dark desert sky, waiting for death to come again, Mea-a-ha truly felt like the last Apache. Wiping her cheeks, she filled with resolve. There would be no pity for herself. This night was for Daniel. He would not see the morning sun.

In the pale blue light, his skin looked ghostly. For the longest time, he didn't move, then he slowly opened his eyes and gazed up lovingly at his sister. "Mea-a-ha, I am sorry."

Folding his limp hand in hers, she kissed it softly. "Rest, my little brother. Be at peace."

Chapter -17-
Standing Tall

From his vantage point on top the high mesa, Jacob watched the riders for miles. Slowly the wavy forms of five horsemen emerged from the shimmering haze. The riders urged their ponies faster than was prudent on a waterless desert.

A trained eye can tell a lot about horsemen several miles away. Trailing Apaches across the open planes, Jacob had honed his talent for reading men at a distance. He could tell if they were looking for a fight or running scared. These men rode with arrogance; trouble was at the end of their trail.

The leader was easy to spot. He wasn't the rider way out front; that was the scout who was often as much a part of the desert as any four-legged critter that struggled for life beneath the unforgiving sun.

The next rider, slightly ahead of the rest, that was the leader. Damon Mathers rode with authority. He had a mixture of confidence that made a man ride easy, and a tension born of meanness, like a rattlesnake ready to strike. It was his way of cowering lesser men. His familiar big white horse made the call easy.

The cowboy to his side would be either the ranch foreman or a gun hand. The next two riders in line were most likely Wyatt and Raithe. Young and restless, they had not learned to sit easy in the saddle. As for the man next to Mathers, Jacob decided he was a gunfighter. He kept low on his mount, his head tilted, looking far ahead.

Mathers wasn't one to ride several days across the desert for a social call. There was going to be trouble. Had it been another time, another place, Jacob might have side-stepped them, but they were on his land. Worse they were making their way towards the cliffs. He wanted no more blood spilled in the Hollow.

The odds were against Jacob, but he was a man who lived by codes. He did what he believed was right and never let the fear of death change how he faced life. Eventually everyone draws the ace of spades. For him, it was not the shuffle of the deck, only how a man played his cards that counted. If death was dealt, he knew there was plenty for everyone. Whoever took him down would collect their winnings with a dying hand.

This lack of fear kept his head clear and his nerves calm when most men would be ready to snap like barbed wire stretched too tight. That's when men make mistakes. It often came down, not to the fastest, but the one waiting patiently for the other to slip. Sholo got too confident. Jacob was hoping Mathers would do the same. The other part of winning is dumb luck.

Following a worn deer trail down the back side of the dusty mesa gave Jacob cover. Mathers' advantage was numbers and a hired gun. Jacob's was knowing the lay of the land. Ahead of the riders was a sparse line of junipers along a dry gulch. The broken land was full of ravines that made access to the mountains difficult. He would use this to his advantage.

Small junipers provided cover, and the gulch was too wide for a horse to jump, making a natural barrier that would stop them from surrounding him. It wasn't much of an edge, but surprising them like this might take the starch out of Damon Mathers and let Jacob deal the first hand.

Once off the mesa, Jacob pushed Major. Getting to the gulch first was everything. Keeping the trees between them, Jacob made for the flat rocky rim of the narrow fissure. At this point it was little more than five feet deep, but it was enough.

Jacob patted Major's thick neck as he often did before a fight. "Okay, boy, let's go."

Over time Major had learned what it meant, and his big heart started pumping. The veteran soldier's heart started beating faster, too.

Moving cautiously up the gulch, Jacob watched the old horse's ears, knowing they would twitch long before he heard the approaching riders. It happened quickly. Within moments came the faint sound of hooves. Listening closely, Jacob matched their speed and direction, trying to guess where the riders would break through the trees.

The moment was now. Easing the Springfield out of the scabbard, Jacob rested it across the pommel and waited in the shadow of a shaggy juniper.

First came the sound of metal horseshoes clopping on flagstone, then the scout came into view. Jacob held cover, waiting for the rest of the party to catch up with the shabby man whose attention was fixed on the problem presented by the gulch. Mathers' voice rang through the sparse trees. "What do you see, Hamp?"

Hamp spit a chew of tobacco. "Looks like we will have ta head east a bit. Thar's a dry wash a blockin' the way." He spit again. "Dang place is filled with 'em. Guessin' that's why no one comes here."

Moments later the riders came into view, lining up along the opposite side of the gulch. Mathers looked irritated as he ripped off his hat and wiped his brow. "I want to get on with this business. How much longer to the nigger's shack?"

From the shadows rolled a deep voice. "You can't get there from here."

The riders jerked to attention, searching for the owner of the voice. Easing forward just enough for the sunlight to glint off the barrel of the big Springfield, Jacob continued. "In fact, you can't get there at all unless you've been invited, and you ain't been invited."

Everyone froze except the gunfighter, who angled his horse for a better position. Without raising the Springfield off the pommel, Jacob moved the large muzzle toward the man.

The hired gun was what Jacob expected; dark, angry eyes set deep in a face void of emotion. Gun-play would start with his hand. The gunman knew the distance across the gulch was too far for the fast draw of a pistol. Any advantage would go to the Springfield. He also knew this was no accident.

Jacob faced the gunfighter, matching his cold sneer. "You got a name?"

The question was meant to let him know who was in charge. Being questioned wasn't to the steely man's liking. His voice, hard and cold, hissed with the threat of death. "The name is Jake Flynn; ya heard of me...boy?"

His reputation as a troublemaker in the mining camps was well known, but why give him the satisfaction? "No, can't say as I have, but I suspect you've heard of me."

Flynn's stone face twitched.

Dismissing the gunman, Jacob turned to Mathers, who was still holding his hat in his right hand. To pull his gun, he would have to drop the hat, signaling his intent. Mathers wouldn't draw – not yet. Wyatt and Raithe had already been cowed by Jacob, nor would they make a move without their father. Hamp was grizzled and sun-baked. His face showed no desire to fight. In fact, he looked a bit amused. While the other faces contorted with hate, Hamp smiled broadly.

Mathers bristled, knowing he had lost the edge – something he prided himself on always having. He intended to get it back. "Well, that's not very friendly, neighbor."

"Wasn't intended to be. State your business, so you can turn around and get off my land."

Mathers spit and cast a glance at the man to his right. If Flynn noticed, he didn't show it. The gunfighter's icy stare remained fixed on Jacob. The next move was up to the rancher.

To Mathers, killing Jacob Keever wasn't murder. He was a darkie, an aberration of nature, no more than a rogue lobo that needed skinning. The fact that he existed in human guise only fueled Damon's hatred. He didn't understand why God created such a mockery of men. Didn't matter, he would wipe him from the face of the earth as he had many men before. To build his empire, he had cleared out entire families of Mexicans who could not prove ownership of their land. Those who didn't go meekly were found hanging in trees. This colored would be just one more carcass rotting beneath the desert sun.

Dusting himself with his hat, Mathers started again, only now acid etched his words. "Kind of uppity ain't 'cha, boy? I said ain't 'cha.. boy?"

Raithe giggled like a schoolgirl, knowing how his pa cut men down to size. Mathers continued, "Mind your place and listen well. I will get off your land when it pleases me. Right now it don't. In fact I think I will be running a few head of cattle on it just to show you I don't take kindly to a dirt farmin' darkie messing in my business."

Mathers looked around surveying the land and uttered a scoffing laugh. "Ya paid four-hundred dollars for ten-thousand acres of alkali dust." He laughed again. "Ya got took boy. Only a darkie. What was ya thinking under that wooly head? Did ya think owning land would make you white? Ya ain't nothin' boy." Mathers' laughed again. "Ain't even good enough for a nigger whore."

The truth burned. Mathers saw the pain flash in Jacob's eyes. He enjoyed whittling his adversary down, but it was hot and wasting time trading words with a colored was demeaning. Mathers wanted it over. "I will take pity on ya, boy. So ya don't go away empty handed, I got a shiny twenty dollar gold piece in my pocket ya can have for your patch-o-dust. From what I hear, you got a little water up in them cliffs and a cabin that might make me a decent line shack."

Reaching into his vest pocket, he tossed the bright coin onto the ground before him. "Pick it up boy, while I'm feelin' generous."

Lifting his gun off the saddle, Jacob leaned forward. "Yes, I've got water, a cabin, and a graveyard that ain't half full."

Mathers cursed at the black man's arrogance. "Give a darkie a medal and it goes to his head." His voice boomed. "There is five of us, boy or can't ya count?"

A smile broke across Jacob's face. "They say I killed ten times that number. That enough math for ya?"

Crazy with hate, Raithe, unable to contain himself, blurted out. "Them was Indians, n' Sholo was dumb as dirt, he couldn't even get rid of that stinkin' Mexican."

Mathers whirled on his son. "Raithe, shut up, ya fool."

Seeing his chance, Jacob butted in. "Your boys don't know when to leave well enough alone. This is the second time I've had to run them off my land."

A look of confusion clouded Mathers' red face. "What?"

Jacob grinned. He'd guessed right. "They didn't tell you how they turned yella' when I caught them beating a defenseless old man?"

Wyatt knew enough to keep his mouth shut, but Raithe didn't. "It weren't that way Pa, he got the drop on us jes' like now and he took our guns."

Crushing his hat in his fist, Mathers lost control. "You damn yellow cowards let this darkie take your guns and you didn't have the guts to tell

183

me?"

Everyone's eyes were on the boys--everyone except Flynn. Mathers' goading had caused Jacob to shift his gun to the rancher. The gunfighter's body sat motionless while his hand, hidden beside the horse, moved with blinding speed. Whipping his shotgun from its scabbard, he swung the deadly barrel toward Jacob. As Flynn thumbed back the broad hammer, fire and smoke exploded from Jacob's Army Springfield, blowing the gunman clean off his horse. Slamming a second cartridge into the breech, Jacob took aim at Mathers. Everyone froze.

Flynn groaned, but surprisingly rose to a sitting position, blood spilling from a hole in his shoulder. The icy expression on his face never changed. He was tough, Jacob would give him that.

Keeping the Springfield on Mathers, Jacob turned his head towards the gunfighter. "Bet you was thinking, 'dumb nigger' when you should have been thinking, 'Mounted Cavalry'." Jacob nodded to the scout. "Hamp, is it? Why don't you poke that dirty scarf hanging around your neck into that hole in his shoulder before he bleeds to death. And make sure it hurts. But first, toss his gun away."

Hamp still seemed amused by the whole affair, and without hesitation, climbed down and tossed the gunman's fancy pearl-handled revolver into the gulch, farther than necessary. If any friendship existed between the two men, it didn't show.

Facing Mathers, Jacob's expression drained of all humor. "You rode two days across the desert, for what? I ought to kill you right now."

Seething with fury, Mathers growled. "Bigger and blacker niggers than you have wound up kicking from trees. They won't let you get away with this."

Gripping the rifle tighter, Jacob exploded. "Who the hell is *they*? Do you think anyone gives a damn about a shot-up gunslinger, or some arrogant rancher and his spoiled brats? No one's riding clear out into the middle of this God-forsaken desert because you got your nose rubbed in the dirt. Hell, they will probably have a good laugh at your expense and tip another glass to the Hero of Apache Springs. So go crying into town and see what it gets you."

Mathers snarled with hate. "Maybe you're right. Maybe no one needs to know about this, but mark my words, you will be licking my boots and calling me master before this is over. Be lookin' over your shoulder, boy. I'll be coming, and I will have drovers and cattle when I do."

Pressing the Springfield to his shoulder, Jacob took aim. "What makes you think you'll be riding away?"

An evil grin twisted Mathers' face. "Because I'm calling your bluff. You ain't no murderer, an' that's your weakness. All you've got is a standoff. So we are backing on out of here, and you can sit on your black ass and watch."

With a curse to the man on the ground to get on his horse, Mathers turned his back on Jacob and arrogantly rode away. The others willingly followed. Jacob's finger tightened on the trigger, "Mathers!" He cursed. "Mathers, you turn and fight."

The rancher laughed. "Just bought yourself a day boy, but you ain't won nothin'."

He was right, it was a standoff. Jacob shook with fury. He played his hand. Mathers threw in his ante and then folded. There would be another game; only next time, Jacob was sure the rancher would shuffle the cards to his liking.

Releasing the trigger, Jacob cooled. He needed his head clear. Too many questions were left unanswered. It didn't add up. Why would Mathers ride all this way to kill a man he didn't even know?

The rancher hadn't heard about Jacob shaming his sons when he started out. He only knew about the money he loaned Luis Rincon, and he saw him with Rose that night in the saloon, but surely that wasn't enough reason for a man to hire a gunfighter and then spend two days crossing an inhospitable desert. It just didn't make sense. There had to be something more. All Jacob knew was the first shot had been fired, and trouble was sure to follow. Mathers would return with a vengeance.

Pulling back from the gulch, Jacob headed west. He wasn't on the trail without reason. Cold empty nights pacing the floor had brought him to the realization that without Mea-a-ha, his beloved Hollow would be just another lonely grave beneath the cliffs.

Fear that she wouldn't come back gnawed at him, but he had to try. His hope was that beneath her anger, love still burned. If he could fan the flames, then there was a chance.

Jacob slapped the reins. The storm had washed away her tracks, but he knew her only chance of survival was returning to the reservation, no matter how unthinkable. One trail led to the Warm Springs reservation. With luck, he hoped to catch her before she reached it. A Buffalo Soldier riding into the village alone would find a cool welcome, but if it had to be, he would ride to hell for this girl.

Chapter -18-
Starlight Trail

The fire burned low. Mea-a-ha held her little brother close and considered letting it burn itself out. Like Daniel, let the last quiet flames flicker and die. No, not yet! She could not bear the thought. In her heart the fire was entwined with her brother. If she could rekindle the flames, then somehow Daniel would go on living. Rising on one elbow, Mea-a-ha tugged a large clump of dry sage from the loose sand and tossed it on the dying embers. The dark coals awoke, igniting the dead brush, sending a thousand tiny sparks into the night sky. A wave of heat washed over them. Daniel stirred, taking a deep breath. He was still with her. Mea-a-ha nuzzled his head under her chin. "I am here, little brother, I am here."

Following a sandy trail through tall clumps of sage, Jacob rode through the night. Visions of Mea-a-ha pushed him on. His tired eyes rolled shut and the reins slipped from his fingers. Major, setting his own course, turned from the dried stream they had followed for several hours and climbed to the top of a brush covered knoll. His huge hooves dug deep into the sand. Maybe he sought the rabbit weed; maybe it was something else, but at the top of the mound, he stopped with a loud snort.

Startled, Jacob opened his eyes, searching his new surroundings. The setting autumn moon cast just enough silver light to reveal a landscape of countless knolls on a sea of sand.

Fighting sleep, Jacob forced his tired mind to see through reluctant eyes. Suddenly a flash of light blazed beyond a distant mound. It burst in the night sky and was gone. "Come on ol' boy, let's see who's keeping late hours way out here." Major stole a large mouthful of brush and started down the other side of the knoll.

Time lulled by. Muffled hoofbeats and the soft creak of worn saddle leather were the only sounds. Both horse and rider hung their heads, surrendering to the night.

Then a faint, familiar scent borne on the crisp night air tickled the gaping nostrils of the old horse snapping him to attention. His gate quickened to a trot. Waking to the sudden urgency of his old companion, Jacob's senses grew keen. Major filled his lungs, releasing an excited whinny.

Mea-a-ha's head lifted from the cold, white sand. "Major!" She knew his husky call as well as any human's.

Jumping to her full height, she searched the darkness. With her heart pounding, she raced blindly to the top of the knoll. Cries of emotion gurgled in her throat as she struggled through the deep sand in a frantic rush.

Reaching the crest, she jolted to a stop. The girl took a breath and held it, listening to the night. Her eyes, wide with expectancy, peered into the darkness... searching. Had she been dreaming? Was it just her grief on a cold empty night?

Then, out of the haze, like a ghostly apparition materialized Major's head, bobbing slowly side to side in the soft, pale light.

Running forward, Mea-a-ha threw her arms around the big horse's neck. "You found me." Tears filled her eyes. "You found me."

In an instant, Jacob stood by her side. Before he could utter a word, she clutched his arm. "Come quick, my brother is hurt bad."

For a moment, he thought she was mad with grief. Teowa was dead, but he allowed her to pull him toward the fire. There lay a young boy, barely in his teens. Jacob's eyes turned to Mea-a-ha, questioning. She continued to tug his arm. "My brother is hurt. Daniel is hurt. Daniel, my brother." Fearful eyes pleaded for a miracle. "Please help him."

Mea-a-ha dropped to her knees and cried. Jacob knelt by the boy and brushed sand from his hair. Beads of perspiration covered the child's gaunt face.

Acting quickly, Jacob pulled away the bandage, revealing the all too familiar hole torn by a heavy bullet. Sliding his hand under the boy's limp body, he checked for an exit wound. There was none. The slug was still inside, no doubt surrounded by infection. It had to come out. Without taking his eyes from the youth, he issued orders to Mea-a-ha. "Build the fire high and boil water. Coffee pot is in the saddle bag." She jumped into action, hope rekindling.

Jacob rested his knife on a stone with the blade in the flames, while he bathed the wound with water from his canteen. "Hold his arms, in case he feels anything."

Obediently, Mea-a-ha pressed Daniel's arms into the sand above his head and turned her face to the side, unable to watch. Water sizzled on the hot blade as Jacob cooled his crude surgical instrument.

Carefully he pushed the sharp knife into the wound. A deep pocket of pus burst, spilling onto the boy's chest. Daniel groaned weakly, but did not wake. Jacob washed it away with the canteen, then pressed the blade deeper, searching. The young boy's flesh was soft and cut easily.

Probing with the blade, he found a broken rib had slowed the bullet's entry. Fortunately, the wound was not deep. Twisting the knife, he removed the slug. Jacob let his incision bleed freely while he heated the blade again to cauterize the wound.

When the knife glowed red, Jacob laid the flat of the blade on the boy's skin. Flesh sizzled and a foul smoke stung Mea-a-ha's nose. She pulled farther away.

Next, Jacob tore his spare shirt into fresh bandages, and lifting the Apache child, carefully bound his wound.

Mea-a-ha took her brother's hand. "Will he live?"

Spreading out his own blanket, Jacob carefully laid the boy on his bedroll. "Only time will tell, but I'm betting on him. The infection is gone, he's young." Grinning, he added. "And besides, he's Apache."

Her bright moist eyes looked to Jacob with deep gratitude. Overwhelming emotions silenced her voice; she could only stare.

Wiping his hands, Jacob leaned over and squeezed her shoulder. "Get some sleep. Come sunup you are going to be busy cooking for a hungry boy."

****

Jacob was jolted awake by a pebble bouncing off his bony noggin. Jerking his head off his saddle, he spied Mea-a-ha with her fingers to her lips. "Shhh. Your snoring will wake him."

Vivid morning colors were already painting the gray dawn landscape. Had she sat there all night? Rubbing his head, Jacob feigned annoyance, trying to hide the joy of waking to Mea-a-ha's comical scolding.

The girl's cute frown quickly melted to a shy smile. She sat with her arms wrapped around her knees, and brown sandy toes peeking out beneath a large blue army shirt. Long raven hair fell loosely over her shoulders, flowing everywhere like dark water cascading over rounded stones. She was beautiful. But it was her large searching eyes that captured Jacob's heart. It had always been her eyes. With a gentle smile, she turned his world around. Her quiet light warmed his heart, allowing the giant man to finally breathe.

Much still lay between them, but darting glances could not hide a nervous delight of being together again. Sliding past Daniel, Jacob sat down by her side. "How'd he sleep?"

"Quietly. He looks much better." She leaned a little towards Jacob, a smile softening her concerned face. "Thanks to you."

Removing his hat, Jacob twisted the brim. "Mea-a-ha, I owe you so much more."

Her wispy voice drifted like soft music, edged with sorrow. "You took a life, you gave a life."

Jacob leaned towards her. Mea-a-ha's small body stiffened, and he pulled back. She was not yet ready to trust. Grief over Teowa still hurt as did Jacob's words that night.

Mea-a-ha looked away filling with emotions. She took a halting breath of air. Slowly her lithe frame began to tremble. Tears filled her eyelashes until they could hold no more.

Burying her head against her knees, the fragile girl struggled for control. Jacob gave her time. Finally, peering up at him through the moist corner of her eyes, her small voice quivered like a doubting child. "Did you come for me?"

He wanted so much to wrap his arms around her and hold her forever,

188

but he knew it was too soon. Jacob looked at the ground. "Yes. I want you to come home."

Turning away, she hid a thin smile. Mea-a-ha wiggled her toes in the sand and took a deep breath. "Many questions. What is home? Is it your home? Is it my home, until you say it is not? Am I just to be a guest again? Many questions."

Jacob nervously bounced the tattered, sweat stained hat on the end of his fingers, then grasping it firmly he forced it down tightly over his head, hiding his eyes. "Many questions."

A lifetime as a soldier had taught him to bury his emotions. She would never know how difficult this was for him. Jacob searched hard for the right words, then giving up, his voice came high and pleading. "Oh Mea-a-ha, I haven't thought that far. All I know is, I love you and I want you back. Isn't that enough?"

Holding her answer, Mea-a-ha pushed back the large blue sleeve and brushed the loose grains of sand, from the top of her brown feet. "You love me?"

She let the words linger. The girl had waited so long to hear them, but they came in the midst of pain. "Maybe it's enough. But things have to be different."

Jacob nodded in silent agreement, while Mea-a-ha continued. "Since I was a little girl, Apaches have lived each day not knowing if it would be the last. I want more than today; I want tomorrow. Can you give me tomorrow?"

Awkward as a schoolboy, Jacob fidgeted uncomfortably. "How can I give you what I don't have? There is much uncertainty for me, too." Lifting her chin on his knuckle, he searched her eyes. "Mea-a-ha, all I can offer is a desperate hope, and my love."

For a moment she sat quietly considering his words, then rising to her knees, she smiled and pressed her fingers softly to his chest. The Apache girl made her decision. "I am used to uncertainty. Love and hope are more than I have ever had. I will return to the Hollow."

Taking her delicate hands in his, Jacob held them to his lips. Her smell, her touch came rushing back to him, calming his heart. He placed a kiss in each palm, then slowly released her. It was as close as he dared for now. Mea-a-ha sat back in the sand, lowering her eyes. "Still many questions, but we have a new beginning."

His words 'I love you,' echoed in her mind, leaving her unable to think. She needed Jacob to give her time.

A weak cough from Daniel turned their attentions to the boy. Jacob stood, pulling Mea-a-ha up. "Well, you better start boiling some water to make a broth; I think he's going to need a little nourishment before too long."

The blackened pot sat balanced on the burning sagebrush, hissing steam. Jacob had ridden out in hopes of finding some game more nourishing than the dried jerky in his saddlebags.

While Mea-a-ha waited, she attended to Daniel, smoothing his shiny black hair. His color looked better and his breaths were long and deep. Jacob had saved his life; she would be forever grateful.

Now if she could get Daniel to leave the warpath. Out of love for her, Jacob would help her little brother, that was the kind of man he was, but he would never tolerate Daniel fighting the soldiers. He lived by deep-rooted codes that not even love could break. If he learned about the attack and a soldier being killed, no telling what he might do.

For now Mea-a-ha hoped Jacob would see Daniel as a very sick little boy who needed his protection.

Off in the distance two quick shots rang out. The rapid succession and high sound told Mea-a-ha that Jacob had used his pistol, which meant they would be having rabbit. It would be tender and cook more quickly into a broth. Daniel stirred, as the gunshots registered in his mind. "Soldiers!"

"No, Daniel." Mea-a-ha pressed his shoulder. "It's breakfast. Do not worry."

Opening his eyes, Daniel saw his sister's reassuring face. He returned a weak smile. "Where is my pony?"

Mea-a-ha laughed. "I sit up all night worrying over you, and your first thought is of your stupid horse. Just like an Apache brave or any man for that matter. Snow Raven is chewing on rabbit weed behind you and that is what you are going to have, rabbit, when it gets here."

Trying to raise his head, Daniel looked around. "Who fired the shots?"

With loving hands, Mea-a-ha pushed him back to the ground. "Well, he was a soldier, once! It is the big old bear I told you about. He found us."

The boy's head jerked up again in alarm. "Will he turn me in?"

"Lie still. Not if he ever hopes of putting his arms around me again." She laughed. "He removed the bullet from you last night. Thanks to him, you are alive."

Relenting, Daniel's head dropped back on the blanket, his eyes closed. A soldier-- not a good thing.

Daniel awoke to his sister lifting his head and touching a spoon to his lips. "Here, sip this."

The warm broth was delicious. Instantly, Daniel felt strength return to his body. Each spoonful was eagerly accepted. Rising on one elbow, he stared into the simmering pot. "Some meat too?"

Mea-a-ha laughed. "Maybe a little."

A spoon clanked against a tin cup behind him. "If he is doing this well, maybe we can risk a short ride to the foothills and camp by water."

The words were spoken in Apache.

Frightened by the deep rolling voice, Daniel twisted his head almost fearing to look. The first thing he saw were tall black boots, then looking up, way up, was the giant bear towering over him with a stern, hard face. "You!"

Daniel tried to pull away. The reassuring hand of his sister halted his retreat. "There is nothing to fear." Then she turned to Jacob. "And you stop your scowling; you're scaring the boy."

Taking the last sip from his cup, Jacob smiled. "Hello, Daniel. See you still got the pony."

Mea-a-ha was stunned, what did Jacob mean? Daniel lay speechless. Kneeling, Jacob rubbed the boy's head and gave Mea-a-ha a wink. "Daniel and I are old friends. We met when he and a fierce band of Apache braves got a good thumping from my friend Jube for stealing his little senorita."

Jerking his head from under the big man's hand, Daniel's face reddened. "Don't make fun of me."

With a hearty laugh, Jacob gave the boy's head another rub. "Not making fun of you, little buck. It turned out all right for everyone, and you got a fine horse."

Still not consoled, Daniel protested. "That Buffalo Soldier nearly killed me when he kicked me off my saddle. He hurt my friends real bad, and we didn't do anything."

Looking more alarmed than confused, Mea-a-ha interrupted. "You stole a girl? And Jubaliah kicked you? I will have more to say to him when I see him again."

Now it was Jacob's turn to look shocked. "Again?"

She flashed Jacob an angry sneer and rumpled Daniel's hair. "Yes, again. Jube and that stupid laugh." A smile of vengeful mischief danced in her eyes. "You are not the only one with secrets. Did you think this shirt was yours? He has seen more of me than you have, so if you want to have fun at Daniel's expense, go right ahead."

Daniel interrupted the banter. "Will you two quit petting me? I am not a dog."

Handing Mea-a-ha his cup, Jacob leaned in with a steely glare. "We will talk later."

Jacob stepped back, letting the bickering die away. "Well, what do you think? It sure would be nice to be near water. We've only got about a quarter of a canteen."

Water was important, but she feared it was too soon in Daniel's weakened condition. "I have Jube's canteen." She drew his name out as a parting shot. "Perhaps if we waited until evening and you made a travois to carry him."

Giving a sigh, Jacob agreed. He would have to travel a ways to find the wooden poles to build a travois, but she was right; it was too soon for the boy to ride.

The cool shadows of the sage grew long as the party headed for the foothills. Daniel had slept most of the day. The travois hung from Major's saddle. Mea-a-ha followed behind, riding Snow Raven. Several miles passed before she satisfied herself that Daniel would be okay if she took her eyes off of him.

Prodding Snow Raven forward, she settled alongside Jacob. After a time, he spoke. His voice was low and controlled. "Do you want to tell me about Jube?"

"Not much to tell. He captured me, but I convinced him to let me go."

The dark shadow of Jacob's hat in the evening light covered his face, but his voice hid nothing. "I bet you did."

The familiar mischievous grin returned as the girl taunted. "Are you jealous?"

"You said he saw more of you than I have."

Her smile broke into a wide grin. "You are jealous!"

Jacob tugged at his dusty brim. "Look, I just don't need the Army breathing down my neck."

"And you are jealous."

His eyes flashed. "It is one thing having an Apache squaw, it's another harboring a buck with a bullet in him. I am not stupid."

"And you're jealous."

Pushing his hat back, his eyes glinted like steel. "Do you want to tell me how Daniel got the bullet? The slug is from a Springfield rifle. That usually means army in these parts."

Answering his question was a bullet she hoped to dodge. "I will tell you about Jube, if you admit you are jealous."

The hat went back down over his eyes. "Play your games if you like, but remember people could get hurt."

The pain in his voice let her know that not all wounds came at the end of a gun. Trust still needed to be rebuilt, and her teasing wasn't helping. She felt ashamed. "I'm sorry. When Jube captured me, I was covered in dust and wearing a ragged loincloth, and my hair was a mess – not much to see. He decided he'd rather set me free than turn me over to the white officer who hates you, so he gave me his shirt and sent me on my way." Nudging her horse in closer, she touched Jacob's arm. "He doesn't know about Daniel."

For awhile they rode in silence as Jacob mulled it over. "Nothing but a loincloth. Maybe a little jealous."

Mea-a-ha ducked her head, letting her flowing hair hide her delight.

Chapter -19-
Second Chance

ℜain fell lightly, sending silver rivulets twisting down the small window panes. A soft light filled the cozy room, making it feel both safe and dreamy. Sitting quietly at the kitchen table, Mea-a-ha stared at the distant flashes of lightning. Sipping her tea, she reflected on the events that were changing her life.

The day before, she had returned to the Hollow riding by Jacob's side. Jacob had carried the boy into the small room and laid him in the bed. This giant man, tenderly holding her little brother like an infant in his arms, stirred emotions deep inside.

Putting down her cup, she slowly stood and pressed her fingers to the stone wall. Mea-a-ha needed to make sure it was real. She was home.

Major and Peaches stood placidly in the shelter of the barn chewing dry grass, while Snow Raven ran circles in the rain, defiantly kicking his heels and making erratic stops.

Leaning against a log saddle tree, Jacob watched idly. This wasn't the life that he planned, but he had made up his mind about Mea-a-ha, and he was going to make it work. This time he was determined he was going to do things right. The boy was a wrinkle that would have to be ironed out.

A squawking magpie embroiled in an argument with the squirrels over the dwindling supply of acorns landed on the windowsill outside the small bedroom and continued his indignant protest.

Daniel stirred and slowly opened his eyes, then bolted upright. Never had he been in a house before. The young warrior pulled the sheet close about him and studied the strange chamber with great fascination.

Over his head, heavy logs were suspended in the air. Thick stone walls surrounded him as he lay in the softest nest. Was this strange cavern the Hollow his sister had spoken of?

The boy's large eyes trailed around the room. Every detail was finely crafted. The giant man must be very rich. No Apache chief ever had a dwelling as fine as this.

From somewhere beyond the chamber drifted his sister's voice softly singing a strange song, in the white man's tongue. 'Oh my darling...' something. It was a strange name he could not pronounce.

Of greater importance to the starving boy was the beckoning aroma of food. Following his stomach's command, Daniel weakly struggled to his feet. A tight bandage around his chest was all he was wearing. Cautiously he stumbled towards the wooden door. Lifting a latch, he quietly peered out. To his amazement, it opened into an even larger chamber with more doors.

Mea-a-ha stood with her back to him, stirring a steaming pot from which the inviting aroma was coming. The scent of venison was sharp in his nostrils, not masked by heavy smoke like the meat cooked over open fires in the village. How strange it was that there were no flames.

Looking around the room, Daniel did not see the big man. He felt relieved. Bracing his hand against the wall, he made his way to his sister. She was still humming as she stirred the pot and did not notice him. "Mea-a-ha, where are we?"

Startled, Mea-a-ha gasped. "What are you doing up?" Taking his arm, she quickly ushered him to a kitchen chair. "Sit before you fall over, foolish child."

The wide-eyed boy repeated his question breathlessly. "Where are we?"

Mea-a-ha brushed back his long black hair and checked his complexion. "We are in the Hollow of healing that I told you about… Jacob's Hollow. Do not fear, you are safe here. He will protect you."

Youthful anger flashed across the boy's brow. "I don't need his protection. I am a warrior!"

Setting a bowl before him, Mea-a-ha bristled at his rebellious nature. "You didn't look like a warrior when he carried you in his arms like a baby. Eat and be grateful for his protection. The soldiers still hunt you."

She gave her brother a light cuff to the back of his head and handed him a spoon. "Now, eat the big man's food, unless you think you can hunt your own."

Deciding it was better to let the subject drop, Daniel toyed with the spoon, then set it aside and dug into the bowl of meat and beans with his fingers.

"No! Here we eat with forks and spoons. We are not savages."

She wiped his hand, then picked up the spoon for him. Mea-a-ha dipped it into the steaming bowl and placed it to his mouth. Famished, he allowed her to feed him. The taste of the delicious food put an end to his belligerence.

With a protesting groan, the heavy outside door swung open and the big man entered. Jacob took in the scene of Mea-a-ha leaning over the table, spoon-feeding her little brother. Daniel knew what the big man was thinking and grabbed the utensil from his sister. "I can feed myself; I am no baby." He sneered at Jacob.

Dancing past her brother, Mea-a-ha threw her arms around Jacob and gave him a big hug. Accepting the cheery embrace, the man smiled warmly. "Looks like your brother is a pretty tough kid."

The unexpected compliment cooled the boy's anger. Visions of his first meeting with the giant sitting on that great horse boldly blocking the trail all by himself, had made the soldier seem larger than life. He was only one man, yet Daniel remembered feeling that day as they rode into the clearing, that all five of them were no match for such a being. Daniel ducked his head. The boy both feared and admired the black man, wishing he could be that brave.

Filling his own bowl, Jacob sat down next to the boy, offering a friendly grin. "Your sister is a pretty good cook. We will have to watch it or we will both wind up fat as ol' Peaches."

With effort, Daniel managed a little smile. Maybe the man was okay after all.

Mea-a-ha sat across the table from the odd pair. Huge and bear-like, Jacob dwarfed the lean, naked boy. They looked odd indeed. She chuckled out loud.

Throughout the meal, Daniel kept looking all around at his new surroundings. Everything was marvelous. Occasionally he would look to his sister for reassurance, but quick shy glances at the big man beside him showed where his real interest lay.

Pushing his bowl away, Jacob turned to the Indian boy. "I put your pony in the corral with the other horses. They are old friends, you know. Snow Raven spent some time here when I built this place, so maybe it is like home to him. I hope it will be home to you."

Not waiting for an answer, Jacob stood and mussed the boy's long, shaggy hair before retiring to his padded leather chair for a nap.

A genuine smiled brightened the boy's face. He watched the big man cross the room, then out of the corner of his eye he caught his sister smiling. Quickly, Daniel bent his head over his bowl, hiding his face.

Resting on his bed, Daniel could hear his sister busying herself in the small room next to his. The sound of water being splashed about piqued his curiosity. Evening had come. Between his napping and Mea-a-ha's constant activity, they had little time to speak. With all that had happened, he needed to talk, or he was sure he would burst.

Suddenly his door swung open. Mea-a-ha danced in and knelt beside him. She touched her hand to his forehead and smiled approvingly.

Pulling back the blanket, she sat on the edge of the bed and removed his bandage. "Your wound looks much better. It is not oozing, but we will be careful."

Helping Daniel to his feet, she guided him to the little room. A single lantern hanging from the ceiling gave the room a warm yellow glow. There was a small, black stove with a bucket of water steaming on it. In the middle of the room was a large tub filled with more steaming water, but what caught Daniel's eye was something magical and strange.

Near the opposite wall stood a flat, shiny, oval object in a large wooden frame nearly as tall as him. In it he could see his reflection perfectly, as though there was another boy standing in the room. Seeing his surprise, Mea-a-ha explained. "It is called a looking glass, isn't it wonderful?"

For a long time Daniel stared at their reflection and marveled, not only at the mirror, but at his appearance. In the hot summer months Apache men often wore only a simple loincloth. Being naked was not something they thought about. Children were usually naked – boys often until they were ten – but looking in the mirror, he realized he was almost a head taller than his sister and no longer a child.

Mea-a-ha and the big man wore fine clothing, yet he was naked and it made him feel uncomfortable. Covering himself, he turned to his sister. "Why did you bring me in here?"

Guiding him towards the tub, Mea-a-ha pointed to the water. "I'm giving you a bath. Now sit in the tub."

Placing his foot in the warm water, Daniel asked. "Do you give the big man a bath?"

A startled laugh burst from Mea-a-ha, revealing the absurdity of the question. "No! I am sure it would not be acceptable in the white man's world. Jacob is a grown man."

Putting his foot firmly back on the floor, Daniel protested. "I am not a child, and I don't need a bath. Let me go to my room."

Mea-a-ha glared. "Get in the tub, little warrior. You are so filthy, you stink like wolf's breath. Now sit or I will call Jacob in to pick you up and put you in the tub."

The threat worked. Grudgingly Daniel settled into the hot water. "When I am well, you will treat me like a man."

Mea-a-ha gently scrubbed his back without responding. Daniel continued. "When I am well, you will take orders from me. You are a woman, and I am an Apache warrior who has fought the Buffalo Soldiers."

Whirling in front of him, Mea-a-ha grabbed his face forcefully, jerking his head towards hers. "Don't think that because you are bigger that you are all grown up. You will be taking orders from me for some time to come."

Anger flew from her eyes as her voice lowered to a harsh whisper. "And my first order to you, little boy, is to never say a thing to anyone about fighting soldiers." She glanced to the door. "Not even to Jacob. Is that clear?"

Lowering his eyes, Daniel muttered. "It's clear."

Mea-a-ha released his face and started soaping his long messy hair. "I know you want to be a great warrior, but for now it is safer if everyone thinks of you as a little boy. The soldiers don't forget when one of their own is killed." Mea-a-ha scrubbed harder, subconsciously trying to wash away the truth.

She realized Daniel must feel miserable. Holding the soap in her hand, she hugged him tenderly to her breast. Her voice grew more consoling. "For my sake, be my little brother for a while longer. There have been too many deaths in our family, and it would kill me to lose you."

Suddenly she thought of Teowa. Surely Daniel knew he was killed. Trembling, she started to ask, then realized that she would have to explain Jacob's part in Teowa's death. Young and rebellious, she feared Daniel would go wild with rage. Maybe later, when he got to know Jacob. She told herself he was too weak for bad news.

Taking the bucket from the stove, she poured the fresh water over Daniel's head. He took in a deep breath and sputtered. "Mea-a-ha. You said a boy, not a child. I don't have to go around naked, do I?"

Setting the bucket on the floor, she laid her cheek next to his. "No. But it might be best if we dress you in white man's clothes. You would be safer, I think. Maybe we should cut your hair."

Closing the door to Daniel's room, Mea-a-ha found Jacob lost in a cup of coffee. Softly she knelt beside him and laid her head on the padded arm of the chair. "It's been a very long day. Times are confusing for an Apache boy, but I think he likes you. Daniel just needs time to get past your having been a soldier."

Looking for reassurance she added. "He is a good boy, don't you think?"

Tweaking her nose, Jacob offered a smile. "With a man like his grandfather and a sister like you, I don't think he could be anything else. You are a most remarkable family."

Mea-a-ha smiled, happy for his kind words, then she timidly took Jacob's hand. "I cut Daniel's hair, but he needs clothes. White man clothes would be best. Do you think it is possible?"

Setting his coffee down, Jacob pulled Mea-a-ha into his lap. "We need supplies. Tomorrow I'm riding into town. It will take about five days. Will you be okay?"

She wrapped her arms around his neck. It seemed too soon to be separated again, but there was no other choice. Needs had to be met. "We will be okay."

"A lot of animal hides are stacking up in the barn. They ought to be worth something, and I still have nineteen dollars. We should be able to get the boy some store-bought clothes."

He hugged her tighter. "It will be slower, but Peaches and the buckboard are best for this trip. That will leave the two saddle horses for you and the boy. If something should happen, if there's danger, don't wait for me. Take the horses and ride out. Make your way to your people. There may still be some Mimbres at Warm Springs. I will find you there."

A shiver ran through her body, but Mea-a-ha tried to put on a brave face. "I know trouble is coming, and you worry about our safety, but I think we still have time. The Hollow is a very long ride for anyone, and its magic will protect us for a while longer. Make your trip. Daniel and I will be safe."

Picking up his cup, Jacob finished his coffee in one long gulp. "Then let's get to sleep. I'll need to get started early."

Mea-a-ha pushed back from Jacob's chest so she could see his face. "While Grandfather was here, I shared the little room with him. Last night I sat up watching my brother. Should I sleep there now so I can take care of Daniel?" Her words were slow and drawn out, asking so much more.

Rising from the padded chair, Jacob stood with Mea-a-ha bundled in his arms. "Yeah, I rode halfway across the desert to fetch you back here just so I could sleep alone. I think all those nights out on the trail changed things just a bit, but you knew that before you ever asked the question."

She couldn't help but giggle. "A girl has to be sure."

As he carried her through the bedroom door, she added, "Especially if she is going to sleep with a ferocious old bear."

Tossing her roughly on to the bed, Jacob gave a low growl. "Girl, you ain't sleeping with no ol' bear, you're his late night snack."

Mea-a-ha giggled as she landed on the mattress with a bounce. Scooting to the back of the bed, she hugged a fluffy pillow for protection, her bright glistening eyes peered over the top.

Jacob's heart raced, he knew this was the moment. His eager hand reached for her. The pillow flew across the room, hitting the wall. With a startled gasp, Mea-a-ha's night shirt quickly followed. She curled into a soft sensual ball, hugging her knees to her breasts waiting, a dark dreamy gaze whispered her heart's desire.

Jacob's muscles rippled as he jerked at his clothing. Tossing his trousers aside, he towered over her, filling his lungs with a hungry breath. His thick, dark, muscular body hinted of a powerful bear. A deep growl rumbled in his throat. "Come here, you."

Slowly Mea-a-ha uncurled, letting her slender legs slide across the sheets. Her arms fell away. Long soft strands of raven hair cascaded over the bed, fanning out in every direction.

Laying her head to the side, her large eyes closed. The dim flicker of the lantern cast a beckoning glow on her reddish velvet skin as she let her body snuggle into the soft white sheets. Jacob caught his breath. "All these years, I been chasing the wrong kind of Indians."

Mea-a-ha let a knee rise and fall. "You talk too much."

Leaning over the bed, Jacob joined her, his powerful hand feeling its way across her soft warm stomach.

Mea-a-ha rose to his strong caress. She buried her face in the sheets. Her mouth opened in a long slow draw of air. The Apache girl was a beauty to see, to touch, to taste. Everything about her overwhelmed his senses. Her fragrance was pure, free of perfumes and lotions.

She was real, not like Rosie. Rosie had been a child's fantasy. Mea-a-ha was a heart, a soul, a mind. She was a woman filled with emotions and desires, yet she was willing to give herself to him completely. He loved her for it, but this night would be for her. This night, and every night to come, he would make sure she knew that his was an act of love.

Gently he lowered himself onto her, kissing her lips. Her delicate body conformed to his. As his weight pushed against her, he halted, fearing he might hurt her, but reassuring hands pulled him tightly back. She trembled to each warm kiss. His open mouth brushed across her skin, smothering her in kisses. They couldn't come fast enough, she wanted more. There was no time to breathe.

With each pounding heartbeat his muscled body tensed, becoming hard as stone. Surrendering, Mea-a-ha lay soft as a helpless kitten. She gave a frightened gasp, cautioning him to be gentle. She was a virgin. He gave her time.

In innocent dreams, she had tried to imagine what it would be like, but never this. Her mind swirled with vibrant sensations, crashing over her like waves, each one greater than the last, washing away her thoughts.

Tiny fingertips dug deep, turning white against his back as unbounded joy pulled her from reality. This is what she had waited her whole life for, but never knew.

Her mind and soul were on fire. Breathing came in gasps to the motion of Jacob's body. Mea-a-ha rose to meet him. Each breath came shorter than the last until she thought she would surely suffocate. Suddenly her mind exploded with a thousand pin pricks of light. Her back arched against pleasure so overpowering it wiped every thought, only this moment remained.

Mea-a-ha collapsed helplessly, her body drained of every last bit of strength. Jacob settled next to her, his huge chest expanding and contracting in deep breaths.

Completely consumed, the Indian girl fought to hold onto her senses, her body and soul reeled. She felt herself slipping away, drowning in emotions new and strange. Physically and mentally exhausted, her body cried sleep.

Jacob kissed her and rolled to the side, cradling her tiny limp form in his arms. All was safe. She melted against him, relenting, falling into sweet dreams, she knew that from this day forth life would be forever changed.

Chapter -20-
Friends

A brisk, autumn wind sent orange and yellow leaves scurrying around the chopping block behind the little house. The Hollow would be in perfect order by Jacob's return, including a well stocked woodpile stacked neatly beneath the eaves.

Wrapped in a wool army blanket, Daniel watched his sister swing the large double-blade ax. She missed more than she hit, but she was getting the job done. Being laid up was boring for a young boy, and it did nothing for his disposition. "Lot of work to run a ranch."

The ax missed its mark, sticking deep in the chopping block. Mea-a-ha tugged on the long handle. "Yes, a lot of work."

"The Apache way is better. Not so much work. A man is free to go where he wants."

The ax would not budge. Mea-a-ha spoke between pants, "Do you see Apache women go wherever they want?"

He ignored her question. "Don't see why you couldn't have married an Apache."

Like most youths, Daniel had a hard time accepting change that did not fit with his view of how things were supposed to be. Since breakfast, the boy had been grumbling.

Mea-a-ha leaned her entire weight on the ax handle, breaking it free. Setting her mind to the task, she continued chopping.

"There are braves that would have you. What about Sam Walking Bird? He does not care that you are old."

A long growl of exasperation rasped through her tight lips. Mea-a-ha shook the two-bladed ax menacingly. "Sam Walking Bird is rightly named. With those long skinny legs, he looks like a crane, and he has about as much brains, following after Cota."

The boy rose to protest but was cut short. "If you think I am so old, and you have all the answers, then maybe you should be taking care of me. Our village is filled with pregnant women whose men will never return. Is that what you wish for me?"

"But, a soldier." Daniel stared into the distance. "I was there when he stood against five of us without fear. He has killed Apaches, I know it."

Mea-a-ha felt her stomach knot. Hiding the truth about Teowa burned deep, but she couldn't tell Daniel, not yet. "When you joined Cota, was not killing in your heart?" She did not wait for his answer. "Jacob is a good man. And he likes you, can't you try to like him?"

"Did he say he likes me?"

Dropping the ax, Mea-a-ha stroked her brother's hair. "Yes. He said you seemed like a good kid. Daniel, nothing is easy these days. The old way is gone. I love Jacob and he loves me. Grandfather wanted Jacob and me to be together. Be happy for me."

The boy's eyes searched his sister's face. "Grandfather liked Jacob?"

"He saw good in him."

A capitulating smile tugged at the edges of Daniel's mouth. "Well it don't seem right, a warrior being friends with a soldier."

Grabbing a tight fist of the boy's hair, Mea-a-ha pulled Daniel's face close to hers.

"Jacob is not a soldier, and while you live in the Hollow, little boy, you are not a warrior."

'A warrior.' The word that once brought pride to her heart, now cut like the double-bladed ax in her hand. For Daniel, being a warrior was a path that could only mean death, as it had for Teowa.

Turning away, the Apache girl buried her face in her hands. It was a truth that she had long denied, but now her brother's life hung in the balance. Mea-a-ha could not bear losing her only sibling. Daniel had to face the cold hard reality – a truth so bitter that all her people refused to see.

Mea-a-ha's voice welled with emotion as she slowly closed the distance between them. "My little brother, I know your hope for our people. It is in the heart of every Apache, but you can never be a warrior again."

"But..."

Silencing the boy's stunned protest, Mea-a-ha cupped his face, begging. "Chief Red Sleeve is dead and with him our last hope, if ever there was any."

Daniel railed. "NO! Beduiat still lives; we are not lost..."

The unbearable grief in his sister's eyes scared him. Her fingers clenched in her long hair, as she suffered the truth. Tears fell, but somehow she found the courage to speak. "Red Sleeve was a great chief with a thousand warriors, and he changed nothing." Her words came fast, born in desperation. "Beduiat has been driven from our land. The Mimbres are now fewer than the beads that hang from my neck. Look at the trees in the wind my brother; there are more soldiers than the leaves falling around you, and each season brings more. All the N'de combined cast a pale shadow that is quickly fading. It is over my dear, sweet brother. The day of the Apache is gone from this earth."

Tears rolled down her cheeks. "I cannot save our people. My only hope is that I can save you, the last of my kin." She wept openly. "Without you, I would die."

Daniel threw his arms around his sobbing sister as she crumbled against him. "I will never accept the end of our people, never! But don't cry. Please, don't cry. I will do what you want, sister. Just don't cry, you will see. Somehow, you will see. We will defeat the soldiers; we will drive them back, somehow…" The boy cried too.

His young heart ached. He held his sister tight, closing his eyes against a truth greater than his years could bear. "You'll see."

A strong, cold breeze shook the branches of the Aspens, swirling leaves about them. All they could hear was the rush of leaves. Leaves everywhere.

Mea-a-ha buried her head against the wind. Brother and sister put the unbearable thought from their minds. They needed time. It was too much to face in one day, or maybe in a lifetime. Daniel sniffed away his tears. "You will see."

Mea-a-ha gave the boy a tender hug, then turned away, wiping her cheek. Daniel's eyes followed his sister. He did not mean to hurt her. She was all he had left, the one person on earth who loved him, and he loved her. "Get busy, old woman. We have a ranch to work."

A much-needed giggle flowed like music from his sister's lips. Stepping close, she gave him a kiss. Then fearing more tears might come, Mea-a-ha quickly picked up the big ax and returned to the chopping block. Daniel sat back down on the pile of wood and wrapped his blanket around him. She would be okay. They were safe in their mountain hideaway.

Seeking refuge from the sadness, Mea-a-ha turned her thoughts to chores and to Jacob. He was a man who could survive the changing winds. This quiet giant was her desperate hope, the Hollow was their enchanted world. Yes, somehow they would survive.

Chopping wood kept her mind busy. With a strong swing, the ax fell, hitting its mark. The wood pile was nearly full, and Jacob would be home tomorrow. Life was good. She needed to hold to that thought.

Mea-a-ha raised the ax over her head, then suddenly froze in mid-swing. Horses! Horses in the Hollow! Turning to Daniel, Mea-a-ha frantically grabbed his arm and pushed him toward the old forest trail. "Hide!" Clutching the ax to her breast with both hands, Mea-a-ha raced through the back door and dropped below the window.

Fighting to calm her breathing, she listened intently. From near the hitching rail, she could hear the horses stomping and muffled male voices, but she couldn't understand the words. Boots scuffed on the porch. Then light steps tapped across the flat stones. A gentle rapping accompanied a soft, woman's voice. "Hello. Is anyone home?"

With a deep sigh of relief, Mea-a-ha sank against the wall. The knocking continued. Still shaking, the frazzled girl stood and leaned against the door. The knock came again. "Hello."

Gathering her courage, Mea-a-ha took a deep breath and cautiously opened the door, just a crack. A thin, beautiful Mexican girl dressed in fine clothes greeted her with a warm smile.

She carried herself with an air of grace and confidence which Mea-a-ha, visibly shaken, clearly lacked. The senorita stood with her feet close together in finely crafted boots that added several inches to her height. She was the most beautiful woman Mea-a-ha had ever seen.

By contrast, Mea-a-ha, her composure completely gone, her eyes puffy from crying, stood barefoot, clad only in Jube's worn army shirt, her tousled hair flecked with wood chips.

Embarrassed, the Apache girl tried to hide behind the door. The fine lady offered her hand through the small opening. "Hello. I would like to introduce myself. My name is Senorita Carmelita Maria Paloma Rincon." Motioning at the two boys behind her, "And these vaqueros are my escorts, Roberto, and Juan."

Prying her fingers from the ax, Mea-a-ha awkwardly accepted her hand. Carmelita waited patiently for a moment, then added, "Please do not be afraid. We are neighbors of Senor Jacob. Is he here?"

Mea-a-ha, regained enough of her senses to speak. "Please come in. Sorry for my rudeness, but you gave me a fright. When I heard your horses I thought you were bad men or sol... Then when I saw you were a beautiful girl, I thought maybe you were someone from town that Jacob once knew..." Mea-a-ha bit her lip. "Sorry, when I get nervous, I tend to rattle. Please excuse me, your question. Jacob went to the village of silver."

"Do you mean Silver City?"

The Apache girl nodded.

A look of concern crossed the Mexican girl's face. She started to speak, then stopped. Extending a slender hand towards a chair, she forced a smile. "May we sit and talk?"

Dropping into a chair, Mea-a-ha voiced her fears. "Is Jacob okay?"

Carmelita reached across and took Mea-a-ha's hand. "I do not know. Let me tell you my small part of the story, and we will start from there."

She gave Mea-a-ha a friendly squeeze and continued. "A messenger brought me word from a soldier that an Indian girl might be living here with Jacob. Do you know a soldier named Jubaliah?"

Mea-a-ha blushed and hid her eyes, wondering if Jube had told her everything. She felt embarrassed to be in his shirt. "Yes. He helped me because I am Jacob's woman, but I don't think he likes Apaches. He called me a naked rat."

Shocked, Carmelita stiffened indignantly. "Well, he will certainly answer for that, but try to forgive him. He is a soldier and he risked a lot to keep you safe. If you haven't guessed, I am Jube's girl. We met right here in the Hollow."

Taking a slow look around the room, Carmelita continued. "This house was only stone walls then... Anyway, believe me I know how soldiers can be. I guess you must, too."

203

A knowing laugh broke from Mea-a-ha's lips. "Yes. I know. It took Jacob a long time to accept me. He didn't like Apaches either. Maybe no one does."

A deep feeling of compassion softened the senoritas eyes. "It is difficult. My family has had our share of trouble with Apache raids. A warrior named Sholo nearly ruined us before Jacob...."

Pain colored Mea-a-ha's face. Carmelita stopped. "Forgive me. I did not mean to offend you. It is difficult for everyone. We Mexicans have had our share of trouble with the gringos also." Carmelita flashed with anger. "There is an evil Gringo who tried to take our land, but Senor Jacob helped us, and now this man, Damon Mathers, is out to get Jacob too."

Mea-a-ha's eyes grew large. "He told me nothing of this, but it is worse. Jacob humiliated this man's sons, protecting me. Maybe he is in much trouble."

Carmelita shook her head. "Then it is truly worse. A rider who came by our place said Mathers is in a rage. Jacob shot a gunfighter he sent to kill him. It is not good for Senor Jacob to be in town."

A shiver went down Mea-a-ha's spine. "Jacob told me none of this. He keeps much from me."

"I am sure he only wants to protect you."

Just then Roberto poked his head through the door and motion to Carmelita, who excused herself and joined him outside. They talked in low voices. After a moment, Carmelita returned to the table while the vaqueros hung in the doorway with their guns drawn. She gathered her thoughts. "Mea-a-ha, please understand that the vaqueros have taken an oath to protect me. My father would skin them alive if I were harmed."

She reached for Mea-a-ha's hand again. "There is a horse in the corral that belongs to a young Apache brave who once kidnapped me. They are worried that there may be other Apache warriors nearby."

Collapsing in tears Mea-a-ha pleaded, "There are no braves here, only a little boy. Please, I beg you, do not hurt my brother. He is young and injured. "

Sliding out of her chair, Carmelita put her arms around Mea-a-ha. "We will not harm your brother, but he must carry no weapons."

Speaking rapidly, Mea-a-ha tried to assure them. "No, Daniel is unarmed. I will get him. He is out back, but tell your vaqueros not to shoot."

Both women rose to their feet. Turning to her escorts, Carmelita spoke. "Boys, put your guns away. I believe her." The boys refused. Carmelita added. "She is Senor Jacob's woman." Roberto and Juan looked at each other, then reluctantly holstered their pistols.

"Come, Mea-a-ha, I will go with you." Roberto stepped forward protesting, but Carmelita brushed past him.

Minutes later the women returned with Daniel clinging to his blanket for protection. The boys stared at each other, unsure, then Juan stepped forward. Smiling, he offered his hand. Daniel grinned with relief and timidly accepted it.

After a moment, Daniel spoke, struggling with a thick accent. "I am much glad to see you, friend. The peace you once offered remains still." Then casting an embarrassed glance at Carmelita, he turned to his sister, speaking in Apache. "Tell the girl, I am sorry I stole her."

Laughing, Mea-a-ha wiped her tears and conveyed the message in English. Everyone laughed.

Ignoring their language barrier, Daniel and Juan seemed eager to be friends. Together, they wandered off to look at the horses. Roberto stayed on the porch, mindful of his duty, while the women sat inside sipping coffee.

Wrinkling her nose, Mea-a-ha put her cup down. "I don't really like coffee but Jacob does, so I keep a pot warm. It reminds me of him." During the conversation Mea-a-ha drifted to the window, idly touching her fingertips to the pane. For a long moment she stood there without speaking, her mind was elsewhere.

Watching as she sipped her own cup, Carmelita studied the Apache girl. Maybe because of her size, she seemed like a child. Being dressed in a man's shirt didn't help. She was cute and comical. Yet it was evident she had done a lot of living. Hope shined from her small, round face, but sadness lay deep in her eyes. "You are worried about Jacob."

Turning back to the table, Mea-a-ha wiped a single tear from her cheek. "He has no fear. A little fear is a good thing if you shoot a gringo." She slumped into her chair. "I asked him to go to town. Why couldn't he have told me there was danger for him?"

Setting down her cup, Carmelita tried to console the Indian girl. "There are some who would be angry when a black man shoots a white man, but people do not like gunfighters. Everyone breathes easier when one is taken down. It is also true that most people around here don't like Damon Mathers and will be quite happy about what Jacob did."

Hope flickered in Mea-a-ha's fragile gaze. "Thank you for telling me, there is much I do not understand."

It was obvious that Jacob had told little to the Apache girl about gringos or himself. Carmelita decided she was going to change all that. "Did you know that Jacob is a very famous hero?"

Astonishment washed across Mea-a-ha's face. "No! I did not."

"Well he is. People love a hero, and he will be treated kindly, unless..."

Her voice trailed off as she regretted her last word.

Mea-a-ha finished the sentence. "Unless he runs into the Mathers."

Standing up, Carmelita pulled Mea-a-ha up by both hands. "It's a big country. Let's be hopeful and have a few surprises when he returns."

Mea-a-ha stared blankly.

Lowering her voice to a whisper, Carmelita explained. "Men do not understand women. They provide food, but never consider that a girl needs much more to feel civilized."

The quizzical look remained on Mea-a-ha's face. "Me, civilized? That would be news to Jacob."

Taking a step back, Carmelita took a long look at Mea-a-ha, studying her up and down. "How many dresses do you own?"

Mea-a-ha tugged at the big blue shirt, knowing that the beautifully dressed Mexican girl would never wear such a thing. She felt embarrassed, but defended her precious shirt. "This is my dress."

"I knew it. Men never think that a woman might like something beautiful."

Hurrying to the door, Carmelita called, "Roberto, unload the pack-horse."

Returning, she pushed Mea-a-ha towards the bedroom. "Since we had to ride all the way up here to warn Jacob, I figured I might bring you some gifts. Jube said you might need some clothes. My closet is full, so I brought you several dresses I have no room for. We will make you so beautiful, Jacob will never go to town again."

Mea-a-ha bounced on her bare feet. "You brought real dresses for me?"

"Yes, and a lot more... shoes, a hairbrush, and combs. I am afraid they are more in the Spanish style than gringo, but you will look beautiful. All we will have to do is shorten them a little."

As the day lulled away, the three boys came inside, hoping for food. Behind the bedroom door they could hear whispers and giggles, but knocks went unanswered, or they were told to go away. Finally Roberto stoked the fire in the stove. "If we are going to eat, it looks like we are going to have to fix it ourselves. When women folk get together, they forget all about us men."

Juan and Daniel hurried off to the smokehouse and soon a meal of meat and beans was ready to eat. There's a camaraderie that all boys share. It is a love of adventure. So there was little eating and lots of laughter. Beans that fell on the table were soon being flicked back and forth. A riotous commotion was building when the bedroom door finally creaked open.

Carmelita slipped through and closed it behind her. She stood, waiting for silence, her face beaming. All laughter in the room died away. The boys realized the great secret was about to be revealed.

With an exaggerated wave of her arm, Carmelita flung the door open wide. As the boys held their breath, Mea-a-ha stepped timidly into view. She was wearing a peach-colored dress with white lace trim on the collar and sleeves. Several layers of crinoline filled out the skirt, making her tiny waist look even smaller. Her long, black hair was pulled back with a tortoise shell comb. Still an Apache, but no longer a savage.

Mustering confidence, she walked into the middle of the room and spun around. The boys were speechless; Juan gave a low whistle. Roberto shoved him and stepped forward. "Senorita, you are most beautiful."

Blushing, Mea-a-ha lowered her eyes and whispered, "Thank you."

Wringing her hand, the Indian girl turned to her brother, hoping for approval. "Do you like?"

Daniel stared at his sister for a long moment. Eyes full of wonder, he glanced toward Carmelita and chose to speak in Apache. "When I first saw this Mexican girl, I thought that no Apache woman could ever be so beautiful. Now I see I was wrong. Clothes change how we see people. Jacob will love it."

Breathing a long sigh of relief, Mea-a-ha hugged Daniel, then turned and hugged Carmelita. "He likes it. Thank you, Senorita. I never thought of myself as beautiful until now."

Taking Mea-a-ha's hand, Carmelita smiled. "Come, let's sit and see if these boys can cook. As the ladies took a seat, Roberto whispered to Juan. The boys suddenly grabbed Daniel by the arms and pulled him backwards off his chair, knocking it over. His blanket fell away, leaving him naked. Startled, Daniel looked at Carmelita and turned bright red. Everyone laughed. Pulling Daniel outside, Roberto hollered over his shoulder. "We will be right back."

Muffled laughter and scuffling came from the front porch. Less than a minute later, Roberto reappeared. Standing in the door with a huge grin, he waved his arm in a great circle, imitating Carmelita. Suddenly, an embarrassed Daniel, sporting a huge grin, was roughly shoved into the room by Juan. He was wearing brown corduroy trousers and a loose, white shirt. They were a bit large, but a tight belt held everything together. Except for his bare feet, he looked a lot like the other boys.

His eyes were fixed on his sister who rose in astonishment. Daniel defended his new look. "You said I should wear white man's clothes."

Mea-a-ha beamed. "You look handsome. Wait until Jacob sees you."

Returning to the table, Juan offered a final comment. "He looks real pretty, and we didn't spend hours hiding in no bedroom giggling." Daniel didn't understand his words, but decided it was his turn to do some shoving and knocked Juan off his chair. Everyone laughed again.

The boys' dinner was simple, but for Mea-a-ha, the new clothes made it a grand affair. She watched every move Carmelita made, wanting very much to be a lady.

Jacob always ate with both arms on the table. Carmelita ate with one hand resting in her lap. While Jacob wolfed down as much food as his spoon could hold, Carmelita took small, dainty bites. There was much to learn about being civilized.

As night fell, the boys rolled out their bedrolls in Daniel's room. Carmelita shared Mea-a-ha's bed. Laughter drifted across the hall from the boys' room and the girls did their own share of giggling about men, relationships and dreams.

As the wicks burned low, the chatter finally waned, giving way to chirping crickets and the sounds of the night. An old hoot owl took up his watch in the shaggy pine boughs over the little cabin. Secure inside the stone walls, the new friends surrendered to a deep sleep. It would be one more day before Jacob returned, but Mea-a-ha fell asleep feeling safe among her new friends.

****

The warm, golden glow from the morning sun peeking over the sleepy cliffs found Mea-a-ha wrapped in her night shirt, balancing on the porch railing with her feet dangling below. Her big blue shirt hung loosely about her; she liked the feel of the crisp, morning air on her bare skin. Everything was perfect.

To Mea-a-ha the Hollow was as a magical place, but magic is hard to touch, and at times she feared it might all disappear. Having neighbors made it seem suddenly very real. She kicked her feet in sheer happiness.

With the protesting moan of the door, Carmelita joined her on the porch and leaned over the railing. "It is a lovely place."

A cheery smile greeted the Mexican girl. "Today it is even lovelier thanks to new friends and wonderful gifts."

Hugging the large cedar column, Mea-a-ha pressed her cheek against the smooth wood and looked across the small meadow. "It is beautiful."

She looked to the road shadowed by aspens. Her face clouded. "But I fear that one day evil will find its way into the Hollow."

As gentle as the morning, Carmelita reached out a hand and played with Mea-a-ha's hair. "There is evil in the world, and maybe there is magic in these old woods, but I think that a lot of the magic can be found in a man named Jacob. He has strength. Trust in him. A good woman gives a man the courage to fight like ten. I think he has found that woman."

The kind words brought a flood of emotions. Mea-a-ha turned away, unable to speak. Stepping behind her, Carmelita wrapped her arms around the Apache girl in a quiet hug. Cheek to cheek, they stared across the bubbling spring. "It truly is enchanting."

Suddenly jumping to her feet, Mea-a-ha could not help but giggle with excitement. "Today Jacob comes home. Won't he be surprised?"

"Let's make it a very special surprise." Carmelita's eyes shone with ideas. Locking hands, the two girls bounced with joy. The conspirators soon laid plans for a great meal. They would roust the boys and send them off to search for wild potatoes, pine nuts, and elderberries.

Ever thoughtful, Carmelita had brought sacks of sugar and flour. There was much to do, and of course the biggest decision of all, which dress should Mea-a-ha wear?

Morning passed quickly with cleaning and cooking. Before midday the boys returned. Roberto carried a sack of wild potatoes and a smaller one of acorns. Juan found elderberries and service berries growing near a tiny spring. Using his sombrero as a basket, he filled it to the brim.

The greatest prize was brought by Daniel. Not able to keep up with the other boys because of his wound, he rested quietly on a shaded log in the forest, waiting for them to return. When a wild tom turkey had the misfortune of wandering into the clearing, Daniel beaned him with a rock. The boy had his sister's arm.

With Carmelita taking care of the final food preparations, Mea-a-ha slipped away for a long soak in the copper tub. Afterwards, the girls retreated to the bedroom once again. Evening was coming on, and everyone kept peering out the window, hoping to see Jacob.

As the waning sun bathed the humble home in a warm, red glow, the creaking of the old wagon and lumbering hooves of a tired horse could finally be heard filtering through the trees. Jacob brought the buckboard to a stop in front of the barn.

Climbing down, he dusted himself off, then gave Peaches some oats and headed toward the house. Extra horses in the corral told him they had guests. The quality of the animals told him it was the Rincons.

Before he reached the porch, the front door opened bringing Jacob to a quick stop. A petite girl in a white dress covered in lace backed out, pulling the latch behind her. Her face was hidden by her neatly combed hair as she shut the door. The last rays of the sun lit the white dress with a dazzling brilliance.

For a moment Jacob thought it was Carmelita, but the girl appeared slightly smaller. Releasing the door handle she whirled to face him. Her bright eyes flashed. "Mea-a-ha!"

Dumbfounded, Jacob stood in disbelief, his hat dropping from his hand. Growing wonder on his astonished face was all the answer the girl needed. She took a tiny step forward, folded her hands and waited.

With long, quick strides, Jacob crossed the distance between them. Still in shock, he took Mea-a-ha's delicate hands in his and stared.

The giant man swallowed several times, but words would not come. His heart was pounding. Mea-a-ha's eyes sparkled with an impish grin, she sugared her words with feminine charm. "I think this is where you tell the girl she is beautiful."

Jacob shook his head in disbelief. "Beautiful seems to come up short, but until they invent another word just for you, darling, you are the most beautiful girl I have ever seen."

Taking her in his arms, Jacob held her tightly. "Now, do you want to tell me what the hell has been going on while I have been gone?"

Giggling, Mea-a-ha pushed away. "We've been busy. We will talk while we eat. Let's go inside. Dinner is on the table."

Laughter echoed through the Hollow as shadows lengthened. All through dinner, a clamoring of voices rang like music with everyone talking and joking over each other.

"I'll take another slice of turkey, please." Jacob motioned to Daniel, who did his best to pass the heavy plate. The big man still scared him just a bit. "So, you killed this bird with a rock. You're just about as amazing as your incredible sister."

Reaching over, he mussed the boy's hair; it had become a joke between them. The boy grinned as he pushed the man's hand away.

Looking across the table to Mea-a-ha, Jacob could see the joy in her face. They had caught him completely by surprise. The bountiful dinner, a house full of people, Daniel's clothes, but nothing compared to Mea-a-ha's transformation. It wasn't just the dress. She carried herself with grace. A side of her that animal skins and alkali dust had hidden burst forth like a spring flower. He couldn't take his eyes off of her. All he wanted was to be alone with the dark-eyed maiden. Carmelita could see it.

With a nod to the boys, she started gathering plates, then turned to Mea-a-ha. "These noisy amigos and I will clean up. Why don't you and Jacob get some fresh air on the porch."

The couple didn't need any more encouragement.

As Jacob pulled the door shut, Mea-a-ha curled her arms around his neck and planted a passionate kiss on his lips. The two held each other tightly in the dark for a long time before easing their embrace.

Giving him one last quick peck, Mea-a-ha turned in Jacob's arms and leaned her back against his chest. "It has been a wonderful day."

Stars filled the moonless sky. The old owl hooted while a soft breeze rattled dry leaves on the stone porch. "Carmelita is so nice."

Jacob rested his chin on Mea-a-ha's head. "You smell great."

"Don't you think Daniel looks wonderful in his new clothes?"

"Do you really think that's what I've got on my mind?"

Mea-a-ha turned again and giggled. "I know what you've got on your mind."

Suddenly lifting her up until her feet dangled in the air, Jacob kissed her long and hard.

Squirming loose, Mea-a-ha whispered. "We have guests."

"I'll saddle their horses."

Mea-a-ha playfully slapped his chest. "Be good. I wouldn't have this dress if it weren't for my new friend."

Ignoring her plea, Jacob took her in his arms again. "I'll saddle our horses; I need to be alone with you." He buried her in kisses and was winning her over. "Honey, let's go to the barn." Suddenly somewhere in the dark, Mea-a-ha heard a faint whimper. "What was that?"

Between kisses Jacob mumbled. "Ignore it, it's just a mangy dog."

She broke free. "You got me a dog? Oh, Jacob, let me see."

Turning, Mea-a-ha ran through the darkness and crossed the little bridge to the wagon with Jacob trailing behind, uttering groans of protest.

"Where is it? I can't see."

Giving up, Jacob stepped to the buckboard and struck a match. "It's in the box."

"In a box? There are many boxes!"

"Yeah, I also got you six chickens and an old rooster."

"Oh, Jacob!"

"Didn't want you thinking our ranch was dumb."

The dog whimpered even louder. Mea-a-ha opened the lid on a wooden crate tucked under the wagon seat and lifted out a small puppy. "Oh, it's just a baby!" She hugged it to her cheek. "And you left it out here all this time. Shame on you."

Jacob howled in pain, dropping the match. "It's an outdoor dog."

Hurrying towards the house, Mea-a-ha hollered over her shoulder. "No, he is not."

Left standing in the dark and knowing full well he had lost to a mangy mutt, Jacob turned to put the hens away before returning to the house. At least the chicken coop would finally serve a purpose.

With his arms full of packages, Jacob kicked the door open with his boot. Sitting on the stone floor with Carmelita and the boys in a circle, Mea-a-ha was playing with the puppy who was wrestling her finger. Looking up, her eyes danced. "I love you. Thank you so much."

Jacob shuffled to the table and dropped his load. "I would ask you where he is going to sleep, but I don't think I could bear the answer."

Turning to Daniel, Jacob tossed him a package wrapped in brown paper and twine. "Here son, now you got two outfits."

Mea-a-ha handed the puppy to Carmelita and went to Jacob, giving him another kiss. "You had enough money?"

"Brought more back than I started with. Got a good price for the hides. The pup came from a lady who had a bigger litter than she could handle. The chickens and a sack of grain was a gift from a farmer who thinks I'm some kind of ---well..."

Mea-a-ha's voice lowered, "Hero? Yes I know. Carmelita told me everything. We are going to have a talk about keeping secrets."

Jacob ducked his head. "It ain't the sort of thing you talk about."

Chapter -21-
Soldiers

He stood for some time in front of the looking glass. It was a marvelous thing. In the desert you had to find a calm pool of water to see your reflection, which wasn't easy, and it sure didn't compare to the perfect image he now saw.

Standing as straight as he could, Daniel tried to convince himself that he was a man. Of course he wasn't as tall as Jacob, but then, nobody was. He was taller than his sister and she was full grown, so he couldn't be a boy, and if he wasn't a boy then he must be a man.

Content with his logic, Daniel turned his attention to the new clothes. Not the ones Juan had given him, these were the duds that Jacob bought just for him. Duds is what Jacob called them. Maybe the big man wasn't so bad after all. He wasn't really a soldier anymore, and he sure made Mea-a-ha happy.

Daniel stepped closer to the looking glass. The light blue shirt and canvas pants made his skinny body look bigger. Licking his hand, Daniel tried to make his hair lay down, but no use. His sister had really chopped it. Next time he would cut his own hair, and she wasn't going to bathe him anymore, either. He was a man, and he would tell her so if she wouldn't get so mad.

By tipping the looking glass in its wooden frame, he could see his boots. Of all his new clothes, the boots were his favorite. Big, black boots like Jacob's.

The bark of a puppy, followed by light footsteps on the porch alerted him that his sister had returned. Quickly he dashed into the big room, just as the door opened.

With the brown and white puppy tugging on her hem, Mea-a-ha stumbled breathlessly into the room. A broad smile lit her face. "You look very handsome. My baby brother is growing up."

He wasn't really sure that was a compliment. "I am grown up. Bigger than you."

"Well, who isn't?" She reached up and straightened his collar. "Jacob will be impressed."

The boy stifled a smile and followed his sister to the table. "You don't think he minds me being here, do you? I mean, he hasn't taken his eyes off you since Carmelita and the boys left. He hasn't said anything about me being in the way, has he?"

Holding the breakfast plates in her hands, Mea-a-ha settled in the wooden chair next to her brother. "Jacob likes you. No one rides a week through the desert to buy you clothes if they don't care about you."

"He is nice to me, but he don't say much, other than to tease me."

Setting the plates on the table, she kissed Daniel's cheek. "That's his way. He doesn't say much to anybody, but I'm working on him. Give him time. After you heal, I am sure he will expect you to work by his side and go hunting with him. You will see."

Lost in thought, Daniel took one of the plates and placed it in front of him, then slid one across the table for Mea-a-ha and set the last one at the head of the table for Jacob. "About me healing, I thought I might stay through the winter if that's okay. I have my own room and all. I won't be in the way."

Giving his hair a brisk rub, Mea-a-ha screeched in exasperation. "You live here. Just try to leave."

The boy heard what he had hoped for. He had a home. "Stop messing my hair."

"You let Jacob do it."

"He's just playing. You do it all sugary."

Returning to the stove, Mea-a-ha retorted. "That's what girls are, sugary."

The door opened again and Jacob stomped in. "The mornin's are getting a bit nippy."

With a sharp bark, the puppy bounced over to greet him. Jacob leaned over and gave him a pat. "Hey, Frog."

A feminine screech interrupted his petting. "Don't call him that. His name is Friendly."

"Ah, he bounces like a frog. Besides, what kind of name is Friendly for a dog?"

Shaking the spatula, Mea-a-ha defended her choice. "It is a good name. He is friendly."

Taking his place at the head of the table, Jacob muttered. "Mathers shows up and we're suppose to say, 'Sic 'em, Friendly.' That'll scare 'em."

As she set a flapjack in front of Jacob, Mea-a-ha frowned. "Don't joke about the Mathers. Maybe they won't come before winter. Maybe by spring they will have forgotten."

"Pass the syrup. They will come. But don't worry, me and Friendly'll get 'em." Jacob leaned over and patted the puppy. "Won't we, Friendly?"

His teasing was going too far. "Jacob, please, it's been wonderful since we returned to the Hollow. If you say bad things, bad things will come. Say it has been wonderful."

Jacob realized he was being insensitive. She was right; it had been wonderful since they returned. "Darling, it has been wonderful. You are more beautiful than a spring morning, and Ol' Friendly here has learned to pee outside. It is wonderful. Now please pass the damn syrup."

Out of the corner of his eye, Jacob caught Daniel watching him and gave a teasing sneer. "What you want, boy?"

"Damn syrup, please."

Her mood not fully restored, Mea-a-ha groaned. "His English is bad enough without you confusing him with swear words."

A sheepish grin met her wrinkled brow. "He said please."

Daniel slumped over his flapjack. "Don't know why we have to speak white man's tongue when none of us are white."

Taking her place at the table, Mea-a-ha saw no point in responding. Unable to ruffle his sister, Daniel turned to Jacob. "If these Mathers come, I will help you kill them."

Mea-a-ha's knuckles whitened as she clenched her fork. Jacob cast the boy a sad smile. "I know you will, but let's hope your sister is right. We need to think good thoughts." Reaching across the table, Jacob gave Mea-a-ha's hand a firm squeeze. "Friendly is a good name."

The familiar smile returned to her round face. "Pass the damn syrup."

****

"Easy, ol' girl; time to earn your keep." Jacob placed a gloved hand on Peaches' massive neck as he hitched her to the buckboard. "Besides, you could do with a little run."

Light footsteps on the small footbridge over the stream turned Jacob's head. Mea-a-ha took hold of Peaches' bridle and slipped her a leftover flapjack. Jacob gave Mea-a-ha a wink. "I'll forget about gathering hay; you can fill the barn with flap jacks and we will feed them to the ponies all winter."

Mea-a-ha stuck out her tongue. "You going to the seep?"

At the mouth of a nameless canyon several miles east, a natural seep provided enough moisture to grow a few acres of wild grama grass. No one knew it was there when they called Jacob a fool for trying to ranch in the middle of the desert. It was his secret, and someday he would have the last laugh. Jacob made repeated trips there to gather feed for the horses to hold them through the coming winter. "It's a good day for it. Don't know how many more we will have."

Looking past Mea-a-ha, Jacob could see Daniel timidly crossing the footbridge. He was trying not to be noticed, but curiosity got the best of him. Giving Mea-a-ha another wink, Jacob turned to the boy. "Could use a little help. Do you feel up to a ride?"

A big smile brightened the boy's face as he hurried over. With a shy grin, he climbed into the wagon, eager to ride in the wondrous contraption. Giving Mea-a-ha a kiss, Jacob climbed in beside him.

For the first mile, Jacob didn't talk, letting Daniel get comfortable with the idea of the two of them being together. The soothing gait of Peaches was like rocking a cradle. Overhead a flock of ibis squawked their way south, adding to the tranquil beauty of the changing seasons.

The occasional cry of red-winged blackbirds carried from a distant line of trees.

Being his first time on a wagon, the boy found it quite exciting. After studying the tack, Daniel finally spoke. "Is driving a wagon hard?"

"Well, with a team of six horses it can be a handful, but ol' Peaches knows where she's going. You just gotta remind her to keep moving. With a cheery grin, Jacob offered Daniel the reins. "Here, let's see if you can handle it."

The wide-eyed boy eagerly accepted. "You trust me?" He hadn't meant to sound so excited and ducked his head.

Jacob made light of it. "Of course I trust you, son. Now keep her steady while I get a little shuteye." Jacob scooted down in the seat and pulled his hat down low over his face, just to show the boy he really did have faith in him.

Encouraged by a new-found pride, the Apache youth sat straight with his arms held high. He took the task seriously. After all, he was a man.

For several miles Daniel gave his full attention to driving the wagon. Today he felt grownup. It seemed like he had always been the youngest. He was the baby of the family, the smallest brave, even smaller than his new best friends. Mea-a-ha treated him like a child, always scolding, but living with Jacob, being part of his family elevated him in the eyes of Roberto and Juan.

It was Juan who asked Daniel if Jacob was now his father. Daniel didn't know how to answer; he was too young to know his real father. He was embarrassed to admit it, but Jacob was like a father, taking care of him, feeding him, buying clothes and protecting him. But Jacob was a soldier and he was a warrior, well at least an Apache – it was difficult.

The wagon wheel dropped over a rock with a bump. Jacob raised his hat. "You're doing fine, son." He lowered his hat and continued his snooze. A smile lit the boy's face. Jacob had called him son.

As Jacob expected, Daniel worked hard by his side cutting grass. There was good stock in the kid, and it was easy for Jacob to take a real liking to him.

After awhile, Jacob had the boy rest while he continued cutting the hay. The wagon was already nearly full of grass. They would be home sooner than he expected. When enough had been harvested to make the trip worth while, Jacob loaded the scythe and pitchfork in the buck board.

Wiping his brow, Jacob pulled his hat down low and retrieved his holster from under the bench seat. As he strapped it on, he caught the boy eyeing the gun. Jacob took the pistol from the holster and handed it to Daniel. "You ever handled one before?"

The gun felt heavy in his small hand. "No." His answer was solemn. He felt its weight, then handed it back. "Are you fast?"

It was the kind of question any boy would ask. "Oh, there are men a lot faster."

For a long moment, the boy struggled with his thoughts. "Sir, the warriors on the reservation tell a story about four Apache braves who came upon a cowboy. They tried to talk with him, but he drew his gun and killed all four of them before they could loose, a single arrow." He paused, thinking about it. "There is not much Indians can do against a gun like that. Sir, can you shoot that fast?"

Jacob kneeled down to eye level with the boy. "Is something bothering you son?"

For a moment Daniel look away, then finding courage, he returned Jacob's gaze. His voice was slow and hesitant. "Roberto and Juan were bragging on you. They say you shot a gunfighter, so you had to be fast. They said you are a famous hero, but they would not say what for; so I guess that you, being a soldier, maybe you killed Apaches." The boy's voice trailed off, fearing to hear the answer.

Now Jacob understood. This is what had been troubling the kid. Killing Apaches was a wall that held the proud little Indian at a distance. Daniel was young and saw things in black and white. If Jacob killed the boy's own kind, how could they be friends?

Jacob had promised Mea-a-ha that he would let her tell Daniel about Teowa in her own way. This question was about other Apaches and needed to be answered. He put his big hand on the boy's shoulder. "Son, seeing what's right ain't always easy. There are a lot of ways for a man to kill – some honorable, some not. A man may murder for greed or even pleasure. He may kill to save his life, or someone else's. He may have to kill in battle. In the end, a man has to ask himself if the killing was just or if it was murder. I know it's hard to understand, but it ain't always easy to tell."

"Sir, have you killed in battle?"

The sounds of distant canons echoed from the dark recesses of Jacob mind. "Daniel, this country is big. The vast desert here is like that tiny fleck of white on Peaches' nose. Once, when I was no older than you, a great war was fought, the likes of which no Apache has ever seen. There were men marching as far as the eye could see. Terrible machines of war, guns called cannons, as big as houses, mortars, and iron ships that floated on vast rivers, all spitting fire and death. The earth exploded, and the land was ripped apart. Black smoke blotted out the sun as brothers against brothers, and fathers against sons, fought for what they believed was right.

In one battle called Bull Run, a number of men far greater than all the Apaches that have lived since the coming of the white man, died in a single day. The land flowed red, and I was a part of it."

Jacob wiped his eyes, trying to erase the terrible vision. "After the war, they sent us black soldiers west. The skirmishes with the Apache didn't seem like battles, not the kind I knew, but men still died. I wish I could tell you I never killed anyone, white or red. All I can tell you is that wars end, and men must find a way to forgive. I guess the hardest part is forgiving yourself."

Jacob lowered his head and thought of Teowa. He was trying to be honest with the boy, but the secret of Teowa was a lie in the middle of his truth.

Jacob gripped Daniel's shoulders with both hands and looked into his eyes. "Son, the color of our skin does not make us enemies. That we were both warriors doesn't make us enemies. After the terrible war, fathers and sons came together because they knew each had followed his heart. Do you understand?"

For awhile Daniel stared at the ground thinking. Finally he looked up. "It is confusing, but I think I understand." With that, Daniel climbed into the buckboard. A smile lit his face. "Can I drive?"

The supper dishes were put away, and Mea-a-ha turned down the kerosene lamp hanging over the table. Tiptoeing to Daniel's room, she found him sleeping like a baby. She then hurried to the back door. This time of the evening, she would often find Jacob sipping his coffee under the tall cedars behind the house, basking in the last rays of the setting sun.

Coming up behind him, she wrapped her arms around his burly chest and rested her cheek against his back. "You wore the poor boy out today."

Jacob took another sip of coffee. "We need to tell him about Sholo and his brother."

Mea-a-ha stiffened.

Stepping in front of Jacob, she folded her arms tightly about herself. "Please Jacob, not yet. Let him learn to love you like I did. It was love that held us together. Let him have that first."

Lifting her in a great bear hug, he held her tightly cheek to cheek. "It rips a hole in me. I feel like I'm lying."

She nuzzled his neck, pretending not to hear. With a sigh of resignation, Jacob gave her a kiss. "We will wait, but I fear we may come to regret it."

"Friendly was so cute today."

Jacob laughed. "You're the one being cute just to change the subject. And I guess it's working."

Giggling, she kissed his ear. "It usually does. There are always reasons to be unhappy, but it is never a good thing to do."

With a final hug, Jacob released Mea-a-ha, chuckling about her wisdom. "If I could bottle you, no one would ever be sad."

Mea-a-ha cocked her head with a quizzical expression. "I do not understand."

Giving her a swat on her backside, Jacob scooted her towards the door. "Good. It's comforting to know there are some things you don't know."

She smiled, it was one of his funny compliments. "Are you coming in?"

"No, while there's still light, I'm going for a walk in the woods to clear my head." With that, he headed down the old forest trail. Mea-a-ha leaned in the doorway and watched him disappear. Daniel would have to be told, but there had been too much pain. Now was a time to heal. She turned and walked through the house.

A beautiful full moon danced on the bubbling spring while the sun faded to a warm, crimson glow. With her chores done, Mea-a-ha wandered to the front porch and gazed at the tall cliffs beneath the amber sky. In the perfect evening light, the gentle beauty seemed to be for her alone.

She thought of how wonderful her life had become. When Mea-a-ha left the reservation with Grandfather, she feared she would be all alone, wandering in the desert without family or hope. Never could she have imagined so many blessings.

Completely lost in reflection, Mea-a-ha did not hear the riders pass the stone gate until it was too late. A horse neighed. The Indian girl looked up. Soldiers! She gasped. Soldiers were in the Hollow.

The serene tranquility turned to horror as a stern white officer leading five black troopers rode right up to the hitching post. A terror that had haunted Mea-a-ha since childhood loomed before her... Soldiers!

Trembling, Mea-a-ha pressed herself against the stone wall, wishing she could fall through it. Her heart beat wildly. There were no demons more terrifying to the Indian girl's mind. Soldiers meant death.

The grim men stared without saying a word. Mea-a-ha braved a tiny glance, into the white officer's snake like eyes, then turned away. She struggled to breathe.

A hungry grin on the man's vile face curled in a sneer. "Looks like Jacob took an Apache squaw, just like Mathers guessed. Figures the nigger couldn't do any better."

"Captain!" Jubaliah protested.

"Keep quiet, sergeant. I will handle this."

Jubaliah turned to Mea-a-ha. "I am sorry miss..."

"I said I will handle this sergeant, that's all."

The captain could hardly contain his sick amusement over the girl's frightened state. "Squaw, you speaky' English? We're looking for some filthy Apaches that murdered a soldier."

He leaned closer. "And where you find one Injun, you find more – like a pack of snarlin' dogs."

Clutching her throat, Mea-a-ha mumbled. "No! I am the only Indian here."

Leaning back in his saddle, the captain broke into a wicked grin. His voice was mocking. "Nooo! Jacob's squaw wouldn't lie, would she? Injuns steal anything ain't nailed down, but they don't lie."

His foul words hit her like fists. She was a woman, and he treated her as if she were an animal. All she could do was shake her head no.

"No, of course not. Stinking Injuns don't lie." Suddenly he spit at her feet, his face contorted in anger. "Then tell me, you lying heathen, why Mathers' men saw Jacob buying boy's clothing, when it seems he prefers putting you in dresses?"

With a loathsome snort, he turned to the men. "Bitch looks almost human."

Mea-a-ha cringed with terror. This captain came to kill Daniel. She pulled herself from the wall. "You go... Go now and take your dirty words."

Reinhart scoffed, "The little dog yaps."

He had his fun, and now his cold heart hungered for blood. "Sergeant, have the men search the house. Kill any Indians you find, and kill this filthy squaw if she gets in the way."

Shamed that he was a part of this, Jube sickened, but he had his orders. "Come on men, search the house, but don't touch the girl."

Jubaliah met Reinhart's angry glare. "Anyone." He repeated himself. "Anyone, who touches the girl, answers to me." He started to climb down when the door slammed open. Jacob rushed past Mea-a-ha with a Winchester held at ready. "Stay in your saddles. The lady told you to go."

The soldiers froze. Jacob's rage hardly contained, eyed his friend. "Jube, stay in your saddle, you're leaving."

Stunned, Jubaliah pleaded with his old friend. "Jacob, we have our orders."

A higher order came in the sound of Jacob pulling back the deadly hammer. His hand shook with fury.

Shouting profanities, Reinhart broke in, "You uppity black son-of-a-bitch, put the gun down or we will take it from you."

Jacob pushed the barrel towards Reinhart. "No need, I'll give it to you, one bullet at a time. There's plenty for everyone."

All color drained from Reinhart's face.

Jubaliah shouted. "Jacob, don't be a fool."

"Stay out of it, Jube."

"We can't. We're soldiers following orders. You taught us that."

Every muscle in Jacob's body readied for a fight. For the first time in his life, he wanted to kill. "This is personal."

Jubaliah angered. "Damn right it's personal. Them murdering savages attacked us while we was sleeping. Young Toby was on guard. When he cried out ta warn us, they put a bullet right through his chest. The boy died in my arms. A boy that idolized you. Or has your love of

Injuns made you forget?"

Jubaliah's words struck hard "Toby dead?" His mouth wrenched in pain. Jacob cast a glance at Mea-a-ha. The guilt on her face told him she knew how Daniel got his wound. She had deceived him.

Visibly shaken by the news of Toby's death, the rifle slipped from Jacob's shoulder, bolstering Reinhart's courage. "It's over, *boy*. Drop your gun. Out of kindness to the squaw, we will take the buck into the woods to kill 'em."

Mea-a-ha gripped Jacob's arm. "Please, Jacob."

The big man glanced to the girl he loved. She had lied, but behind those terrified eyes was a woman who had proven her worth. He raised his gun. "If there's killin' in the woods, it won't be Apache."

Reinhart screamed. "Ya damn fool, you'll die with the heathens."

Jacob pushed Mea-a-ha out of the way. "Talk's over, captain. Order the attack you're famous for. Only this time, the Indians win."

Jubaliah threw his arms wide. "You would kill yo' own soldiers?"

Only his respect for Jube stayed his gun. "Jube, this is my last word. You talk about being soldiers. You are supposed to uphold the law. I taught you that too. So uphold it. You are on private property. Bring me a court order, and you can search my home. But until then, get off my land, or I'll kill the first man who puts a boot on the Hollow."

A friendship since childhood faced the final test at the point of a gun. Their eyes locked, unwavering, both men knowing they would kill if it came to it. Jacob could see the sense of betrayal in the eyes of his old friend. "Jube, I am truly sorry about Toby, he was a good kid, but this is my home."

Once again Reinhart scoffed. "Niggers don't own land."

The veins in Jubaliah's neck bulged. He sat straight in the saddle. "This one does. So if you want to search without a warrant, you will have to do it yourself."

Reinhart went livid. "Sergeant, I order you to search this house."

Jubaliah sat motionless, resolve chiseled in his stone face. "Damn your hide, sergeant." Reinhart turned to the men searching for obedience. He was met with total silence as each trooper stared forward. Air hissed from Reinhart's snarling lips. He wanted to kill them all, but it was beyond his power. He screamed. "You call yourselves soldiers, you're not even men."

Hatred burned in his eyes "I gave you an order, you damn sons-of-bitches. Are you too black to understand the meaning of duty?"

An awkward hush turned the seconds into eternity. The grim troopers swallowed their shame. Reinhart scoffed at Jube. "So these are the heroes of Apache Springs!"

Someone had to give or die. Without a word, Rolley pulled his reins, and backing away, rode from the Hollow. One by one, the others silently followed.

Staring in disbelief, Reinhart turned on Jube, who remained. "You don't deserve your stripes. You're a bunch of black cowards. Never should have made you soldiers. Might as well come with women."

Reinhart turned to Jacob. "I will be back with a search warrant and when I do, we will tear this place apart stone by stone." Twisting in his saddle, he once again faced Jube. "And if these darkies are too cowardly to follow orders, I will bring real soldiers."

Whirling his horse around, he hurled one last threat at Jacob. "I don't forget." Then, he turned on Jubaliah repeating his threat. "I don't forget." Spurring his mount, the captain raced from the Hollow.

Jubaliah lingered, his head hung in shame, his tired voice fell from his lips in a raspy whisper. "Good lord Jacob, do you know how much those men risked for you?"

The rifle dropped to Jacob's side. "Jube, this is my family."

"Jacob, don't know what's got into ya, willin' to kill yo' own men over an Injun. I hope she's worth it."

Pulling the reins, Jubaliah backed away. "When I come back, you'll have ta kill me, Jacob."

Jacob stepped off the porch. "Jube, what if you were standing here, and I was sitting in your saddle hunting Mexicans?"

For a moment Jubaliah hesitated, then spurring his horse, the stricken soldier disappeared into the dark.

Lowering the hammer, Jacob slumped against the log column. "You knew."

Frantic, Mea-a-ha fell against him pleading. "Daniel didn't kill your friend. He only had a bow and arrow. Please Jacob, not Daniel."

"I don't blame the boy, he did what he believed was right. It was you, hiding the truth that nearly got him killed, got us all killed tonight."

To her surprise, he took her in his arms. "No more secrets. If this family is going to survive, we must trust each other."

Turning to the door, Jacob ushered Mea-a-ha back inside. Daniel was crouching by the inner wall. Quickly he stood up, hiding his tears. Mea-a-ha reached for Daniel, but he stepped past her to Jacob. "You didn't let them take me."

Gently, Jacob ruffled the boy's hair. "It's okay."

Daniel tried to be brave, but suddenly fell against Jacob crying. "No. Everybody is in danger because of me. It's my fault. I'm sorry, I'm sorry."

Jacob took the boy into his arms. "Listen to me, son. This has got nothing to do with you. Nothing at all."

Lifting his head, the doubting boy searched the big man's face, desperately wanting to believe. "Son, that white officer and a nasty rancher are gunning for me. They set their sights long before I met you.

They're just using you as an excuse. This is my battle. I'm the one who is sorry."

Mea-a-ha was stunned. "Jacob, is this true?"

Rubbing the weariness from his eyes, Jacob turned. "Do you think the army would ride several days across this God-forsaken desert, just for a wounded boy? No. It's me they're after."

Jacob balled his fist. "But why, I don't know. One thing is for sure, Reinhart didn't come all the way out here on his own. Somehow he is tied with Mathers, I just don't know how."

Mea-a-ha shook her fist. "They are bad men, filled with much hatred. That is why."

Looking down, Jacob sought to make sense of it. "No. Hatred will drive a man to kill, but they are going to too much trouble. It just doesn't make sense." He gave a sigh of resignation.

Reaching out, Jacob gathered his family in his arms. "Next time they will come to kill. So set your mind to it."

Wringing her hands, Mea-a-ha clung to hope. "Maybe the Buffalo Soldiers will not follow his orders?"

Jacob kissed her gently on the forehead. "The soldiers are good men. When they believe Reinhart has the law on his side, they will follow orders, even if it means killing me."

"Jacob, where can we go?"

With a gentle smile, Jacob brushed Mea-a-ha's hair from her face. "We can go to bed, it's late."

His reasoning was lost on the girl. "But there's so little time. We need to leave now."

"No, Mea-a-ha. It is time to stand. If a man does not draw a line beyond where he can't be pushed, then he can never hold anything of value. We are family and the Hollow is our home. It is worth fighting for."

Finding courage, Daniel threw back his shoulders. "I will fight."

Jacob took the boy's head in his hand and pressed it to his chest.

Mea-a-ha reached for Jacob's rifle. She had never held one before, but now she bravely clutched it to her breast and stared into Jacob's eyes. "We will all fight."

The hour grew late. Mea-a-ha lay curled in Jacob's leather chair, wrapped in a warm blanket. Daniel had fallen asleep in front of the fire, so Jacob carried him to bed, then returned to his task of cleaning the guns. Spread on the table were four rifles: Jacob's army Springfield, the two Winchesters he had taken from the Mathers' boys when he first rescued Mea-a-ha; and Sholo's Winchester with the beadwork in the stock. They would be cleaned and loaded for the coming battle.

It had been a very long day. Jacob wanted to scoop Mea-a-ha up and go to bed, but it was not to be. Life doesn't happen in equally measured doses. Sometimes it comes like a gale force wind that never lets up. So it was beneath the dark pines of their quiet home.

As Jacob finished loading the last gun, the whinny of horses once again filtered through the thick stone walls. Every muscle in the big man tensed. It couldn't be soldiers; Jube wouldn't let them return to murder in the middle of the night. Had Mathers come with his men after the army failed? Quickly Jacob blew out the lantern. Picking up his Army Colt .45, he pressed himself against the door, listening.

Mea-a-ha awoke with a sense of danger and hurried to Jacob's side. As their eyes grew accustomed to the light of a full moon piercing through the window, they could see the silhouettes of a dozen Indians. "The rifles are loaded. Wake Daniel and stay inside." Opening the door a crack, Jacob squeezed onto the porch.

With the moon to their backs, the Indian sat his mount like a dark statue. Edging into the silver light, Jacob spoke the Apache tongue. "Welcome to my home."

A powerfully built warrior rode forward. "I am Cota, war chief of the Apache. You are Jacob, Buffalo Soldier. Apaches have known of Soldier Jacob for many years."

The Indian's voice was solemn, but held respect. Jacob responded in kind. "I am Jacob, but no longer a soldier. Your name is known to me; you led the raid in which Daniel was hurt."

The young chief raised in the saddle, taking a tone of authority. "Braves are few, I have come for him."

Typical of many Apaches Jacob had met, Cota used few words. There was little room for misunderstanding or debate. Jacob stood his ground. "The boy is safe here."

Squaring his shoulders, Cota's voice became stern. "I say I have come for him."

Just as stern, was Jacob's reply. "I say he stays with me."

"I could order my warriors to kill you."

Jacob clenched his gun, making its presence known. "And I could kill you before the words left your mouth." A smile crossed his face. "Both our threats are mighty weak."

The young brave paused, impressed by his courage. "It is said, you killed Sholo. He was a great warrior."

Jacob wondered who told him, but could guess why. "He chose violence and died by his choice."

"Why do you help the long knives?"

Lowering his gun, Jacob hoped words might prevail where bullets could not. "We are different, Cota, you and I, but maybe not so different. We are both trying to survive in the white man's world. The Apache are fading. I am one man alone trying to make a place of my own. We both want peace, yet we stand with guns."

223

Cota found truth in the black man's words. "Yes, we are both trying to survive, but I will not find a place in the white man's world. Fighting is all I have."

"Fighting must serve a purpose. That is why I'm no longer a soldier. Your killing serves no purpose."

A lifetime of injustice bred defiance in the young brave's heart. "Should good surrender because evil is stronger?"

"Brave Cota, if you fight, you will die. If you choose peace, then might not some good survive? You will live to teach your children so that the Apache might not die completely." A big grin spread across Jacob's face. "Or would you rather leave the teaching of your young to an old Buffalo Soldier like me?"

His jest made the Apache smile. "At least let there be peace between us. Daniel has ridden the warpath. He is a man now. Let him decide the trail he takes."

Jacob turned to Mea-a-ha who was peering behind the crack of the door. He pushed it open. Mea-a-ha shook her head, her eyes pleading.

Jacob understood her fear, but it was not her decision. "Cota's words are fair. We must let Daniel choose his destiny."

At Jacob's motioning, Daniel stepped out the door. "Son, you have heard our words. What do you say?"

The boy rubbed his hands against his trousers, fighting for courage. He cast nervous glances at the two imposing figures. To Daniel they were the mightiest of men, his heroes, but on opposing sides. Cota was his chief who led him into battle against a mighty foe, and Jacob the man who was willing to die for him, like a father for a son. He must now turn his back on one of these great men to whom he owed so much.

For the young boy it was the hardest decision of his short life, yet it was time to stand as a man or be marked a child. Pulling himself to his full height, he dug deep inside, searching for the strength his heroes had given him. He could be no less than them. His voice rang strong. "Yes, I have heard your words...All of them."

He faced Jacob. "Words you have not told me before." His voice shook with grief. "You killed Sholo, and so you killed Teowa." Daniel's voice broke as he thought of his beloved brother. He clenched his teeth, trying not to cry. "These are words you should have told me. You talk of trust, then you hide the truth."

Daniel waited, searching the big man's face. Jacob met his stare but did not answer. He would offer no defense. Daniel must decide for himself.

The boy struggled, trying to understand. Jacob had been a soldier, but to Daniel he was so much more. Slowly, his anger faded. Jacob had already answered his question. 'Fathers and sons must look into each other's hearts.'

224

The boy turned to his sister and stared until she hid her eyes. Daniel scolded. "I am not a child, and it is not for you to steal the truth either. You say I am not old enough to make my own decisions, but you let fear make yours. You tell me I am small and need Jacob to protect me. I tell you sister, it will always be true for you, but tonight I am a man."

Mea-a-ha bowed her head.

Slowly the boy turned and faced his chief. Daniel had found the courage to speak his mind. Now it was time to proclaim his decision. The night was cool, yet his face burned with the blood of a warrior. "Great Cota, I will honor the ways of the Apache and I will ride with you if you command me, but Jacob has put his life between me and the soldiers, and if you say it is my choice, then I choose to stay with my family. I have growing to do."

Cota looked hard at the boy, then smiled. "So it is. A brave must go willingly. Maybe someday you will be the one who will teach the Apache children, if any survive."

Prodding his pony forward, Cota turned his attention to the shining eyes of the Apache girl. "Little Mea-a-ha. You have grown, not so much taller maybe, but you have grown away from your own people, and you have taken this young warrior from them."

He held her gaze. "You wear the clothes of our enemy. Beneath them are you still Apache? Or does your skin turn white?"

Mea-a-ha pushed away from Jacob and stepped into the moonlight. Her small fists clenched by her side. "Proud Cota, you teased me when we were young, but we are no longer children, so do not taunt me now. Follow the path you are on and when you lay in your own blood, remember that little Mea-a-ha survives when the great Cota could not. Then ask, who is the mightier Apache."

The brave's stern face broke into a smile, and he laughed out loud. "I leave Daniel in good hands." Cota turned to Jacob. "Find peace with the long knives if you can, but if you hope for peace with this Mimbre woman, use a stout switch."

With no further word, Cota led his small band of braves into the night.

Jacob wrapped his arms around his family. Mea-a-ha leaned her head on Jacob's chest. "How did Cota know Daniel was here?"

Jacob shook his head. It was plain there was more going on than he knew. "Cota could not have followed Daniel's trail. Somebody wanted him to know he was here, hoping there would be a fight, but who? Mathers knows Reinhart, but how would he know Cota, or even how to find him?"

"There was a white man." Daniel spoke up. "There was a white man who came to our camp a few times with firewater, bullets, and messages. He was old and shaggy, and looked like the desert. He was always grinning."

A light flashed in Jacob's eyes. "Let's go inside."

Late into the night, Mea-a-ha sat with Daniel in his room remembering Teowa. The boy had the heart of a warrior and held no blame, yet tears fell just the same. Apaches do not speak of the dead, but Mea-a-ha was taught by the priest and felt talking would help ease Daniel's grief. For now he had a family, and the fear of losing it made forgiveness easier.

After he drifted off to sleep, Mea-a-ha found Jacob sitting in his padded leather chair, lost in contemplation. She kissed his cheek. "Come, darling, let's go to bed. It has been a long day."

Roused from his thoughts, Jacob slowly rose to his feet and returned her kiss. "Let me snuff out the lamp, and I'll join you."

His mind struggled for answers as he watched the Indian girl disappear through the doorway. Leaning over to blow out the lantern on the table, Jacob looked down at the Winchesters glinting in the yellow light. Suddenly his eyes grew intense. Pieces of the puzzle began to fall into place. "That's it!"

Chapter -22-
Desperate Plan

There were dining places quainter than the Dona Anna Hotel; quieter too, but the Dona Anna had become popular as the place to be. Its large dining room off the grand lobby made for an inviting entrance where guests could meet. Tall windows allowed for a good view of the comings and goings of the citizenry. While sitting at its cloth-covered tables, guests could watch people arriving on the stage right in front of the hotel. Silver City was growing so fast that the Butterfield Stage made two trips each day.

The morning stage from Santa Fe had brought no less a person than the Territorial Judge, D. Hein; a jolly man who liked his cigar and enjoyed a good laugh. On the bench he was quite serious, but right now he was laughing. Across the table sat Colonel Aaron McCrae, commanding officer of Fort Cummings. Colonel McCrae, with some annoyance and a measure of humor, was grilling newly promoted Captain Lawrence Reinhart, who was standing rather stiffly by the table. "This couldn't wait until I got back to the fort? You had to chase me into town?"

Hein knew Reinhart to be arrogant, so he was enjoying watching his friend McCrae take the captain down a notch. Reinhart grew red-faced as he tried to defend his actions. "Sir, I was told at the fort that you would be meeting Judge Hein, and since I needed a search warrant, it seemed like the ideal opportunity, sir."

McCrae's voice rose with aggravation. "Search warrant? What the hell do you need a search warrant for in the middle of the damn desert? You're chasing Indians; since when do you need a search warrant to apprehend Indians?"

Judge Hein's belly laughs only added to the color of Reinhart's face. "Sir, I have reason to believe that Jacob Keever is harboring a young Apache that was involved in the attack in which the black trooper Toby Waters was killed, sir."

Puffing out his cigar, Judge Hein interrupted with some excitement. "Why, I know of Sergeant Jacob Keever. I've got a paperback novel about him by Barnabas Kane, right here in my coat pocket. Been reading it on the stage. The man is a real hero. Took on nearly sixty Indians almost single handedly."

Hearing Jacob being called a hero for the hundredth time made Reinhart boil. Everywhere he went, people offered praise for the great Jacob Keever and seemed to forget that he was the officer that supposedly led the raid. The captain knew his black troopers had fed outlandish tales to Barnabas Kane and it galled him. "Begging your pardon, Judge, but Keever left the army and has taken up with an Apache squaw. He is holed up in the mountains on a place he's got, and won't let anyone search it without a warrant."

Taking on an official air, Judge Hein plucked his cigar from his mouth and defended his hero. "Lots of good men take squaws out here in the territory. Ain't nothing wrong in that. And if he is on his land, he's got a right to demand a search warrant."

Realizing it was useless talking to the judge, Reinhart returned his flustered plea to McCrae. "Sir, Keever was seen buying children's clothing right here in town." As soon as he said it, Reinhart regretted his choice of words. "Sir, I mean…"

Tiring of the conversation, McCrae had enough. "Listen here, captain, you are supposed to be mopping up Indians that are accosting the good citizens of this territory, not harassing a popular hero for buying baby clothes. If Keever is up there in the mountains with a squaw, leave him be. You stick to patrolling the main roads through the desert and guarding the watering holes as ordered. Is that clear?"

Seeing his position as hopeless, Reinhart gave a crisp salute, added an about face, and hightailed it out the door before he burst. He would find another way to get Jacob Keever, but get him he would.

Across town on a steep narrow side street sat the Glory Hole Saloon. It too had a small restaurant, but that is where its similarities to the Dona Anna ended. The Glory Hole did see its share of wealthy men, though the types of business conducted at the two establishments were quite different.

In the rooms above the Glory Hole resided the fancy ladies of Madam Sarah Danes' House of Pleasure. So the lamps were lowered, and the windows of the Saloon were painted over, giving a degree of anonymity.

The patrons of the Glory Hole found it best to mind their own business. No one cared to notice when a distinguished gentleman with a saucy girl wrapped around his arm slid from a cozy table in a darkened alcove and stumbled up the stairs, sloshing a bottle of wine. Their laughter blended with the raucous tenor of the dingy saloon. Nor did anyone pay any attention to a tall, dark man standing in the shadows by the back door. He lingered for sometime, finishing a frothy brown beer. The stranger was in no hurry.

Even though the good bartender had graciously said the drink was on the house, the big man tossed fifty cents on the bar, paying for the beer and a generous tip. He upended his glass and quietly took the stairs himself.

On the landing he watched a door to one of the rooms open, allowing a portly little man to come out carrying two empty buckets. Before the door closed, the pretentious laughter of the noisy couple could again be heard ringing from inside.

Damon Mathers leaned over the edge of the copper bathtub, puffing hard on a large imported cigar as Rosie Montier, kneeling next to the tub, held a match to it. Rosie had stripped to her pink satin petticoat to avoid ruining her beautiful dress, as Damon splashed water everywhere. After taking a long drag on the expensive weed, Damon leaned back in the tub and blew smoke rings into the air. Rosie dipped a washcloth into the water and started washing the burly rancher's hairy chest.

A deep voice rolled from the doorway. "Touching."

Damon coughed, choked and sputtered, dropping the French cigar into the sudsy water. A giant of a man moved closer, towering over the stunned couple. "Hi, neighbor, please don't get up."

Mathers' lower jaw hung like a broken hinge. Jacob nodded to the girl crouching behind him.

"Hi, Rosie. Looks like you were right, you do have all the water you want, but you still have to clean up the dirt."

Mathers gripped the edge of the tub with both hands. "You're a dead man, you son-of-a..."

Shoving the flat of his boot against the rancher's chest, Jacob knocked him back into the tub. "Let's keep it friendly. We've all had so many good times in this room."

Mathers boiled with outrage. "Why, you black nigger bastard..."

"Damon!" Rose protested.

Mathers exploded. "Shut up, bitch, and get me a towel."

Rose glanced at Jacob, then quickly hid her eyes.

"Poor Rosie, this tiny room is your whole world. You put on your pretty dresses and pretend, just like the men who buy you. The difference is they are free to go as they will, while you remain, a captured bird in a gilded cage."

"She's a darkie that knows her place. Something I'm gunna' teach you, before I kill ya."

Jacob smiled affably. "Now there's no need for all this unpleasantness, I've just come to see my neighbor. You paid me a visit; I'm payin' you one."

Casting a glance around the room, Jacob's voice filled with mock disappointment. "Looks like those twenty burly cowboys you been bragging on can't nursemaid you all the time. Guess in the end, a man has got to stand alone and face his own music. So best you pick your tune carefully."

Mathers' cursed at the black man's impudence. "The tune I pick will be the sound of cattle thundering across your worthless scrap of lizard droppings."

Jacob kept his smile. "Much obliged, I could use a little beef for the winter. Best bring all your drovers; wouldn't want you to embarrass yourself again."

With a quick wink to Rosie, he leaned over the naked man. "Looks like you keep comin' up short."

Cursing, Mathers covered himself and thrust a stiff arm at the girl, knocking her over backwards. "Damn it, whore, I said get me a towel!"

Obediently, Rosie reached for a towel lying near Jacob's feet. Stooping, Jacob grabbed the stunned girl by the wrist, pulling her up on her toes. Then without warning, he leaned down and forced a long, hard kiss full on her painted lips.

Releasing her, Jacob cocked his head with a thoughtful expression. "Nope, nothing." He offered a friendly smile and gave her a shove. Rose fell over backwards, landing square on Mathers with a splash. Amid the hollering and screams, Jacob tipped his hat and backed out of the alcove. "If you'll excuse me, I'm havin' a little trouble with the army that's gunna' take me south of the border for a bit, but I'll be back, so keep off my land or I'll bury you with the Indians."

Struggling to his feet, Mathers threw the drenched whore to the floor and stood stark naked, clutching his soaked cigar. "You're dead, you black son-of-a-bitch. Four days and I'll be running cattle on your land. Four days, Keever. You watch for me. I'm comin'."

Picking up Mathers' trousers on the way out, Jacob ducked out the door, with the threats of the irate rancher echoing down the hall. "Four days. Four days!"

The dented lantern sitting on top of a wooden barrel burned cheerfully in the cluttered stall of the livery stable that old Tatum used for an office. Leaning back on a milking stool, the grizzled teamster awkwardly rested his head on a saddle blanket draped over the railings, his dirty bare feet propped on a bale of hay. His snoring ended with an abrupt snort, as the rusty hinges on the small side door screeched open. "Tatum, your snorin' could be heard all the way to the Glory Hole."

Rubbing his whiskered face, the old man came to life. "It keeps the horses calm, n' scares away the wolves. Didja' find the polecat?"

Stepping into the light, Jacob plopped down on a wooden keg. "Sure did. So happy to see me, he promised another visit. Did you get any information for me?"

Bright blue eyes twinkled above a toothless grin. "Yup. The only ones a moving freight like that would be me or Parker's Freight Company, n' 'cept for the one delivery I took to Damon Mathers' ranch, ain't nobody done none. Tom Parker told me so his self."

The old man licked his lips with a large, flat tongue and rubbed his weathered hands, hardly able to contain his excitement. "It gets better. The numbers ya gived' me are right here on the bill o' ladin'." With that, he reached deep into a torn pocket of his overalls and pulled out a poorly folded piece of paper along with bits of straw.

A broad smile showed Jacob's delight as he eagerly stuffed it into his shirt. "Thanks, Tatum, I owe you one."

Tatum gave an evil cackle. "I figure ya wouldn't go ta the trouble of askin' iffin' ya weren't plannin' some discomfort for that high-steppin' rancher and his no-account cubs."

Dropping his saddle on Major's back, Jacob leaned over the horse. "Keep this between us. Wouldn't want to spoil the surprise. Just remember what I told you if anyone asks."

Tatum stood outside the livery stable watching Jacob disappear down the dark road. The loose dirt felt cool on his bare feet. The old man chuckled quietly to himself. "That boy's got grit."

A commotion on the side street across from his stable caught the old man's attention. Two men were hurrying towards him, quarreling as they came. Seeing Tatum standing under a lamp, the taller man shouted. "You there, Tatum. Hold a minute."

Tatum waited politely as they crossed the street. "Kin I help ya Captain? Always willin' ta be o' service to the army. Was a soldier once myself 'til they kicked me out."

Reinhart and Mathers came to a blustering halt. "Did Jacob Keever stable his horse here today?"

Rubbing his shock of snow white hair, Tatum gave the question considerable thought. He scratched his neck, dug his toe into the dirt and gave it a little more. "Hmm. Kin ya describe him?"

Stomping his boot, Mathers swore. "Damn it, old man. He's a big colored."

The old man continued rubbing his hair. "What color?"

Anger rising, Reinhart broke in. "Black! What the hell color do you think a colored man is, you old fool?"

Unruffled, Tatum continued to smile. "Meant the horse. Don't remember men, jes' horses."

Mathers whirled around, tearing at the brim of his hat. "He rides a huge bay with a U.S. Army brand."

Giving off with a chuckle, Tatum slapped his hands on the side of his overalls as if it finally came to him. "Oh, ya mean that tall dark feller. Thought he jes' had too much sun. Yep, he did stable his horse. Said he didn't want 'em out in the corral where people could see. Come on in."

The two men pushed past the old man, nearly knocking him down. Tatum stepped through the rickety door after them. Reinhart hurried down the row of stalls. "Where is it?"

Again, Tatum looked confused. "Where's what?"

"The bay horse, you old dotard."

"Oh! The bay. He's gone."

Reinhart started yelling. "Then why the hell did you have us come in?"

231

The old man looked hurt. "Jes' trying to be of help. Thought ya might want ta know what he said. You bein' army n' all."

Mathers hissed through clenched teeth. "Well what did he say?"

Once again, Tatum went back to rubbing his messy white hair. "Not so much what he said, jes' small talk. This n' that, ya know. He did take some extra canteens, mutterin' somethin' 'bout Mexico. That, and how we sure was havin' nice weather. And if anybody asked, not to say anythin', but you bein' army n' all..."

The information improved the humor of the men. Reinhart cheered to disagreeable. "Listen carefully, old man. Did he have anyone with him?"

"No, not as I 'ken say. Asked about the old Mimbre trail, paid 'es nickel for some extra oats, and left."

The two men hurried out the door with Reinhart talking excitedly. "So he's going to make a run for the border, but he'll have to go back to the Hollow to get the buck. That buys some time. Keever will have to cross the Mimbre trail south of his property if he figures on getting that Apache over the border. I will have troops there waiting for him. This time, we will kill them both."

Mathers sneered. "Just the same, I'm drivin' cattle right through his Hollow. If you don't get him, I will. No more witnesses. We'll kill the squaw and end this thing once and for all."

****

A sea of stars floated in the moonless sky. Their serene light was just enough to see the trail. On the outskirts of town where the road dipped through Pinos Creek, Jacob turned his horse upstream, just in case he was followed. Few would be able to track him on the road at night; fewer still would be able to follow him up the stream. Maybe Luther, but he was likely at the fort.

Speed was essential if he was going to stay one jump ahead of Reinhart and Mathers. The information he got from Tatum verified his suspicion. Now he needed time. Jacob hoped his little ruse about going to Mexico would stop Reinhart from returning directly to the Hollow.

It was the best he could do to keep his family safe. His gun no longer offered protection from the soldiers.

To win this battle he would have to draw the enemy out into the open, in more ways than one. Jacob hoped they would tip their hand, for as yet he had no evidence tying Mathers and Reinhart together, though an idea of what they were hiding was beginning to take shape in Jacob's mind. He would follow up on his hunch in time, but for now he had a little mischief to attend to. Mathers and Tatum were his first two calls; by tomorrow he would make one more.

Before dawn, Jacob stopped on a high knoll. He had made good time.

As of yet, no one was dogging his trail. Prodding Major, he hurried on. Towards noon the sky darkened, and a gusty wind whipped up white dust off the desert, allowing Jacob to make speed riding in the open, instead of winding through arroyos.

By evening the wind had blown itself out, replaced by a light steady rain. His hard ride had taken him to a series of narrow, rugged canyons half a day's ride northwest of the Hollow and northeast of Mathers' spread.

The terrain was a labyrinth of low, rocky ridges and sparse pines with so little foliage, life was difficult for anything larger than a squirrel. Small, spindly pinyons were scattered about the mouths of the deep cuts into the hills, making it impossible to tell if they petered out or opened into hidden canyons. Jacob counted three cuts before heading into the mountains. The trail was steep at first as it wound through a narrow, rocky draw, but suddenly turned north and started a gradual incline. The canyon widened, allowing for smaller gullies to open along the trail.

Eventually a small stream trickled from a side canyon, high up the wall. It was rare to find a flowing stream this late in the year. Dry grasses spread out from the tiny brook, and the small pines became more numerous.

After following the trail for about a quarter mile, Jacob turned Major into the denser trees to avoid being seen and continued quietly forward. He slowed to a cautious pace. A light rain dampened any sound.

The narrow walls of the canyon offered a quiet solitude, but it did nothing to put Jacob at ease. Ahead, he could see sky through the trees as he approached a clearing. Staying close to the western slope, he was able to ride into the small meadow without being spotted by the two Apache braves standing guard.

Sitting around a fire were a dozen warriors. Jacob was on them before they knew he was there. Screams erupted from the startled Indians as they scrambled for their rifles.

Riding boldly into a circle of raised weapons, Jacob smiled. "Greetings, Cota."

Chapter -23-
Mimbres

perched on the log fence behind the barn, Mea-a-ha pressed her bare toes against the rough bark of the railing. Grain tumbled through her slender fingers as she idly watched the chickens scratch and peck the small patch of bare ground.

A fat gray hen with black speckles bobbed its head near the girl's feet. Jacob said it was a Plymouth Rock. Mea-a-ha named her Mother Gray Feathers.

Strutting near the small, wooden door of the hen house like a warrior guarding his squaws stood a tall, reddish brown rooster with a long, flowing tail. He was a Rhode Island Red. His name was Chief Noise in the Morning. Jacob said they were named after far away places. Mea-a-ha hoped to someday see the strange land of chickens.

Stamping his brown and white paws impatiently, Friendly cocked his ear and offered an eager yap at the hungry birds. Mea-a-ha tossed some seeds at him and smiled. "Be nice." Backing his rump in the tall grass next to the fence post, Friendly gave an excited whine but tried to be good.

A crisp morning breeze blowing across the pond tossed Mea-a-ha's hair and stung her cheeks. She wondered when the first snow would come. Somehow she felt winter would wrap the Hollow in a protective blanket, keeping the bad men away. Maybe they would forget by spring, or whatever the trouble was wouldn't matter after a long winter.

A woman in the wilderness is dependent on the protection of her man, and right now it made her feel helpless. The danger coming looked too big for any one man, even Jacob.

Mea-a-ha needed to believe in something greater. She had been taught Christian beliefs, but as a little girl in her village she learned that the great spirit Ussen sent mountain spirits called Gahns to protect the Apache, and even the white man would have to bow to the angry spirit of winter. Maybe the first snow would come soon.

A long low whistle in the clear air caught Mea-a-ha by surprise.

"Why, if you don't look prettier every day."

"Jacob!"

Grudgingly, the chickens inched aside as Major carefully maneuvered his large hooves between the birds. Jacob leaned over and plucked Mea-a-ha off the fence. She threw her arms tightly around his neck, giving him a big kiss. "I missed you."

The Indian girl nuzzled her cheek against his worn leather coat, loving the smell of horse and man. The morning lost its chill.

234

Holding the girl in a tight embrace that said more than words, Jacob headed the big horse back to the house, but Mea-a-ha tugged at the reins. "Let's go to the cemetery."

Jacob tensed, his breath caught in his chest, but the Indian girl's dark eyes spoke of love, calming his fears.

Without a word he turned Major around and started down the deep narrow winding path with Friendly dancing about his hooves.

Resting her head under his chin, Mea-a-ha closed her eyes, enjoying the short ride. "Did everything go okay?"

Jacob smiled and kissed her. "I think so, but I must leave again soon."

"Jacob, no." She hung tightly to his neck.

"You've got to be strong. I'm taking Daniel with me."

Her body slumped. She would be alone. Worse, she would be waiting, fearing that they might never return. Mea-a-ha hadn't asked Jacob about his plans, and wasn't sure she wanted to know. She would trust her man. "Jacob, do you think you can win against so many bad men?"

"Darling, when fightin' starts, a man never knows if he is gunna' live or die, no matter what the odds. But you never give up. If you are the last man standing, you won. Mea-a-ha, I got to believe that the good win, that they have some extra advantage that sees them through." Jacob hugged her tightly. "Honey, I promise I will return. For the first time, I have something too valuable to lose...and maybe that's it. Maybe that is the advantage."

At the end of the pond where the lush reeds abruptly gave way to small desert plants, Mea-a-ha wiggled loose and slid from the saddle. Her large eyes looked up at Jacob, filling with emotion. Turning, she bent near the dark green cattails and picked a tiny blue Showy Daisy; it was the last of the flowers. In small loving hands she held it close, then quickly turned and hurried down the path with her little treasure. Major followed without any prodding from his master. The old horse dearly loved the girl.

Jacob watched the tiny figure, lost in the big blue shirt, her bare feet scurrying down the cold dirt trail, intent on her business. Her innocence was comical and sweet. If one word described this beautiful woman-child, it was 'Love.' Amid all the suffering, she had the courage to give her heart, but those who love the most, hurt more deeply and he feared what lay ahead might be too much. He had news to tell her. Jacob saddened; it could wait a while longer.

Along the trail, the sparse yellow grasses swayed in the chilled autumn breeze. The pale morning sun hid behind the border trees, offering a soft cool light.

Catching up, Jacob halted Major at the closest headstone. The earth around the graves had been cleared of weeds. Mea-a-ha had spent some time here while he was gone.

The stones were laid in two rows of six graves, plus one larger stone on the left end of the back row, which was Sholo's. Kneeling near the second stone from the opposite end, Mea-a-ha placed her single flower and looked up. "This one is Teowa's."

Jacob didn't doubt that somehow the little Indian girl knew. Mea-a-ha held out her hand inviting Jacob to come down. As he climbed from the saddle, pain was visible on his face.

Standing on tiptoes, she offered a tender kiss and slipped her hand into his with a reassuring smile. "This is our home; there should be no sadness in the Hollow. Teowa died a warrior. Being here near him, I feel only his love. My brother found peace beneath these cliffs, and so must you."

Mea-a-ha pressed a small hand to his face, holding his eyes with a will stronger than his own. She would not allow him to carry the pain any longer. "Even good men walk a stony trail. Such is life. Do not blame yourself for a path you did not choose."

****

Mea-a-ha awoke to a distant cock-a-doodle-doo. Chief Noise in the Morning had given his permission to the day. The Indian girl's delicate brown hand reached for her man before the sleep had left her eyes.

Jacob was gone. Pushing the blankets back, Mea-a-ha sat up. Worry erased the sleep from her sweet face. The invincible giant had tossed and turned all night.

Leaning his elbows on the railing of the small bridge that crossed the bubbling spring, Jacob tried to lose himself in the mystical waters. If there were healing powers in this ancient stream, he wished it would work its magic now. He loved Mea-a-ha. In the darkest hours when others floundered in despair, this girl found reason to be happy. Her laughter chased away the blackest night, but she also cried easily and let pain cut her deep.

Jacob buried his head in his hands. He should have told her yesterday. But how could he tell her?

Caring fingers slipped around his arm. Coming out of his gloom, Jacob looked into the questioning eyes of the woman he loved. Mea-a-ha did her best to offer a brave smile. "No more secrets, my hero."

She nuzzled her head against his shoulder then looked up again. "You have bad news, and you are trying to protect me."

The stone soldier looked across the water. A gentle hand rubbed his arm, calling him back. Jacob slowly turned and faced her imploring gaze, knowing he was about to destroy her world.

Mea-a-ha had suffered so much, and she didn't deserve this. Jacob's face darkened. Gathering her in a great bear hug, he shuttered.

Frightened, Mea-a-ha leaned back to see his face. This giant was stronger than any warrior she had ever known, but he was waging a battle for control. "Oh, Jacob! I am not so fragile, that you have to be so strong. Tell me or I will die from your pain."

The big man clenched his jaw. There was no way around it. He slowly released her and boldly came to attention, but a trembling hand on the railing, betrayed him. "My darling, you must be very strong."

He gave her a moment to brace herself, then spoke his doom. "There's news from town. It is your people. Victorio is dead."

Mea-a-ha jolted. Her mouth opened, but there was no word that could express her anguish. The girl's eyes spoke the grief that words could not; pleading it wasn't true.

Jacob hated that it was he who must tell her the tragic story. "Darling, there was a terrible battle with Mexican troops in the mountains of Tres Castillos. The warriors ran out of ammunition."

The girl struggled to speak as tears flowed from a shattered heart. She had to know. "My people!" She finally screamed. "What of my people?"

Kneeling, Jacob took her hands. "I'm sorry. The braves were killed to the last man. The women and children that survived the bloody night were taken into slavery in Mexico. They are scattered to the winds. Your people are no more."

"The babies, there were babies. Mary Lost Pony had a beautiful baby before I left."

Wailing as though death had taken her also, Mea-a-ha collapsed on the bridge. "There were so many Mimbres with him. Are, are... they all dead?"

Jacob pulled her close. He wished more than anything to kiss away her tears, but she had to hear it all. "All those with Victorio are lost. Word has it, that a few Mimbre warriors are somewhere in the desert, maybe a dozen, but your tribe is gone. Warm Springs lies empty."

Unable to believe, Mea-a-ha searched for any hope. "No! There's Cota and the boys, Sam Walking Bird, Sauto. Maybe some women, and, and babies." Her eyes pleaded.

Jacob shook his head. "Time has run out. Maybe one last battle for Cota, but there's nowhere to go now. No home to protect, no women to fight for. The days of the Mimbres are over."

Mea-a-ha wept. Her people were no more. Everyone the little girl had ever known was gone, wiped from the earth.

Jacob scooped up his Apache maiden and carried her back to the house. His heart ached for her. How alone she must feel. In all the land, he knew of no other Mimbre woman. The warriors he once hunted lay slaughtered on a lonely hillside, their scalps cut away.

A race of proud people had come to an end. Their crime was being

237

Indians, and now he held one of the last in his arms. Jacob put her to bed, then went and got Daniel. The three hugged each other beneath the covers, and silently suffered their loss.

When the Mimbres had offered their friendship to the strangers in their land, the white man's words said, "Fear us not." As war ravaged their villages, more words pledged peace. When they huddled, starving on the reservation, words promised food. Wrapped now in each other's arms, words no longer held any value; for in death, the true value of the white man's words were known.

Midday offered only the sounds of shuffling feet. Jacob busied himself in the kitchen making a barley soup. Maybe no one would eat, but life had to go on. The bedroom door creaked opened, and Mea-a-ha silently came out holding her puppy. She attempted a smile. "Friendly would let me be sad no longer."

Jacob set a steaming bowl on the table and pulled a chair out for her. "Barley with a little wild onion. How's Daniel?"

Mea-a-ha hugged the puppy to her cheek, hiding a tear. "He is strong. A precious dream is dead, but he weeps more for me, I think. Daniel is a good boy. He told me we have a new family and as long as we live, our people live, and someday the Mimbres will return."

Mea-a-ha rested a spoon on the rim of her bowl and stared into the distance. "I do not think this is true, but Teowa always said Daniel was the smartest, so maybe..."

As Jacob finished setting the bowls on the table, the door opened once more and Daniel joined them. His eyes were red, but held a look of unshakable determination. The boy was a fighter. He lifted his young face to the big man and gritted a pained smile. Jacob pulled the boy to him in a big hug. "Yes sir, you are a most remarkable family."

Mea-a-ha reached a hand to him. "We are a most remarkable family."

They ate their meal in silence, taking strength from the food, and from each other. The emptiness they felt could only be filled with love. It was the one thing they had in abundance. Mea-a-ha looked out the window at their secret world unchanged by time. Here in Jacob's Hollow, the Mimbres would survive.

Chapter -24-
Hard Ride

The horses burst from the wall of scrub oak far below the Hollow and dashed on to the open foothills. Leaving home in such haste fired the boy's heart. Daniel was young and eager for adventure. He knew they were riding into danger, and his skin prickled with excitement. Consequences were far from his mind.

The enticing desert lay before them. Snow Raven had been too long in the corral and wanted to run. By the pace Jacob set, it was clear there was great urgency. Fortunately, the trail led almost due south, in a steady decline to the desert floor. The horses could go a great distance without tiring.

Daniel gazed at the big man with wonder. It seemed that with each beat of the thundering hooves, Jacob grew stronger, more invincible. Every muscle in his chiseled face turned hard as stone. He burned with an intensity that the boy felt no living man could withstand.

What lay ahead was a mystery, but Daniel did not worry about the outcome. He reached down and felt the shiny Winchester in the scabbard by his leg. He had never fired a gun but when trouble came he knew he would fight side by side with his father. He dared not call him father, not yet, but in his heart, Daniel knew what role the big man played in his life.

They rode throughout the morning and midday with little talking. The unlikely pair pushed on as evening approached, only pausing briefly to share some pemmican and water from the canteen while Jacob searched the horizon with his field glasses.

The winds had changed. Daniel sensed it. No longer would they wait for evil men to decide their fate. From now on, this quiet giant would carry the battle forward.

Ahead lay the deep twisting cut of Sand Creek that marked the southern boundary of Jacob's land. From the high ground, it looked like a dark line drawn on the desert floor. Rains were seldom, but when they came they were fast and furious. Torrents of water rushing to the lowest point cut the steep, narrow gorge that stretched for miles.

From the flatlands, the scar was invisible, but from its rim, a sheer drop of fifteen to twenty feet of deeply eroded sand made a formidable barrier. While roaming with the ragtag band of Indian boys on that old jenny mule, Daniel had learned the desert and this creek well. They had spent many nights hiding in its twisting folds.

On the opposite rim of Sand Creek was the Old Mimbre Trail that followed the cut some distance before turning south to the border. The Apache often rode through the bottom of the gorge, evading the soldiers who patrolled the desolate land above.

Veering west, Jacob climbed the last high bluff and dismounted. The empty desert flattened out in all directions, no more knolls or ravines, except Sand Creek. Far to the east lay the lonely Dona Anna Mountains. South lay old Mexico.

The strange country meant nothing to the Apache, but it was a magical line that the soldiers could not cross. This political distinction, time and again, allowed the warriors to escape the pursuing army. Daniel had never been to the border. It was a long way. In truth, it was a long way to anywhere.

The young boy turned his face into the wind and waited. All the big man's attention was on what peril lay before them. Standing like a mighty oak anchored to the ground, Jacob vigilantly searched the horizon with his field glasses.

Daniel's waiting came to an end when all of a sudden Jacob tensed, focusing in one direction. A thin wisp of dust was slowly moving towards them. The recent rains had dampened the desert floor. Any dust at all would mean many horses riding fast.

Casting a glance at the cold sun resting low on the flat horizon, Daniel guessed it was less than an hour before dark, and about the same time for the riders to reach them. Jacob said nothing about who the riders were. He had never mentioned his plans, but with a growing sense of urgency, the big man climbed into the saddle. "Mount up, little buck."

Surprisingly, they turned around and headed back in the direction they had come, staying to the low side of the knoll. It was clear to Daniel that Jacob wanted to avoid the riders.

They continued for some time. Suddenly, Jacob took a sharp turn due west, climbing the nearest ridge, where he stopped and faced south once again.

On the high ground they were exposed. It was all confusing to Daniel. The faint dust cloud was bigger now with an orange cast as the sun spread its last rays across the desert sand. The distant horizon burned a crimson red.

As the clouds grew dark about them, Daniel's sense of adventure quailed before an impending reality of danger. Death was riding towards them.

Atop the knoll, Jacob waited once more. In the last minutes before twilight, the desert air is clear, and vibrant colors burst forth where moments before only dusty gray cloaked the barren land. All things are revealed in their true glory.

With the red light dancing in his eyes, a sly grin broke across Jacob's strong face. "Race you to Sand Creek, little buck."

With a kick of his heels, Jacob tore down the embankment leaving the boy alone on the ridge. For a moment Daniel watched Jacob, stunned in disbelief. Then, summoning a high pitched yell, the Apache boy shot after him like an arrow.

What was Jacob doing? Racing down the ridge would surely make them visible to the approaching riders. Suddenly Daniel understood... Jacob wanted to be seen. This was his game.

Leaning close to Snow Raven's neck, the Indian boy yelled to his pony. "Fly, my friend. Today we show the big man that size does not matter."

With a burst of speed, he tore down the ridge. Rock and sand exploded into the air as Snow Raven's hooves dug deep into the earth, going faster with each thunderous beat. The pony was sure-footed, never faltering. He was bred to run; this chase was to his liking.

Ahead, charging into the setting sun was the dark silhouette of Major, his powerful legs responding to the challenge like countless times before. Major's massive hooves struck the crumbling ridge throwing up a huge cloud of dust.

The old horse was as mighty as his master. Seeing them ride boldly filled Daniel with awe. It was as though fate had brought the stone soldier and immense war horse together for some great purpose. They were meant to be, this was their destiny. From a time now past, they were the last of the great warriors.

Daniel pressed his cheek tighter into his pony's neck. "Take wing. It is our day."

Snow Raven understood and rose to the challenge. As the ridge flattened out, the boy and pony raced past Jacob, whooping and cheering. The brisk wind pulled tears of excitement from the corners of his eyes.

Racing into the orange glow of the setting sun, Snow Raven increased the lead. Soon they broke onto the open plane, a small boy on a painted pony flying across a vast white sea. On they went with only the beating of hooves to remind them they were not soaring in the twilight sky. They too had a destiny.

Dashing to the edge of the gorge, Snow Raven braced his feet and came to an abrupt stop. Breathless, Daniel raised in his saddle, shouting with joy. "We won, we won." The last rays of light brought fiery brilliance to his dusty red skin. A lineage of proud warriors shined in the boy's face.

Moments later, Jacob came riding to a breathless halt. Daniel repeated his claim. "We won." Grinning wide, the old soldier leaned over and mussed Daniel's thick black hair, glowing with pride. "I knew you could."

Jacob looked past the boy to the approaching horsemen who had quickened their pace. The mad race down the hill had not gone unnoticed. Surprisingly the riders were only minutes away. With a setting sun to their backs, it was impossible to see who they were. Jacob's face returned to stone, his voice, just as hard. "Now the race begins for real, little buck. Follow me, stay close as skin."

Whirling the big horse around, Jacob headed west following the rim. The distance between them and the dark riders narrowed. Daniel's heart raced. Every sound carried in the clear desert air, the slap of dry leather, the clank of cold steel, tired horses snorting exhaustion and dust, each making the shadowy figures seemed so close they could reach and pluck him from his saddle.

Upon reaching the gorge, the dark riders veered west along the south rim, keeping pace with Jacob's great steed on the north. Not more than a few hundred feet now separated them. An eerie hush hung over the charged scene. The time for words had passed. This night was meant for blood.

A thin ribbon of light between the distant horizon and the thick, menacing clouds surrendered to a cold, damp night. "Close as skin" echoed in Daniel's mind as he sought Jacob in a sea of black. "Close as skin."

Hooves tramping on the broken rock drummed a warning, 'Death is near.' A rising bitter wind hissed in Daniel's ears, adding to the haunting cadence.

The unseen host took on a demonic peril for the boy. Daniel fought to calm his growing fears as time lost all meaning. Blinded by the murky night, the lines between reality and a child's imagination ceased to exist. His thin body grew cold. Shivers ran down his spine. Could the dark riders hear him shaking? Could they read his mind?

The unrelenting drum of the hooves on broken rocks changed to muffled thuds. The Apache boy choked back a scream. They had reached a point along the gorge where the steep walls gave way to sandy slopes. Here was the Mimbre Crossing. The protection of the gorge was gone. The evil was no longer held at bay.

Daniel pressed Snow Raven closer to Major's flank. Slowly, they edged forward, step by step, waiting. A sound! Only yards away, the faint creaking of a saddle; the enemy was upon them. The boy's heart pounded in terror. What was Jacob doing? Had they come to die?

A whispered word broke from the blackness. "Now!" With a hard slap of his reins and a blood curdling yell, Jacob charged directly towards the host. Startled horses reared amid screams of confusion. A rider near Daniel fell with a heavy thump. The boy held to Jacob's side as the big man swiftly turned, racing into Sand Creek like devils were on his tail.

All Daniel could do was follow as he had been told, "Close as skin." A clamor of hooves, layered with murderous cries, told the story. The dark riders were in deadly pursuit.

At the speed Jacob was pushing the horses, Daniel was sure the big man must know the gorge like birds know wind. Any hidden rock in the dark could spell disaster for the horses. The boy wisely gave Snow Raven his head, trusting the horse's senses over his own.

Sounds once more became muted by sandy cliffs, the narrow walls of the gorge had returned. Now they were boxed in with only one direction to go.

Around snaking curves and tight bends, Jacob set a dangerous pace. Unseen branches of willows lining the dark walls whipped and stung Daniel's face. Snow Raven stumbled on boulders buried in the unforgiving blackness, shaking his confidence. The great stallion was having trouble keeping up with Major's powerful stride. Racing in the open in bright daylight was one thing. Now Daniel learned, not all races could be won by speed alone.

With eyes closed, the boy hung desperately to his pony's neck, small fingers tightly wove deep into the stallion's damp, flowing mane. On they went, twisting and turning, slowing, then bursting forth. The sound of Snow Raven's breathing grew louder and louder.

Neither horse nor men could keep up this pace much longer through the dangerous terrain. After a stretch where they pulled ahead, Jacob slowed to a trot, the hunters and the hunted accepting the reality that the chase was going to be long.

Slowly Daniel rose in the saddle, allowing himself to breathe. For the first time, the boy became aware that he was soaked from a drizzling rain.

After some distance the gorge began to open up. Echoes faded, and lightning strikes illuminated the jagged walls which were now several hundred feet apart. Tall, pungent sagebrush filled the sandy creek. Slowing to a walk, Jacob led Daniel into the open area. The Indian boy judged it to be longer than an arrow could fly.

Thunder rolled, and the rain came hard. Halting the horses, Jacob waited for the next bolt of lightning to illuminate the trail ahead. While they waited, the rain beat in loud torrents. A heavy rumble, and lightning glowed inside a thick, dark cloud. Daniel tried to look ahead and behind at once. Jacob found the trail and pushed on. Deep sand, made heavy by the downpour, caused the horses to struggle. Each flash of lightning revealed water rising around Snow Raven's hooves. An emerging stream splashed where minutes before there was only dry sand.

Once across the clearing, the gorge quickly narrowed again, and the water that had spread out now churned in the confined space.

Without warning, Jacob grabbed Snow Raven's bridle and pulled them up a narrow path between the willows. Here he waited. A brilliant bolt of lightning struck directly overhead, illuminating the path behind them. Elongated shadows of the dark riders wavered ominously on the distant wall of the gorge. The pursuers had not followed them through the clearing. Their love of life was greater than their lust to kill. They feared the growing stream.

To Daniel's great surprise, with the next clap of thunder, Jacob spurred the horses up a steep narrow cut hidden behind a dense brush, taking them to the rim in moments. The boy's heart raced; they were free. Was it that easy? A chilling wind blowing off the desert seemed a good trade for the dread below.

Pulling back from the rim, Jacob dismounted and whispered for Daniel to stay with the horses. Then, bending low, he headed back to the gorge on foot.

Thunder continued to rumble, and the wind drove the rain with new fury. Daniel scrambled to the ground. Holding the bridles tightly, he squeezed between the horses for shelter. With teeth chattering, Daniel shivered uncontrollably and laid his head on Snow Raven's wet shoulder seeking warmth.

Eternity passed for the young boy before Jacob finally returned. The man's voice was calm. "Water is raging in the creek, but they are safe where they are. I saw a small fire, and it looks like they are going to stay at the opposite side of the gorge. It would be crazy for them to enter the narrows again with it flooding."

Trying to control the quiver in his voice, Daniel did his best to speak. "Is, is it soldiers?"

The familiar hand rubbed his soaking wet hair. "Did you think it was ghosts?"

Daniel shivered. "Maybe." Wiping the rain from his face, he asked hopefully, "Do you think they have given up?"

"No. It is my guess they think we are stuck just like they are until the rain lets up."

Without another word Jacob mounted up, back tracking the way they had came. The Apache boy did not understand what had happened, but at least they had escaped. For Indian children, soldiers were the demons in their nightmares; and to Daniel, their race had been a terrifying experience. His last run-in with soldiers had nearly cost him his life.

Eventually they reached the sandy crossing where their frightening race down the gorge had started. Instead of heading home, Jacob turned back into the creek, now behind the riders. None of it made any sense. All Daniel could do was follow and accept his fate.

Their pace was much slower and cautious this time. Pulling Snow Raven alongside Major, Daniel struggled for the courage to speak. "I don't understand."

He got a reassuring pat on the shoulder. "Lookin' for an opportunity. I need to talk with a friend, so we're having a little fun."

Fun! This was fun? What would it be like when it got serious? The young boy began to realize how bold the big man was, and how much he would have to grow to be like him.

Fearing what lay ahead, Daniel hoped his own courage would not fail. He wanted to make Jacob proud of him.

The swollen creek made their second trip all the more treacherous. Swirling water, knee-deep, made it difficult for Snow Raven to keep his footing. Only their slower pace saved them from tumbling into the cold, black water.

It took them almost an hour to return to where the soldiers were camped. The boy hoped they were sleeping. No figures could be seen standing around the fire that flickered under the sheltered face of the sandy cliff.

Once more, Jacob had Daniel stay back with the horses while he went ahead on foot. Through it all, the patter of rain droned in the boy's ears, jumbling his thoughts. The thunder had silenced, and the downpour lessened, but it was going to be a very wet night.

When Jacob returned, he was chuckling. "Just as I guessed, they put the horses behind them, and left them saddled for a fast chase. The army is nothing if not predictable."

Kneeling down, Jacob wrapped his arm around the boy holding him close for a long moment. He rubbed his small shoulders, bringing life back into his cold limbs. Jacob's arms offered warmth and caring the boy had never known. Daniel leaned against him and wished the big man would never let go.

For the boy's sake, Jacob would risk a few more minutes. "Do you see their campfire?"

"Yes."

"Stare at it. It will give you warmth."

Daniel concentrated on the distant flames. Suddenly he was not so cold. His chattering teeth calmed.

"Rest a bit, son." Jacob brushed the water from the boy's hair. "Winter's coming on. I will get you a cowboy hat to keep you dry when we get home."

Daniel smiled. "I want one like yours."

Surrendering a smile of his own, Jacob gave the boy's hair a final rub. "Little buck, we best get moving. You need to stay with me, no matter what. Ride low and fast, there may be shooting this time. Let's mount up."

In the soldier camp, Luther Tomes sidled up to Jube. "Sarge, this don't seem right; somethin' is about to bust, I can feel it."

Jube leaned in until the brims of their rain-soaked hats were touching. "Just follow orders. Offer nothin'; this is between the captain n' Jacob, let them fight it out."

Pulling his collar up, Luther moved away from the fire and faded into the cracks of the high wall.

Adrenalin surged, warming Daniel's blood. Cautiously they moved forward. Before the boy realized, it they were among the soldier's horses.

One word escaped Jacob's lips. "Ride!"

The two of them bolted forward at full speed, diving through the huddled soldiers, with Jacob's pistol firing into the air. Daniel hung close to the saddle, praying Snow Raven's speed would save him. In the dim firelight, he kept his eyes glued to the big man. A kick of Jacob's heels drove Major into the white officer, sending the flailing man crashing head- first into the mud.

Blinded by their own campfire, startled troopers scrambled to get out of the way. Frantic screams filled the air, wild shots rang out. Major plowed through the sage and sand making his own trail. Snow Raven fought to keep pace. By the time they reached the other side of the clearing, the soldiers were in hot pursuit. Curses echoed through the night.

Down into the surging steam Jacob charged, through an ever-narrowing gorge. Water splashed from Snow Raven's pounding hooves, soaking Daniel to the bone. Soldiers close behind hollered at their mounts, urging them faster through the churning foam.

Major never faltered under Jacob's command, always pushing forward, giving everything he had.

Twisting past one more bend, Jacob whirled the great horse around and disappeared into a steep cut that was not visible from the direction they came. There was barely enough room for Snow Raven to squeeze beside him. In the dark, driving rain the irate soldiers flew past them and on down the gorge. From feet away, Jacob did his best to count the thundering horses. "three, four, five, ...only five."

Moments later, terrified screams from men and horses reverberated up the gorge. Daniel listened in disbelief. "What happened?"

Turning Major back the way they came, Jacob laughed until his shoulders shook. "If I were a betting man, I'd say Reinhart and the boys burst over a low waterfall just around the bend, crashing into a deep pool of icy water, and are right now bobbin' around like a bunch of bruised apples."

Daniel laughed out loud. "You knew."

Jacob gave an evil chuckle. "The only way out for them is miles down the gorge. Now let's get back to that warm fire they were kind enough to build for us."

Daniel took a deep breath and followed Jacob. With the Mimbres gone, the Indian was the last of his kind. It struck him, so was the big man.

Nearing the campsite, Daniel was suddenly alarmed to see a lone soldier sitting on a log, warming himself. He paid little attention to them. Climbing down, Jacob approached the man. "Evening Jube, any coffee?"

The soldier tipped his head, rain drained off the brim of his hat. "Guess ya had fun, loosing my cinch?" He looked mad enough to fight. "Must have had a good laugh thinking of me falling off old Buck into a pool o' water."

Jacob laughed again. "Well, it's better than what happened to the rest of the boys. And I see you didn't chase after me."

"No. When I realized ya only loosened my cinch, I figured ya wanted ta talk. I owed ya that."

Slowly, Jube stood up. Anger rang in his voice. "Reinhart is gunna' kill you for this."

"Damn it, Jube, he was gunna' kill me anyway."

Jube motioned towards the figure on the horse. "You is harboring a murderin' Injun. Jacob, have you gone plum crazy?"

"Jube, you've known me too long. It has nothing to do with the boy."

Waving his arm, Jacob motioned Daniel to join them in the light. Timidly, the Apache youth climbed off his horse and hid behind Jacob. The scowling soldier standing before him was as big as Jacob. Daniel held back, fearing that at any moment, the angry man would attack him.

Jacob, his eyes beaming like a proud father, took the boy by the shoulders, and brushing back his wet hair, held him before him. "I would like you to meet Daniel, Mea-a-ha's little brother."

With a trembling breath, Daniel tried his best English. "Hello, Mr. Soldier man."

Surprised, Jube reached out his hand and held the boy's face. "He's just a child."

"Jube, you named it the Battle of Apache Springs. I saw the pain in your face when you looked down at the body of a boy no older than Daniel. Do you still want to kill him?"

Releasing the young buck, Jube looked to Jacob. "No, guessin' I don't, but what do ya mean, it ain't nothin' ta do with the Injun?"

"Jube, do you really think a lazy no-good dandy like Reinhart would ride all the way to the Hollow after a wounded child, when he really should be tracking Cota?"

The absurdity of the idea, invoked a nervous chuckle from Jube. "I found that one a might hard to swallow, myself. But I follow orders. So tell me what it's all about."

Jacob knelt by the fire and fished two tin cups out of the sand. Filling them with warm coffee, he handed one to Daniel. After a long sip, He looked to his old friend. "There's some tie between Reinhart and Mathers. Don't know what it is, but I'm sure of it. There's something they don't want me to find out, and they're willin' to kill me to keep it hidden."

"Ya got any proof?"

Proof was the problem, Jacob shook his head. "No, but I got somethin' else. Mathers has been sellin' guns to the Apaches. I have the bill-of-sale to prove it."

Turning to Daniel, "Son, get our rifles."

Quickly, Daniel pulled the rifles from the scabbards and returned to the fire. Jacob took the Winchesters and handed them to Jube. "The one with the feather you know, it's Sholo's. The other I took off Mathers' boy. Check the serial numbers."

Leaning over the fire, Jube turned the guns so he could see the stampings. He wiped away the rain with his thumb. "They's only one number different."

He stared at Jacob, letting the meaning sink in. "Damn it. Damn it to hell. The bastard gave Sholo guns in exchange for raiding the Rincons' cattle, so it would leave 'em broke an' he could steal their land."

"You got it."

Jube handed the guns back. "The Rincons nearly lost everything. Poor Carmelita. This makes it personal."

Jumping to his feet, Jube thundered in anger. "Folks died because of them guns. Do ya figure Mathers suspects you know?"

"Not sure. Somethin' tells me there's more to it."

"Ya think there's a part where Reinhart figures in?"

"Jube, whenever Sholo raided the Rincons' we were someplace far away on Reinhart's orders. Think Jube, even then we doubted his leadership, but had no reason to suspect him, an officer of the United States Army, of aiding the enemy. It's unthinkable."

The sergeant jerked as the truth hit him. "That son of a bitch. For over a year we done chased Sholo through ice and hellfire. And Reinhart knew where he was all the time. No wonder he stayed behind."

Furious, Jube stomped back and forth, thinking it through. "We didn't catch Sholo until ya led us into the hills against orders."

Jacob hung his head, his voice grew husky. "Sholo didn't post guards that night because he knew we were supposed to be someplace else."

His friend's meaning was not lost on Jube. "Maybe it weren't a fair fight Jacob, but neither was the year chasin' him. Sholo had Reinhart on his side, an' we had a crusty ol' sergeant, ornery enough to disobey orders. In the end we got 'em. That evens things out, but Reinhart made us look like a bunch of bumbling' black fools, too dumb ta catch a band of starvin' Injuns."

"Jube, there's one more thing. When Reinhart gave his report on the battle the morning we returned to the fort, he told the colonel that the Indians had repeater rifles. I never mentioned that when I briefed him."

"Damn him!" Jube squared with Jacob and offered his rain-soaked glove. "Forgive me old friend, I've been a fool. What is it ya want me ta do?"

Jacob took his hand. "Talk to the boys. Buy me some time to find proof."

The soldier's voice rang loud. "Oh, I'll talk to the boys; you gots' all the time ya need. We'll turn the tables on that white bastard. We'll track ya every place ya ain't, just like we did Sholo."

A broad smile broke beneath the dripping brim of Jacob's hat. "Great. Tomorrow Mathers is driving cattle onto my land to draw me into a fight. It would help if the boys were tracking me to Mexico so I can take this in smaller bites."

With a braying laugh, Jube reached for his reins. "We is as good as there. Saw ya hightail it south myself, I did."

He reached down and patted Daniel's head. "You and this mighty dangerous Indian brave here."

Not sure if he was being complimented or teased, Daniel hid a shy grin. The men drained their cups and parted.

For a very tired Indian boy, the rest of the night was spent beneath a sparse stand of wavy leaf oak some miles north of Sand Creek. The crackling of a small fire roused him from his sleep. Poking his head out of the damp blanket, Daniel saw Jacob hunched over the low flames, roasting snake meat on a stick. A big smile welcomed the boy to the new day. "Have you recovered?"

Boys live from moment to moment. What happened the night before was only a memory. Daniel, none the worse for the wear, was ready for another adventure. "If I can dry out I will be okay."

"Good. Your part is over; you're headin' home."

Daniel's face fell. He sat bolt upright in his bedroll, his voice pleading. "I did good last night. Snow Raven and I stayed right with you. We did good. We outran the horse soldiers. Now we are going to help you fight the bad man."

"It's not about that, son. You did good, real good. Where I'm going, there's gunna' be killing, and I don't want you a part of it. What matters is that your sister is all alone and may be in danger. She needs your protection."

The boy slumped. For the first time in his life, Daniel had been on the winning side. He wanted more than anything to be with the big man who had become his hero, but he had a duty to obey. Mea-a-ha needed him at home. Slowly Daniel crawled out of his bedroll, the pout of a child evident as he did his best to shoulder the responsibility of a man.

The matter being settled, Jacob mounted up. Tugging on the reins, he faced the boy one last time. "Have breakfast, then head out."

The face of the big man softened. "Tell your sister not to worry about the soldiers anymore. Tell her I love her, and tell her that I am proud, very proud of her little brother. He brings honor to our family."

A lump caught in the boy's throat as he watched Jacob whirl the great horse around and ride away.

Chapter -25-
Separate Trails

Throughout the morning, Jacob pushed hard toward the western boundaries of his land. Speed was critical. Mea-a-ha was in the Hollow. By wit or by gun he must not let the rancher and his cowboys get past him. If he followed Sand Creek, he could stay in the flats and make better time than he would by trying to traverse the rolling foothills. Still, there was a full day's ride ahead.

Daniel's ride north to the Hollow would take less time if he pushed it. Chuckling to himself, Jacob thought of Jube leading Reinhart south. Jube was so mad, he might take the mangy bastard all the way to Mexico and leave him. He would do it too, if he thought he could get away with it. Last night's game worked pretty well. Now all the players of the late night misadventure were heading lickety-split in three different directions.

Major sensed the urgency of his master and increased his stride. There was a lot of thinking to do. Jacob really didn't have a plan, leastways not one all figured out. He had kept the soldiers and Mathers from joining forces. Now he must keep the rancher out of the Hollow. How he was going to manage that – well, that part he had to work on. Trouble was, he felt like a one-legged rabbit charging a pack of hungry wolves.

By midday, Sand Creek had pretty much played out, becoming little more than a ditch disappearing into a large sink. The sink spread across the barren terrain leaving crusty patches of surface clay that cracked and curled like dried paint flaking away. Foul pools of water from last night's rain dotted the bleak landscape. On the sink's western border, several small rolling gullies drained the low foothills. The gullies were wide, separated by eroded sandy knolls, most no higher than a tall saguaro. Foliage was sparse at best, a scattering of greasewood and creosote added little color to the dismal scene.

Jacob had only come this way once before, but turned aside from the maze of hills, preferring to make better speed further north. This time however, something had caught his eye.

For some distance, the faint signs of cattle tracks had begun to appear. They were old, but it takes a good deal of wind and rain to completely erase the deep scars of a cattle drive.

Jacob was beginning to have a pretty good idea that the tracks led from the Rincon ranch. After all, this used to be part of the Rincon range before he came along. It was also a good bet these might be the track of the cattle rustled during the Indian raids.

Time was short, but curiosity pushed him on. Why would Sholo drive the herd so far south and risk running into army patrols when there were hungry Apaches on the reservation further north who were desperate for food? It didn't add up.

Suddenly the mystery grew. Wagon tracks joined the trail. Not Conestoga wagons like settlers used, or buckboards, but large freight wagon tracks. There weren't too many freighters in this part of the desert. The tracks led into a single gully completely surrounded by knolls just high enough to offer a little shelter from the wind or perhaps from prying eyes. The gully was only a couple hundred feet wide, making a natural corral.

Cautiously, Jacob rode into the center of the depression and stopped. Nothing. It was just a big alkali sink.

Rising high in the saddle, Jacob let his dark eyes scan the empty bowl. The only thing he could tell for sure was the wagons came in. The wagons went out. The cattle didn't. At least not on their own hooves. It appeared that Sholo was quite a businessman, not only dealing in guns, but also a regular cattle baron. Question was, who was the buyer?

With a tap of the reins, Jacob rode up the ridge to the top of the knolls. Slowly he started to make his way around the rim.

At one point, the unmistakable glint of metal caught Jacob's eye. Dropping to the ground, he plucked a bullet casing from the sand. Looking around, he saw several more scattered about. Gazing down into the sink, it became apparent to Jacob that after herding the cattle into the center of the bowl, the Apaches opened up on the poor beasts with rifles from the high ground, slaughtering them all. Crude, but effective. Gathering up a handful of cartridges, Jacob stuffed them in his pocket and mounted up.

Across the sink was a dry water course where the ground showed signs of being disturbed. Jacob had a pretty good hunch what he would find there. Spurring Major, he quickly headed to the spot. As he approached, the putrid smell of death filled his nostrils. Carelessly buried, were the discarded remains of the slaughtered cattle.

Climbing from the saddle, Jacob moved from mound to mound kicking the partially exposed carcasses loose from the dirt, until he finally found what he was looking for. There, plain as day, was a piece of hide with the Rincon brand. It looked like an "R" with the upper loop made in the shape of a horseshoe. Taking out his knife, Jacob cut a square around the brand and stuffed it into his saddlebag. Then, walking to the middle of the sink, he took it all in trying to make sense of it. "Now we know how and where, but not why or who, except for Sholo of course."

Thinking hard, Jacob tried to piece it all together. "Since we know Sholo was trading for guns with Mathers, we can tie the rancher in, but he sure didn't need the meat, and he wouldn't have heavy freight wagons. Only the army--"The army!"

Suddenly it all came together. Jacob was stunned as the full plot unfolded. The plan was so simple, yet no one had any reason to put all the culprits together.

As the biggest rancher, Mathers had the contract to supply the army with beef for the reservation. Instead of selling his own beef, he obviously found it more profitable to sell the army Rincon's beef, while disposing of the evidence of the cattle rustling at the same time. The rancher must have had quite a chuckle over his own cleverness.

Everything fell into place. Part of Reinhart's responsibilities at the fort was to pick up the beef from Mathers and haul it to the reservation. This he always did with a couple of hand-picked soldiers. The scheme was simple, and so were the reasons behind it. The greedy rancher wanted Rincon's huge Spanish land grant so he could build the biggest spread in the territory. He got Sholo to do the dirty work by trading him rifles. The enterprising Reinhart probably got a healthy cut of the profits for keeping the soldiers away, and for hauling off the stolen beef.

Placing the army freight wagons at this location where the rustled herd was slaughtered, instead of Mathers' ranch where they should have been, was the key to the puzzle. It firmly tied both Mathers and Reinhart to a crime of selling stolen beef to the army, not to mention selling guns to the Indians and cattle rustling.

So there it was, the great Damon Mathers, respected cattle baron, and the famous Captain Lawrence Reinhart, hero of a battle he never fought, exposed for what they were, a pair of low down scoundrels.

These were hanging offenses, and the unscrupulous pair feared that with Jacob living in the Hollow, the risk of him stumbling on to this place and putting it all together was too great.

Now Jacob understood why Reinhart and Mathers wanted him dead. Yessir, there it was, but knowing the truth and proving it were two different things. Jacob knew full well that the word of a colored dirt farming squaw man, crazy enough to set up digs in the middle of the desert would mean nothing against a decorated army officer and the wealthiest cattle rancher in the territory. With Sholo dead and the rustling stopped, time would eventually erase all evidence. The lone bullet Jacob fired into Sholo's heart on that fateful morning had ended Mathers' game. Jacob shook his head; it was one more reason why the rancher wanted him dead. That brought Jacob back to the task at hand.

Knowing the truth can be a powerful thing but it wasn't going to stop Mathers from reaching the Hollow. Turning the rancher away would be much harder than sending Reinhart traipsing off to Mexico. Jacob had friends, but against Mathers and his cowboys, he would be alone. The big man patted Major's thick neck. "Twenty men. If we pull off this one old friend, maybe we will deserve our own dime novel."

With a slap of the reins, Jacob headed for his showdown with Damon

Mathers.

A bitter wind hissed through the naked rocks atop the lonesome ridge, biting Jacob's exposed flesh. The warm campfires of the drovers were visible from the bluff where the weary rider watched from the saddle of his horse. "Yessir, Major, it's going to be a cold one tonight."

The storm clouds of the previous day had cleared out, leaving brilliant stars hanging in a frigid sky. Tiny ice crystals floated in the chilled desert air, prickling Jacob's skin.

In the camp below, a dog barked. "Well, so much for running off their horses during the night. Best we get some rest, Major, and see if the morning scares up some luck for us. We're gunna' need it."

Easing from the saddle, Jacob found a little shelter from the wind by wedging himself in a narrow crag. "At least it's got a nice view."

Jacob looked to his horse as though he expected a reply. The big man turned away and did his best to get comfortable at the base of a gnarled juniper growing from a ledge above his head.

From here he could keep an eye on his adversary and hopefully catch a few winks. Major seemed content tucked in the cut between the rocks that had brought them to this overlook. He sniffed the dried juniper needles scattered about his hooves in this narrow passage, then closed his aging eyes. Sleep took him easily. Jacob wedged his back deeper into the crevasse. "Yessir, it is going to be a cold one tonight."

Smoke from the cowboys' fire carried the taunting aroma of hot food to Jacob's nostrils. Probably steak and beans, a far cry better than his stiff, rancid jerky. "Sure would love some hot coffee." Reaching for his canteen, he sipped some stale water and resigned himself to his fate.

How close the men seemed. Jacob was maybe sixty feet higher and little less than a pistol shot away. He stretched out his freezing hand, half hoping to feel the warmth of their fires.

Fragments of conversation drifted on the crisp night air. The drovers were engaged in good natured ribbing of each other. Occasionally laughter would rise, then fall, but Jacob could never catch the joke. They were certainly in happy spirits standing around their nice warm fire.

A cold, hard stone pushed into Jacob's back making the camp below seem inviting. He wished he could join the men, yet tomorrow these same good-natured fellows intended to kill him. Jacob pulled his collar about him and closed his eyes.

Eventually the fires and voices died low. The drovers snuggled in their bedrolls, while Jacob remained on guard. By morning the men would be refreshed and well fed. He would be stiff from a cold, sleepless night.

Not one to give up, Jacob held his hands to his mouth and made his best coyote howl. Instantly the dog took to barking. A satisfied smile crossed his tired face. As the yammer died away, Jacob howled again and the hound started all over. An evil chuckle escaped his lips... the cold seemed a little more bearable.

Whiffs of steam swirled from the cold damp sand as the sleepy sun yawned above the edge of the weathered bluff. Damon Mathers rose late, pushed back the heavy canvas flap on his tent and poked his head out. Beads of ice cold dew pooled together in the folds and spilled on to the rancher's bare neck, evoking an angry curse.

This was his second trip into the disagreeable desert, and he wasn't happy one bit. The Buffalo Soldier would pay dearly for his meddling. Death would not come easily.

Clay Bohanan, Mathers' foreman, stepped forward, ready with a tin cup of hot coffee. "Welcome up, Mr. Mathers, take a chew on old Scully's coffee, it'll burn off the morning chill, if it don't kill you first. Daresay its deadlier n' bullets."

Sour-faced, Mathers took the cup. "Hell, if that's the case, pour the rest of the pot down that damn hound of yours, kept me awake all night."

For a long moment the two men stood silently sipping the evil brew. Their bitter expressions gave testimony to the accuracy of Bohanan's description of Scully's coffee.

Slowly, a rangy old man in a battered hat and a buckskin coat left his place amongst the cowboys standing by the fire. He sidled up to the somber pair, courageously contending with his own cup of black tar. Mathers cast him a disgruntled glance then returned to staring at nothing in particular. "Morning, Hamp. Any idea when we'll find that black son-of-a-bitch? I'd like to give him a cup of this swill."

Rubbing his whiskered jaw, Hamp chuckled. "Well, that would be cruel indeed. If I find him right quick-like would there be extra pay?"

The ill-humored rancher grunted. "I'll shoot the cook so you never have to taste this evil brew."

Hamp's deep, wrinkled face broke into a toothy grin as he braved another sip. "Well, sir, I'd rather have the money but guess I got ta earn my pay. So put a gun ta Scully's head, 'cuz that's the famous hero right thar'."

Stunned, Mathers jerked in every direction. Hamp took time to choke down a long swallow before continuing. "That's him up thar' 'bout five hundred yards away on the bluff with the sun to his back. Been there since first light."

High on the ridge, the men spied the silhouette of a large man sitting a tall horse nearly lost in the sun behind him. The rising steam made the shadowed rider waver like a desert mirage.

Bohanan swore. "Why didn't you say something sooner?"

Stirring his cup with a crooked finger, the old scout took his time. "No need. He ain't going nowhere or else he woulda' already went."

Mathers' face turned bright red and he angrily threw his cup to the ground. Bohanan gripped the butt of his revolver. "I'll have some men ride up and we will drag that uppity black bastard out of his saddle."

Stepping forwards, Mathers faced the man on the bluff. "No, Hamp is right. That's just what he wants. The darkie is goading us. He met us way out here because he's an old cavalry soldier and he wants some fighting room. Like nothing better than to get four or five of these young cowboys up there so he could cut them to pieces."

The foreman looked incredulous. "You can't be serious?"

"He's cavalry an' he can fight from the saddle at a dead run. Ain't none of these callow boys can steady a gun while charging up that hill. Most likely shoot their horses in the back of the head. That's what he wants alright. He's goading us."

Clenching his fist, Bohanan fumed. "Do you think he's that good?"

Mathers didn't break his stare. "Don't underestimate him. He got the drop on Flynn, which ain't easy, took the guns away from Raithe and Wyatt who are 'most as fast as Flynn, and he sure as hell killed Sholo."

Taking a few steps forward Mathers shook his head. "No, I won't underestimate him again. I'll kill 'em. That's the truth, but I won't underestimate 'em."

Throwing his cup beside Mathers, Bohanan stomped ahead of his boss. "We can't just stand here. What if we all open up on him right now? Hero or not, ain't no way he can survive twenty Winchesters spitting lead."

Hamp cut in. "No, don't want ta get him started shootin', some of these young boys will get kilt. I was watching him through my spyglass. His horse is sporting two scabbards. Guess one is his 45-70 Army Springfield. He'll jes' ride out of our range and pick us off. He wouldn't be sitting out there iffin' he thought he was in any danger."

Completely flustered, the foreman turned to Mathers. "Then what the hell are we 'spose ta do?"

"Nothin'. He'll be his own undoing. The good Sergeant Keever, Hero of Apache Springs, is a man of honor. He'll never shoot first. That's why he's goading us. So we'll just keep pushing the herd and let him be the one that stews. This time I won't underestimate him, no sir."

Exasperated, Bohanan ripped off his hat adding it to the dented tin cups. "Well, that's a hell of a way to kill a man. We'll just ignore him 'til he ups n' dies on his own."

Mathers offered a wicked grin. "It's the perfect way. We will just ignore him and drive these steers right up to his precious Hollow, where we'll have him trapped against the cliffs, and then while he's busy protecting his squaw, we'll close in and cut him down."

Turning around, Mathers laughed and rubbed his thick hands. "Scully, get me another cup of that delicious coffee, and some breakfast too."

The drovers were given strict orders to stay clear of the rider as they went about their business of breaking camp. The men worked while casting uneasy glances at the dark motionless figure looming above them.

Sizing it all up, Mathers was glad he had left his worthless sons to guard the ranch, albeit to punish them. They would have just embarrassed him more, and they'd be hard to control with the Buffalo Soldier sitting up there taunting them – especially Raithe, who would just get stupid crazy.

Bohanan leaned against the lone chuck wagon as the boys loaded in Mathers' heavy canvas tent. Hamp chuckled. "Kind of gives you the willies, him watchin' like a hungry wolf. But I 'spec Mathers is right. It would be too costly to take him now."

Bohanan tightened a rope on the wagon. "It ain't right. We got him twenty to one. It ain't right,"

Mounting his pony, Hamp looked down. "It ain't right what we is doing, so I guess we can't complain that it's all wrong."

An angry frown clouded the foreman's face. "Best keep that kind of talk to yourself if you want to ride for this outfit."

Looking up at the lone horseman, Hamp spoke more to himself. "Ya got ta respect him."

Throughout the morning, the cowboys pushed the small herd of a dozen cattle toward the cliffs, ever mindful of the rider in the lead. It seemed as though the man they were chasing was riding scout for them. He knew the direction they were going and rode just ahead, choosing the trail they would take.

Old Hamp headed his pony through the herd, listening to the young drovers. Some were getting edgy, hungering for a kill, others were less eager, finding admiration for the brave Hero of Apache Springs.

By midday they had pushed deep into the foothills. The vast desert gave way to small, rolling gullies, and the cattle bunched closer together. As the herd neared the crest of a steep hill, the drovers looked up from their work, surprised to see the lone rider dismount and make his way to a large rock.

The whole procession came to a quick halt as uneasy men tried to figure out what he was doing. Noticing their concern, Jacob tipped his hat and pulled a large piece of jerky and a biscuit from his coat pocket, then began eating. There was a sigh of relief. Even Mathers chuckled. "I guess he's right, it is time to break for lunch."

Barking an order, the rancher climbed out of the saddle. "Scully, you murdering cook, build a fire and heat some grub."

The adversaries sat eating their lunch together, Mathers' small army and the condemned man with little more than a dozen cattle strung between them. Clay Bohanan dug another scoop of beans from his plate. "It don't seem right. It don't seem right at all."

Stuffing his mouth with a piece of bread, Mathers tried to be more philosophical. "A condemned man is entitled to a last meal. Nothing says he has to eat it alone."

Rising to his feet, Hamp cleared his gravelly throat. "That's about as true a word as I've heard all day."

Walking over to the chuck wagon, he grabbed two plates of beans, and tucking a loaf of bread under his arm, started up the hill. All the drovers watched in disbelief. Even Mathers sat dumbfounded. Bohanan shook his head in bewilderment. "If that don't beat all. It just keeps getting' stranger by the moment."

From his rock perch, Jacob watched with some amusement as the grizzled old scout stumped up the trail. Hamp was the first to speak. "Didn't spill a bean." He laughed and continued. "Thought ya might like some warm vittles."

Returning the kindness, Jacob greeted him with a tip of his hat. "Mighty neighborly. Living on jerky gets tiring. Much obliged."

The two men ate quietly for awhile, just enjoying the moment, then Jacob spoke again. "A right nice herd of cattle you brought me there. You must thank Mathers for me."

The old scout took a few more bites. "It may get ugly."

"Been ugly for some time."

Lowering his plate, Hamp eyed Jacob hard. "Is there any other way? Can't you high tail it outta here?"

"If everyone ran, where would we be?"

Turning his fork over, Jacob idly stirred his beans. "Are you so married to the idea of killin' me?"

The old scout winced. "It won't be my bullet that finds you. I promise you that. I may have sunk low enough in my old age to scout for a snake, but he'll have to do his own killin'."

"I appreciate it; saves me a bullet. Tell me Hamp, if I kill Mathers, will the others give it up?"

Hamp sopped up some beans with a slice of bread and took a thoughtful chew. He stared at the cowboys below, some were his friends. "No. They won't give it up. They're young n' full of fire. Killin' the ol' skunk would be like pourin' kerosene on 'em."

"Kinda figured that. Being young and full of fire will make 'em reckless. Countin' on that too."

"Do you really think you have a chance?"

A thin smile cracked the soldiers face. "Legend has it I gunned down sixty warriors at Apache Springs."

The old scout grinned and shook his head. "I heard they was swarmin' like flies. So what's the truth?"

Jacob took time for another bite. "It is truly amazing how things get blown out of proportion. I have to laugh at it myself. The honest truth, Mr. Hamp, is I only shot two bullets that mornin'." He gave a reflective chuckle. "And now it looks like ten times that won't be enough, but the thing is, people give up too easy. Makes no sense to throw in your hand when it's all that stands between you and a bad day."

"Son, I hope ya got a few aces up your sleeve; you're gunna' need 'em."

Taking a large bite of bread, Jacob pondered his words. "You seem like a straight sort of fellow. It may be a might strange, but I want to ask you a favor."

"Ain't nothing that ain't strange about this day. Ask your favor and I'll see what I can do."

Finishing his bread, Jacob cleared his throat. "If it goes bad for me... make sure the Indian girl gets out. Don't let them have her."

Hamp stared into the tired face of the Buffalo Soldier and saw fear... not for himself, but for a girl. There's something about love that can make a man shed his life as if it were only a thin layer of skin. Hamp now understood why this man would stand to his dying breath. The Hero of Apache Springs was more than just a myth.

Giving a sad smile, the old scout nodded. "If I see you fall, I'll ride out and get ta her first. They won't put their dirty hands on her, I promise ya that."

Jacob handed his plate back. "It's been a good meal, Mr. Hamp, I thank you most kindly."

The two men shook hands. No matter how this day would end, for the scout and the soldier, it would be as friends.

Standing up, Jacob threw his shoulders back and filled his lungs. "Now for the ugly part you were mentioning. I was hoping for some good news, but I can't wait any longer. We settle it here. So I recommend you find yourself some high ground."

Hurrying down the hill, Hamp had no idea what Jacob was planning, but he knew it was going to get interesting real quick. He strolled right past the men, every eye begging to know what was said. Tossing the plates on the chuck wagon, he went right to his horse. Mathers exploded. "Well, what the hell did he say?"

Hamp tightened the cinch, without looking back. "He said to tell you thanks for the cattle."

One of the drovers stood up and pointed. "Look, he's gone."

Everyone gaped, wondering what it meant. No one dared move, no one but Hamp who mounted to the saddle.

Suddenly, from the crest of the hill, Jacob's Winchester exploded in rapid fire, spending every shell. His volley broke like thunder. The tranquil meal erupted into pandemonium as screaming bullets tore into the earth beneath the startled cattle.

The crazed steers bolted, stampeding down the gully right through the bewildered drovers. Frightened cowboys scrambled frantically out of

258

the way of bullets and trampling hooves. Rearing horses broke free in panic. The team harnessed to the chuck wagon whirled around and headed down the hill, spilling the wagon and its contents. There was no chance to return fire; every man ran for his life as the charging herd raced into the desert.

It was over as quick as it had started, Jacob had played his hand. Clay Bohanan jumped up coughing in a cloud of dust. Brandishing his pistol, he fired wildly at the empty ridge. Mathers climbed from behind the upturned wagon, shouting orders. "Put that damn thing away and get the horses."

Bohanan bellowed to his drovers. "Round up the horses and cattle."

Mathers spit. "To hell with the cattle. Get the horses, damn it. We'll end it here."

The men went racing down the hill on foot. Dusting himself off, Mathers turned, saw Hamp sitting on his pony halfway up the hill, and went livid. "You knew, you son-of-a-bitch. You knew he was going to do this."

Too old for fear, the grizzled scout scoffed. "Ya hired me ta scout, not ta do your fightin'."

Venting his rage at the only one he could, Mathers roared. "You could have warned us, you old bastard."

"It ain't my job ta nursemaid ya."

Drawing his pistol Mathers continued roaring. "You're fired and you can join the nigger in hell."

The rancher fired a round, but it fell short. The old scout spurred his mount, heading for the top of the ridge. Before Mathers could take another shot, a mounted rider came tearing up the gully at full gallop, screaming all the way. Astonished, Mathers turned. It was Raithe.

Plowing to a halt, Raithe, sweat-stained and haggard, jumped out of the saddle landing in front of his angry father. "They're gone. They're all gone."

"Make sense, boy. Who's gone?"

"The herd. The entire herd."

Dropping his gun into the dirt, Mathers grabbed his son by his vest with both hands. "What do you mean the herd is gone? There are four thousand head. You and your brother were supposed to guard them. What were you doing?"

Terrified, Raithe pleaded. "It weren't my fault pa. I think it was Indians."

The older man, roared. "Indians!"

"Pa, they burned down everything." The boy whimpered. "The house, the barn. The ranch is gone, Pa. We got nothin'."

Mathers face contorted as if every blood vessel in his head was going to burst. He had spent years building a cattle dynasty, and now it had vanished in an instant.

Consumed by madness, Damon Mathers shook his son so violently the poor boy fell to his knees. "I'm ruined, you stupid fool. Didn't you try to stop them?"

Tears streamed down the frightened boy's face. "They came at night. I was all alone."

"Alone? Where was Wyatt?"

"He's gone."

Mathers stopped shaking the boy and waited for him to continue.

"He's gone Pa. Wyatt didn't like being left behind, so he said he would meet up with you in the Hollow. He was going to finish with the Indian girl."

Throwing his boy to the ground, Mathers turned and took several stumbling steps, his shoulders slumped. "Fools. I raised fools."

Suddenly he threw back his head and glared at the ridge with vengeance burning in his eyes. "Damn you, Jacob Keever, this is your doing. You had a hand in the Indians stealing my herd. I know it."

Clenching his fists, he roared like a wounded lion. "You got my herd, but listen to me, Jacob Keever, my boy Wyatt has your stinking squaw."

As madness overcame the rancher, rage suddenly turned to laughter. "Mark my word, I will get my herd back. Can you say the same for your squaw?"

Whirling around and around, Mathers searched the ridge. "Did you hear me, Keever? Can you say the same for your filthy squaw?"

There was no answer. Jacob was gone.

Chapter -26-
Never Give Up

When something is so important you can hardly wait, time goes slow. For Mea-a-ha it had come to a stop. She wished so deeply for Jacob's safe return that the time between each heart beat seemed an eternity. The girl felt as though she would die before she could breathe again. Pulling her gaze from the window, she tried to quiet her mind.

Even though she had lost her appetite, Mea-a-ha stood over the stove cooking her supper same as always. Slicing a single rib from a side of smoked elk, she placed it in a pan of boiling water along with a pinch of salt. The rib was large enough that she might be able to pass the remaining daylight nibbling the meat from the large, curved bone. Maybe she would eat it curled up in Jacob's big cozy chair, pretending the battle was over, and she was safe in his arms.

The day was waning, and Mea-a-ha dreaded nights the most. She would lay awake for long dark hours, tormented by her imagination. Jacob had forbidden her from letting the new puppy climb into bed with them, but now curling up with Friendly was her only comfort on these lonely nights.

Friendly was more than a pet, he was Mea-a-ha's constant companion. At the slightest sound, his ears would prick up. Occasionally he would growl, then just as quickly go back to play, as if to say everything was okay.

The small puppy's vigilance gave the Apache girl some comfort in her lonely hours. Friendly was also her confidant. He would listen to her intently, cocking his head to one side as though he really understood. Mea-a-ha believed he did. As she saw it, in their little family there was a giant man, a rebellious boy, a pretty girl, and a fuzzy dog. Every size, shape, and color. All different, but equally important.

Setting the plate with the single rib on the table, Mea-a-ha stepped to the door to see where Friendly had gotten to. He loved to race down to the pond and root through the cattails, scaring up birds.

When he didn't answer her call, Mea-a-ha strolled down to the barn to search for him. Birds were getting scarce; maybe he was whining at the hens as they clucked away in their nesting boxes refusing to come out and play. She called again, but faint barks on the far side of the pond told her he was too busy with important matters to answer her call.

As Mea-a-ha made her way through the barn she came to the ladder leading to the loft. The loft was one of her favorite places in the Hollow. She let her fingers trace the wooden rungs. Up there she was tall. From the two windows on either end, she could see most of their beloved

Hollow. Drawn by innocent joy, she scurried up the ladder and in a moment, was gazing out toward the road. The road would bring Jacob home. Oh, how she wished he would come right now. She would race from the barn and throw her arms around him before he could even get out of the saddle. He would pretend to be annoyed, and she would giggle.

Picking up a piece of straw, the dreamy eyed girl placed it to her lips and leaned against the window sill. It was cooler after yesterday's rain. An afternoon breeze felt refreshing. The sun's deep red glow brought a warmth that seemed to work from the inside out. How beautiful everything was, if only Jacob was there to share it with her.

As she sat daydreaming Mea-a-ha noticed something. Beneath the dark green branches of the evergreens that canopied over the road, she could see the front legs of a horse standing still. Everything else was hidden. For just the briefest moment her heart leaped, thinking it was Jacob, but no, the legs were too thin to be Major's.

Just then, the rider prodded the horse into the naked aspens. The young girl threw a hand to her mouth, stifling a scream. Astride the tall stallion sat Wyatt Mathers. Mea-a-ha's legs went weak. She collapsed to the hay covered floor, her heart pounding in her breast.

Nightmarish visions of her poor grandfather being beaten by Wyatt's cruel hand amid his sick, twisted laughter screamed in her mind, overwhelming her with nausea.

Fighting back panic, Mea-a-ha raised just enough to peer out the window. Had he seen her? Should she run or stay hidden. He would catch her if she ran. All she could do was watch, hoping he would search the house and go away. It seemed like that might happen.

Wyatt rode right to the door and boldly walked in as though he own the place. He had heard that the black soldier had lit out for Mexico. Courage came easy when there was only a girl to face. He could unleash his cruelty in the light of day.

While the rancher's son was out of her sight, Mea-a-ha managed to control her breathing. Jacob had left her the other Winchester for protection, but she had left it leaning in a corner by the bed. He had told her to keep it with her, but she hadn't. Foolish girl. Riding Peaches was out of the question. Hiding was her only choice.

All too soon the front door pushed open wide and Wyatt reappeared, swaggering on to the porch. Clutched in his hand was her dinner. Mea-a-ha felt violated. He had stolen her meal. A small wrong compared to what she knew he was planning, but it outraged her just the same. How she wished he would choke on that bone.

Gnawing the rib, Wyatt tossed the china plate to the ground, shattering it without a care. He then made his way to the barn as though he were on a Sunday stroll. Terrified, Mea-a-ha scrambled to a corner of the loft and dove beneath the hay. Her eyes grew wide. He was coming.

The monster was coming, coming for her.

Mea-a-ha covered her mouth with her hands, trying to muffle her cries. Below she could hear his lumbering footsteps as he stepped inside. His evil voice hissed up through the rafters, paralyzing her with fear. "Hey, little Papoose, are you in here? Tasty meat, but I think your flesh shall be more delicious."

Wyatt's heavy footsteps moved from the door, coming closer to the ladder. "Hey, little Papoose, come out and play."

Mea-a-ha could hear him kicking at the hay piled below. She dared not breathe. "I will find you, little Papoose. You know I will. We need to finish the game we started before that darkie of yours spoiled our fun. You knew I had plans for you. Didn't you?"

Slowly he moved around the cluttered barn poking in shadows, turning over crates and saddle trees, all the while pouring out his sick hate. "My pa has probably got that nigger hanging from a tree by now. His neck stretched, eyes all bulgy."

Wyatt laughed. "Yea, I would like to see that." His voice turned angry. "If my pa had let me go with him, I'd of skinned that darkie too."

His resentment turned to a pathetic whine. "But Father ordered me to stay home like I was a little kid. He thinks I'm weak. I'll show him. When he comes and finds I got here first and have already taken care of pretty little you, he will see."

The oldest brother's thoughts quickly changed. "Bet you're sweet as candy beneath them buckskins." His perverse hiss returned. "Come out, little Papoose, maybe you will enjoy it. Them rutting braves must've had you before that darkie. Now you get to find out what it's like to be taken by a white man."

Every stomp of his boot, each ugly word, added to her madness. Closer he came, nearer then farther. With a loud bang, the grain room door was kicked open. Boxes and sacks tipped over. He continued his taunting, and slowly returned to the ladder as he had many times before. "Hey little Papoose are you up there waiting for me on a bed of straw? Answer me, little Pap—, well what do we have here? Hi, little fella', where is your sweet little Injun princess hiding?"

Her mind reeled. No! Not Friendly. Not in the grip of that evil monster! An innocent yap, and her heart sank. Mea-a-ha pressed her head against the floor and curled into a little ball, her whole body shaking. Crying silently, she prayed over and over. "Please don't let him hurt Friendly, please don't let him hurt my puppy."

Wyatt's deep, evil voice came sickly sweet. "Here little pooch, would you like a bone? That's it come closer. Closer boy. That's it." A startled yelp told her Wyatt had the helpless pup in his grasp. She rose through the hay to a sitting position, pulling her knees in a tight embrace. Tears streamed past her gaping mouth as the panic stricken girl shook helplessly in the corner. She had to go down and save her puppy, but terror nailed her to the floor. Her body and mind were being torn apart.

A painful whine burst from a frightened puppy who did not understand. "Little Papoose, I got your dog. Come out, little Papoose or I might have to break his tiny neck."

Friendly struggled to free himself, his pleading whimpers ended in a high pitch gurgle. He was suffocating. "If I squeeze his neck any tighter it's going to snap. You better come down."

Losing all control, Mea-a-ha wailed with rage. She clawed her way to the ladder, screaming through her tears. "Don't you hurt my puppy. Please don't hurt him."

With choking garbled pleas for mercy, she scrambled down the ladder in a frantic rush. Limbs flaying madly, Mea-a-ha fell to the ground hard. Rolling over she held out her arms to the monster towering over her. "Please, give me my puppy. I will do anything. Please don't hurt him."

The evil voice crackled with mockery. "Does the Papoose want her little puppy?"

Reaching from the shadows he dangled the helpless animal above her. Sobbing, Mea-a-ha stretched her arms higher. A twisted grin broke across Wyatt's dark face. "Well then, come get him, little Papoose."

The only thought in the tortured girl's mind was for her puppy. Crawling closer, she reached her tormentor's boot. Again she stretched her arms up, pleading. His evil laugh smote like thunder, reverberating through the timbers.

Slowly, Wyatt lowered Friendly temptingly towards her hands, only to jerk the puppy back as she got close, laughing at his own amusement.

As her anguish grew unbearable, he lowered the puppy again, until her fingertips just barely touch the puppy's dangling paw, then suddenly with Friendly almost in her grasp, he snatched his arm back and with despicable cruelty, hurled the helpless ball of fur across the barn. The puppy slammed high into the wall with a final painful yelp, then dropped lifelessly behind the haystack. Mea-a-ha screamed in horrid disbelief. Throwing herself into the hay, she crawled frantically towards her puppy.

Laughing insanely, Wyatt let his prey scramble a few feet before grabbing a bare leg and dragging her back. She clawed furiously at the straw, mindless of Wyatt's intent. The evil pitch of his laugh grew as he lifted her off the ground by her ankle.

Tossing her about like a little rag doll, he flipped her around and crushed her to his chest. The girl's legs kicked helplessly in the air, her fists beat furiously on his shoulders.

Growing crueler with each breath, the malicious brute grabbed her hair. Yanking her head back, he pressed his lips to hers. Mea-a-ha's wild blows went unnoticed as he forced her mouth open. She would not relent. The cowardly beast had killed her puppy.

Fighting with all she had, she bit completely through his lip. Wyatt gave a high pitched yowl and slapped her hard. His eyes burning at her affront, he spit his blood in her face.

Seething with rage, the crazed boy grabbed the tail of her shirt, and dropped her to the ground. With the thin fabric clenched in his fists, he violently shook her out of her dress as though he was dumping a sack of potatoes.

Falling hard but free, Mea-a-ha twisted and crawled back into the hay. Her screams and his laughter filled the barn. Wyatt wiped his bloody mouth on the shirt, then threw it away. His eyes glazed with insanity, fired by the vision of the dark, naked beauty sprawled before him.

Lunging forward, Wyatt's heavy body dropped on the fragile girl, nearly crushing her ribs. "Where you going, Papoose? Would you prefer your dead puppy over me?"

Mea-a-ha gasped helplessly for air.

Rolling her over, Wyatt pinned her wrists above her head with one hand, then reaching down, unbuckled his gun belt and tossed it aside.

Bringing his hand back, he let it slide slowly over her naked skin. "Soft little Papoose, so soft." His voice grew cold. "I fear this is going to hurt you more than you can ever imagine." Callused fingers dug deep into her tender breast. The girl whimpered.

"Gunna make love to you little Injun 'til you're all used up."

All of a sudden Wyatt grunted as a flying weight struck him from behind. "Get off my sister, you..."

Daniel, unaware of what was happening until he stepped into the barn, came unarmed. Yet in an instant, he was on the man wrapping his thin arm around Wyatt's neck in a choke hold. The young boy pulled back with all his might.

Gagging, Wyatt released Mea-a-ha and rose to his feet, taking the youth with him. Squeezing tighter, Daniel refused to release his grip. Only four years separated the two adversaries, but it was enough. One had the body of a man, and the other was still a boy.

Red faced, eyes bulging, Wyatt stumbled backwards, slamming Daniel's thin frame into a heavy log beam, knocking the wind out of him, but the boy held on.

Leaning forward, Wyatt threw himself back again with all his force, crushing Daniel against the unyielding timber. A scream of agony escaped Daniel lips as his ribs cracked. Knocked senseless, the courageous youth crumbled to the ground.

The brute whirled around coughing and cursing. Enraged by Daniel's interference, he swung his leg back and kicked the boy, square in the stomach. Daniel shuddered under the impact of the heavy boot. "Damn you Injun." Wyatt reached down. Grabbing Daniel by the hair, he jerked him violently to his knees.

Going for the kill, Mathers hardened his huge fist and raised it high. Before he could release his lethal blow, Mea-a-ha screamed and threw herself on his back. He struggled to ignore her, but she tore at him like a she-bear protecting her cub. Pulling herself higher, Mea-a-ha dug her fingers into his eyes, scratching and gouging.

Howling in excruciating pain, Wyatt dropped the boy and grabbed Mea-a-ha's wrists, hauling her into the air.

Lifting her over his head, he twisted around and with all his force, hurled her down, driving Mea-a-ha's fragile body against the hard packed earth. Every last breath of air was forced from her lungs in a heavy gasp. Her arm buckled beneath her with a loud snap.

Covering his bloody eye socket, Wyatt screamed with fury. "Filthy bitch, you blinded me!"

Consumed with madness, Wyatt raised his foot and stomped on her soft stomach with the flat of his boot. Mea-a-ha's limbs flailed wide, she convulsed, struggling to breathe.

Fighting for consciousness, she could only stare helplessly at the blurry madman looming over her, roaring vengeance. His wrath unabated, he cast about for a weapon, and jerked a pitchfork from the hay. Stumbling forward, he straddled her naked body, his dripping blood painting her skin. "You will pay, Injun. You will pay." He raised the sharp, deadly tines high above her exposed stomach and plunged it downwards.

In the same instant, Daniel pushed himself up with one arm. His fingers clasped around something in the straw; it was a discarded rib bone. Screaming the bloodthirsty cry of a savage warrior, Daniel hurled himself high onto the man's shoulders, his small hand locked into Wyatt's hair, pulling his head back. Wielding the curved bone with all his might, the boy drove it deep into the side of Wyatt's neck.

Writhing in agony, Wyatt's aim went wild, the pitchfork slammed into the dirt, one tine cutting a deep gash in Mea-a-ha's side. With blind fury, Wyatt pulled Daniel over his shoulder, slamming him to the ground. The boy's head hit with a sharp thud and all went black.

Wyatt staggered a few feet. "Damn Injuns--Pa..."

Mea-a-ha floated in and out of a dream. Visions of holding Friendly for the first time while sitting on the floor of their safe home stirred her mind. He eagerly licked her face. She tried to raise her arm to pet him but it would not obey. Searing pain shot from her fingertips all the way to her neck.

Mea-a-ha struggled to come to her senses. It was pitch black. She was cold and naked. The dream of sitting on the warm floor of their home vanished, but the soft tongue, lapping about her face continued. Friendly! He was alive. In the darkness, the little dog had found her. "My puppy." Tears of joy streamed down the girl's cheeks. "My dear puppy."

266

Raising up on her left arm, Mea-a-ha inched her way over to a lantern that sat on an old barrel. Reaching it she felt around for the matches and lit the wick.

Blinking away the darkness, her vision returned. There sat brave little Friendly as happy as ever. He tried to come to her but as soon as he put weight on his right paw, he yelped in pain and sat back down. "Poor Friendly."

Looking into the shadows, Mea-a-ha spied the lifeless body of Wyatt Mathers. She cringed. His head was lying in a black pool of blood, her dinner bone sticking out of his neck.

The bone might have been nothing more than a weapon of opportunity, but to the Indian girl, it was the magic of the Hollow answering her prayers. The bone could have fallen anywhere, but it "happened" to be in just the right spot for the hand of a courageous boy.

Daniel! Mea-a-ha's eyes frantically searched the dark. In the shadows under the log railings of the stall, Mea-a-ha could make out the thin shape of her brother flattened against the ground. Nauseating pain washed over her as she pulled herself to him with one arm. "Daniel, Daniel," she pleaded. "Daniel."

Slumping by his side, she laid her cheek next to his. He was breathing. Gently, she stroked his hair and called his name.

Coming to his senses, he opened his eyes then closed them. "Hi."

Mea-a-ha nuzzled her head to his, her eyes blurry with tears. Daniel swallowed and struggled for words. "Where is the man?"

Mea-a-ha snuggled closer. "He is dead."

The trio cuddled in the same bed. Even though he was cracked and bruised, Daniel had managed to bind Mea-a-ha's broken arm, and he had bound Friendly's injured limb, too. Mea-a-ha made him tend to Friendly before he could splint her arm or bandage her ribs.

It was nearly dawn before they had doctored their wounds. Fatigue finally won over frazzled nerves. Mind and bodies spent, they slept curled together through the rest of the day.

That was how Jacob found them, in deep sleep. Even Friendly, snoozing in the middle of the bed, did not stir when Jacob crept into the room. Mea-a-ha's bandaged arm, resting outside the covers, told much of the story. It was best to let them sleep. Jacob would hear the details later, but most of it he could already guess.

Chapter -27-
The Last Stand

The soft crackling of embers in the fireplace awakened Mea-a-ha. A warm, red glow danced on the rough stone wall outside her room. Jacob was home. As she raised her head, a firm hand from the shadows pressed her back into the pillow. "Rest, my darling."

"Oh, Jacob." The girl's voice was weak and buried in emotion. She could not finish her sentence. Jacob placed a tender kiss on her forehead. A day would come to face the horror of that terrible night, but now was a time to heal.

Over the next few days Mea-a-ha would often wake to the smell of food, or open her eyes and find Jacob dozing, wrapped in a blanket in the chair by the side of her bed. She would fall asleep knowing he would be there when she woke again.

For his part, Jacob spent his time moving between the two bedrooms. Daniel was in better condition physically, but Jacob could tell the violent killing of Wyatt Mathers weighed heavy on the young boy's heart. He was silent and slept little.

After several restless nights, Jacob went into Daniel's room and sat on the edge of the small bed. "Son, it's time to talk."

Daniel's face winced with pain. Jacob pulled the boy into his arms. Tears began to roll down his young face. "Sir, it wasn't like I expected. Killin' I mean. There's no glory. It was like you said, the hardest thing is forgiving yourself."

Jacob smoothed the boy's hair. "You also saved a life, little buck." Jacob paused and whispered. "You took a life, you gave a life." He pulled the boy closer. "It ain't always easy being grownup, but you did what I told you to do. You protected your sister. I'm proud of you. You stood tall as any man."

Daniel nuzzled his head beneath Jacob's square jaw. "If it's okay, I just want to be a boy awhile longer."

Smiling, Jacob rocked Daniel in his arms. "Sure, son; growin' up takes time."

"Sir? Can I really be your son?"

Jacob closed his eyes and held the boy tighter. "You already are."

On the fourth day, Mea-a-ha had Jacob carry her into the big room and placed her in his stuffed chair. She snuggled in a cozy blanket. The curtains were pulled back, bathing the room in cheery light. Clattering pans, Jacob hurried about preparing a special stew. His ingredients were simple: antelope, wild potatoes, and onions. Watching from her padded nest, Mea-a-ha giggled. "That is way too much food. It will take us days to eat it."

Dropping more meat into the pot, Jacob gave her a wink. "I don't tell you how to cook. We will have it all eaten today."

This Mea-a-ha seriously doubted. "Add a little fat and some flour, it will thicken the broth."

The banter continued. "Look, little lady, would you like to go back to eating my beans?"

Mea-a-ha, eyes beaming in mock terror, quickly shut her mouth while shaking her head. Jacob added more meat.

The excited barking of little Friendly awoke her sometime later. Rubbing the sleep from her eyes, she could see him bouncing excitedly by the door on three legs. Jacob was already opening it wide.

Mea-a-ha almost fell out of her chair. Eager voices told her they had company. Stepping on to the porch Jacob shook hands with three strange men. Suddenly an elderly lady pushed past them and made her way into the room, followed by Carmelita.

Mea-a-ha gave a sigh of relief. Love and sadness showed in the old woman's face as she looked at Mea-a-ha. "It is as we feared, you have been hurt."

Rushing to Mea-a-ha, Carmelita knelt beside her and gave her a kiss. "It is good to see you, this is my mother, Senora Elena Rincon. The older woman bent over Mea-a-ha and took her face in her wrinkled hands. "My daughter has told me so much about you, I feel I already know you."

Mea-a-ha loved the old lady instantly. Elena took charge, asking all sorts of questions. "Are you in pain? Has he been taking good care of you? Have you been eating?" She left little time for Mea-a-ha to answer her questions, other than to smile and nod. The caring woman turned to Carmelita. "Tell the boys to bring in our bags, wounds need proper tending."

Carmelita smiled and kissed Mea-a-ha again, then hurried out the door. While she was gone, Elena's voice grew soft. "You poor child. Are you okay?"

Mea-a-ha understood what she meant. Her eyes teared, as she answered. "Yes, my little brother Daniel came in time to protect me. He was very brave."

Elena leaned over and hugged Mea-a-ha to her bosom. "You are with friends now; you will be fine."

The old woman's words were like medicine. Mea-a-ha sobbed uncontrollably for the first time since that terrible night. For Jacob she tried to be brave, but in the arms of a consoling mother, she found permission to cry. Releasing her hold on Elena, Mea-a-ha sniffed. "You will stay awhile, won't you?"

Brushing back the Indian girl's hair, Elena gave her a reassuring smile. "Of course we will darling. I had Luis bring the covered wagon.

We will stay as long as you like."

Just then the door burst open. Carmelita returned with Roberto and Juan in tow – their arms filled with baskets and sacks. Once again, Elena started issuing orders. "Put it on the table, and don't drop anything. Be quick."

The men followed them inside. Jacob went to Mea-a-ha and squeezed her hand. "I would like you to meet Senor Luis Rincon, our neighbor."

The snowy haired man made a deep bow, and taking her hand from Jacob, gave it a kiss. "I knew it would take a beautiful girl to capture Jacob's heart. It is a great pleasure to meet you."

All she could do was stare in wonder at this old gentleman. With a smile baked on by the sun and dark sparkling eyes, he reminded her of Grandfather.

Clearing his voice Jacob interrupted. "And this, my dear, is the honorable Victor Ramirez, our attorney and trusted friend."

Victor blushed at the introduction and bowed awkwardly several times, blustering his words, as though he had more to say than he could in a short greeting. "Most happy to meet you. Most happy to meet you indeed."

He seemed like the friendliest man Mea-a-ha had ever met. His face was broad and sported a cheery grin. Mea-a-ha offered her hand for another kiss. "It is nice to meet you. Is an A-tt-orn-ney like a chief or medicine man?"

Everyone laughed. Victor blushed again and looked to Jacob. "Victor makes a different kind of medicine. His last medicine made Damon Mathers very ill."

Everyone laughed again, including Victor. It was contagious, and Mea-a-ha joined in. "If your magic did that, then you are truly a great medicine man."

Stepping forward, Roberto made a low bow to Mea-a-ha, trying to behave like the men. He took her hand, giving it a quick peck then quickly retreated. Juan went right to what was on his mind. "Where is Daniel?"

Mea-a-ha tilted her head toward the bedroom door. "In his room, probably scared out of his wits, wondering what's going on. You go on in."

Without another word, the boys disappeared. Next, Mea-a-ha turned a questioning eye to the scruffy gent who waited patiently near the door. Lifting his arm, Jacob motioned the man to step forward. "This old desert fox is Hamp, a friend who gave up his job for me and then rode several days to bring our friends here."

A confused look crossed Mea-a-ha's face as she offered her hand to the generous stranger.

Seeing her puzzlement, Jacob added. "He was one of the men who tried to kill me."

Hamp coughed, nearly choking. "A pleasure," were the only words he offered with a hardy handshake. Then seeing Mea-a-ha's questioning eyes, he added in defense of Jacob's little joke. "Your man has a way of growing on ya kinda' quick like."

Still not knowing what to think, and preferring the kiss to the pumping of her arm, Mea-a-ha politely nodded. "If you are not planning on killing him anytime soon, welcome to our home."

"Yes, ma'am, I mean, no, ma'am."

Lifting her head towards Jacob, she gave his hand a reproachful shake. "You knew they were coming; that's why you cooked so much food."

Grinning wide, Jacob gloated. "I told you it would all be eaten."

Dinner was quite merry. Everyone was happy to be together. None of the guests truly understood how much they meant to the Indian girl. Sadly, too many people in her life were gone. Apaches were fading from the earth, and at times Mea-a-ha felt as though she too would disappear. But now the Mimbre girl had new friends. Her world was growing. Tonight there was hope.

With the setting sun, Mea-a-ha ate dinner in Jacob's chair wrapped in a big handmade quilt Elena had brought. When they finished eating, Jacob sat down on the hearth next to her and tended the fire. The boys lay on an elk skin rug, and everyone else pulled up chairs from the kitchen table, finding peace by the warm flickering hearth.

It was late, and the lamps were turned low. Jacob tossed another log on the fire. The light of the flames danced across contented faces. Hamp, sitting on the opposite side of the hearth, rubbed his full belly then spoke from the shadows. "Jacob, I have come the long way about getting' here; lost my job n' nearly my life in the process. I would sure like ta know how ya orchestrated the disappearance of Damon Mathers' four thousand head of cattle while leading us single handedly on a wild goose chase through the desert."

A murmur of surprise rose from the darkened room. Mea-a-ha knew nothing of this; her interest piqued. "You made that evil man's entire herd disappear? I think I would like to hear this story, too."

She looked to Elena for sympathy. "He tells me nothing."

All eyes went back to Jacob. Their eager expression told Jacob a story was expected. "Well, there's nothing much to tell really."

The silence persisted, only louder.

Resigning to his fate, Jacob rested a large hand on the log mantle and cleared his throat. "It is just like in the army. You have to know what your adversary is doing so you can keep one step ahead of him. That is partly why I went to town, to goad Mathers into action. It's better to know that a man is coming after you, instead of waiting around wondering. Kind of like watching a hornet's nest – knock it down and deal with it. I got lucky when Mathers lost his temper and told me he was bringing all his cowboys after me in four days."

Engrossed in the tale, Hamp burst in without thinking. "There was twenty of us." Realizing his error, he swallowed hard. "I mean them."

Juan rose up off the floor in awe. "Twenty against one. Wow!"

Nervously, Jacob glanced to Mea-a-ha. Her eyes were wide with fear. Jacob forced an amused grin. "Don't worry, I don't want to give away the ending, but I live."

Taking a breath, he continued. "Anyway, after his failed attempt with the gunfighter, it was a good bet he would bring all his men. In fact, I was counting on it. Everything else just seemed to fall into place. It was Daniel here that made it possible, when he told me how to find Cotas camp." He gave the boy a wink.

Eyes darted towards Daniel, who blushed with embarrassment at being included in the story. Jacob gave Daniel his moment then went on. "I found my way into Cota's camp and..."

Victor's voice rose in surprise. "He didn't kill you? My word."

"Well, I guess I should tell you that Cota came here looking for Daniel one night and we sort of made a truce."

It was now Luis's turn to interrupt. "You made a truce?"

Before Jacob could answer, Mea-a-ha chimed in with great pride. "Cota wanted Daniel, but Jacob wouldn't let Cota take him. He was very brave. Apaches respect bravery."

A murmur of agreement floated across the shadowed room. Self-conscious, Jacob protested. "We're getting far a field here. As I was saying, I went to Cota's camp and let him know he was fighting a losing battle if he was going to keep butting heads with the army, something he had already figured out the hard way. So I told him if he really wanted to make a difference, he could turn the tables, so to speak, on the biggest rancher in these parts and maybe drive him out. That would really make a difference."

Everyone nodded in agreement with Jacob's logic. Having their approval, he added. "I just told him I would draw off the cowboys. Cota did the rest."

Assuming he was done, Jacob took a long sip on a cup of coffee, but eager eyes burning holes into his silence said otherwise.

Putting his cup down, Jacob tried his best to accommodate his guest. "Timing was the tough thing. It all hinged on Mathers keeping his word about four days, which gave him time to return to his ranch and round up his men. I just had to slow him down. Anyway, Cota was to watch Mathers' ranch and stay out of sight, then after Mathers left, wait until dark and steal the herd. Well, not actually steal the herd, just scatter the cattle across the desert and foothills until there was no possible way for

Mathers to round them up before winter. That would give Cota a real victory. It also gives Luis here a little well deserved vengeance."

Shocked by this statement, Luis spoke up. "What do you mean, give me vengeance? Mathers wanted my land, but he didn't get it thanks to you, Jacob. Why should I need vengeance?"

Once again, Jacob took a long sip on his cup of coffee. Longer than necessary, having his own sweet vengeance upon his demanding guest. The room remained silent, waiting for Jacob's answer. He milked the moment a bit longer before letting the cat out of the bag. "Try to stay calm, my friend. Mathers was the one stealing your cattle."

Aghast, old Luis jumped to his feet, blustering with outrage. Everyone was talking at once. The roar died down, and once again all faces looked to their host. By now, Jacob had his hands up as if to say no more. "I believe I have answered Hamp's original question. As for Mathers stealing Luis's cattle, that is another story."

Before there could be any protest, Jacob pointed to Mea-a-ha. "It can wait for tomorrow. Mea-a-ha has had too much excitement for today, and we must get her to bed."

Elena voiced her agreement and cleared a path, while Jacob scooped up the girl and headed for the bedroom, quite pleased with himself.

Chapter -28-
Fort Cummings

The horses stamped impatiently outside the little stone house. Luis and Victor sat mounted and ready to ride, their breath steaming in the cold mountain air. Jacob lingered beside his great horse, taking his time cinching down his saddlebags. When it looked as though he could delay no longer, Carmelita opened the door. "Jacob, she is awake and would like to see you before you leave."

Without a word, Jacob hurried inside. Mea-a-ha sat propped up on pillows in her bed. "Are you sure you have to go?"

Her face hung in a pout. Jacob leaned over and kissed her. "They will just keep coming if I don't."

Mea-a-ha gave his hand a nervous squeeze. "I know. It's just that since I was a little girl, the army has hunted my people from that evil fort. Now they hunt you, and your plan is to ride inside its walls. The soldiers have never listened to the words of the Apache, but you expect them to listen to you. It is difficult to believe."

Kneeling beside the bed, Jacob pressed her hand to his lips. "I won't lie to you. There's a risk the army won't listen to me either, but at some point we must trust, or go on fighting forever. This is our only chance."

"I know, but I don't have to like it."

Her pout gave way to a smile. "I made a gift for you."

"A gift?"

"Yes. I made it before I was... Well, while you were gone."

Reaching under her pillow, she withdrew her tightly closed fist and clutched its secret to her breast. Her bright eyes glistened with excitement. Slowly stretching her hand towards Jacob, she spread her fingers wide, revealing a small leather pouch decorated with tiny colored beads. It hung from a thin rawhide cord.

Mea-a-ha's voice came in an excited whisper. "It is a medicine bag to keep you safe." Eagerly, her eyes waited for Jacob's response. His large hand slowly reached out cupping hers. Unable to speak, he swallowed hard. Mea-a-ha had learned that when Jacob spoke the least, he felt the most.

Holding it high with her good arm, Mea-a-ha placed it around his neck. "You must wear it. I filled it with magic from the Hollow. There are little stones and sprinklings of earth. They hold the Hollow's healing power. There's a small feather from the old raven that lives on the cliffs. He gives you wisdom. There's a wolf's tooth to give you strength."

Mea-a-ha's sweet voice filled with emotion. "And there is a lock of my hair, so you will know you are loved." She placed her hand softly on his cheek. "And that wherever you go, I go with you."

The big man cleared his throat several times and opened his mouth as though he was going to speak, but no words would come. Teasing, Mea-a-ha feigned a comical pout. "You do like it, don't you?"

Gently, he took her by the shoulders and held her to his chest. "Yes. I like it very much. It is just that no one has ever given me a gift before."

Mea-a-ha pulled back in surprise. "Never?"

"It hasn't been that kind of life."

Shaking off the emotions that were about to overwhelm him, Jacob took a deep breath. "It is beautiful. I love it."

"You must wear it at the fort; it is good medicine."

"I will wear it always."

The three men rode from the cold shadow of the pines and into the pale rays of the sun, breaking through the spindly white aspen now bare of leaves. Dew hung on the rocky trail. Jacob tucked the medicine bag inside his coat and pulled his collar close to his neck. He took comfort knowing Elena and Carmelita would look after Mea-a-ha.

With Hamp and the three boys, there was enough firepower to discourage anyone. Besides, she was in the Hollow; the ancient cliffs and the magic spring would protect her still.

As the trail broadened, Luis spurred his pinto, bringing him alongside Jacob. "Don't mean to be morbid, just curious what you did with Wyatt Mathers' body. Hate to think of that monster being buried in the Hollow."

Jacob frowned. "I would have fed him to the wolves before I let his body foul the soil of the Hollow. Evil or no, a son should be returned to his father. I wrapped him in his bedroll and tied him over his saddle. While Mea-a-ha slept, I rode him out of the foothills and gave his horse its head. It should have made its way home by now."

Old Luis grimaced. "Damon Mathers will go insane. Are you sure he won't come hunting you on your mountain?"

"Damon Mathers is one of those sad people who spends most of his life in a rage. He hates losing more than even losing a son. At some point he'll come a killin', but right now he'll be bent on finding his cattle."

The trio spent the night at an outcropping of weathered rocks known as Robbers' Knoll, so named because the labyrinth of stone slabs provided hiding places for outlaws who ambushed unwary travelers – usually miners hauling their precious silver. It lay on the Old Spanish Trail about halfway between the Hollow and Fort Cummings. The large stones made good shelter from the wind.

As they sat around their campfire, Victor paced in deep thought. "We have a long ways to go, and a lot to talk about before we get to the fort. It won't be easy. There is a lot to be said, and some that shouldn't."

He held his warm cup of coffee with both hands looking uncommonly serious. "I think it best we keep Daniel's part in Wyatt's death quiet. It will only raise the army's hackles." He looked sympathetically at Jacob. "To save the boy, you are going to have to take the blame and pay the price."

Jacob nodded. "Wouldn't have it no other way."

Victor took another sip of his coffee. "Yessir', we have a lot to talk about."

Captain Lawrence Reinhart paced back and forth in front of Jubaliah Jackson who stood stiffly at attention. Jube hoped the arrogant son-of-a-bitch would walk off some of his anger. Instead, the red-faced captain stopped in front of the obliging sergeant glaring eye to eye, looking as though he wanted to strike him.

A twitch in his upper lip was something Jubaliah had not seen before. "Damn it boy, if I could prove you led me on a wild goose chase, I would have your stripes right now. And peel your black hide to boot."

Doing his best to look injured by the accusation, Jubaliah threw his shoulders back in a dramatic snap to attention. "Sir, no, sir. We coloreds did our best for you, sir. Look at how long it took us to get Sholo. And we wouldn't of done that iffin' Sergeant Jacob hadn't done got lost in them mountains. No, sir, I bet ol' Jacob is over the Mexican border sippin' Mescal right now, yessir 'I surely do."

"Don't think me a fool boy; you're standing in deep sand. You play dumb when it suits you. Well, right now you better get real smart."

Reinhart's face was growing redder by the second. "I turned in a report to Colonel McCrae saying we spent the better part of a week chasing Jacob Keever and an Apache warrior to the Mexican border. It would be very embarrassing if it turned out he was someplace else. Now I am going to ask you one last time. Were we chasing Keever or not?"

"It's hard ta say sir. We sure started out chasing him, that we did sir. Where he done lost us is a mystery."

Reinhart paced again, then paused at the window. His voice came shrill as he fought for control. "Did you know Damon Mathers rode in here last night to plead with Colonel McCrae for more time to fulfill his beef contract with the army?"

This time Jubaliah's ignorance was genuine. "Sir, why would he need more time?"

"It seems someone ran off his entire herd of over four thousand cattle."

"Do tell, sir! Who could do such a thing?"

"Damn it sergeant, it was Keever! Now are you going to tell me you don't know anything about this?"

"Jacob's got a big appetite, but he ain't got no use for that many cattle. Maybe Mr. Mathers should go back and count them again, sir."

The Captain slammed his fist down on his desk. "Damn it, boy! You think this is funny, do you? Well, do you think it funny that Mathers' oldest son was murdered and your clever friend is going to hang for it?"

The humor left Jubaliah's face. Leading a fool's chase was one thing; murder was another.

Thrusting his face at the sergeant, Reinhart bristled with unbridled rage. "You led me on a fool's ride to Mexico while your friend murdered the son of a prominent rancher, and I filed a false report. Jacob was never south of Sand Creek, and you knew it. If the colonel finds out, I will make sure your fat neck stretches right alongside that black son-of-a-bitch's."

Jube ended his game. His voice rang cold. "Maybe we all have somethin' we're hiding that could stretch our necks."

Reinhart thrust his chin towards Jube and hissed through clenched teeth. "What do you mean?"

Jubaliah stood silently at attention.

A telling fear stretched the captain's voice even tighter. "What do you think you know?"

Just then the door banged open, and a trooper burst into the room saluting. "Sir."

"What the hell is it, corporal?"

"Sir, three men are riding towards the fort."

"Tell somebody else, I'm busy."

"Sir, one of them looks like Jacob Keever."

Flames exploded in Reinhart's eyes. He whirled screaming. "Sippin' Mescal in Mexico, is he? Corporal, arrest the sergeant and put him in irons; I will deal with him later." Reinhart raced from his office, knocking the startled trooper into the door.

Jubaliah stood shocked. If Jacob was here, he couldn't have chosen a worse time. With the captain's rage and Mathers' grief, it would be a violent collision.

As the corporal regained his footing and struggled with how best to arrest the sergeant, Jube pushed past him, knocking the flustered soldier into the door again.

Without delay, Jubaliah rushed for the fort's large gate with the hapless corporal in tow. If it was Jacob, it was too late to turn him away. Hurrying past the guard at the gate, Jubaliah looked out. The riders were a ways off, but no mistaking his old friend – a huge man on a giant horse, dwarfing the shorter men by his side. All hell was about to break loose, and Jubaliah wondered if Jacob had any clue. Did he know the rancher was here right now?

Looking over his shoulder, Jubaliah saw Reinhart dart into the guest quarters, no doubt to tell Mathers.

The word spread quickly. Troopers, black and white, were peeking out of windows and doors. Men wandered from the mess hall carrying their tin plates. This would be something to see.

Riding under the archway of the sally port gate, Jacob nodded to his old friend. Jubaliah shook his head, signaling that things were bad. Jacob read Jube's distraught face and motioned for his companions to stop, then proceeded on alone.

Hoping for a peaceful ending, he had stuffed his pistol in his saddle bag. His Winchester lay tied in the scabbard by his leg. For Jacob, this was a time for words, not war.

Soldiers moving about the parade ground stopped in mid-stride and watched as Jacob Keever entered the fort. He was one of them returned, a lowly Buffalo Soldier, now famous and infamous. He was the Hero of Apache Springs. Every man knew him, had read the stories printed about him, and formed their own opinions as to whether he was a hero or a fool. Still, the quiet strength of the dark figure sitting the tall horse left no doubt, this was a time of reckoning. Something was about to bust.

Moving cautiously, the large, plodding hooves of the great horse on the dusty parade grounds slowly pounded out the final seconds. All other sounds faded away. When the rider stopped, it was safe to bet somebody was going to have a bad day.

Reaching the middle of the square, Jacob pulled up on the reins as a wide-eyed black maid rushed up to him from the guest quarters wringing her hands in her apron. "Mr. Jacob, you bes' flee. They's comin' to kill you."

Jacob realized things weren't going to go as he had hoped. His voice strained with urgency. "Mattie, leave the fort now!"

He reached to untie the Winchester, but too late. All of a sudden the door of the guest quarters burst open. Damon and Raithe Mathers tore out, followed by Reinhart. Raithe, gripping his Winchester in both hands, screamed as he charged onto the dusty square.

The Mathers' were a hard breed who dealt their own justice, and even the imposing walls of the fort weren't going to change that. Nobody would fault them for killing the murderer of their kin. The younger Mathers went crazy at the sight of the black man. It was Raithe who discovered his dead brother draped cold and gray over his horse outside their burned-out home. The image tormented his sick mind. The boy may have fought with his sibling, but Wyatt was the only friend the disturbed youth had. Crying over his dead brother, Raithe had vowed that he would settle the score.

"You filthy black murderer, I'll kill you!" Blinded by hatred, he threw the rifle to his shoulder and chambered a round. At the same instant, Jubaliah grabbed the carbine from the guard at the gate and brought it to bear. His voice thundered loud and clear, bringing Raithe to an abrupt halt. "Drop the gun or I'll kill ya dead." The booming command was not to be ignored.

Raithe froze at the black soldier's promise of death. A tenuous balance of fury and fear held the boy in check. He loved his brother enough to kill for him, but not to die for him.

Reinhart pounded the railing with a balled fist. He knew Jacob would never ride so boldly into the fort unless he had discovered their crime. If the young Mathers would shoot, the problem would be solved.

Frantically he shouted his command. "Sergeant Jackson, lower your rifle! That's an order."

Jubaliah stood like iron, the deadly Springfield fused to his shoulder.

The captain raged. "I gave you an order."

Unflinching, the sergeant's eyes remained locked on his quarry, his finger tight against the trigger.

Livid, Reinhart yelled at the trooper by Jube's side. "Corporal, I told you to arrest this black son-of-a-bitch, now take the sergeant's rifle."

Turning pale, the nervous corporal awkwardly pulled his revolver from his holster and thrust it towards Jube. Behind him the unmistakable sound of rifles cocking brought the frightened soldier to an abrupt halt. Rolley Dupree and Luther Tomes stood grim beneath the flagpole, their dark unwavering eyes sighting down their barrels at the unenviable corporal.

The captain stood dumbfounded. How dare they? How dare this inferior black scum defy his authority! Casting his eyes at the white soldiers standing about, he barked another order. "Troopers, arrest these darkies."

A stunned silence prevailed as the soldiers hesitated, every face questioning the command. "Now. Damn it, now!" Reinhart's voice screeched like an old woman's.

Unwillingly, pistols and carbines slowly glinted in the cold morning sun, as soldiers struggled between duty and reason. The dull slap of reluctant hands on wood and metal brought a ragged line of weapons to bear, changing the tenor of the parade ground to one of utter disbelief. The haunting cadence rose and trailed away as the last guns picked their targets. Then it stopped.

Silence once again claimed the yard. Young Luther cast a nervous glance at the large gaping bore of the deadly Springfields now trained on him; they looked like cannons. This time he wouldn't go unnoticed. Rolley gave him a tight grin. "Ya didn't spec' to live forever."

The distraught captain's lip twitched and parted for the final command, when suddenly, the familiar dull slap rose anew, but this time the hands were dusty black and the rifles worn. Hands trained to mind their place could no longer be cowered. They would not stand by and watch their comrades murdered. Not a soldier on the parade grounds could believe what was happening.

Inside the cold adobe walls, guns shifted and shifted again, finding new targets. Carbines pointed in every direction as men, black and white struggled to do what they believed was right. The low metallic clamor died away for the final time. If a hammer fell, there would be carnage inside the fort walls.

The flapping of the flag overhead offered the only protest to the heavy silence. On this cold December first morn, every man held his breath, knowing the next move was insanity. Still, it only takes one trigger to start a war, one twisted mind to seal the fate of all.

Raithe, never having faced so many guns, pleaded to his pa in a weak, trembling voice. Mathers gripped his revolver. "Captain, are you in charge or not? Kill the nigger, or I will."

Sweat beading on his lip, Reinhart lost his final grip on reality. His voice rose shrill. "Shoot them, shoot them all. Shoot, shoot, shoot!"

Sanity held a heartbeat longer.

From behind Reinhart, a door banged open wide. Colonel McCrae stared in disbelief. "What the... Captain, what in Sam hell is going on here?"

Reinhart was wild with fear. "Sir, the darkies are siding with that criminal." He pointed a shaking gun at Jacob. "They are disobeying my direct orders sir. It's a mutiny."

Pushing past the captain with disgust, the colonel pulled a large cigar from his mouth. McCrae slammed his hands down on the railing and thrust out his chin, making his presence felt. "Now every one of you sons-a-bitches listen to me. Lower your weapons now for Christ sake."

With a collective sigh of relief, all guns fell in quick order, as comrades stepped back from the brink of death.

Sanity prevailed, but common sense was not a trait found in the wild-eyed Mathers youth. The fear that stayed Raithe's hand was gone while his fury remained. He was a Mathers, and he was above the law. "Nigger, I'll be damned if you take another breath." His thumb slipped from the hammer. Jube was ready. The large Springfield roared with smoke and flame. Raithe Mathers hurled backwards through the air, his own shot hissing past Jacob's ear. The thunder of the big gun had not ended before Damon Mathers charged forward, living a father's worst nightmare – his seeds wiped from the earth. The brutal man's revolver leaped, spitting lead and vengeance. Jube stumbled and fell.

Mathers' gun turned quickly on the mounted rider, but Sholo's Winchester, ripped from the scabbard, jumped in Jacob's hand. Damon Mathers saw the smoke curling about the barrel of the angry gun. From the churning mist, he caught a glint of the bullet in the morning light, then grabbed a red spot on his chest. The would-be king stumbled a few steps in disbelief before collapsing over his son, their blood pooling together on the ground.

No matter how high a throne a man pretends to, he is still mortal, and what will kill a peasant, will fell a king. With a single ounce of lead, the Mathers' reign had come to an ignoble end. The illusion of greatness could not protect him. In the dirt lay a man who would not be mourned.

In an instant, Jacob was by Jubaliah's side, holding his friend. "Why, Jube?"

Weakly, Jubaliah lifted his head amid sounds of a distant battlefield, the image of a brave young boy with a bloody bayonet fading before his eyes. A feeble smile parted his lips. "We're even, friend." The big soldier closed his eyes.

Screaming for help, Jacob pressed his hand to the flowing wound above Jube's heart. "Somebody, please. Please!"

The fort's surgeon pushed through the crowd to the fallen man, calling orders to the troopers. "Get him to the infirmary."

The crush of men, black and white, who moments before were ready to take each other's lives, joined hands to help their fallen comrade.

Jacob, left kneeling, stared at the blood on his hand. He had never imagined anything like this, not Jube. Mea-a-ha had warned him. Anybody but Jube.

Reinhart shoved through the troopers. "Arrest this man."

Jacob raised his head, murder in his eyes. The bonds that shackled his rage were shattered by the stain on his hands. Charging up from the blood-soaked earth, Jacob's huge fist caught Reinhart in the pit of his stomach, lifting him off the ground. Another pounded into the stunned captain's chin, knocking him senseless. Soldiers rushed to subdue the crazed man, but to no avail. Buried in bodies, Jacob battled forward, raging and kicking at the prostrate captain. His grief carried him on, blind to all.

Suddenly there was Rolley, the only man bigger than Jacob. His voice was calm. "It's no good, Sarge. This ain't the way."

The storm in Jacob's eyes quelled. Rolley pushed the other soldiers back. "Get away from him. Let him be."

Jacob slumped, consumed with sorrow. "Jube." Reinhart no longer mattered.

The deep commanding voice of Colonel McCrae again took charge as he issued an order to Rolley. "Corporal, take this man to the stockade."

From out of the crowd of soldiers, a small figure burst forward. Luis Rincon's voice crackled with indignation. "You will not arrest Jacob. He has done no wrong. If you want to arrest somebody, let it be that criminal on the ground."

Colonel McCrae turned and faced the white-haired gentleman. He knew of Luis Rincon and his family's respected position in the territory.

McCrae was something Reinhart was not, an officer of breeding. "Senor Rincon, my apologies, but this is a military matter. We will handle it."

Stepping forward, Victor Ramirez bowed politely and cleared his throat. "Excuse me sir. I mean no disrespect, but this is not a military matter. Jacob is a civilian. The man he shot was a civilian, and if it comes to trial, it would be in a civilian court. Allow me to introduce myself. I am Victor Ramirez, attorney-at-law and an officer of the court."

He offered his hand to the colonel. "Perhaps we could resolve this matter in your office, if you would allow us to present you with certain facts."

Without waiting for an answer, the affable attorney took Jacob's arm and escorted him to the door of Colonel McCrae's office, then politely waited for the colonel to enter.

Taken aback by the confidence of the portly gent, McCrae chomped his cigar, and followed them into his office.

As the crowd pressed into the darkened room, Victor whispered to his friend. "Let me do the talking." Jacob only stared at the blood of his friend on his hands. Nothing else mattered.

Rolley entered with McCrae, pushing the door closed behind him. Before they were seated a clamor arose on the porch. Captain Reinhart slammed into the door, knocking it wide open. Cursing and screaming, he stumbled into the room. "Colonel, I want Sergeant Keever arrested for murder." Rubbing his chin, he added, "And assaulting a superior officer."

The colonel was in no mood for any more ruckus. "Captain, be silent. I want to hear what these men have to say."

"But, Colonel, I protest."

McCrae treated the captain with indifference. "Protest to your friends in Washington. Here you sit down and shut up."

With that, the colonel put a match to his cigar and dropped back in his chair. Reinhart looked around the room nervously, then slid a chair away from the rest.

After taking several long puffs, Colonel McCrae leaned his arms on his desk. "Now, what's this all about?"

The captain opened his mouth, but an angry look from the colonel quickly closed it. Old Luis also started to speak, but the gentle hand of Victor Ramirez silenced him as well.

Rising from his chair, Victor, stepping into the center of the room, took a moment to look at each person then faced McCrae. "My good colonel, I will try to be brief, but serious crimes have been committed and in the interest of justice, please allow me to tell the complete story so that you might have all the facts. As an honorable man, I am sure you want nothing less than the absolute truth."

Leaning back in his chair, the colonel warned. "I will let you tell your story, but this is not a courtroom, so no long-winded theatrics; just keep to the facts."

The attorney bowed and continued. "Very well. As you know, Luis Rincon was the victim of numerous Indian raids led by the Apache, Sholo. His losses were so great that he nearly lost his vast Spanish land grant to the deceased, Damon Mathers, who held a note against it for a loan. Many times Senor Rincon came to you directly, pleading for army assistance to end these raids, yet they continued for over a year."

Feeling this was an accusation, Colonel McCrae became agitated. "Look here, if you are insinuating that the army failed in its duty to provide protection, I want to point out that it was your own Sergeant Keever who was charged with apprehending the renegades."

Victor apologized. "Not at all, sir. The army responded most promptly. And we are aware of Sergeant Keever's part."

The attorney then turned and faced Captain Reinhart, his voice becoming cold for the first time. "As well as the captain's."

Regaining his polite composure, he returned to his story. "Regardless of the army's effort, Senor Rincon would have lost his family's home if it were not for the timely intervention of Jacob here, who provided the funds Senor Rincon needed to pay off his debt to the deceased."

The colonel raised his eyes, obviously surprised by this bit of information. Seeing the colonel's interest, Victor couldn't help but add a little courtroom flair, and threw his arms wide. "You see, sir, this is where the real culprits got nervous and started making mistakes."

Pulling his cigar from his mouth the colonel interjected. "You saying it wasn't Sholo who committed the raids?"

The skillful attorney avoided the question, wetting the colonel's curiosity. "Excuse me, I am getting ahead of myself. It was much more than random Indian raids. Behind it was a clever plot to steal Senor Rincon's land by running him into bankruptcy, in order to build a vast cattle empire."

Victor let this sink in before continuing. "The criminals, worried that Jacob would uncover their plot, made several attempts to do away with him."

As Victor continued to talk, he shot glances at Reinhart, making the captain more nervous with each moment. Reinhart had no way of knowing what the attorney knew about his part, if any, though he feared the worst.

Impatient, the colonel demanded Victor get to the point. "Look here. If it is your intent to say that Damon Mathers was behind the raids, and that is what led up to the incident outside, then say it and offer your proof."

Victor again bowed. "Very well, sir. Yes. I am saying it was Damon Mathers behind the raids. As for our proof," Victor reached into his vest pocket and pulled out a slip of paper. "Here is a bill of sale for several cases of Winchester rifles delivered to Damon Mathers, the deceased." He handed the bill of sales to McCrae. "Listed are the serial numbers. Lying outside in the yard is the rifle Jacob took from Sholo, in the now-famous Battle of Apache Springs. If you want to examine it, you will find that the number on the gun is also on the list you hold. It is also likely that the same holds true for the rifle Raithe tried to kill Jacob with."

Examining the paper, McCrae turned to Rolley. "Corporal, retrieve the rifles."

Taking the opportunity of the break, Victor walked over and stood right in front of Reinhart. "Do you find this interesting, captain?"

Swallowing hard, Reinhart snarled. "So far you have proved nothing."

Strolling back into the center of the room, Victor smiled. "Oh, but I will. I most certainly will."

Corporal Rolley returned and handed the pair of rifles to the colonel. After a moment's inspection the colonel spoke, beating Victor to the punch. "Well, I'll be. So it is your contention that Mathers gave rifles to the Indians in exchange for his raiding Senor Rincon's herd, thus preventing him making good on his note."

Victor seemed almost disappointed. "Why yes, that's it exactly. Mathers feared Jacob could expose him, so Mathers tried to dispose of Mr. Keever."

Leaning back in his chair, McCrae thought for a moment. "Do you have any other proof?"

Once again the attorney stepped to the middle of the room. "Yes, sir, we do. If it were Sholo acting alone, he might have driven the cattle anywhere, but certainly not across the Southern reaches of the desert in a direct line towards Mathers' ranch, where he would likely be spotted by regular cavalry patrols that passed along Sand Creek. But that is exactly what he did. Jacob found faint tracks of a cattle herd and followed them."

Reaching into his satchel, Victor produced the square of hide, that Jacob had given him and tossed it on the colonel's desk. "Here sir, is a piece of hide cut from a fallen steer, with the Rincon brand plainly visible on it."

Picking up the hide, McCrae studied it. His head bobbed as the truth became apparent. "Your story makes sense. The hide and the bill of sale back it up. Selling guns to the Indians is a serious crime. Not to mention attempted murder and cattle rustling. Plenty of reason for Mathers to try and silence the sergeant when he saw him ride in."

The colonel looked at the stocky Mexican attorney with new respect. "You have proven your case to my satisfaction. What happened here today was a clear cut case of attempted murder and self-defense. I won't tolerate a thief no matter his station. Mathers was a scoundrel that got what he deserved."

Opening his mouth, Victor started to speak, but the colonel held up his hand. "Which leaves us with the crime of assault on Captain Reinhart." The colonel paused, casting a glance towards Reinhart, who was willing to sit silent, hoping that maybe his part had been overlooked.

Seeing no desire on Reinhart's part to speak, the colonel continued. "I won't mince words here. A former black soldier striking his superior white officer would be considered a serious offense, even out here in the West, but both these men have become heroes for their actions at Apache Springs, which has in turn been good press for the fort's reputation, and I for one don't want to see that blemished, so I am willing to let it pass, if it is agreeable to the captain."

Relieved, and hoping for a quick conclusion, Reinhart simply nodded in agreement. Colonel McCrae smiled. "Then that's it. We let the matter be buried with the dead. You men may take your leave, and we will let Jacob here, see to his friend."

Luis placed a sympathetic hand on Jacob's shoulder, who sat silently through it all. Slowly Reinhart rose from his chair, eager to leave unscathed.

This was the moment the attorney had been waited for. "Not so fast, captain."

His icy stare froze Reinhart in his tracks. "I am sorry, colonel, but that is not the end of it. Sadly, it is far from settled."

Stunned, the colonel dropped back in his chair. "You won, Mr. Ramirez, what more is there?"

The small attorney faced Reinhart. "Sit down, captain. You did not go unnoticed. There will be justice here today. All debts will be paid."

Throwing his arms wide, Reinhart hollered, "Colonel, this is ridiculous. It is pointless to let this absurd little Mexican ramble on any longer. Send them on their way. He should be grateful I am not pressing charges."

Chomping on his cigar, Colonel McCrae studied the two men facing each other; a tall, heroic cavalry officer and a short, aging Mexican, standing toe to toe. What intrigued the colonel was that the only fear was in the face of the officer. It disgusted him. "Captain, sit down! There seems to be a story here, and I want to hear it."

"But, Colonel…"

"I said sit down."

Slowly Reinhart sank into his chair, his face draining of color.

Victor's icy stare melted away as he again addressed the colonel. "It is evident that Damon Mathers was greedy and corrupt. He was so greedy, in fact, that with all his wealth, he could not pass up even the slightest chance to make a profit." Turning once again, Victor pointed his chubby hand towards Reinhart. "And this is where the good Captain Reinhart, hero of Apache Springs, enters our little story."

Reinhart swallowed hard, but all he could do was sit and watch as the little man destroyed his career.

Victor's presence commanded the room. "Colonel, to put it simply, Damon Mathers sought to hide the stolen beef by selling it to the army."

The colonel's shock was evident. Victor continued. "To do this, he enlisted the help of Captain Reinhart, which wasn't hard since the captain was already in his employment, making sure the Buffalo Soldiers were never around when Sholo made his raids on poor Senor Rincon's herd."

An involuntarily curse escaped McCrae's lips. Captain Reinhart jumped from his chair. "It's a lie! It's a lie! Jacob is out to get me, and he is using this Mexican to do it!"

Reinhart lunged at Victor, but Rolley stepped into his path. Rising from his chair, McCrae thundered. "Enough of this ruckus! Captain, sit down." He then raised a cautioning finger toward the attorney. "Be very careful, Senor Ramirez, you are leveling serious charges against an officer of the U.S. Army. What you speak of is treason."

"Colonel, sir, I understand the gravity of my charges, and I would never make them if I were not absolutely sure. You see, where Jacob found the hides, he also found tracks of heavy freight wagons joining them. Freight wagons like those used by the army and few others in these parts. To dispose of the beef, Captain Reinhart and a few hand-picked soldiers would help slaughter the herd and take the meat to the Indian reservation."

Reaching into his pocket, Victor tossed a handful of shells on McCrae's desk. "Mixed with the Winchester shells that were used to slaughter the cattle, were Army Springfield cartridges."

Taking a deep breath, the little man humbly folded his hands. "Sir, in the end, I admit my evidence is circumstantial, and it comes down to me asking you to choose the word of a colored, and a couple of humble Mexicans over one of your most trusted officers – a man decorated for bravery in battle, a man lauded in the press as a true hero for his leadership in the Battle of Apache Springs and the death of the Indian chief, Sholo."

The attorney paused and paced the room, then returned to the colonel. "Sir, Jacob Keever may be a poor negro foolishly trying to ranch in the middle of the desert, but he is an honest man and a true hero; neither of these terms apply to Captain Reinhart. For you see, he is a low-down scoundrel living a lie, and a blemish on the army. He never was in the Battle of Apache Springs. Instead, the good captain was holed up in a whorehouse while Jacob single-handedly led his men into those mountains against Reinhart's direct orders."

Victor stepped back from the desk and held his arms out wide. "And that is the simple truth."

Seizing on his only chance, Reinhart jumped from his chair. "You heard him, colonel, it is all circumstantial. He made it all up. There's no proof. They are lying, trying to ruin my good name."

For a long time, Colonel McCrae strummed his fingers on his desk, mulling it all over. He rose, walked to the window, then turned and looked at each man. Finally he returned to his chair. "Senor Ramirez, it would seem that the only man who could offer proof for your fantastic story is lying dead outside in the yard. You killed your only witness."

The colonel leaned forward. "There is truth and there is reality. The reality, Senor Ramirez, is that if Captain Reinhart was to stand trial, it would be in a military court of white officers. The only one to testify would be a negro with no hard evidence. The press would have a field day, and Washington would have my head for allowing a man they decorated to be brought to trial. Fort Cummings and the men that have honorably served here, including the black soldiers, would have their bravery forever tarnished by these accusations. It may be disappointing to you, but that is the reality."

The poor attorney stood speechless, while Reinhart gloated. "You are lucky I don't press charges, but as the colonel said, a trial would be a blemish on Fort Cummings."

McCrae brought his fist down heavy on the desk. "Captain, shut UP!" The tone of his voice put Reinhart back in his chair. Stubbing out his cigar, McCrae nodded his tired face towards Rolley. "Corporal."

Stepping forward, Rolley saluted. "Sir, yes sir."

"Tell me about the Battle of Apache Springs."

Taking a moment to look down at his ex-sergeant, Rolley eyes shined with respect. "Sir, Captain Reinhart seldom accompanied us on patrol. Didn't like our smell, sir. It was Sergeant Jacob, sir, who tracked them Injuns where no one else could. It was Sergeant Jacob who led us men, outnumbered and outgunned, up that hill. He fired the first shot and the last shot. He killed Sholo."

The big man saluted again and started to step back, then stopped. "Sir, we all owe our lives to Sergeant Jacob. We would follow him to hell, sir. That is why we stood by him on the parade ground today. There's no finer man. I think that's what galls the captain. With all his fancy rank and position, he'll never be as good a soldier as the Sarge."

For a long moment, the room was silent. Realizing the change in mood, Reinhart growled deep and angry. No attempt was made to hide his hatred. "Colonel, this is ridiculous, he is one of them. He would say anything his old sergeant wanted him to. Darkies stick together."

287

In a slow, somber voice McCrae added. "As they should, as they should." The colonel faced Victor. "As I said there is the truth and the reality."

He paused before going on, sadness showed in his eyes. "And the truth is, I believe the corporal, and I believe you."

His voice filled with anger as he faced Reinhart. "Every single word. Captain, you disgrace your uniform. You sicken me. However, what I said still holds true, you will not face trial. But this fort will not suffer your presence a moment longer. I want your request for transfer on my desk within the hour. Go back east to your wealthy friends or wherever you want, but get the hell out of the territory."

Reinhart knew it was over. He had lost, but he was lucky to escape with his skin and his rank. Eager to be gone from their presence, the captain raised his hand to salute. Colonel McCrae stopped him short. "Don't you dare salute me. Just crawl out of my sight. Corporal, escort this sorry son-of-a-bitch to his quarters."

Discredited and dishonored, Reinhart, dared one final curse at Jacob. "You think you won. Your kind never wins!" The room rattled with his mocking laugh. "After all your brave honorable deeds, ask yourself. Who's headed to Washington, a decorated hero and who can never be anything more than what he is, a poor black dirt farmer."

Jacob raised his head, his eyes clear. "I never wanted to be a hero. Being a dirt farmer is good enough."

Rolley gripped Reinhart's arm and pushed him roughly through the door.

Everyone in the room sat quietly, relieved it was finally over. Regaining his composure, Colonel McCrae tried to make what amends he could. "Sergeant, I am sorry. You deserved better. If there's any comfort in it, you will always be welcome at Fort Cummings. What you did may never be known in Washington, but you are the true hero."

Turning to the gentle attorney who spoke so eloquently, McCrae's sad face managed a smile. "Senor Ramirez, well done. If this were a court of law, your client would have received more justice than I was able to give here today. It is an honor to have met you." Victor bowed politely.

Taking a more official air, McCrae folded his hands before him and faced Luis Rincon. "Senor Rincon, I am deeply sorry for the injustice you had to endure, dealt in part by an officer of this fort. It seems however, that I am now in serious need of an honest rancher to fill the army's beef contract. If you want it, the contract is yours."

Chapter -29-

Going Home

The death of Mathers and the disgrace of Captain Reinhart were pushed to the dark recesses of Jacob's mind. Jubaliah had written his friendship in his own blood, and now lay at death's door.

For the next three days, Jacob sat by Jube's side. The bugler had blown Taps and Fort Cummings settled in for the night. Scooting his chair close to the bed, Jacob turned the lamp to a faint glow. It reminded him of other nights not long ago, sitting by Mea-a-ha's bedside after her fight with Wyatt Mathers. He pulled the medicine bag she had made him from his shirt and held it tightly in his hand, hoping this would be his last bedside vigil.

As the evening grew late, the door quietly opened. Jacob, half dozing, raised his head to see Rolley slip inside. The big man leaned his carbine against the wall and stepped near the bed. "Pulled guard duty. Thought I'd see if there was any change."

Jacob nodded and turned his attention back to Jube.

Taking a chair, Rolley joined the vigil. "Who'd a guessed such a thing? The battle up on that mountain 'most a year ago, and shots still bein' fired. Ol' Jube as sure a victim as Sholo." Turning his gaze to Jacob, the big soldier's gentle face showed understanding. "That day set a lot of changes for you too; a home, a woman, bein' a famous hero."

Jacob stirred uncomfortably. After a thoughtful pause, Rolley continued. "Most men dream of bein' a hero, but you take ta hidin' like it's somethin' shameful."

Shaking his head, Jacob stared at the floor. "It ain't shame. Funny, Jube called me a hero. Hell, someone writes a book, and everyone calls me a hero. Don't even know me."

"I know ya; Jube knows ya."

"Well there's others who call me a fool of a dirt farmer. Guess there's truth in that, too."

Rolley gave a soft chuckle. "Twixt a fool and a hero."

Pushing his hands against his knees, Jacob sat straight. "Don't care what they say, just trying to find the truth. A man should know his own truth."

With a heavy sigh, Rolley stood to leave. "Don't know that any of us ever does. Twixt a fool and a hero. Guess that sums up every man."

Rolley turned as he reached the door. "While other men hide from their fears, you dared to dream. Ought to be a medal for that. Good night, Sarge."

Sometime before dawn, as Jacob's head slowly nodded, a weak cough brought him to attention. Jube's hand, lying on the covers, gave a slight twitch. Jacob took it in his own and held it to his chest. In the faint light, Jube's eyes blinked, then closed. "This don't mean we's goin' steady."

Jube took a weak breath and fell into a deep sleep. Later in the night, he woke long enough to take a drink of water, then faded off again. It wasn't much, but he was back among the living.

With the pall of death lifted, Jacob did not wait for his friend to regain consciousness. Knowing Mea-a-ha would worry herself sick about his failure to return, Jacob said his goodbyes, sure he would see his friend again.

It was decided Luis and Victor would wait until Jubaliah could travel, then take him by wagon to Luis's ranch, where he could heal.

Riding across the parade grounds, Jacob paused. Blood still stained the hard packed earth. It was a sight that would haunt him for years to come. Kicking his heels, Jacob slowly moved on.

It was over, and they had won. To Jacob it didn't feel like a victory. There had been too much ugliness, and no one's hands were clean. Right and wrong should be clear as the morning sun, but he couldn't see it.

Riding through the adobe walls, Jacob pulled up short. A large detachment of the Ninth Cavalry came riding in. At the end of the procession were two bodies laying over their saddles, wrapped in blankets.

Captain McArthur tipped his hat to Jacob and disappeared beneath the sally port gate. Sergeant Bolley pulled out of line. "Mornin' Jacob. Its good to see ya."

They paused in respect, as the bodies of the dead soldiers passed by. "Privates Soderquist and Judi, good men." Bolley raised his eyes. "Caught up with the Apaches that rustled Mr. Mathers' cattle."

A shiver ran down Jacob's spine. Sergeant Bolley spoke as much to himself. "Ambushed them by a watering hole; cut 'em down. Should have ended there Jacob, but that crazy Injun, Cota. He made it to his horse. Coulda' fled; instead, he charged our line, whoopin' like a wild savage. Must of shot him a dozen times, but he kilt Soderquist and Judi before fallin' off his pony." Bolley shook his head. "Senseless."

Looking past the Sergeant at the endless desert, Jacob remembered Cota's last words. "He'd find no place in the white man's world." It was a big country, and still there was no place for Victorio's people. The Mimbre were gone. "Yes Bolley, senseless." Jacob started to turn away then paused. "Did you bury them?"

Sergeant Bolley looked confused. "What for, Jacob? They's Injuns."

Pausing on a bluff to look back at his old fort, Jacob filled his lungs, but the air seemed bitter. So much death. It had been less than a year since he gave up the army life to follow his dream.

The dream had changed and so had he. There had been some good. He'd learned to look at the color of a man's heart and not his skin. His reward was a love far greater than he ever dreamed. It had not come without pain, but nothing of value ever does. Jacob slapped the reins; Major moved on.

In the early afternoon, Jacob reached Robbers' Knoll. Pulling up short near an outcropping of sandstone rocks that stood like a loaf of sliced bread, Jacob took a long draw on his canteen, then wiped his lips. Looping the canteen back over the saddle horn, he eased his Winchester from the scabbard. Sholo's feathers still hung from the barrel. Each time Jacob saw the feathers, it reminded him of how it all began. It was there, in the moment when Sholo died, that he found the courage to leave the army and follow his dream.

Never could he have imagined all the events that decision would set in motion. Like a single stone rolling down a hill, bumping and dislodging other stones, until there was an avalanche that nothing could stop.

Here among these weathered rocks, the violent collisions would finally end. Jacob filled his lungs. The voice of the old Buffalo Soldier shattered the silence, as it rang from stone to stone. "Reinhart. Let's finish it."

A cold wind hissed over the parched earth, carrying a mournful reply of its own. Sparse patches of dried brown grass waved to and fro, ghostly reminders that all life must end. As Jacob waited, death held its breath.

At last a bitter voice added its icy discourse to the chill autumn breeze. "How did you know I would be here?"

The sergeant laughed scornfully. "You're too filled with hate to just ride away. That, and I saw your tracks."

"You think you're clever." The captain sneered from his hiding place. "The great Jacob Keever, loved and respected by all." Resentment, long hidden, poisoned the air. "Why you? I am a cavalry captain in the U.S. Army, for hell sake. Instead of leading real soldiers to glory, I got stuck parading a bunch of howling monkeys that the fools in Washington put in uniforms."

Festering hatred erupted like puss from a foul wound. "And you, smelling of stable dung, think you are a better soldier than me, an officer trained at West Point."

While Reinhart spewed his vomit, Jacob leaned an ear to the wind, searching the rocks. The disgruntled captain droned on. "You couldn't stay in your place, boy. You had to get Sholo, prove you were a hero, and ruin my plans."

Sliding silently from the saddle, Jacob slipped around the nearest stones, moving to out flank his old lieutenant.

The captain's pathetic whining echoed through the empty passages. "I won't live the rest of my life with everyone thinking you're a better man than me. When they find your body, they will know who was the real soldier."

Levering a bullet into the chamber, Jacob knew this was one killing he wasn't going to regret. The acrid voice of his adversary rattled on about the injustice he endured. With slow deliberate steps, Jacob closed the distance on his quarry.

"You're not as good as you think. You hear me, Jacob Keever? You're just lucky."

As he skirted to his left, the voice grew closer. Jacob planned to come up behind Reinhart and end the captain's whining forever. As he slipped between the rocks listening to the hatred, Jacob thought "Just keep talking, you pompous windbag."

Reinhart did not disappoint him. "A real soldier doesn't rely on luck. He thinks things through, develops a strategy. Your kind don't think. Killing you will be nothin', like stomping a snake."

Quietly, Jacob edged forward. Reinhart's loud ramblings made stalking him easy. In fact, too easy. With a sinking feeling, the hair on the back of his neck bristled. Whirling around, Jacob fell backwards roaring at the top of his lungs, all the while firing like a madman.

Leveling the Winchester as fast as he could, Jacob sent four bullets tearing through the cold air. Their reverberating roar was joined by the sharp crack of a fifth. Blood exploded from Jacob's left leg as he hit the ground, writhing in pain. His own shots went wild, but succeeded in foiling his assassin.

Continuing to fire, Jacob dragged himself backwards as rapidly as he could, finding refuge in a narrow passage.

"Did you get him?" Reinhart yelled from the rocks below.

A steely voice answered, sending a tremor down Jacob's spine. "Winged him, but the wooly rat crawled into a hole."

It was the gunfighter, Jake Flynn.

Cursing his arrogance, Jacob realized he had foolishly fallen into a trap, and was surrounded.

With his back pressed against the wall, his mind raced as he desperately tried to watch both ends of the passage at once. Sandwiched between two tall rock walls with nowhere to go, he was completely exposed. Death waited at both ends.

Reinhart gloated. "A good officer out-thinks his adversary. Did you really expect me to just shoot it out with you like a couple of drunken cowboys?"

Jacob tried to stop the bleeding. Because of the angle of the bullet's entry, it had traveled up his leg. The wound went deep, badly tearing up muscle. Racked with pain, Jacob swallowed several gulps of air, trying to control the nausea rising in his stomach. He would be lucky to stand, let alone walk. Right now he desperately needed to buy time.

Mustering a weak chuckle, Jacob struggled to calm his voice. "Well, yes, captain, I guess I did expect a fair fight. Thanks for the lesson."

From the rocks above, Flynn broke in. "Here's another lesson. If you shoot somebody, make sure you kill 'em."

Stuffing his neckerchief into the hole in his trousers, Jacob arched against the pain, then forced his words. "You're right Flynn..." He took a heavy breath. "This time I'll make sure you're dead."

Reinhart's laugh was closer. "Brave to the last."

Jacob could hear boots scraping on stone at the bottom of the passage, the end was near. Blood dripping through his fingers, Jacob gripped his Winchester. "Since you're giving so much good advice, let me give you some. I wouldn't poke my head in here if I was you, captain. Likely to get it blown plum off."

The officer mocked Jacob's feeble threat. "I know you're stalling. But it doesn't matter, you're a dead man."

Enjoying his victory, Reinhart continued his taunt. "It galled me how you always won against better men. Mathers was better. His boys were better, even Sholo was better, but you still won. Then I realized, you always had friends to back your play. Darkies, Mexicans, Indians, even whites, that whiskered old scout. Somebody was always there to bail you out. Jacob Keever, friend to everyone. But this time it's different; you're all alone. You didn't find me here, I chose this spot. There's no one to save you this time. You'll die alone." Reinhart's sick laugh echoed up the narrow chute. "A final, sad chapter for Barnabas Kane."

Flynn had been silent too long. Jacob, knew that at any moment, the gunfighter would be at the upper end of the passage, firing down on him from high ground. Whatever Jacob was going to do, had to happen now. Flynn was the greater danger. Any chance Jacob had against the gunfighter was at a distance, with his rifle. Pushing the butt of the Winchester into the sand, Jacob raised himself to a standing position and leaned against the rocks. Searing pain brought beads of sweat to his forehead. He didn't know how long he could last.

Gritting his teeth, he edged towards the lower end of the passage. Blood rolled down his boot, writing its tale in the sand.

Only steps separated him from the opening, only seconds from death. He could hear Reinhart's breathing and could see the officer's pale shadow on the cold sandstone, not yards away. The moment had come, Jacob took a final breath. His voice grew calm. "By the way captain, thanks for reminding me about friends. No shame in sayin' they've always been there for me."

Filling his lungs, Jacob gave a loud whistle. Reinhart glanced about nervously. Jacob whistled again. His call was answered by the heavy pounding of hooves on hard stone. From below, old Major came racing to his master's call. The great warhorse headed straight for the narrow passage. The jerking motion of Reinhart's shadow, showed he had turned to face the thundering steed.

Instinctively, Reinhart raised his rifle, firing at Jacob's loyal friend. At the top of the chute came the metallic sound of a six gun being hammered. Instantly Jacob dove forward, twisting in mid air as he did. Sholo's rifle barrel stabbed into Reinhart's rib cage. In an explosion of flame and smoke, the bullet tore its path, straight through the captain's bitter heart. He would hate no more.

Struggling frantically to his knees, Jacob rose to a stream of bullets fanned from Flynn's lightning fast revolver. Jacob had never faced anything like it. Holding steady, he levered another round into the chamber, but Flynn's bullet found its target first, ripping through Jacob's chest. Another bullet burned across his neck, and a third cut the back of his hand.

Ignoring the hail of lead, Jacob squeezed off a single round, drilling the gunfighter through the brain. The roar of his gun trailed away, leaving only the icy wind.

Collapsing backwards, Jacob's mind whirled as he fought for consciousness. The tall rocks wavered like deathly specters waiting to claim the man who dared to dream. His eyes blurred and closed, beyond his control. All his senses cried out, "It's over, let go!"

Clenching his teeth, the Buffalo Soldier forced a defiant growl. Death may come, but not this moment. He roared again to jolt his senses and fought to breathe. Caked in blood and dirt, he slowly began to crawl towards Major. The great horse was down. His chest heaved as he sucked in air, fighting his own valiant battle with death.

Growing weaker, Jacob clawed his way to his faithful companion. With his last bit of strength, he hauled himself upon Major's heaving shoulder. He felt his friend's pain more deeply than his own. How many years had they been together? How many battles had they fought?

Reaching out his bloody hand, Jacob clenched Major's silky mane. His voice sputtered in a raspy whisper. "It's okay, old friend, we did our best." His words ended in a cough of blood. "At least we'll die together."

As if he understood, Major struggled to raise his head. A mournful groan came from deep within. He pressed his soft muzzle to Jacob's arm, then closed his eyes forever. The faithful horse lay still.

Shutting his own eyes, sobs of anguish caught in Jacob's throat. His loss was too great to bear. Jacob buried his head against his dear friend. For the first time, he was truly alone. Maybe death's kind hand would take him, too. Perhaps it was meant to be this way. Darkness filled every corner of his mind. Pain relinquished its hold.

Life is fleeting, but the cold wind blows on forever, carrying no pity for the dying and the dead. Yet in its mournful howl is the breath of life. Catch it if you can. From out of darkness, fragments of memories swirled in the soldier's mind like shards of glass from a shattered mirror. Each would flash, then whirl away as if carried by the wind. He struggled to put the pieces together. When he had collapsed, his head was resting on Major's strong shoulder; now he was floating, nothing was real. A breeze brushed his cheek, or was it kisses, sweet tender kisses.

Warm tears moistened his dirty face. He struggled to open his eyes, but all was cold and black, save for a pale, phantom moon that would not be ignored.

Floating in the shimmering light, a vision of Mea-a-ha's gentle, loving face faded in and out. Her eyes glistened like jewels in the heavens. Each tear caught the magical light as they fell from her cheek. Her soft voice echoed as if from far away.

Filled with grief, her anguished face turned towards the moon, and she broke into an Indian chant. Each syllable bore more pain than her heart could bear. The chant crumbled into sobs, then started again.

The dream washed over him like sparkling waves in a sea of darkness. Jacob struggled to form a word, but none came, only a shallow gasp. It was enough for her desperate heart. Mea-a-ha's beautiful eyes turned down, anxiously searching his face. There was a flicker of life beneath half opened lids ... *Jacob*.

She pressed her lips to his. Her warmth chased away the chill. Death bowed to love's gentle embrace.

The wheel of the old buckboard dropped hard over a stone. Pain shot through his body, telling him it was all real. Wrapped in a blanket, cradled by his sweet Mea-a-ha, he longed to speak. She read his thoughts. "I know, lie still." She cried for him.

Slipping into deep peaceful dreams, Jacob slept as the wagon rocked gently under Peaches' slow gate. Hamp went easy on the reins. Carmelita, sitting quietly by his side, wiped tears of her own. Elena reached down and stroked the Indian girl's hair. A sleepy puppy lay curled by her side, and three somber boys rode behind in the gloomy shadows of the full moon. The procession rolled silently through the night.

Mea-a-ha was the only one Jacob was aware of, but he was among friends just the same.

Chapter -30-
A time, a place

It was a most amazing place. In truth, she had never seen anything like it. Even the somber mood did not alter the fact that it was the most amazing place Mea-a-ha had ever been. In addition to the grand hacienda, there were at least a dozen outbuildings surrounding beautiful courtyards and stone walkways.

Many men and women worked and lived at the Rincon's ranch. Why, there were three cooks that Mea-a-ha knew of. One was a woman who lived in the great house and cooked for the Rincons, and two men who cooked for all the ranch hands. The sprawling adobe buildings seemed more like Mea-a-ha had imagined a town would be, though she had never actually seen one.

People dressed in fine Mexican clothing were coming and going all day long, yet the ranch seemed as tranquil as sitting by the bubbling spring in the Hollow. The serenity comforted Mea-a-ha during her long vigils by Jacob's bed. Several days had come and gone since they had found him at Robbers' Knoll.

When he had not returned from that dreadful fort, she had a feeling something was terribly wrong and insisted on searching for him. Elena finally relented and had Hamp make a bed for her in the wagon. The three boys came along for protection. It was the boys who discovered Reinhart's and Flynn's horses grazing near the road, not far from where Jacob had fallen. Then they found Jacob and the dead men. It was a terrible sight for the boys.

When they arrived at the hacienda, Elena took action. There was no doctor, and the bullets were buried deep. Everyone feared for his life.

Elena's hands were old, but in her years she had served as a midwife and doctored her share of wounds. A grim man who took care of the animals joined her. He was skilled with a knife. Together they worked on Jacob. Mea-a-ha held his hand through it all. An eternity passed for the girl, while each bullet was slowly removed and dropped into a pan. Finally, the wounds were stitched closed. Elena stepped back and folded her hands. "It is up to God now."

Mea-a-ha stayed by Jacob's side through the night. She refused to believe he could die. If he was going to live, then she had to act like he was going to live. In the days that followed, she allowed herself to take walks around the great house and even venture out into the courtyard for fresh air. Jacob was strong, and she would be strong too.

First thing every morning, a worried Daniel would peek in. The boy would stand by Jacob's bed and touch his hand, assuring himself that the big man was breathing. He would come again at night.

Without any knowledge of Luis and Victor's fate, everyone feared the worst, but several days later the two of them came riding in on an army wagon with Jubaliah resting in the back. Everyone was shocked at the turn of events. Carmelita was frightened to tears, but the whole story was finally told. It was a great relief that the fighting was over.

Mea-a-ha and Carmelita spent time together, talking and consoling each other, now that both of their men lay hurt.

"Hey, wake up. I been jawin' at ya for hours and all ya do is snore. Don't know why they wheeled me in here to see ya, if all you is gunna' to do is sleep."

Jubaliah shouted across the large room at his friend. "I looks for a little sympathy, and ya go n' upstage me. Always been like that."

Jubaliah had been talking aloud to his friend for some time, hoping he would respond. Carmelita and Mea-a-ha had left their daily vigil to take some food. A pale sun lulling in the south facing window washed the shadows from the white stucco walls of Jacob's room. "It ain't fair. I takes one bullet and ya takes two. I kills one varmint, ya kills three. You's' jes' greedy, Jacob Keever."

A thick, garbled voice interrupted Jubaliah's grumbling. "I'll trade you bullet holes if it'll shut you up."

Jube pounded his hand on the arm of the chair and brayed for joy. "It's about time. I was getting' bored with my own company. Which is right hard since I'm mighty interestin' company if I do say so ma..."

"Where's Mea-a-ha?"

"Well, that's a fine how-de-do. I did save yo' life ya know, and if ya had been a might faster, I wouldn't be a sittin' here with a bullet hole in me. So excuse me for intrudin' on yo' precious time. It's not like ya gots any place to g..."

"God, I've gone to hell."

"All right, take it easy. I gots the brass bell they gave me right here."

The loud clattering brought Carmelita rushing back into the room. Jube pointed towards his old friend. "Get the Injun girl; seems like my company ain't good enough." Jube laughed.

Just then, Mea-a-ha returned to the room. Seeing Carmelita's excitement, she hurried to Jacob's side. A weak smile greeted her hopeful face. Ever so gently she took his hand. Her eyes beamed as all her fears faded away, like closing a frightening old book.

Against all odds they had prevailed, and a new story was about to begin. From the first day on the desert when Jacob became her reluctant rescuer, it had been a terrifying journey. Two hearts bound by fire. As

Jacob had said, "No matter how hopeless, never give up." She kissed his cheek. "Hey, sleepy, it's time you woke."

The big man squeezed the Indian girl's small hand. "You're beautiful. Been dreamin' 'bout you." Jacob drifted back to sleep.

It was a month they called December. It meant little to Mea-a-ha, but it was a time of celebration at the hacienda. People scurried about making plans. The house was decorated for a big occasion. A tree was brought into the great room and adorned with ribbons and candles.

When Mea-a-ha was a little girl, a priest came to her village and told them about the birth of a child in a far away land. As near as she could figure, this was what all the fuss was about. The occasion was made all the more special because their men were on the mend, and everyone was together at last.

Occasionally, Mea-a-ha would help Elena and Carmelita with the decorations, but often she would sit chatting away the hours with Jacob. Mostly he would listen, sometimes attentively, other times with a far away gaze. Still, he was by her side, and it filled Mea-a-ha with joy.

They would take gentle walks in the courtyard when the sun was bright, and in the evening sit inside by a huge fire, where Jacob would teach her to read.

There were lots of books. They read books about great men and books about animals that could talk. These were her favorite. The words below the beautiful pictures of funny animals were small, and she could read them easily. Someday she would own books.

At times, Jubaliah and Carmelita joined them. The men played a game called checkers on a small wooden board, while Carmelita taught Mea-a-ha to sew. These were good days. There was no hurry, no urgent matters to attend to. Plenty of willing hands made life safe and peaceful.

Daniel would still come daily. The boy seldom spoke, he just needed to know the big man was okay. Finally a morning came when Daniel missed his visit. Mea-a-ha could see the disappointment on Jacob's face.

Giving him a hug, she told him a heavy snow had fallen up on Robbers Knoll the night he was shot. It was melting. Hamp and the boys went to bury old Major. Jacob's eyes misted over. When Daniel returned that night, he hugged him tightly. There were no words, but the boy handed him a braided lock of Major's silky mane, then hurried from the room.

Once the day of the celebration came, Mexican families began arriving at the ranch by early in the afternoon. The Rincons were one of the oldest and most respected families in the territory, and so their hacienda was the center of Mexican culture for miles around.

As the hour of celebration neared, everyone gathered in the great room. Often Mea-a-ha came to this room just to stare in wonder. It was bigger than their entire house of stones in the Hollow. The ceiling was so high, a rider standing in the stirrups on a tall horse could not have touched it with his outstretched hand. White stucco columns rising from the stone floor formed graceful arches leading to hallways and smaller rooms where guests chatted with old friends.

Gaily dressed vaqueros stood at one end of the great room with strange instruments, making beautiful music. Some had strings that were plucked, others were blown into by men with bright red faces. There were no drums.

More than anything else, it was the food that amazed the Apache girl the most. Tables were set everywhere, covered with pots and platters piled high with delicacies of every kind. The hall filled with the delicious aroma of tempting new dishes. She swore for the rest of her years that there was more food that night than she had seen in her whole life.

So many friends crowded the room that Mea-a-ha could hardly see. Roberto and Juan were dressed in fine Mexican clothes with gold braid. Broad sombreros hung on their backs. Of course Daniel was with them as always, dressed in borrowed Mexican garb. Carmelita had trimmed his hair, and Mea-a-ha thought he looked quite handsome. Apparently, so did a group of girls with shy grins, hovering close, as they pointed and giggled at the dashing new boy. Mea-a-ha couldn't help teasing. "They are not Apache, but quite pretty, don't you think?" Daniel ducked his head.

Bewhiskered old Hamp sat contentedly on a small stool in the corner with his tattered hat drooping down over a mess of silver hair. He was sipping from a glazed jug that he held tightly. It must have been good; he smiled a lot, nodding to passersby.

Cheery Victor Ramirez, his face carefree as always, watched from the side, holding a plate of food, while his wife chatted with a group of women.

A priest dressed in black, clutching a book in his hands, milled slowly about the room. He reminded Mea-a-ha of the priest who had come to her village long ago.

Old Luis, sitting in a carved wooden high-back chair with Elena by his side, looked like a great chieftain, which Mea-a-ha thought perhaps he was, for his home was far grander than her entire village.

A young, well-built man with an air of authority stood next to them. It was Vicente, Carmelita's handsome brother.

The guests were all talking at once while laughing children ran between men's legs and around women's flowing dresses, sometimes hiding under them making for a lot of commotion.

Mea-a-ha had never experienced a celebration like this. In her village there was dancing and singing, but this was not a war dance or a dance for a great hunt. The people gathered here danced for joy.

Jubaliah was fit enough to try a little jig with Carmelita. He was surprisingly good. Everyone clapped their hands. Mea-a-ha thought how brave they were to perform in front of all the people. Carmelita's crimson dress sparkled in the firelight as she twirled. She was so beautiful.

Mea-a-ha looked down at her own dress. It was a long white gown that Carmelita had altered just for her. They had stayed up late for several nights adding lace and sequins, making it the loveliest dress Mea-a-ha could imagine. She called it her party dress, and it made her feel like a princess. Her hair was pulled back with ribbons and combs. Everybody told her how beautiful she was. It was embarrassing, and she loved it.

Music and laughter filled the room as other couples tried to dance. Perhaps it was a bit much for Jacob. He stood under a large, shadowed archway, leaning on a cane. Mea-a-ha strolled to his side. People she had never met shook his hand and made polite conversation. Some spoke in English, others in Spanish. No matter which, Jacob answered in either tongue. It was apparent Jacob was held in great esteem. Mea-a-ha's eyes glistened with pride.

Down the hallway, Mea-a-ha could see a servant open the front door. A tall, distinctive white soldier in fine dress stepped inside, accompanied by a younger white officer, followed by four Buffalo Soldiers. She recognized them from the dark night in the Hollow when they came hunting Daniel. At first she clung tightly to Jacob, but seeing the smile on his face, she realized everything was okay.

Jacob snapped to attention and saluted the white soldier, then turned to Mea-a-ha. "Darling, I would like to introduce you to Colonel McCrae, ferocious chief of the evil Fort Cummings." He was teasing her, and she blushed.

The colonel laughed as he took her hand, giving it a kiss. "My dear lady, I hope you will give me a chance to redeem myself, or at least judge me only for my own sins and not those of a nation." His eyes were warm and shining with sincerity. He did not seem such a monster on this night.

Old Luis motioned to the vaqueros, and the music stopped. Pressing his weathered hands on the arms of the chair, he rose to greet Colonel McCrae, who crossed the floor offering his hand. "Senor Rincon, thank you for the invitation to your beautiful hacienda on this Christmas Eve. I am honored."

Matching the officer's erect posture, Luis pushed back his shoulders. The old Mexican was less in stature, but no less dignified. "Dear Colonel, welcome to my home. It has been many years since a commander of the fort has seen fit to visit my hacienda. The honor is ours."

The colonel nodded to the young officer by his side, who quickly produced folded papers from a leather satchel. McCrae handed them to Luis. "As a Christmas gift, I thought I would bring the army beef contract myself. May it build a lasting friendship between us for years to come."

Taking the papers, Luis's eyes sparkled. "Thank you, it means so much to us all."

Then holding them above his head for all to see, Luis cleared his throat and did his best to make a worthy speech. "My dear friends, for a very long time we have struggled just to survive. This room is filled with brave men who risked their lives fighting for what they knew was right, because that is what good men do. This document brings prosperity to those who stood tall when it mattered most."

Old Luis stopped and shook Colonel McCrae's hand. Everyone cheered. Luis raised his hand again. "There is more. We will be moving a lot of cattle, and that means I will need a few more men. So I am offering jobs right now to some of those very same men who made this possible."

As his shining eyes searched the room, old Luis called out names. "First, Jube, who has become like a son to me," He grinned towards his daughter. "I hope he plans to stay on permanently."

Carmelita hid her eyes and blushed as the guest laughed at the innuendo. Luis continued. "Jube, we could use a good foreman to help Vicente. Who better than a tough army sergeant?" Jube smiled and looked to Carmelita. "Thank you, sir, 'cuz I gots some branding of my own ta do." Everyone laughed again.

Turning toward the three boys, Luis continued. "We will need strong young men who can sit a good horse. Daniel, since you and these young rascals are inseparable; you might as well get paid for it."

Once again the crowd cheered while Daniel gave a shy grin. Juan leaned in to explain. "He means you can live here with us."

Daniel nudged him with an elbow. "I know."

Everyone crowded around old Luis offering congratulations.

Watching from the archway, Jacob was glad some good had finally come from such darkness. He loved seeing Mea-a-ha being pulled across the room by so many people eager to meet this mysterious Apache. He knew how much friends meant to her. She was having the time of her life.

Suddenly, standing before him was Daniel. A sweet, dark haired girl hung a few steps back. The young boy's face told a story of admiration for the big man that needed no words. He took the girl's arm and stepped forward trying his best English. "Sir, please you to know Juan's sister, Maria. She wishes to meet my--my Pa." The final word brought a lump to Daniel's throat. "You being, you know, famous and all."

Jacob swallowed a lump of his own. Bowing low, he took the young girl's hand and offered a kiss. Maria blushed, but found the courage to speak. "It is an honor to meet you Senor Keever. I teach the younger children at our school. Carmelita gave me a book about you that I read to them. They will be so excited when I tell them I actually met you."

Tonight, for Daniel's sake, Jacob did not protest. Children need heroes, and he would willingly play the part, though he couldn't help sharing a little of the glory. "If you want the children to meet a real hero, take my son to school with you." Jacob lovingly mussed the boy's hair. "He has had many brave adventures of his own."

Maria giggled. "Si, Juan has told me much, but Daniel is like his famous father and won't talk about himself."

Jacob laughed. "Well, take him anyway and teach him to read."

The girl smiled with delight. "Si, Senor Keever. I will, most happily." Slipping her arm into Daniels', the starry-eyed girl pulled the young boy away, eager to show him off to her friends. It was Daniel's first Christmas. His gift was a new life with new friends. The old way was gone, but the Mimbres would survive.

Jacob turned his gaze back to the merriment, thinking to himself. Yes, some good had come from the darkness.

And so the festivities of the evening continued. Carmelita made sure Mea-a-ha met everyone. The Indian girl did her best to try and remember all their names, but it was hopeless. Mea-a-ha found fame of her own. She had known Sholo as well as the Hero of Apache Springs.

While most women stayed home dreaming of adventure, Mea-a-ha had been right in the middle of the greatest tale. She soon learned why Jacob found it embarrassing to talk about himself. Feeling overwhelmed, Mea-a-ha escaped to one of the many alcoves and from the shadows, savored the gaiety with her eyes closed, letting her senses calm.

"Mea-a-ha." The Mimbre girl looked up. It was Jube. The anxious eyes of the big man glistened. Awkwardly, he took her tiny hand in his. "Mea-a-ha, I, ah...well..." He cleared his throat several times. "I wanted ta..." Jube swallowed a deep breath and tried again. "Mea-a-ha, its, its... Well...a... Hey, look at you layered in lace. Why, you is prettier than the first day I met ya ."

Mea-a-ha giggled and Jube turned red. "I mean..." He lowered his head, feeling miserable.

The Indian girl closed the distance between them. "I know, Jube. You're a good man." She raised on her toes and kissed his cheek.

He gave a sad smile. "Jacob gots himself a good woman, an' I'll lick the man that says he ain't." Jube squeezed her hand and hurried away.

Mea-a-ha watched Jube disappear in the crowd. He was a soldier and she, an Apache. Some things take time. It had for Jacob.

Thinking of her old bear, she suddenly needed a big hug. Mea-a-ha searched the corners of the room. Jacob was gone.

The fresh night air in the courtyard calmed Jacob's mind. Wisps of fog, rolling slowly across the ground, curled and disappeared into the star-filled sky. A dim glow of yellow light broke the solitary moment as Mea-a-ha opened and closed the tall wooden door.

Quietly, she joined Jacob by the low adobe wall surrounding the courtyard. Taking his thick arm, she wrapped it around her like a warm blanket and nuzzled close. "So many good people; it is wonderful here."

Her words did not break his silence. Sliding in front of him, she pressed her back against his chest and wrapped his other arm around her as well. "You miss the Hollow."

His hand slid to her face and a finger traced her cheek. "It was the dream that set all this in motion. A dream that led down a long trail of pain and death. I wonder if it was all worth it. Maybe the dream will always be shadowed by what has happened."

Twisting in his arms, Mea-a-ha circled his neck. Her smile pierced the darkness. "There is magic in the Hollow that has endured. It is still there, keeping the dream safe. That is what magic is for, protecting the desires of the heart. There is no shadow so dark that love will not shine through. You will see."

Again she caught Jacob by surprise. "Quite the little philosopher. You figured that out by yourself?"

She hugged tighter, burying her face deeper against his chest. "Yes, and I talk to Grandfather. I can hear him whispering in the wind."

Mea-a-ha leaned back, taking an air of authority, she lowered her voice to a deep, comical tone. "He says, 'Mea-a-ha, you stay with Jacob. He good man. You get pregnant, have lots of children.'"

They both laughed. Jacob became quiet, and after a moment, spoke softly. "After living in this beautiful hacienda with all these nice people and a friend like Carmelita, are you sure you could return to our little house of stone? They would let you stay here, you know."

Mea-a-ha snuggled deeper into Jacob's arms. "The Rincon's hacienda is beautiful. Maybe I had to come here to learn that there are good places in the world beyond the Hollow, so I did not use it as a hiding place. The Hollow is where I fell in love for the first time, where I found hope. The hacienda will always be here, filled with friends, but the Hollow is home."

Taking her by the waist, Jacob lifted her onto the low stone wall and looked into her beautiful eyes. "Then let's go home, darling. Tonight. Right now."

The girl's heart fluttered with excitement. On a cold night in a month they called December, she knew the time had come. They were going home to the Hollow. "We must tell the Rincons. They will be upset if our leaving spoils their celebration."

Jacob twirled her around and set Mea-a-ha on the ground. "It won't. In fact, we'll make it a night they'll never forget. Come."

Taking Mea-a-ha by the hand, Jacob hurried through the door. Inside, Jacob grabbed Jubaliah's arm. "Jube, get Luis and the padre."

Releasing Mea-a-ha's hand, Jacob and the men scooted away, talking hurriedly amongst themselves. Carmelita, seeing the men's excitement, stepped next to Mea-a-ha. "What are our boys up to now?"

Mea-a-ha could only shrug her shoulders. "Jacob said it would be a night we won't forget."

Carmelita laughed. "Jacob is a quiet man, but not one to be ignored."

The men's discussion ended as quickly as it had started. Old Luis stepped to the center of the room and once again, signaled for the music to stop. Straightening his coat, he did his best to look serious, but a twinkle in his eyes betrayed his excitement. "My dear guests, on this eve of Christmas, we have gathered together friends and family, in peace and love. It is a most joyous occasion, but I think this year it is indeed a most memorable Christmas."

Luis paused, smiling at his guest, building suspense. "Now our dear friend, and local legend, Sergeant Jacob Keever, retired, plans to make it a Christmas we will truly never forget. He has something he would like to say."

Luis stretched his arm towards Jacob, offering him the floor. Rubbing his hands on his breaches, Jacob licked his lips and stepped to the center of the room. Mea-a-ha had never seen him so nervous. He glanced about the room, then settled his gaze on her. Leaning on his cane, he held out his hand and motioned her to join him.

Aware that all eyes were upon her, Mea-a-ha scurried across the floor, and slipped the tips of her fingers into his big hand. Rising on her toes, Mea-a-ha whispered between clenched teeth. "Please don't make me dance in front of all these people."

He laughed at her innocence. Clearing his throat, Jacob took on a somber expression and raised his voice for all to hear. "Mea-a-ha, tonight we are surrounded by our friends."

Her large frightened eyes cast about the room. "I know, it's scary."

She had not meant to speak so loud; everyone laughed. Jacob continued. "Darling, I want to spend the rest of my life with you."

Leaning on his cane, Jacob bent to one knee. "Mea-a-ha, will you marry me?"

Suddenly, she realized what he was doing and laughed. "I thought we were married. You give me a house and take in my family. What man does that if not married? Apache way much simpler."

Once again everyone laughed and cheered.

Not giving up, Jacob persisted. "Let me win just this once."

More laughter and prodding flowed across the room. Taking Jacob's face in her gentle hands, Mea-a-ha met his eyes. "Yes."

Jacob wrapped her in a bear hug and stood up amid cheers, twirling her in the air. Men slapped him on the back and women cried. As the clamor died down, Mea-a-ha's innocent voice could once again be heard. "Now we are married?"

The padre was called over, and an official ceremony was held. Mea-a-ha learned new words like best man and bridesmaid as Jube and Carmelita stood by their sides. Afterwards, the guests crowded around. Teary-eyed women hugged her, and every man in the room kissed her. It was all very strange. Still, it was a bit more memorable than the Apache way.

In the dark hours before morning as most of the guests finally slept, Jacob harnessed Peaches to the buckboard while Elena and Carmelita loaded the wagon with supplies. Every time Mea-a-ha protested it was too much, they brushed it off with the words, "Wedding gifts."

Finally, old Luis and the boys brought over two beautiful horses with new saddles and tied them to the back of the buckboard. One was a small pinto mare, and the other a tall buckskin stallion. Jacob was overcome. Seeing his awkwardness, Luis tried to make light of it. "It is nothing. We have too many horses here. Now you go start your own herd. They are a fine pair. Maybe someday I will buy horses from you."

The men shook hands and stepped apart. Elena and Carmelita hugged Mea-a-ha and promised to visit in the spring. Silently, Daniel stepped from the shadows. All fell silent, giving him his time. Awkwardly, the young boy searched for words, blending Apache and English. "My sister, I want to thank you for saving my life. I don't think I ever did that." His eyes cast about at the boys and Luis. "Senor Rincon has offered me work here. There is so much I can learn."

Juan interrupted. "There are girls."

Daniel shoved him and everyone laughed. "I wish to stay with my friends if it is okay."

Mea-a-ha melted as she hugged her brother. "You will always have two homes."

Stepping apart from his sister, Daniel stood before Jacob. The boy could find no words to express his feelings. Suddenly he threw his arms around the big man and buried his head against his chest. Jacob mussed his hair. "Little Buck, work hard and learn about ranching. When you come home, you can teach me. I love you, my son." Mea-a-ha hugged her brother once more, then Jacob lifted her onto the buckboard.

Finally, Jube came forward and shook Jacob's hand. He cleared his throat. "Well, Sergeant, it's been one hell of a ride. Who would a' thought such an amazin' day would have come for the likes of us. Once I made fun 'a yo' dream, and now I's happy to be part of it..."

His voice would no longer hold together. Carmelita took his arm. "We are all a part of it." She playfully reached up and pinched Jube's cheek. "And if Jube knows what is good for him, he will find the courage you did tonight."

Giving the reins a snap, they headed home, leaving Jube grinning from ear to ear.

On the evening of the third day, they came into the Hollow. Jacob eased the wagon to a gentle stop past the stone pillars. From the canopy of trees, the little stone house could be seen snuggled beneath the pine boughs. It was just as they had left it. Mea-a-ha was right. There was magic in the Hollow that would hold as long as their love endured. Gently he nudged his sleeping bride, wrapped in a blanket on his shoulder. "Darling, wake up. We're home. Let's go inside, it's snowing."

Mea-a-ha opened her eyes. Large, perfect snowflakes fell softly on her cheek and eyelashes. The Hollow was frosted in a fresh layer of white. Her sleepy voice filled with contented joy. "It is our time, our place to stop walking, just the two of us. The snow will come heavy and deep, locking the world outside until spring. We are finally home."

Timeframe for Jacob's Hollow

Historical Events:

1864   Black soldiers form the Ninth & Tenth Calvary and head west.

1878 October   Mimbres forced to leave Warm Springs. Victorio goes to war.

1880 October 15   Victorio and the last free Mimbres killed at Tres Castillo Mexico.

1887   Last of the Apaches surrender & are taken from their homeland.

Jacob Keever:

1847 February 16   Jacob born in Kentucky

1861   Fought in the Civil War at age 14 until the war ended in 1865.

1866   Joined the Ninth Calvary in Louisville, Kentucky

1875   Sent from Texas to New Mexico

1880 March 4   Led attack at Apache Springs

1880 March 6   Left army at age 34 after twenty years of service

1880 March 9   Acquired Jacob's Hollow and 10,000 acres of surrounding land.

1880 December 24   Married Mea-a-ha

1881   Followed the Mimbre Trail

1884   Added two bedrooms and a new bathroom off the back door of their little stone house. The addition had a large second story loft.

1886   Because of his knowledge of the land and friendship with the Indians and Mexicans, Jacob was hired as a Deputy Sheriff and served until 1900.

1887   Trailed killer Joe Bascomb into Colorado

1900   Sold 100 horses to the U.S. Army. A friend of Gen. Pershing. Sold horses until the end of WWI.

1910   Bought a Model A Ford. First car in the Hollow

1935 May 9   Died at age 88 in Jacob's Hollow

Mea-a-ha:

1860   Born in the Fall at Ojo Caliente New Mexico (Warm Springs)

1880 Dec 24   Married Jacob Keever

1883 Feb 20   Gave birth to baby boy named Jube Jacob

1884 Jun 13   Gave birth to baby boy named Teo Daniel

1886 Oct 16	Gave birth to baby girl named Mia Spring
1887 Jul 17	Gave birth to baby girl named Mary Summer

Note: Jacob chose the children's first names and Mea-a-ha chose the middle names.

1892	Took the family to spend a week in the grotto to see the little room.
1896	Wrote first book titled "The Magical Spring."
1897	Old Friendly died at age 16
1898	Wrote a children's book, "Friendly the Bouncing Pup."
1904	Mia marries a German photographer. Mea-a-ha gets first camera.
1906 April	Made Jacob take a trip to Seattle to see Mia's first baby. (Firsts: First visit to a town, first boat ride, SF to Seattle.)
1911	Another first: Convinced Jacob to teach her to drive. Took trip with Carmelita Jackson to Santa Fe. Girls only. First wreck.
1920	First photo exhibit and book signing.
1935	Left Hollow when Jacob died, after 54 blissful years. She was 72.
1937	Mea-a-ha became wealthy selling the 10,160 acre ranch and large horse herd to the Rincon family.
1939	Published her twelfth book. Her writings were about Jacob's Hollow and later of Yosemite. She wrote several books about New Mexico and one about the San Francisco Earthquake, including pictures she took on her first trip there with Jacob. Mea-a-ha was always proud that she supported herself after Jacob's death. Her last book was "Whisper in the Wind." A book about Grandfather.
1958	Took her last trip to Seattle and her first plane ride.
1961 Jan 03	Died at the age of 101 at the home of her grandson, Jacob Daniel Keever, near Yosemite California. Jacob Daniel was the son of Teo Keever and Jubilee Jackson.

Mea-a-ha's brother Daniel, born 1865, took the last name of Keever. To him it was the family name and Jacob was his father. After living three years with the Rincons where he went to school and learned to read and write, Daniel moved back to the Hollow, helping Jacob with the ranch and playing the part of big brother to his nephews. Having a home in the Hollow saved him from the forced relocation by the government to

Florida in 1887 with the last of the Apaches. At age 24, he married Juan's sister Maria and became Jacob's foreman. They built a small cabin just inside the old forest. Maria and Mea-a-ha spent much time together while the men worked the horses. Daniel died Jan. 1948.

Jubaliah Jackson and Carmelita Rincon were married in 1882. Jube and Vicente ran the ranch jointly after Louis's death in 1890. Carmelita had five children. She died in the winter 1934 of pneumonia at the age of 74. Jube died in the spring 1935 at 86. He said it was time. Mea-a-ha attended both funerals. She returned to Jacob's Hollow in 1950 to put flowers on the graves. It was her last trip. Some thought it was a bit strange she had Jacob buried in the Apache cemetery. She said he had finally found peace there, his place to stop walking forever. "Besides," she said, "How else could I bury him next to ol' Friendly?"

Her family laid her to rest by Jacob's side. It was her last request.